The House on the Borderland

And Other Creepy Stories

William Hope Hodgson

FANTASTIC TALES

The House on the Borderland

And Other Creepy Stories

William Hope Hodgson

**With an author biography by
Jake Jackson**

451
FLAME TREE

This edition is Published in 2014 by Flame Tree 451
The House on the Borderland was originally
published by Chapman and Hall, 1908;
'From the Tideless Sea' in *The Monthly Story Magazine, 1907;*
'The Voice in the Night' in *Blue Book Magazine, 1907;*
'The Mystery of the Derelict' in *Story-teller, 1907;*
'The Derelict' in *The Red Magazine*, 1912.

FLAME TREE 451
Crabtree Hall, Crabtree Lane, Fulham,
London SW6 6TY, United Kingdom
www.flametree451.com

Flame Tree 451 is an imprint of Flame Tree Publishing Ltd
www.flametreepublishing.com

A CIP record for this book is available from the British Library

Print ISBN 978-1-78361-236-9
ePub ISBN 978-1-78136-198-6

Acknowledgements
Jake Jackson (Author Biography) has written, edited and contributed to
over 20 books, including Myths and Legends, Celtic Myths and Norse Myths.
Related works include studies of Babylonian creation myths, the philosophy
of time and William Blake's use of mythology in his visionary literature.

Judith John (Glossary) is a writer and editor specializing in literature
and history. Judith's major research interests include Romantic
and Gothic literature, and Renaissance drama.

Printed and bound by
CPI Group (UK) Ltd, Croydon, CR0 4YY

Contents

A TASTE FOR THE FANTASTIC

From mystery to crime, supernatural to horror and fantasy to science fiction, the terrific new range of paperbacks and ebooks from Flame Tree 451 offers a healthy diet of werewolves and mechanical men, blood-lusty vampires, dastardly villains, mad scientists, secret worlds, lost civilizations and escapist fantasies. Discover a storehouse of tales gathered specifically for the reader of the fantastic.

Great works by H.G. Wells and Bram Stoker stand shoulder to shoulder with gripping reads by titans of the gothic novel (Algernon Blackwood, Charles Brockden Brown, Arthur Machen), and individual novels by literary giants (Jane Austen, Gustave Flaubert, Charles Dickens, Emily Brontë) mingle with the furious intensity of H.P. Lovecraft and the pure psychological magic of Edgar Allan Poe.

Of course there are classic Conan Doyle adventures, Wilkie Collins mysteries and the outlandish fantasies of Robert E. Howard, Edgar Rice Burroughs and Mary Shelley, but there are so many other tales to tell: *The White Worm, Black Magic, The Murder Monster, When the World Screamed, The Centaur* and more.

So, let the inimitable Sherlock Holmes, fearless secret agent Nick Carter and the braggadocio of Conan of Cimmeria lead you to an indulgence of fantastic fiction, night-time interventions, ghostly wanderings and sheer pulpy murder.

Check our website for regular updates and new additions to our incredible, curated range of speculative fiction: www.flametree451.com

The House on the Borderland

William Hope Hodgson

From the manuscript discovered in 1877 by Messrs. Tonnison and Berreggnog in the ruins that lie to the South of the Village of Kraighten, in the West of Ireland. Set out here, with notes.

TO MY FATHER

(Whose feet tread the lost aeons)
Open the door,
And listen!
Only the wind's muffled roar,
And the glisten
Of tears 'round the moon.
And, in fancy, the tread
Of vanishing shoon—
Out in the night with the Dead.

"Hush! And hark
To the sorrowful cry
Of the wind in the dark.
Hush and hark, without murmur or sigh,
To shoon that tread the lost aeons:
To the sound that bids you to die.
Hush and hark! Hush and Hark!"
Shoon of the Dead

Author's Introduction to the Manuscript

Many are the hours in which I have pondered upon the story that is set forth in the following pages. I trust that my instincts are not awry when they prompt me to leave the account, in simplicity, as it was handed to me.

And the MS. itself—You must picture me, when first it was given into my care, turning it over, curiously, and making a swift, jerky examination. A small book it is; but thick, and all, save the last few pages, filled with a quaint but legible handwriting, and writ very close. I have the queer, faint, pit-water smell of it in my nostrils now as I write, and my fingers have subconscious memories of the soft, "cloggy" feel of the long-damp pages.

I read, and, in reading, lifted the Curtains of the Impossible that blind the mind, and looked out into the unknown. Amid stiff, abrupt sentences I wandered; and, presently, I had no fault to charge against their abrupt tellings; for, better far than my own ambitious phrasing, is this mutilated story capable of bringing home all that the old Recluse, of the vanished house, had striven to tell.

Of the simple, stiffly given account of weird and extraordinary matters, I will say little. It lies before you. The inner story must be uncovered, personally, by each reader, according to ability and desire. And even should any fail to see, as now I see, the shadowed picture and conception of that to which one may well give the accepted titles of Heaven and Hell; yet can I promise certain thrills, merely taking the story as a story.

WILLIAM HOPE HODGSON December 17, 1907

Chapter 1

The Finding of the Manuscript

Right away in the west of Ireland lies a tiny hamlet called Kraighten. It is situated, alone, at the base of a low hill. Far around there spreads a waste of bleak and totally inhospitable country; where, here and there at great intervals, one may come upon the ruins of some long desolate cottage—unthatched and stark. The whole land is bare and unpeopled, the very earth scarcely covering the rock that lies beneath it, and with which the country abounds, in places rising out of the soil in wave-shaped ridges.

Yet, in spite of its desolation, my friend Tonnison and I had elected to spend our vacation there. He had stumbled on the place by mere chance the year previously, during the course of a long walking tour, and discovered the possibilities for the angler in a small and unnamed river that runs past the outskirts of the little village.

I have said that the river is without name; I may add that no map that I have hitherto consulted has shown either village or stream. They seem to have entirely escaped observation: indeed, they might never exist for all that the average guide tells one. Possibly this can be partly accounted for by the fact that the nearest railway station (Ardrahan) is some forty miles distant.

It was early one warm evening when my friend and I arrived in Kraighten. We had reached Ardrahan the previous night, sleeping there in rooms hired at the village post office, and leaving in good time on the following morning, clinging insecurely to one of the typical jaunting cars.

It had taken us all day to accomplish our journey over some of the roughest tracks imaginable, with the result that we were thoroughly tired and somewhat bad tempered. However, the tent had to be erected and our goods stowed away before we could think of food or rest. And so we set to work, with the aid of our driver, and soon had the tent up upon a small patch of ground just outside the little village, and quite near to the river.

Then, having stored all our belongings, we dismissed the driver, as he had to make his way back as speedily as possible, and told him to come across to us at the end of a fortnight. We had brought sufficient provisions to last us for that space of time, and water we could get from the stream. Fuel we did not need, as we had included a small oil-stove among our outfit, and the weather was fine and warm.

It was Tonnison's idea to camp out instead of getting lodgings in one of the cottages. As he put it, there was no joke in sleeping in a room with a numerous family of healthy Irish in one corner and the pigsty in the other, while overhead a ragged colony of roosting fowls distributed their blessings impartially, and the whole place so full of peat smoke that it made a fellow sneeze his head off just to put it inside the doorway.

Tonnison had got the stove lit now and was busy cutting slices of bacon into the frying pan; so I took the kettle and walked down to the river for water. On the way, I had to pass close to a little group of the village people, who eyed me curiously, but not in any unfriendly manner, though none of them ventured a word.

As I returned with my kettle filled, I went up to them and, after a friendly nod, to which they replied in like manner, I asked them casually about the fishing; but, instead of answering, they just shook their heads silently, and stared at me. I repeated the question, addressing more particularly a great, gaunt fellow at my elbow; yet again I received no answer. Then the man turned to a comrade and said something rapidly in a language that I did not understand; and, at once, the whole crowd of them fell to jabbering in what, after a few moments, I guessed to be pure Irish. At the same time they cast many glances in my direction. For a minute, perhaps, they spoke among themselves thus; then the man I had addressed faced 'round at me and said something. By the expression of his face I guessed that he, in turn, was questioning me; but now I had to shake my head, and indicate that I did not comprehend what it was they wanted to know; and so we stood looking at one another, until I heard Tonnison calling to me to hurry up with the kettle. Then, with a smile and a nod, I left them, and all in the little crowd smiled and nodded in return, though their faces still betrayed their puzzlement.

It was evident, I reflected as I went toward the tent, that the inhabitants of these few huts in the wilderness did not know a word of English; and when I told Tonnison, he remarked that he was aware of the fact, and, more, that it was not at all uncommon in that part of the country, where the people often lived and died in their isolated hamlets without ever coming in contact with the outside world.

"I wish we had got the driver to interpret for us before he left," I remarked, as we sat down to our meal. "It seems so strange for the people of this place not even to know what we've come for."

Tonnison grunted an assent, and thereafter was silent for a while.

Later, having satisfied our appetites somewhat, we began to talk, laying our plans for the morrow; then, after a smoke, we closed the flap of the tent, and prepared to turn in.

"I suppose there's no chance of those fellows outside taking anything?" I asked, as we rolled ourselves in our blankets.

Tonnison said that he did not think so, at least while we were about; and, as he went on to explain, we could lock up everything, except the tent, in the big chest that we had brought to hold our provisions. I agreed to this, and soon we were both asleep.

Next morning, early, we rose and went for a swim in the river; after which we dressed and had breakfast. Then we roused out our fishing tackle and overhauled it, by which time, our breakfasts having settled somewhat, we made all secure within the tent and strode off in the direction my friend had explored on his previous visit.

During the day we fished happily, working steadily upstream, and by evening we had one of the prettiest creels of fish that I had seen for a long while. Returning to the village, we made a good feed off our day's spoil, after which, having selected a few of the finer fish for our breakfast, we presented the remainder to the group of villagers who had assembled at a respectful distance to watch our doings. They seemed wonderfully grateful, and heaped mountains of what I presumed to be Irish blessings upon our heads.

Thus we spent several days, having splendid sport, and first-rate appetites to do justice upon our prey. We were pleased to find how friendly the villagers were inclined to be, and that there was no evidence of their having ventured to meddle with our belongings during our absences.

It was on a Tuesday that we arrived in Kraighten, and it would be on the Sunday following that we made a great discovery. Hitherto we had always gone up-stream; on that day, however, we laid aside our rods, and, taking some provisions, set off for a long ramble in the opposite direction. The day was warm, and we trudged along leisurely enough, stopping about mid-day to eat our lunch upon a great flat rock near the riverbank. Afterward we sat and smoked awhile, resuming our walk only when we were tired of inaction.

For perhaps another hour we wandered onward, chatting quietly and comfortably on this and that matter, and on several occasions stopping while my companion—who is something of an artist—made rough sketches of striking bits of the wild scenery.

And then, without any warning whatsoever, the river we had followed so confidently, came to an abrupt end—vanishing into the earth.

"Good Lord!" I said, "who ever would have thought of this?"

And I stared in amazement; then I turned to Tonnison. He was looking, with a blank expression upon his face, at the place where the river disappeared.

In a moment he spoke.

"Let us go on a bit; it may reappear again—anyhow, it is worth investigating."

I agreed, and we went forward once more, though rather aimlessly; for we were not at all certain in which direction to prosecute our search. For perhaps a mile we moved onward; then Tonnison, who had been gazing about curiously, stopped and shaded his eyes.

"See!" he said, after a moment, "isn't that mist or something, over there to the right—away in a line with that great piece of rock?" And he indicated with his hand.

I stared, and, after a minute, seemed to see something, but could not be certain, and said so.

"Anyway," my friend replied, "we'll just go across and have a glance." And he started off in the direction he had suggested, I following. Presently, we came among bushes, and, after a time, out upon the top of a high, boulder-strewn bank, from which we looked down into a wilderness of bushes and trees.

"Seems as though we had come upon an oasis in this desert of stone," muttered Tonnison, as he gazed interestedly. Then he was silent, his eyes fixed; and I looked also; for up from somewhere about the center of the wooded lowland there rose high into the quiet air a great column of hazelike spray, upon which the sun shone, causing innumerable rainbows.

"How beautiful!" I exclaimed.

"Yes," answered Tonnison, thoughtfully. "There must be a waterfall, or something, over there. Perhaps it's our river come to light again. Let's go and see."

Down the sloping bank we made our way, and entered among the trees and shrubberies. The bushes were matted, and the trees overhung us, so that the place was disagreeably gloomy; though not dark enough to hide from me the fact that many of the trees were fruit trees, and that, here and there, one could trace indistinctly, signs of a long departed cultivation. Thus it came to me that we were making our way through the riot of a great and ancient garden. I said as much to Tonnison, and he agreed that there certainly seemed reasonable grounds for my belief.

What a wild place it was, so dismal and somber! Somehow, as we went forward, a sense of the silent loneliness and desertion of the old garden grew upon me, and I felt shivery. One could imagine things lurking among the tangled bushes; while, in the very air of the place, there seemed something uncanny. I think Tonnison was conscious of this also, though he said nothing.

Suddenly, we came to a halt. Through the trees there had grown upon our ears a distant sound. Tonnison bent forward, listening. I could hear it more plainly now; it was continuous and harsh—a sort of droning roar, seeming to come from far away. I experienced a queer, indescribable, little feeling of nervousness. What sort of place was it into which we had got? I looked at my companion, to see what he thought of the matter; and noted that there was only puzzlement in his face; and then, as I watched his features, an expression of comprehension crept over them, and he nodded his head.

"That's a waterfall," he exclaimed, with conviction. "I know the sound now." And he began to push vigorously through the bushes, in the direction of the noise.

As we went forward, the sound became plainer continually, showing that we were heading straight toward it. Steadily, the roaring grew louder and nearer, until it appeared, as I remarked to Tonnison, almost to come from under our feet—and still we were surrounded by the trees and shrubs.

"Take care!" Tonnison called to me. "Look where you're going." And then, suddenly, we came out from among the trees, on to a great open space, where, not six paces in front of us, yawned the mouth of a tremendous chasm, from the depths of which the noise appeared to rise, along with the continuous, mistlike spray that we had witnessed from the top of the distant bank.

For quite a minute we stood in silence, staring in bewilderment at the sight; then my friend went forward cautiously to the edge of the abyss. I followed, and, together, we looked down through a boil of spray at a monster cataract of frothing water that burst, spouting, from the side of the chasm, nearly a hundred feet below.

"Good Lord!" said Tonnison.

I was silent, and rather awed. The sight was so unexpectedly grand and eerie; though this latter quality came more upon me later.

Presently, I looked up and across to the further side of the chasm. There, I saw something towering up among the spray: it looked like a fragment of a great ruin, and I touched Tonnison on the shoulder. He glanced 'round, with a start, and I pointed toward the thing. His gaze followed my finger, and his eyes lighted up with a sudden flash of excitement, as the object came within his field of view.

"Come along," he shouted above the uproar. "We'll have a look at it. There's something queer about this place; I feel it in my bones." And he started off, 'round the edge of the craterlike abyss. As we neared this new thing, I saw that I had not been mistaken in my first impression. It was undoubtedly a portion of some ruined building; yet now I made out that it was not built upon the edge of the chasm itself, as I had at first supposed; but perched almost at the extreme end of a huge spur of rock that jutted out some fifty or sixty feet over the abyss. In fact, the jagged mass of ruin was literally suspended in midair.

Arriving opposite it, we walked out on to the projecting arm of rock, and I must confess to having felt an intolerable sense of terror as I looked down from that dizzy perch into the unknown depths below us—into the deeps from which there rose ever the thunder of the falling water and the shroud of rising spray.

Reaching the ruin, we clambered 'round it cautiously, and, on the further side, came upon a mass of fallen stones and rubble. The ruin itself seemed to me, as I proceeded now to examine it minutely, to be a portion of the outer wall of some prodigious structure, it was so thick and substantially built; yet what it was doing in such a position I could by no means conjecture. Where was the rest of the house, or castle, or whatever there had been?

I went back to the outer side of the wall, and thence to the edge of the chasm, leaving Tonnison rooting systematically among the heap of stones and rubbish on the outer side. Then I commenced to examine the surface of the ground, near the edge of the abyss, to see whether there were not left other remnants of the building to which the fragment of ruin evidently belonged. But though I scrutinized the earth with the greatest care, I could see no signs of anything to show that there had ever been a building erected on the spot, and I grew more puzzled than ever.

Then, I heard a cry from Tonnison; he was shouting my name, excitedly, and without delay I hurried along the rocky promontory to the ruin. I wondered whether he had hurt himself, and then the thought came, that perhaps he had found something.

I reached the crumbled wall and climbed 'round. There I found Tonnison standing within a small excavation that he had made among the débris: he was brushing the dirt from something that looked like a book, much crumpled and dilapidated; and opening his mouth, every second or two, to bellow my name. As soon as he saw that I had come, he handed his prize to me, telling me to put it into my satchel so as to protect it from the damp, while he continued his explorations. This I did, first, however, running the pages through my fingers, and noting that they were closely filled with neat, old-fashioned writing which was quite legible, save in one portion, where many of the pages were almost destroyed, being muddied and crumpled, as though the book had been doubled back at that part. This, I found out from Tonnison, was actually as he had discovered it, and the damage was due, probably, to the fall of masonry upon the opened part. Curiously enough, the book was fairly dry, which I attributed to its having been so securely buried among the ruins.

Having put the volume away safely, I turned-to and gave Tonnison a hand with his self-imposed task of excavating; yet, though we put in over an hour's hard work, turning over the whole of the upheaped stones and rubbish, we came upon nothing more than some fragments of broken wood, that might have been parts of a desk or table; and so we gave up searching, and went back along the rock, once more to the safety of the land.

The next thing we did was to make a complete tour of the tremendous chasm, which we were able to observe was in the form of an almost perfect circle, save for where the ruin-crowned spur of rock jutted out, spoiling its symmetry.

The abyss was, as Tonnison put it, like nothing so much as a gigantic well or pit going sheer down into the bowels of the earth.

For some time longer, we continued to stare about us, and then, noticing that there was a clear space away to the north of the chasm, we bent our steps in that direction.

Here, distant from the mouth of the mighty pit by some hundreds of yards, we came upon a great lake of silent water—silent, that is, save in one place where there was a continuous bubbling and gurgling.

Now, being away from the noise of the spouting cataract, we were able to hear one another speak, without having to shout at the tops of our voices, and I asked Tonnison what he thought of the place—I told him that I didn't like it, and that the sooner we were out of it the better I should be pleased.

He nodded in reply, and glanced at the woods behind furtively. I asked him if he had seen or heard anything. He made no answer; but stood silent, as though listening, and I kept quiet also.

Suddenly, he spoke.

"Hark!" he said, sharply. I looked at him, and then away among the trees and bushes, holding my breath involuntarily. A minute came and went in strained silence; yet I could hear nothing, and I turned to Tonnison to say as much; and then, even as I opened my lips to speak, there came a strange wailing noise out of the wood on our left.... It appeared to float through the trees, and there was a rustle of stirring leaves, and then silence.

All at once, Tonnison spoke, and put his hand on my shoulder. "Let us get out of here," he said, and began to move slowly toward where the surrounding trees and bushes seemed thinnest. As I followed him, it came to me suddenly that the sun was low, and that there was a raw sense of chilliness in the air.

Tonnison said nothing further, but kept on steadily. We were among the trees now, and I glanced around, nervously; but saw nothing, save the quiet branches and trunks and the tangled bushes. Onward we went, and no sound broke the silence, except the occasional snapping of a twig under our feet, as we moved forward. Yet, in spite of the quietness, I had a horrible feeling that we were not alone; and I kept so close to Tonnison that twice I kicked his heels clumsily, though he said nothing. A minute, and then another, and we reached the confines of the wood coming out at last upon the bare rockiness of the countryside. Only then was I able to shake off the haunting dread that had followed me among the trees.

Once, as we moved away, there seemed to come again a distant sound of wailing, and I said to myself that it was the wind—yet the evening was breathless.

Presently, Tonnison began to talk.

"Look you," he said with decision, "I would not spend the night in that place for all the wealth that the world holds. There is something unholy—diabolical—about it. It came to me all in a moment, just after you spoke. It seemed to me that the woods were full of vile things—you know!"

"Yes," I answered, and looked back toward the place; but it was hidden from us by a rise in the ground.

"There's the book," I said, and I put my hand into the satchel.

"You've got it safely?" he questioned, with a sudden access of anxiety.

"Yes," I replied.

"Perhaps," he continued, "we shall learn something from it when we get back to the tent. We had better hurry, too; we're a long way off still, and I don't fancy, now, being caught out here in the dark."

It was two hours later when we reached the tent; and, without delay, we set to work to prepare a meal; for we had eaten nothing since our lunch at midday.

Supper over, we cleared the things out of the way, and lit our pipes. Then Tonnison asked me to get the manuscript out of my satchel. This I did, and then, as we could not both read from it at the same time, he suggested that I should read the thing out loud. "And mind," he cautioned, knowing my propensities, "don't go skipping half the book."

Yet, had he but known what it contained, he would have realized how needless such advice was, for once at least. And there seated in the opening of our little tent, I began the strange tale of The House on the Borderland (for such was the title of the MS.); this is told in the following pages.

Chapter 2

The Plain of Silence

I am an old man. I live here in this ancient house, surrounded by huge, unkempt gardens.

The peasantry, who inhabit the wilderness beyond, say that I am mad. That is because I will have nothing to do with them. I live here alone with my old sister, who is also my housekeeper. We keep no servants—I hate them. I have one friend, a dog; yes, I would sooner have old Pepper than the rest of Creation together. He, at least, understands me—and has sense enough to leave me alone when I am in my dark moods.

I have decided to start a kind of diary; it may enable me to record some of the thoughts and feelings that I cannot express to anyone; but, beyond this, I am anxious to make some record of the strange things that I have heard and seen, during many years of loneliness, in this weird old building.

For a couple of centuries, this house has had a reputation, a bad one, and, until I bought it, for more than eighty years no one had lived here; consequently, I got the old place at a ridiculously low figure.

I am not superstitious; but I have ceased to deny that things happen in this old house—things that I cannot explain; and, therefore, I must needs ease my mind, by writing down an account of them, to the best of my ability; though, should this, my diary, ever be read when I am gone, the readers will but shake their heads, and be the more convinced that I was mad.

This house, how ancient it is! though its age strikes one less, perhaps, than the quaintness of its structure, which is curious and fantastic to the last degree. Little curved towers and pinnacles, with outlines suggestive of leaping flames, predominate; while the body of the building is in the form of a circle.

I have heard that there is an old story, told amongst the country people, to the effect that the devil built the place. However, that is as may be. True or not, I neither know nor care, save as it may have helped to cheapen it, ere I came.

I must have been here some ten years before I saw sufficient to warrant any belief in the stories, current in the neighborhood, about this house. It is true that I had, on at least a dozen occasions, seen, vaguely, things that puzzled me, and, perhaps, had felt more than I had seen. Then, as the years passed, bringing age upon me, I became often aware of something unseen, yet unmistakably present, in the empty rooms and corridors. Still, it was as I have said many years before I saw any real manifestations of the so-called supernatural.

It was not Halloween. If I were telling a story for amusement's sake, I should probably place it on that night of nights; but this is a true record of my own experiences, and I would not put pen to paper to amuse anyone. No. It was after midnight on the morning of the twenty-first day of January. I was sitting reading, as is often my custom, in my study. Pepper lay, sleeping, near my chair.

Without warning, the flames of the two candles went low, and then shone with a ghastly green effulgence. I looked up, quickly, and as I did so I saw the lights sink into a dull, ruddy tint; so that the room glowed with a strange, heavy, crimson twilight that gave the shadows behind the chairs and tables a double depth of blackness; and wherever the light struck, it was as though luminous blood had been splashed over the room.

Down on the floor, I heard a faint, frightened whimper, and something pressed itself in between my two feet. It was Pepper, cowering under my dressing gown. Pepper, usually as brave as a lion!

It was this movement of the dog's, I think, that gave me the first twinge of real fear. I had been considerably startled when the lights burnt first green and then red; but had been momentarily under the impression that the change was due to some influx of noxious gas into the room. Now, however, I saw that it was not so; for the candles burned with a steady flame, and showed no signs of going out, as would have been the case had the change been due to fumes in the atmosphere.

I did not move. I felt distinctly frightened; but could think of nothing better to do than wait. For perhaps a minute, I kept my glance about the room, nervously. Then I noticed that the lights had commenced to sink, very slowly; until presently they showed minute specks of red fire, like the gleamings of rubies in the darkness. Still, I sat watching; while a sort of dreamy indifference seemed to steal over me; banishing altogether the fear that had begun to grip me.

Away in the far end of the huge old-fashioned room, I became conscious of a faint glow. Steadily it grew, filling the room with gleams of quivering green light; then they sank quickly, and changed—even as the candle flames had done—into a deep, somber crimson that strengthened, and lit up the room with a flood of awful glory.

The light came from the end wall, and grew ever brighter until its intolerable glare caused my eyes acute pain, and involuntarily I closed them. It may have been a few seconds before I was able to open them. The first thing I noticed was that the light had decreased, greatly; so that it no longer tried my eyes. Then, as it grew still duller, I was aware, all at once, that, instead of looking at the redness, I was staring through it, and through the wall beyond.

Gradually, as I became more accustomed to the idea, I realized that I was looking out on to a vast plain, lit with the same gloomy twilight that pervaded the room. The immensity of this plain scarcely can be conceived. In no part could I perceive its confines. It seemed to broaden and spread out, so that the eye failed to perceive any limitations. Slowly, the details of the nearer portions began to grow clear; then, in a moment almost, the light died away, and the vision—if vision it were—faded and was gone.

Suddenly, I became conscious that I was no longer in the chair. Instead, I seemed to be hovering above it, and looking down at a dim something, huddled and silent. In a little while, a cold blast struck me, and I was outside in the night, floating, like a bubble, up through the darkness. As I moved, an icy coldness seemed to enfold me, so that I shivered.

After a time, I looked to right and left, and saw the intolerable blackness of the night, pierced by remote gleams of fire. Onward, outward, I drove. Once, I glanced behind, and saw the earth, a small crescent of blue light, receding away to my left. Further off, the sun, a splash of white flame, burned vividly against the dark.

An indefinite period passed. Then, for the last time, I saw the earth—an enduring globule of radiant blue, swimming in an eternity of ether. And there I, a fragile flake of soul dust, flickered silently across the void, from the distant blue, into the expanse of the unknown.

A great while seemed to pass over me, and now I could nowhere see anything. I had passed beyond the fixed stars and plunged into the huge blackness that waits beyond. All this time I had experienced little, save a sense of lightness and cold discomfort. Now however the atrocious darkness seemed to creep into my soul, and I became filled with fear and despair. What was going to become of me? Where was I going? Even as the thoughts were formed, there grew against the impalpable blackness that wrapped me a faint tinge of blood. It seemed extraordinarily remote, and mistlike; yet, at once, the feeling of oppression was lightened, and I no longer despaired.

Slowly, the distant redness became plainer and larger; until, as I drew nearer, it spread out into a great, somber glare—dull and tremendous. Still, I fled onward, and, presently, I had come so close, that it seemed to stretch beneath me, like a great ocean of somber red. I could see little, save that it appeared to spread out interminably in all directions.

In a further space, I found that I was descending upon it; and, soon, I sank into a great sea of sullen, red-hued clouds. Slowly, I emerged from these, and there, below me, I saw the stupendous plain that I had seen from my room in this house that stands upon the borders of the Silences.

Presently, I landed, and stood, surrounded by a great waste of loneliness. The place was lit with a gloomy twilight that gave an impression of indescribable desolation.

Afar to my right, within the sky, there burnt a gigantic ring of dull-red fire, from the outer edge of which were projected huge, writhing flames, darted and jagged. The interior of this ring was black, black as the gloom of the outer night. I comprehended, at once, that it was from this extraordinary sun that the place derived its doleful light.

From that strange source of light, I glanced down again to my surroundings. Everywhere I looked, I saw nothing but the same flat weariness of interminable plain. Nowhere could I descry any signs of life; not even the ruins of some ancient habitation.

Gradually, I found that I was being borne forward, floating across the flat waste. For what seemed an eternity, I moved onward. I was unaware of any great sense of impatience; though some curiosity and a vast wonder were with me continually. Always, I saw around me the breadth of that enormous plain; and, always, I searched for some new thing to break its monotony; but there was no change—only loneliness, silence, and desert.

Presently, in a half-conscious manner, I noticed that there was a faint mistiness, ruddy in hue, lying over its surface. Still, when I looked more intently, I was unable to say that it was really mist; for it appeared to blend with the plain, giving it a peculiar unrealness, and conveying to the senses the idea of unsubstantiality.

Gradually, I began to weary with the sameness of the thing. Yet, it was a great time before I perceived any signs of the place, toward which I was being conveyed.

"At first, I saw it, far ahead, like a long hillock on the surface of the Plain. Then, as I drew nearer, I perceived that I had been mistaken; for, instead of a low hill, I made out, now, a chain of great mountains, whose distant peaks towered up into the red gloom, until they were almost lost to sight."

Chapter 3

The House in the Arena

And so, after a time, I came to the mountains. Then, the course of my journey was altered, and I began to move along their bases, until, all at once, I saw that I had come opposite to a vast rift, opening into the mountains. Through this, I was borne, moving at no great speed. On either side of me, huge, scarped walls of rocklike substance rose sheer. Far overhead, I discerned a thin ribbon of red, where the mouth of the chasm opened, among inaccessible peaks. Within, was gloom, deep and somber, and chilly silence. For a while, I went onward steadily, and then, at last, I saw, ahead, a deep, red glow, that told me I was near upon the further opening of the gorge.

A minute came and went, and I was at the exit of the chasm, staring out upon an enormous amphitheatre of mountains. Yet, of the mountains, and the terrible grandeur of the place, I recked nothing; for I was confounded with amazement to behold, at a distance of several miles and occupying the center of the arena, a stupendous structure built apparently of green jade. Yet, in itself, it was not the discovery of the building that had so astonished me; but the fact, which became every moment more apparent, that in no particular, save in color and its enormous size, did the lonely structure vary from this house in which I live.

For a while, I continued to stare, fixedly. Even then, I could scarcely believe that I saw aright. In my mind, a question formed, reiterating incessantly: 'What does it mean?' 'What does it mean?' and I was unable to make answer, even out of the depths of my imagination. I seemed capable only of wonder and fear. For a time longer, I gazed, noting continually some fresh point of resemblance that attracted me. At last, wearied and sorely puzzled, I turned from it, to view the rest of the strange place on to which I had intruded.

Hitherto, I had been so engrossed in my scrutiny of the House, that I had given only a cursory glance 'round. Now, as I looked, I began to realize upon what sort of a place I had come. The arena, for so I have termed it, appeared a perfect circle of about ten to twelve miles in diameter, the

House, as I have mentioned before, standing in the center. The surface of the place, like to that of the Plain, had a peculiar, misty appearance, that was yet not mist.

From a rapid survey, my glance passed quickly upward along the slopes of the circling mountains. How silent they were. I think that this same abominable stillness was more trying to me than anything that I had so far seen or imagined. I was looking up, now, at the great crags, towering so loftily. Up there, the impalpable redness gave a blurred appearance to everything.

And then, as I peered, curiously, a new terror came to me; for away up among the dim peaks to my right, I had descried a vast shape of blackness, giantlike. It grew upon my sight. It had an enormous equine head, with gigantic ears, and seemed to peer steadfastly down into the arena. There was that about the pose that gave me the impression of an eternal watchfulness— of having warded that dismal place, through unknown eternities. Slowly, the monster became plainer to me; and then, suddenly, my gaze sprang from it to something further off and higher among the crags. For a long minute, I gazed, fearfully. I was strangely conscious of something not altogether unfamiliar— as though something stirred in the back of my mind. The thing was black, and had four grotesque arms. The features showed indistinctly, 'round the neck, I made out several light-colored objects. Slowly, the details came to me, and I realized, coldly, that they were skulls. Further down the body was another circling belt, showing less dark against the black trunk. Then, even as I puzzled to know what the thing was, a memory slid into my mind, and straightway, I knew that I was looking at a monstrous representation of Kali, the Hindu goddess of death.

Other remembrances of my old student days drifted into my thoughts. My glance fell back upon the huge beast-headed Thing. Simultaneously, I recognized it for the ancient Egyptian god Set, or Seth, the Destroyer of Souls. With the knowledge, there came a great sweep of questioning—'Two of the— !' I stopped, and endeavored to think. Things beyond my imagination peered into my frightened mind. I saw, obscurely. 'The old gods of mythology!' I tried to comprehend to what it was all pointing. My gaze dwelt, flickeringly, between the two. 'If—'

An idea came swiftly, and I turned, and glanced rapidly upward, searching the gloomy crags, away to my left. Something loomed out under a great peak, a shape of greyness. I wondered I had not seen it earlier, and then remembered I had not yet viewed that portion. I saw it more plainly now. It was, as I have said, grey. It had a tremendous head; but no eyes. That part of its face was blank.

Now, I saw that there were other things up among the mountains. Further off, reclining on a lofty ledge, I made out a livid mass, irregular and ghoulish. It seemed without form, save for an unclean, half-animal face, that looked out, vilely, from somewhere about its middle. And then I saw others—there were hundreds of them. They seemed to grow out of the shadows. Several I recognized almost immediately as mythological deities; others were strange to me, utterly strange, beyond the power of a human mind to conceive.

On each side, I looked, and saw more, continually. The mountains were full of strange things—Beast-gods, and Horrors so atrocious and bestial that possibility and decency deny any further attempt to describe them. And I—I was filled with a terrible sense of overwhelming horror and fear and repugnance; yet, spite of these, I wondered exceedingly. Was there then, after all, something in the old heathen worship, something more than the mere deifying of men, animals, and elements? The thought gripped me—was there?

Later, a question repeated itself. What were they, those Beast-gods, and the others? At first, they had appeared to me just sculptured Monsters placed indiscriminately among the inaccessible peaks and precipices of the surrounding mountains. Now, as I scrutinized them with greater intentness, my mind began to reach out to fresh conclusions. There was something about them, an indescribable sort of silent vitality that suggested, to my broadening consciousness, a state of life-in-death—a something that was by no means life, as we understand it; but rather an inhuman form of existence, that well might be likened to a deathless trance—a condition in which it was possible to imagine their continuing, eternally. 'Immortal!' the word rose in my thoughts unbidden; and, straightway, I grew to wondering whether this might be the immortality of the gods.

And then, in the midst of my wondering and musing, something happened. Until then, I had been staying just within the shadow of the exit of the great rift. Now, without volition on my part, I drifted out of the semi-darkness and began to move slowly across the arena—toward the House. At this, I gave up all thoughts of those prodigious Shapes above me—and could only stare, frightenedly, at the tremendous structure toward which I was being conveyed so remorselessly. Yet, though I searched earnestly, I could discover nothing that I had not already seen, and so became gradually calmer.

Presently, I had reached a point more than halfway between the House and the gorge. All around was spread the stark loneliness of the place, and the unbroken silence. Steadily, I neared the great building. Then, all at once, something caught my vision, something that came 'round one of the huge buttresses of the House, and so into full view. It was a gigantic thing, and moved with a curious lope, going almost upright, after the manner of a man. It was quite unclothed, and had a remarkable luminous appearance. Yet it was the face that attracted and frightened me the most. It was the face of a swine.

Silently, intently, I watched this horrible creature, and forgot my fear, momentarily, in my interest in its movements. It was making its way, cumbrously 'round the building, stopping as it came to each window to peer in and shake at the bars, with which—as in this house—they were protected; and whenever it came to a door, it would push at it, fingering the fastening stealthily. Evidently, it was searching for an ingress into the House.

I had come now to within less than a quarter of a mile of the great structure, and still I was compelled forward. Abruptly, the Thing turned and gazed hideously in my direction. It opened its mouth, and, for the first time, the stillness of that abominable place was broken, by a deep, booming note that sent an added thrill of apprehension through me. Then, immediately, I became aware that it was coming toward me, swiftly and silently. In an instant, it had covered half the distance that lay between. And still, I was borne helplessly to meet it. Only a hundred yards, and the brutish ferocity of the giant face numbed me with a feeling of unmitigated horror. I could have screamed, in the supremeness of my fear; and then, in the very moment of my extremity and despair, I became conscious that I was looking down upon the arena, from a rapidly increasing height. I was rising, rising. In an inconceivably short while, I had reached an altitude of many hundred feet. Beneath me, the spot that I had just left, was occupied by the foul Swine-creature. It had gone down on all fours and was snuffing and rooting, like a veritable hog, at the surface of the arena. A moment and it rose to its feet, clutching upward, with an expression of desire upon its face such as I have never seen in this world.

Continually, I mounted higher. A few minutes, it seemed, and I had risen above the great mountains—floating, alone, afar in the redness. At a tremendous distance below, the arena showed, dimly; with the mighty House looking no larger than a tiny spot of green. The Swine-thing was no longer visible.

Presently, I passed over the mountains, out above the huge breadth of the plain. Far away, on its surface, in the direction of the ring-shaped sun, there showed a confused blur. I looked toward it, indifferently. It reminded me, somewhat, of the first glimpse I had caught of the mountain-amphitheatre.

With a sense of weariness, I glanced upward at the immense ring of fire. What a strange thing it was! Then, as I stared, out from the dark center, there spurted a sudden flare of extraordinary vivid fire. Compared with the size of the black center, it was as naught; yet, in itself, stupendous. With awakened interest, I watched it carefully, noting its strange boiling and glowing. Then, in a moment, the whole thing grew dim and unreal, and so passed out of sight. Much amazed, I glanced down to the Plain from which I was still rising. Thus, I received a fresh surprise. The Plain—everything had vanished, and only a sea of red mist was spread far below me. Gradually as I stared this grew remote, and died away into a dim far mystery of red against an unfathomable night. A while, and even this had gone, and I was wrapped in an impalpable, lightless gloom.

Chapter 4

The Earth

Thus I was, and only the memory that I had lived through the dark, once before, served to sustain my thoughts. A great time passed—ages. And then a single star broke its way through the darkness. It was the first of one of the outlying clusters of this universe. Presently, it was far behind, and all about me shone the splendor of the countless stars. Later, years it seemed, I saw the sun, a clot of flame. Around it, I made out presently several remote specks of light—the planets of the Solar system. And so I saw the earth again, blue and unbelievably minute. It grew larger, and became defined.

A long space of time came and went, and then at last I entered into the shadow of the world—plunging headlong into the dim and holy earth night. Overhead were the old constellations, and there was a crescent moon. Then, as I neared the earth's surface, a dimness swept over me, and I appeared to sink into a black mist.

For a while, I knew nothing. I was unconscious. Gradually, I became aware of a faint, distant whining. It became plainer. A desperate feeling of agony possessed me. I struggled madly for breath, and tried to shout. A moment, and I got my breath more easily. I was conscious that something was licking my hand. Something damp swept across my face. I heard a panting, and then again the whining. It seemed to come to my ears, now, with a sense of familiarity, and I opened my eyes. All was dark; but the feeling of oppression had left me. I was seated, and something was whining piteously, and licking me. I felt strangely confused, and, instinctively, tried to ward off the thing that licked. My head was curiously vacant, and, for the moment, I seemed incapable of action or thought. Then, things came back to me, and I called 'Pepper,' faintly. I was answered by a joyful bark, and renewed and frantic caresses.

In a little while, I felt stronger, and put out my hand for the matches. I groped about, for a few moments, blindly; then my hands lit upon them, and I struck a light, and looked confusedly around. All about me, I saw the old, familiar things. And there I sat, full of dazed wonders, until the flame of the match burnt my finger, and I dropped it; while a hasty expression of pain and anger, escaped my lips, surprising me with the sound of my own voice.

After a moment, I struck another match, and, stumbling across the room, lit the candles. As I did so, I observed that they had not burned away, but had been put out.

As the flames shot up, I turned, and stared about the study; yet there was nothing unusual to see; and, suddenly, a gust of irritation took me. What had happened? I held my head, with both hands, and tried to remember. Ah! the great, silent Plain, and the ring-shaped sun of red fire. Where were they? Where had I seen them? How long ago? I felt dazed and muddled. Once or twice, I walked up and down the room, unsteadily. My memory seemed dulled, and, already, the thing I had witnessed came back to me with an effort.

I have a remembrance of cursing, peevishly, in my bewilderment. Suddenly, I turned faint and giddy, and had to grasp at the table for support. During a few moments, I held on, weakly; and then managed to totter sideways into a chair. After a little time, I felt somewhat better, and succeeded in reaching the cupboard where, usually, I keep brandy and biscuits. I poured myself out a little of the stimulant, and drank it off. Then, taking a handful of biscuits, I returned to my chair, and began to devour them, ravenously. I was vaguely surprised at my hunger. I felt as though I had eaten nothing for an uncountably long while.

As I ate, my glance roved about the room, taking in its various details, and still searching, though almost unconsciously, for something tangible upon which to take hold, among the invisible mysteries that encompassed me. 'Surely,' I thought, 'there must be something—' And, in the same instant, my gaze dwelt upon the face of the clock in the opposite corner. Therewith, I stopped eating, and just stared. For, though its ticking indicated most certainly that it was still going, the hands were pointing to a little before the hour of midnight; whereas it was, as well I knew, considerably after that time when I had witnessed the first of the strange happenings I have just described.

For perhaps a moment I was astounded and puzzled. Had the hour been the same as when I had last seen the clock, I should have concluded that the hands had stuck in one place, while the internal mechanism went on as usual; but that would, in no way, account for the hands having traveled backward. Then, even as I turned the matter over in my wearied brain, the thought flashed upon me that it was now close upon the morning of the twenty-second, and that I had been unconscious to the visible world through the greater portion of the last twenty-four hours. The thought occupied my attention for a full minute; then I commenced to eat again. I was still very hungry.

During breakfast, next morning, I inquired casually of my sister regarding the date, and found my surmise correct. I had, indeed, been absent—at least in spirit—for nearly a day and a night.

My sister asked me no questions; for it is not by any means the first time that I have kept to my study for a whole day, and sometimes a couple of days at a time, when I have been particularly engrossed in my books or work.

And so the days pass on, and I am still filled with a wonder to know the meaning of all that I saw on that memorable night. Yet, well I know that my curiosity is little likely to be satisfied.

Chapter 5

The Thing in the Pit

This house is, as I have said before, surrounded by a huge estate, and wild and uncultivated gardens.

Away at the back, distant some three hundred yards, is a dark, deep ravine—spoken of as the 'Pit,' by the peasantry. At the bottom runs a sluggish stream so overhung by trees as scarcely to be seen from above.

In passing, I must explain that this river has a subterranean origin, emerging suddenly at the East end of the ravine, and disappearing, as abruptly, beneath the cliffs that form its Western extremity.

It was some months after my vision (if vision it were) of the great Plain that my attention was particularly attracted to the Pit.

I happened, one day, to be walking along its Southern edge, when, suddenly, several pieces of rock and shale were dislodged from the face of the cliff immediately beneath me, and fell with a sullen crash through the trees. I heard them splash in the river at the bottom; and then silence. I should not have given this incident more than a passing thought, had not Pepper at once begun to bark savagely; nor would he be silent when I bade him, which is most unusual behavior on his part.

Feeling that there must be someone or something in the Pit, I went back to the house, quickly, for a stick. When I returned, Pepper had ceased his barks and was growling and smelling, uneasily, along the top.

Whistling to him to follow me, I started to descend cautiously. The depth to the bottom of the Pit must be about a hundred and fifty feet, and some time as well as considerable care was expended before we reached the bottom in safety.

Once down, Pepper and I started to explore along the banks of the river. It was very dark there due to the overhanging trees, and I moved warily, keeping my glance about me and my stick ready.

Pepper was quiet now and kept close to me all the time. Thus, we searched right up one side of the river, without hearing or seeing anything. Then, we crossed over—by the simple method of jumping—and commenced to beat our way back through the underbrush.

We had accomplished perhaps half the distance, when I heard again the sound of falling stones on the other side—the side from which we had just come. One large rock came thundering down through the treetops, struck the opposite bank, and bounded into the river, driving a great jet of water right over us. At this, Pepper gave out a deep growl; then stopped, and pricked up his ears. I listened, also.

A second later, a loud, half-human, half-piglike squeal sounded from among the trees, apparently about halfway up the South cliff. It was answered by a similar note from the bottom of the Pit. At this, Pepper gave a short, sharp bark, and, springing across the little river, disappeared into the bushes.

Immediately afterward, I heard his barks increase in depth and number, and in between there sounded a noise of confused jabbering. This ceased, and, in the succeeding silence, there rose a semi-human yell of agony. Almost immediately, Pepper gave a long-drawn howl of pain, and then the shrubs were violently agitated, and he came running out with his tail down, and glancing as he ran over his shoulder. As he reached me, I saw that he was bleeding from what appeared to be a great claw wound in the side that had almost laid bare his ribs.

Seeing Pepper thus mutilated, a furious feeling of anger seized me, and, whirling my staff, I sprang across, and into the bushes from which Pepper had emerged. As I forced my way through, I thought I heard a sound of breathing. Next instant, I had burst into a little clear space, just in time to see something, livid white in color, disappear among the bushes on the opposite side. With a shout, I ran toward it; but, though I struck and probed among the bushes with my stick, I neither saw nor heard anything further; and so returned to Pepper. There, after bathing his wound in the river, I bound my wetted handkerchief 'round his body; having done which, we retreated up the ravine and into the daylight again.

On reaching the house, my sister inquired what had happened to Pepper, and I told her he had been fighting with a wildcat, of which I had heard there were several about.

I felt it would be better not to tell her how it had really happened; though, to be sure, I scarcely knew myself; but this I did know, that the thing I had seen run into the bushes was no wildcat. It was much too big, and had, so far as I had observed, a skin like a hog's, only of a dead, unhealthy white color. And then—it had run upright, or nearly so, upon its hind feet, with a motion somewhat resembling that of a human being. This much I had noticed in my brief glimpse, and, truth to tell, I felt a good deal of uneasiness, besides curiosity as I turned the matter over in my mind.

It was in the morning that the above incident had occurred.

Then, it would be after dinner, as I sat reading, that, happening to look up suddenly, I saw something peering in over the window ledge the eyes and ears alone showing.

'A pig, by Jove!' I said, and rose to my feet. Thus, I saw the thing more completely; but it was no pig—God alone knows what it was. It reminded me, vaguely, of the hideous Thing that had haunted the great arena. It had a grotesquely human mouth and jaw; but with no chin of which to speak. The nose was prolonged into a snout; thus it was that with the little eyes and queer ears, gave it such an extraordinarily swinelike appearance. Of forehead there was little, and the whole face was of an unwholesome white color.

For perhaps a minute, I stood looking at the thing with an ever growing feeling of disgust, and some fear. The mouth kept jabbering, inanely, and once emitted a half-swinish grunt. I think it was the eyes that attracted me the most; they seemed to glow, at times, with a horribly human intelligence, and kept flickering away from my face, over the details of the room, as though my stare disturbed it.

It appeared to be supporting itself by two clawlike hands upon the windowsill. These claws, unlike the face, were of a clayey brown hue, and bore an indistinct resemblance to human hands, in that they had four fingers and a thumb; though these were webbed up to the first joint, much as are a duck's. Nails it had also, but so long and powerful that they were more like the talons of an eagle than aught else.

As I have said, before, I felt some fear; though almost of an impersonal kind. I may explain my feeling better by saying that it was more a sensation of abhorrence; such as one might expect to feel, if brought in contact with something superhumanly foul; something unholy—belonging to some hitherto undreamt of state of existence.

I cannot say that I grasped these various details of the brute at the time. I think they seemed to come back to me, afterward, as though imprinted upon my brain. I imagined more than I saw as I looked at the thing, and the material details grew upon me later.

For perhaps a minute I stared at the creature; then as my nerves steadied a little I shook off the vague alarm that held me, and took a step toward the window. Even as I did so, the thing ducked and vanished. I rushed to the door and looked 'round hurriedly; but only the tangled bushes and shrubs met my gaze.

I ran back into the house, and, getting my gun, sallied out to search through the gardens. As I went, I asked myself whether the thing I had just seen was likely to be the same of which I had caught a glimpse in the morning. I inclined to think it was.

I would have taken Pepper with me; but judged it better to give his wound a chance to heal. Besides, if the creature I had just seen was, as I imagined, his antagonist of the morning, it was not likely that he would be of much use.

I began my search, systematically. I was determined, if it were possible, to find and put an end to that swine-thing. This was, at least, a material Horror!

At first, I searched, cautiously; with the thought of Pepper's wound in my mind; but, as the hours passed, and not a sign of anything living, showed in the great, lonely gardens, I became less apprehensive. I felt almost as though I would welcome the sight of it. Anything seemed better than this silence, with the ever-present feeling that the creature might be lurking in every bush I passed. Later, I grew careless of danger, to the extent of plunging right through the bushes, probing with my gun barrel as I went.

At times, I shouted; but only the echoes answered back. I thought thus perhaps to frighten or stir the creature to showing itself; but only succeeded in bringing my sister Mary out, to know what was the matter. I told her, that I had seen the wildcat that had wounded Pepper, and that I was trying to hunt it out of the bushes. She seemed only half satisfied, and went back into the house, with an expression of doubt upon her face. I wondered whether she had seen or guessed anything. For the rest of the afternoon, I prosecuted the search anxiously. I felt that I should be unable to sleep, with that bestial thing haunting the shrubberies, and yet, when evening fell, I had seen nothing. Then, as I turned homeward, I heard a short, unintelligible noise, among the bushes to my right. Instantly, I turned, and, aiming quickly, fired in the direction of the sound. Immediately afterward, I heard something scuttling away among the bushes. It moved rapidly, and in a minute had gone out of hearing. After a few steps I ceased my pursuit, realizing how futile it must be in the fast gathering gloom; and so, with a curious feeling of depression, I entered the house.

That night, after my sister had gone to bed, I went 'round to all the windows and doors on the ground floor; and saw to it that they were securely fastened. This precaution was scarcely necessary as regards the windows, as all of those on the lower storey are strongly barred; but with the doors—of which there are five—it was wisely thought, as not one was locked.

Having secured these, I went to my study, yet, somehow, for once, the place jarred upon me; it seemed so huge and echoey. For some time I tried to read;

but at last finding it impossible I carried my book down to the kitchen where a large fire was burning, and sat there.

I dare say, I had read for a couple of hours, when, suddenly, I heard a sound that made me lower my book, and listen, intently. It was a noise of something rubbing and fumbling against the back door. Once the door creaked, loudly; as though force were being applied to it. During those few, short moments, I experienced an indescribable feeling of terror, such as I should have believed impossible. My hands shook; a cold sweat broke out on me, and I shivered violently.

Gradually, I calmed. The stealthy movements outside had ceased.

Then for an hour I sat silent and watchful. All at once the feeling of fear took me again. I felt as I imagine an animal must, under the eye of a snake. Yet now I could hear nothing. Still, there was no doubting that some unexplained influence was at work.

Gradually, imperceptibly almost, something stole on my ear—a sound that resolved itself into a faint murmur. Quickly it developed and grew into a muffled but hideous chorus of bestial shrieks. It appeared to rise from the bowels of the earth.

I heard a thud, and realized in a dull, half comprehending way that I had dropped my book. After that, I just sat; and thus the daylight found me, when it crept wanly in through the barred, high windows of the great kitchen.

With the dawning light, the feeling of stupor and fear left me; and I came more into possession of my senses.

Thereupon I picked up my book, and crept to the door to listen. Not a sound broke the chilly silence. For some minutes I stood there; then, very gradually and cautiously, I drew back the bolt and opening the door peeped out.

My caution was unneeded. Nothing was to be seen, save the grey vista of dreary, tangled bushes and trees, extending to the distant plantation.

With a shiver, I closed the door, and made my way, quietly, up to bed.

Chapter 6

The Swine Things

It was evening, a week later. My sister sat in the garden, knitting. I was walking up and down, reading. My gun leant up against the wall of the house; for, since the advent of that strange thing in the gardens, I had deemed it wise to take precautions. Yet, through the whole week, there had been nothing to alarm me, either by sight or sound; so that I was able to look back, calmly, to the incident; though still with a sense of unmitigated wonder and curiosity.

I was, as I have just said, walking up and down, and somewhat engrossed in my book. Suddenly, I heard a crash, away in the direction of the Pit. With a quick movement, I turned and saw a tremendous column of dust rising high into the evening air.

My sister had risen to her feet, with a sharp exclamation of surprise and fright.

Telling her to stay where she was, I snatched up my gun, and ran toward the Pit. As I neared it, I heard a dull, rumbling sound, that grew quickly into a roar, split with deeper crashes, and up from the Pit drove a fresh volume of dust.

The noise ceased, though the dust still rose, tumultuously.

I reached the edge, and looked down; but could see nothing save a boil of dust clouds swirling hither and thither. The air was so full of the small particles, that they blinded and choked me; and, finally, I had to run out from the smother, to breathe.

Gradually, the suspended matter sank, and hung in a panoply over the mouth of the Pit.

I could only guess at what had happened.

That there had been a land-slip of some kind, I had little doubt; but the cause was beyond my knowledge; and yet, even then, I had half imaginings; for, already, the thought had come to me, of those falling rocks, and that Thing in the bottom of the Pit; but, in the first minutes of confusion, I failed to reach the natural conclusion, to which the catastrophe pointed.

Slowly, the dust subsided, until, presently, I was able to approach the edge, and look down.

For a while, I peered impotently, trying to see through the reek. At first, it was impossible to make out anything. Then, as I stared, I saw something below, to my left, that moved. I looked intently toward it, and, presently, made out another, and then another—three dim shapes that appeared to be climbing up the side of the Pit. I could see them only indistinctly. Even as I stared and wondered, I heard a rattle of stones, somewhere to my right. I glanced across; but could see nothing. I leant forward, and peered over, and down into the Pit, just beneath where I stood; and saw no further than a hideous, white swine-face, that had risen to within a couple of yards of my feet. Below it, I could make out several others. As the Thing saw me, it gave a sudden, uncouth squeal, which was answered from all parts of the Pit. At that, a gust of horror and fear took me, and, bending down, I discharged my gun right into its face. Straightway, the creature disappeared, with a clatter of loose earth and stones.

There was a momentary silence, to which, probably, I owe my life; for, during it, I heard a quick patter of many feet, and, turning sharply, saw a troop of the creatures coming toward me, at a run. Instantly, I raised my gun and fired at the foremost, who plunged head-long, with a hideous howling. Then, I turned to run. More than halfway from the house to the Pit, I saw my sister— she was coming toward me. I could not see her face, distinctly, as the dusk had fallen; but there was fear in her voice as she called to know why I was shooting.

'Run!' I shouted in reply. 'Run for your life!'

Without more ado, she turned and fled—picking up her skirts with both hands. As I followed, I gave a glance behind. The brutes were running on their hind legs—at times dropping on all fours.

I think it must have been the terror in my voice, that spurred Mary to run so; for I feel convinced that she had not, as yet, seen those hell creatures that pursued.

On we went, my sister leading.

Each moment, the nearing sounds of the footsteps, told me that the brutes were gaining on us, rapidly. Fortunately, I am accustomed to live, in some ways, an active life. As it was, the strain of the race was beginning to tell severely upon me.

Ahead, I could see the back door—luckily it was open. I was some half-dozen yards behind Mary, now, and my breath was sobbing in my throat. Then, something touched my shoulder. I wrenched my head 'round, quickly, and saw one of those monstrous, pallid faces close to mine. One of the creatures, having outrun its companions, had almost overtaken me. Even as I turned, it made a fresh grab. With a sudden effort, I sprang to one side, and, swinging my gun by the barrel, brought it crashing down upon the foul creature's head. The Thing dropped, with an almost human groan.

Even this short delay had been nearly sufficient to bring the rest of the brutes down upon me; so that, without an instant's waste of time, I turned and ran for the door.

Reaching it, I burst into the passage; then, turning quickly, slammed and bolted the door, just as the first of the creatures rushed against it, with a sudden shock.

My sister sat, gasping, in a chair. She seemed in a fainting condition; but I had no time then to spend on her. I had to make sure that all the doors were fastened. Fortunately, they were. The one leading from my study into the gardens, was the last to which I went. I had just had time to note that it was secured, when I thought I heard a noise outside. I stood perfectly silent, and listened. Yes! Now I could distinctly hear a sound of whispering, and something slithered over the panels, with a rasping, scratchy noise. Evidently, some of the brutes were feeling with their claw-hands, about the door, to discover whether there were any means of ingress.

That the creatures should so soon have found the door was—to me—a proof of their reasoning capabilities. It assured me that they must not be regarded, by any means, as mere animals. I had felt something of this before, when that first Thing peered in through my window. Then I had applied the term superhuman to it, with an almost instinctive knowledge that the creature was something different from the brute-beast. Something beyond human; yet in no good sense; but rather as something foul and hostile to the great and good in humanity. In a word, as something intelligent, and yet inhuman. The very thought of the creatures filled me with revulsion.

Now, I bethought me of my sister, and, going to the cupboard, I got out a flask of brandy, and a wine-glass. Taking these, I went down to the kitchen, carrying a lighted candle with me. She was not sitting in the chair, but had fallen out, and was lying upon the floor, face downward.

Very gently, I turned her over, and raised her head somewhat. Then, I poured a little of the brandy between her lips. After a while, she shivered slightly. A little later, she gave several gasps, and opened her eyes. In a dreamy, unrealizing way, she looked at me. Then her eyes closed, slowly, and I gave her a little more of the brandy. For, perhaps a minute longer, she lay silent, breathing quickly. All at once, her eyes opened again, and it seemed to me, as I looked, that the pupils were dilated, as though fear had come with returning consciousness. Then, with a movement so unexpected that I started backward, she sat up. Noticing that she seemed giddy, I put out my hand to steady her. At that, she gave a loud scream, and, scrambling to her feet, ran from the room.

For a moment, I stayed there—kneeling and holding the brandy flask. I was utterly puzzled and astonished.

Could she be afraid of me? But no! Why should she? I could only conclude that her nerves were badly shaken, and that she was temporarily unhinged. Upstairs, I heard a door bang, loudly, and I knew that she had taken refuge in her room. I put the flask down on the table. My attention was distracted by a noise in the direction of the back door. I went toward it, and listened. It appeared to be shaken, as though some of the creatures struggled with it, silently; but it was far too strongly constructed and hung to be easily moved.

Out in the gardens rose a continuous sound. It might have been mistaken, by a casual listener, for the grunting and squealing of a herd of pigs. But, as I stood there, it came to me that there was sense and meaning to all those swinish noises. Gradually, I seemed able to trace a semblance in it to human speech—glutinous and sticky, as though each articulation were made with difficulty: yet, nevertheless, I was becoming convinced that it was no mere medley of sounds; but a rapid interchange of ideas.

By this time, it had grown quite dark in the passages, and from these came all the varied cries and groans of which an old house is so full after nightfall. It is, no doubt, because things are then quieter, and one has more leisure to hear. Also, there may be something in the theory that the sudden change of temperature, at sundown, affects the structure of the house, somewhat—causing it to contract and settle, as it were, for the night. However, this is as may be; but, on that night in particular, I would gladly have been quit of so many eerie noises. It seemed to me, that each crack and creak was the coming of one of those Things along the dark corridors; though I knew in my heart that this could not be, for I had seen, myself, that all the doors were secure.

Gradually, however, these sounds grew on my nerves to such an extent that, were it only to punish my cowardice, I felt I must make the 'round of the basement again, and, if anything were there, face it. And then, I would go up to my study, for I knew sleep was out of the question, with the house surrounded by creatures, half beasts, half something else, and entirely unholy.

Taking the kitchen lamp down from its hook, I made my way from cellar to cellar, and room to room; through pantry and coal-hole—along passages, and into the hundred-and-one little blind alleys and hidden nooks that form the basement of the old house. Then, when I knew I had been in every corner and cranny large enough to conceal aught of any size, I made my way to the stairs.

With my foot on the first step, I paused. It seemed to me, I heard a movement, apparently from the buttery, which is to the left of the staircase. It had been one of the first places I searched, and yet, I felt certain my ears had not deceived me. My nerves were strung now, and, with hardly any hesitation, I stepped up to the door, holding the lamp above my head. In a glance, I saw that the place was empty, save for the heavy, stone slabs, supported by brick pillars; and I was about to leave it, convinced that I had been mistaken; when, in turning, my light was flashed back from two bright spots outside the window, and high up. For a few moments, I stood there, staring. Then they moved—revolving slowly, and throwing out alternate scintillations of green and red; at least, so it appeared to me. I knew then that they were eyes.

Slowly, I traced the shadowy outline of one of the Things. It appeared to be holding on to the bars of the window, and its attitude suggested climbing. I went nearer to the window, and held the light higher. There was no need to be afraid of the creature; the bars were strong, and there was little danger of its being able to move them. And then, suddenly, in spite of the knowledge that the brute could not reach to harm me, I had a return of the horrible sensation of fear, that had assailed me on that night, a week previously. It was the same feeling of helpless, shuddering fright. I realized, dimly, that the creature's eyes were looking into mine with a steady, compelling stare. I tried to turn away; but could not. I seemed, now, to see the window through a mist. Then, I thought other eyes came and peered, and yet others; until a whole galaxy of malignant, staring orbs seemed to hold me in thrall.

My head began to swim, and throb violently. Then, I was aware of a feeling of acute physical pain in my left hand. It grew more severe, and forced, literally forced, my attention. With a tremendous effort, I glanced down; and, with that, the spell that had held me was broken. I realized, then, that I had, in my agitation, unconsciously caught hold of the hot lamp-glass, and burnt my hand, badly. I looked up to the window, again. The misty appearance had gone, and, now, I saw that it was crowded with dozens of bestial faces. With a sudden access of rage, I raised the lamp, and hurled it, full at the window. It struck the glass (smashing a pane), and passed between two of the bars, out into the garden, scattering burning oil as it went. I heard several loud cries of pain, and, as my sight became accustomed to the dark, I discovered that the creatures had left the window.

Pulling myself together, I groped for the door, and, having found it, made my way upstairs, stumbling at each step. I felt dazed, as though I had received a blow on the head. At the same time, my hand smarted badly, and I was full of a nervous, dull rage against those Things.

Reaching my study, I lit the candles. As they burnt up, their rays were reflected from the rack of firearms on the sidewall. At the sight, I remembered that I had there a power, which, as I had proved earlier, seemed as fatal to those monsters as to more ordinary animals; and I determined I would take the offensive.

First of all, I bound up my hand; for the pain was fast becoming intolerable. After that, it seemed easier, and I crossed the room, to the rifle stand. There, I selected a heavy rifle—an old and tried weapon; and, having procured ammunition, I made my way up into one of the small towers, with which the house is crowned.

From there, I found that I could see nothing. The gardens presented a dim blur of shadows—a little blacker, perhaps, where the trees stood. That was all, and I knew that it was useless to shoot down into all that darkness. The only thing to be done, was to wait for the moon to rise; then, I might be able to do a little execution.

In the meantime, I sat still, and kept my ears open. The gardens were comparatively quiet now, and only an occasional grunt or squeal came up to me. I did not like this silence; it made me wonder on what devilry the creatures were bent. Twice, I left the tower, and took a walk through the house; but everything was silent.

Once, I heard a noise, from the direction of the Pit, as though more earth had fallen. Following this, and lasting for some fifteen minutes, there was a commotion among the denizens of the gardens. This died away, and, after that all was again quiet.

About an hour later, the moon's light showed above the distant horizon. From where I sat, I could see it over the trees; but it was not until it rose clear of them, that I could make out any of the details in the gardens below. Even then, I could see none of the brutes; until, happening to crane forward, I saw several of them lying prone, up against the wall of the house. What they were doing, I could not make out. It was, however, a chance too good to be ignored; and, taking aim, I fired at the one directly beneath. There was a shrill scream, and, as the smoke cleared away, I saw that it had turned on its back, and was writhing, feebly. Then, it was quiet. The others had disappeared.

Immediately after this, I heard a loud squeal, in the direction of the Pit. It was answered, a hundred times, from every part of the garden. This gave me some notion of the number of the creatures, and I began to feel that the whole affair was becoming even more serious than I had imagined.

As I sat there, silent and watchful, the thought came to me—Why was all this? What were these Things? What did it mean? Then my thoughts flew back to that vision (though, even now, I doubt whether it was a vision) of the Plain of Silence. What did that mean? I wondered—And that Thing in the arena? Ugh! Lastly, I thought of the house I had seen in that far-away place. That house, so like this in every detail of external structure, that it might have been modeled from it; or this from that. I had never thought of that—

At this moment, there came another long squeal, from the Pit, followed, a second later, by a couple of shorter ones. At once, the garden was filled with answering cries. I stood up, quickly, and looked over the parapet. In the moonlight, it seemed as though the shrubberies were alive. They tossed hither and thither, as though shaken by a strong, irregular wind; while a continuous rustling, and a noise of scampering feet, rose up to me. Several times, I saw the moonlight gleam on running, white figures among the bushes, and, twice, I fired. The second time, my shot was answered by a short squeal of pain.

A minute later, the gardens lay silent. From the Pit, came a deep, hoarse Babel of swine-talk. At times, angry cries smote the air, and they would be answered by multitudinous gruntings. It occurred to me, that they were holding some kind of a council, perhaps to discuss the problem of entering the house. Also, I thought that they seemed much enraged, probably by my successful shots.

It occurred to me, that now would be a good time to make a final survey of our defenses. This, I proceeded to do at once; visiting the whole of the basement again, and examining each of the doors. Luckily, they are all, like the back one, built of solid, iron-studded oak. Then, I went upstairs to the study. I was more anxious about this door. It is, palpably, of a more modern make than the others, and, though a stout piece of work, it has little of their ponderous strength.

I must explain here, that there is a small, raised lawn on this side of the house, upon which this door opens—the windows of the study being barred on this account. All the other entrances—excepting the great gateway which is never opened—are in the lower storey.

Chapter 7

The Attack

I spent some time, puzzling how to strengthen the study door. Finally, I went down to the kitchen, and with some trouble, brought up several heavy pieces of timber. These, I wedged up, slantwise, against it, from the floor, nailing them top and bottom. For half-an-hour, I worked hard, and, at last, got it shored to my mind.

Then, feeling easier, I resumed my coat, which I had laid aside, and proceeded to attend to one or two matters before returning to the tower. It was whilst thus employed, that I heard a fumbling at the door, and the latch was tried. Keeping silence, I waited. Soon, I heard several of the creatures outside. They were grunting to one another, softly. Then, for a minute, there was quietness. Suddenly, there sounded a quick, low grunt, and the door creaked under a tremendous pressure. It would have burst inward; but for the supports I had placed. The strain ceased, as quickly as it had begun, and there was more talk.

Presently, one of the Things squealed, softly, and I heard the sound of others approaching. There was a short confabulation; then again, silence; and I realized that they had called several more to assist. Feeling that now was the supreme moment, I stood ready, with my rifle presented. If the door gave, I would, at least, slay as many as possible.

Again came the low signal; and, once more, the door cracked, under a huge force. For, a minute perhaps, the pressure was kept up; and I waited, nervously; expecting each moment to see the door come down with a crash. But no; the struts held, and the attempt proved abortive. Then followed more of their horrible, grunting talk, and, whilst it lasted, I thought I distinguished the noise of fresh arrivals.

After a long discussion, during which the door was several times shaken, they became quiet once more, and I knew that they were going to make a third attempt to break it down. I was almost in despair. The props had been severely tried in the two previous attacks, and I was sorely afraid that this would prove too much for them.

At that moment, like an inspiration, a thought flashed into my troubled brain. Instantly, for it was no time to hesitate, I ran from the room, and up stair after stair. This time, it was not to one of the towers, that I went; but out on to the flat, leaded roof itself. Once there, I raced across to the parapet, that walls it 'round, and looked down. As I did so, I heard the short, grunted signal, and, even up there, caught the crying of the door under the assault.

There was not a moment to lose, and, leaning over, I aimed, quickly, and fired. The report rang sharply, and, almost blending with it, came the loud splud of the bullet striking its mark. From below, rose a shrill wail; and the door ceased its groaning. Then, as I took my weight from off the parapet, a huge piece of the stone coping slid from under me, and fell with a crash among the disorganized throng beneath. Several horrible shrieks quavered through the night air, and then I heard a sound of scampering feet. Cautiously, I looked over. In the moonlight, I could see the great copingstone, lying right across the threshold of the door. I thought I saw something under it—several things, white; but I could not be sure.

And so a few minutes passed.

As I stared, I saw something come 'round, out of the shadow of the house. It was one of the Things. It went up to the stone, silently, and bent down. I was unable to see what it did. In a minute it stood up. It had something in its talons, which it put to its mouth and tore at....

For the moment, I did not realize. Then, slowly, I comprehended. The Thing was stooping again. It was horrible. I started to load my rifle. When I looked again, the monster was tugging at the stone—moving it to one side. I leant the rifle on the coping, and pulled the trigger. The brute collapsed, on its face, and kicked, slightly.

Simultaneously, almost, with the report, I heard another sound—that of breaking glass. Waiting, only to recharge my weapon, I ran from the roof, and down the first two flights of stairs.

Here, I paused to listen. As I did so, there came another tinkle of falling glass. It appeared to come from the floor below. Excitedly, I sprang down the steps, and, guided by the rattle of the window-sash, reached the door of one of the empty bedrooms, at the back of the house. I thrust it open. The room was but dimly illuminated by the moonlight; most of the light being blotted out by moving figures at the window. Even as I stood, one crawled through, into the room. Leveling my weapon, I fired point-blank at it—filling the room with a deafening bang. When the smoke cleared, I saw that the room was empty, and the window free. The room was much lighter. The night air blew in, coldly, through the shattered panes. Down below, in the night, I could hear a soft moaning, and a confused murmur of swine-voices.

Stepping to one side of the window, I reloaded, and then stood there, waiting. Presently, I heard a scuffling noise. From where I stood in the shadow, I could see, without being seen.

Nearer came the sounds, and then I saw something come up above the sill, and clutch at the broken window-frame. It caught a piece of the woodwork; and, now, I could make out that it was a hand and arm. A moment later, the face of one of the Swine-creatures rose into view. Then, before I could use my rifle, or do anything, there came a sharp crack— cr-ac-k; and the window-frame gave way under the weight of the Thing. Next instant, a squashing thud, and a loud outcry, told me that it had fallen to the ground. With a savage hope that it had been killed, I went to the window. The moon had gone behind a cloud, so that I could see nothing; though a steady hum of jabbering, just beneath where I stood, indicated that there were several more of the brutes close at hand.

As I stood there, looking down, I marveled how it had been possible for the creatures to climb so far; for the wall is comparatively smooth, while the distance to the ground must be, at least, eighty feet.

All at once, as I bent, peering, I saw something, indistinctly, that cut the grey shadow of the house-side, with a black line. It passed the window, to the left, at a distance of about two feet. Then, I remembered that it was a gutter-pipe, that had been put there some years ago, to carry off the rainwater. I had forgotten about it. I could see, now, how the creatures had managed to reach the window. Even as the solution came to me, I heard a faint slithering, scratching noise, and knew that another of the brutes was coming. I waited some odd moments; then leant out of the window and felt the pipe. To my delight, I found that it was quite loose, and I managed, using the rifle-barrel as a crowbar, to lever it out from the wall. I worked quickly. Then, taking hold with both bands, I wrenched the whole concern away, and hurled it down—with the Thing still clinging to it—into the garden.

For a few minutes longer, I waited there, listening; but, after the first general outcry, I heard nothing. I knew, now, that there was no more reason to fear an attack from this quarter. I had removed the only means of reaching the window, and, as none of the other windows had any adjacent water pipes, to tempt the climbing powers of the monsters, I began to feel more confident of escaping their clutches.

Leaving the room, I made my way down to the study. I was anxious to see how the door had withstood the test of that last assault. Entering, I lit two of the candles, and then turned to the door. One of the large props had been displaced, and, on that side, the door had been forced inward some six inches.

It was Providential that I had managed to drive the brutes away just when I did! And that copingstone! I wondered, vaguely, how I had managed to dislodge it. I had not noticed it loose, as I took my shot; and then, as I stood up, it had slipped away from beneath me ... I felt that I owed the dismissal of the attacking force, more to its timely fall than to my rifle. Then the thought came, that I had better seize this chance to shore up the door, again. It was evident that the creatures had not returned since the fall of the copingstone; but who was to say how long they would keep away?

There and then, I set-to, at repairing the door—working hard and anxiously. First, I went down to the basement, and, rummaging 'round, found several pieces of heavy oak planking. With these, I returned to the study, and, having removed the props, placed the planks up against the door. Then, I nailed the heads of the struts to these, and, driving them well home at the bottoms, nailed them again there.

Thus, I made the door stronger than ever; for now it was solid with the backing of boards, and would, I felt convinced, stand a heavier pressure than hitherto, without giving way.

After that, I lit the lamp which I had brought from the kitchen, and went down to have a look at the lower windows.

Now that I had seen an instance of the strength the creatures possessed, I felt considerable anxiety about the windows on the ground floor—in spite of the fact that they were so strongly barred.

I went first to the buttery, having a vivid remembrance of my late adventure there. The place was chilly, and the wind, soughing in through the broken glass, produced an eerie note. Apart from the general air of dismalness, the place was as I had left it the night before. Going up to the window, I examined the bars, closely; noting, as I did so, their comfortable thickness. Still, as I looked more intently, it seemed to me, that the middle bar was bent slightly from the straight; yet it was but trifling, and it might have been so for years. I had never, before, noticed them particularly.

I put my hand through the broken window, and shook the bar. It was as firm as a rock. Perhaps the creatures had tried to 'start' it, and, finding it beyond their power, ceased from the effort. After that, I went 'round to each of the windows, in turn; examining them with careful attention; but nowhere else could I trace anything to show that there had been any tampering. Having finished my survey, I went back to the study, and poured myself out a little brandy. Then to the tower to watch.

Chapter 8

After the Attack

It was now about three a.m., and, presently, the Eastern sky began to pale with the coming of dawn. Gradually, the day came, and, by its light, I scanned the gardens, earnestly; but nowhere could I see any signs of the brutes. I leant over, and glanced down to the foot of the wall, to see whether the body of the Thing I had shot the night before was still there. It was gone. I supposed that others of the monsters had removed it during the night.

Then, I went down on to the roof, and crossed over to the gap from which the coping stone had fallen. Reaching it, I looked over. Yes, there was the stone, as I had seen it last; but there was no appearance of anything beneath it; nor could I see the creatures I had killed, after its fall. Evide] ntly, they also had been taken away. I turned, and went down to my study. There, I sat down, wearily. I was thoroughly tired. It was quite light now; though the sun's rays were not, as yet, perceptibly hot. A clock chimed the hour of four.

I awoke, with a start, and looked 'round, hurriedly. The clock in the corner, indicated that it was three o'clock. It was already afternoon. I must have slept for nearly eleven hours.

With a jerky movement, I sat forward in the chair, and listened. The house was perfectly silent. Slowly, I stood up, and yawned. I felt desperately tired, still, and sat down again; wondering what it was that had waked me.

It must have been the clock striking, I concluded, presently; and was commencing to doze off, when a sudden noise brought me back, once more, to life. It was the sound of a step, as of a person moving cautiously down the corridor, toward my study. In an instant, I was on my feet, and grasping my rifle. Noiselessly, I waited. Had the creatures broken in, whilst I slept? Even as I questioned, the steps reached my door, halted momentarily, and then continued down the passage. Silently, I tiptoed to the doorway, and peeped out. Then, I experienced such a feeling of relief, as must a reprieved criminal—it was my sister. She was going toward the stairs.

I stepped into the hall, and was about to call to her, when it occurred to me, that it was very queer she should have crept past my door, in that stealthy manner. I was puzzled, and, for one brief moment, the thought occupied my mind, that it was not she, but some fresh mystery of the house. Then, as I caught a glimpse of her old petticoat, the thought passed as quickly as it had come, and I half laughed. There could be no mistaking that ancient garment. Yet, I wondered what she was doing; and, remembering her condition of mind, on the previous day, I felt that it might be best to follow, quietly—taking care not to alarm her—and see what she was going to do. If she behaved rationally, well and good; if not, I should have to take steps to restrain her. I could run no unnecessary risks, under the danger that threatened us.

Quickly, I reached the head of the stairs, and paused a moment. Then, I heard a sound that sent me leaping down, at a mad rate—it was the rattle of bolts being unshot. That foolish sister of mine was actually unbarring the back door.

Just as her hand was on the last bolt, I reached her. She had not seen me, and, the first thing she knew, I had hold of her arm. She glanced up quickly, like a frightened animal, and screamed aloud.

'Come, Mary!' I said, sternly, 'what's the meaning of this nonsense? Do you mean to tell me you don't understand the danger, that you try to throw our two lives away in this fashion!'

To this, she replied nothing; only trembled, violently, gasping and sobbing, as though in the last extremity of fear.

Through some minutes, I reasoned with her; pointing out the need for caution, and asking her to be brave. There was little to be afraid of now, I explained—and, I tried to believe that I spoke the truth—but she must be sensible, and not attempt to leave the house for a few days.

At last, I ceased, in despair. It was no use talking to her; she was, obviously, not quite herself for the time being. Finally, I told her she had better go to her room, if she could not behave rationally.

Still, she took not any notice. So, without more ado, I picked her up in my arms, and carried her there. At first, she screamed, wildly; but had relapsed into silent trembling, by the time I reached the stairs.

Arriving at her room, I laid her upon the bed. She lay there quietly enough, neither speaking nor sobbing—just shaking in a very ague of fear. I took a rug from a chair near by, and spread it over her. I could do nothing more for her, and so, crossed to where Pepper lay in a big basket. My sister had taken charge of him since his wound, to nurse him, for it had proved more severe than I had thought, and I was pleased to note that, in spite of her state of mind, she had looked after the old dog, carefully. Stooping, I spoke to him, and, in reply, he licked my hand, feebly. He was too ill to do more.

Then, going to the bed, I bent over my sister, and asked her how she felt; but she only shook the more, and, much as it pained me, I had to admit that my presence seemed to make her worse.

And so, I left her—locking the door, and pocketing the key. It seemed to be the only course to take.

The rest of the day, I spent between the tower and my study. For food, I brought up a loaf from the pantry, and on this, and some claret, I lived for that day.

What a long, weary day it was. If only I could have gone out into the gardens, as is my wont, I should have been content enough; but to be cooped in this silent house, with no companion, save a mad woman and a sick dog, was enough to prey upon the nerves of the hardiest. And out in the tangled shrubberies that surrounded the house, lurked—for all I could tell—those infernal Swine-creatures waiting their chance. Was ever a man in such straits?

Once, in the afternoon, and again, later, I went to visit my sister. The second time, I found her tending Pepper; but, at my approach, she slid over, unobtrusively, to the far corner, with a gesture that saddened me beyond belief. Poor girl! her fear cut me intolerably, and I would not intrude on her, unnecessarily. She would be better, I trusted, in a few days; meanwhile, I could do nothing; and I judged it still needful—hard as it seemed—to keep her confined to her room. One thing there was that I took for encouragement: she had eaten some of the food I had taken to her, on my first visit.

And so the day passed.

As the evening drew on, the air grew chilly, and I began to make preparations for passing a second night in the tower—taking up two additional rifles, and a heavy ulster. The rifles I loaded, and laid alongside my other; as I intended to make things warm for any of the creatures who might show, during the night. I had plenty of ammunition, and I thought to give the brutes such a lesson, as should show them the uselessness of attempting to force an entrance.

After that, I made the 'round of the house again; paying particular attention to the props that supported the study door. Then, feeling that I had done all that lay in my power to insure our safety, I returned to the tower; calling in on my sister and Pepper, for a final visit, on the way. Pepper was asleep; but woke, as I entered, and wagged his tail, in recognition. I thought he seemed slightly better. My sister was lying on the bed; though whether asleep or not, I was unable to tell; and thus I left them.

Reaching the tower, I made myself as comfortable as circumstances would permit, and settled down to watch through the night. Gradually, darkness fell, and soon the details of the gardens were merged into shadows. During the first few hours, I sat, alert, listening for any sound that might help to tell me if anything were stirring down below. It was far too dark for my eyes to be of much use.

Slowly, the hours passed; without anything unusual happening. And the moon rose, showing the gardens, apparently empty, and silent. And so, through the night, without disturbance or sound.

Toward morning, I began to grow stiff and cold, with my long vigil; also, I was getting very uneasy, concerning the continued quietness on the part of the creatures. I mistrusted it, and would sooner, far, have had them attack the house, openly. Then, at least, I should have known my danger, and been able to meet it; but to wait like this, through a whole night, picturing all kinds of unknown devilment, was to jeopardize one's sanity. Once or twice, the thought came to me, that, perhaps, they had gone; but, in my heart, I found it impossible to believe that it was so.

Chapter 9

In the Cellars

At last, what with being tired and cold, and the uneasiness that possessed me, I resolved to take a walk through the house; first calling in at the study, for a glass of brandy to warm me. This, I did, and, while there, I examined the door, carefully; but found all as I had left it the night before.

The day was just breaking, as I left the tower; though it was still too dark in the house to be able to see without a light, and I took one of the study candles with me on my 'round. By the time I had finished the ground floor, the daylight was creeping in, wanly, through the barred windows. My search had shown me nothing fresh. Everything appeared to be in order, and I was on the point of extinguishing my candle, when the thought suggested itself to me to have another glance 'round the cellars. I had not, if I remember rightly, been into them since my hasty search on the evening of the attack.

For, perhaps, the half of a minute, I hesitated. I would have been very willing to forego the task—as, indeed, I am inclined to think any man well might—for of all the great, awe-inspiring rooms in this house, the cellars are the hugest and weirdest. Great, gloomy caverns of places, unlit by any ray of daylight. Yet, I would not shirk the work. I felt that to do so would smack of sheer cowardice. Besides, as I reassured myself, the cellars were really the most unlikely places in which to come across anything dangerous; considering that they can be entered, only through a heavy oaken door, the key of which, I carry always on my person.

It is in the smallest of these places that I keep my wine; a gloomy hole close to the foot of the cellar stairs; and beyond which, I have seldom proceeded. Indeed, save for the rummage 'round, already mentioned, I doubt whether I had ever, before, been right through the cellars.

As I unlocked the great door, at the top of the steps, I paused, nervously, a moment, at the strange, desolate smell that assailed my nostrils. Then, throwing the barrel of my weapon forward, I descended, slowly, into the darkness of the underground regions.

Reaching the bottom of the stairs, I stood for a minute, and listened. All was silent, save for a faint drip, drip of water, falling, drop-by-drop, somewhere to my left. As I stood, I noticed how quietly the candle burnt; never a flicker nor flare, so utterly windless was the place.

Quietly, I moved from cellar to cellar. I had but a very dim memory of their arrangement. The impressions left by my first search were blurred. I had recollections of a succession of great cellars, and of one, greater than the rest, the roof of which was upheld by pillars; beyond that my mind was hazy, and predominated by a sense of cold and darkness and shadows. Now, however, it was different; for, although nervous, I was sufficiently collected to be able to look about me, and note the structure and size of the different vaults I entered.

Of course, with the amount of light given by my candle, it was not possible to examine each place, minutely, but I was enabled to notice, as I went along, that the walls appeared to be built with wonderful precision and finish; while here and there, an occasional, massive pillar shot up to support the vaulted roof.

Thus, I came, at last, to the great cellar that I remembered. It is reached, through a huge, arched entrance, on which I observed strange, fantastic carvings, which threw queer shadows under the light of my candle. As I stood, and examined these, thoughtfully, it occurred to me how strange it was, that I should be so little acquainted with my own house. Yet, this may be easily understood, when one realizes the size of this ancient pile, and the fact that only my old sister and I live in it, occupying a few of the rooms, such as our wants decide.

Holding the light high, I passed on into the cellar, and, keeping to the right, paced slowly up, until I reached the further end. I walked quietly, and looked cautiously about, as I went. But, so far as the light showed, I saw nothing unusual.

At the top, I turned to the left, still keeping to the wall, and so continued, until I had traversed the whole of the vast chamber. As I moved along, I noticed that the floor was composed of solid rock, in places covered with a damp mould, in others bare, or almost so, save for a thin coating of light-grey dust.

I had halted at the doorway. Now, however, I turned, and made my way up the center of the place; passing among the pillars, and glancing to right and left, as I moved. About halfway up the cellar, I stubbed my foot against something that gave out a metallic sound. Stooping quickly, I held the candle, and saw that the object I had kicked, was a large, metal ring. Bending lower, I cleared the dust from around it, and, presently, discovered that it was attached to a ponderous trap door, black with age.

Feeling excited, and wondering to where it could lead, I laid my gun on the floor, and, sticking the candle in the trigger guard, took the ring in both hands, and pulled. The trap creaked loudly—the sound echoing, vaguely, through the huge place—and opened, heavily.

Propping the edge on my knee, I reached for the candle, and held it in the opening, moving it to right and left; but could see nothing. I was puzzled and surprised. There were no signs of steps, nor even the appearance of there ever having been any. Nothing; save an empty blackness. I might have been looking down into a bottomless, sideless well. Then, even as I stared, full of perplexity, I seemed to hear, far down, as though from untold depths, a faint whisper of sound. I bent my head, quickly, more into the opening, and listened, intently. It may have been fancy; but I could have sworn to hearing a soft titter, that grew into a hideous, chuckling, faint and distant. Startled, I leapt backward, letting the trap fall, with a hollow clang, that filled the place with echoes. Even then, I seemed to hear that mocking, suggestive laughter; but this, I knew, must be my imagination. The sound, I had heard, was far too slight to penetrate through the cumbrous trap.

For a full minute, I stood there, quivering—glancing, nervously, behind and before; but the great cellar was silent as a grave, and, gradually, I shook off the frightened sensation. With a calmer mind, I became again curious to know into what that trap opened; but could not, then, summon sufficient courage to make a further investigation. One thing I felt, however, was that the trap ought to be secured. This, I accomplished by placing upon it several large pieces of 'dressed' stone, which I had noticed in my tour along the East wall.

Then, after a final scrutiny of the rest of the place, I retraced my way through the cellars, to the stairs, and so reached the daylight, with an infinite feeling of relief, that the uncomfortable task was accomplished.

Chapter 10

The Time of Waiting

The sun was now warm, and shining brightly, forming a wondrous contrast to the dark and dismal cellars; and it was with comparatively light feelings, that I made my way up to the tower, to survey the gardens. There, I found everything quiet, and, after a few minutes, went down to Mary's room.

Here, having knocked, and received a reply, I unlocked the door. My sister was sitting, quietly, on the bed; as though waiting. She seemed quite herself again, and made no attempt to move away, as I approached; yet, I observed that she scanned my face, anxiously, as though in doubt, and but half assured in her mind that there was nothing to fear from me.

To my questions, as to how she felt, she replied, sanely enough, that she was hungry, and would like to go down to prepare breakfast, if I did not mind. For a minute, I meditated whether it would be safe to let her out. Finally, I told her she might go, on condition that she promised not to attempt to leave the house, or meddle with any of the outer doors. At my mention of the doors, a sudden look of fright crossed her face; but she said nothing, save to give the required promise, and then left the room, silently.

Crossing the floor, I approached Pepper. He had waked as I entered; but, beyond a slight yelp of pleasure, and a soft rapping with his tail, had kept quiet. Now, as I patted him, he made an attempt to stand up, and succeeded, only to fall back on his side, with a little yowl of pain.

I spoke to him, and bade him lie still. I was greatly delighted with his improvement, and also with the natural kindness of my sister's heart, in taking such good care of him, in spite of her condition of mind. After a while, I left him, and went downstairs, to my study.

In a little time, Mary appeared, carrying a tray on which smoked a hot breakfast. As she entered the room, I saw her gaze fasten on the props that supported the study door; her lips tightened, and I thought she paled, slightly; but that was all. Putting the tray down at my elbow, she was leaving the room, quietly, when I called her back. She came, it seemed, a little timidly, as though startled; and I noted that her hand clutched at her apron, nervously.

'Come, Mary,' I said. 'Cheer up! Things look brighter. I've seen none of the creatures since yesterday morning, early.'

She looked at me, in a curiously puzzled manner; as though not comprehending. Then, intelligence swept into her eyes, and fear; but she said nothing, beyond an unintelligible murmur of acquiescence. After that, I kept silence; it was evident that any reference to the Swine-things, was more than her shaken nerves could bear.

Breakfast over, I went up to the tower. Here, during the greater part of the day, I maintained a strict watch over the gardens. Once or twice, I went down to the basement, to see how my sister was getting along. Each time, I found her quiet, and curiously submissive. Indeed, on the last occasion, she even ventured to address me, on her own account, with regard to some household matter that needed attention. Though this was done with an almost extraordinary timidity, I hailed it with happiness, as being the first word, voluntarily spoken, since the critical moment, when I had caught her unbarring the back door, to go out among those waiting brutes. I wondered whether she was aware of her attempt, and how near a thing it had been; but refrained from questioning her, thinking it best to let well alone.

That night, I slept in a bed; the first time for two nights. In the morning, I rose early, and took a walk through the house. All was as it should be, and I went up to the tower, to have a look at the gardens. Here, again, I found perfect quietness.

At breakfast, when I met Mary, I was greatly pleased to see that she had sufficiently regained command over herself, to be able to greet me in a perfectly natural manner. She talked sensibly and quietly; only keeping carefully from any mention of the past couple of days. In this, I humored her, to the extent of not attempting to lead the conversation in that direction.

Earlier in the morning, I had been to see Pepper. He was mending, rapidly; and bade fair to be on his legs, in earnest, in another day or two. Before leaving the breakfast table, I made some reference to his improvement. In the short discussion that followed, I was surprised to gather, from my sister's remarks, that she was still under the impression that his wound had been given by the wildcat, of my invention. It made me feel almost ashamed of myself for deceiving her. Yet, the lie had been told to prevent her from being frightened. And then, I had been sure that she must have known the truth, later, when those brutes had attacked the house.

During the day, I kept on the alert; spending much of my time, as on the previous day, in the tower; but not a sign could I see of the Swine-creatures, nor hear any sound. Several times, the thought had come to me, that the Things had, at last, left us; but, up to this time, I had refused to entertain the idea, seriously; now, however, I began to feel that there was reason for hope. It would soon be three days since I had seen any of the Things; but still, I intended to use the utmost caution. For all that I could tell, this protracted silence might be a ruse to tempt me from the house—perhaps right into their arms. The thought of such a contingency, was, alone, sufficient to make me circumspect.

So it was, that the fourth, fifth and sixth days went by, quietly, without my making any attempt to leave the house.

On the sixth day, I had the pleasure of seeing Pepper, once more, upon his feet; and, though still very weak, he managed to keep me company during the whole of that day.

Chapter 11

The Searching of the Gardens

How slowly the time went; and never a thing to indicate that any of the brutes still infested the gardens.

It was on the ninth day that, finally, I decided to run the risk, if any there were, and sally out. With this purpose in view, I loaded one of the shotguns, carefully—choosing it, as being more deadly than a rifle, at close quarters; and then, after a final scrutiny of the grounds, from the tower, I called Pepper to follow me, and made my way down to the basement.

At the door, I must confess to hesitating a moment. The thought of what might be awaiting me among the dark shrubberies, was by no means calculated to encourage my resolution. It was but a second, though, and then I had drawn the bolts, and was standing on the path outside the door.

Pepper followed, stopping at the doorstep to sniff, suspiciously; and carrying his nose up and down the jambs, as though following a scent. Then, suddenly, he turned, sharply, and started to run here and there, in semicircles and circles, all around the door; finally returning to the threshold. Here, he began again to nose about.

Hitherto, I had stood, watching the dog; yet, all the time, with half my gaze on the wild tangle of gardens, stretching 'round me. Now, I went toward him, and, bending down, examined the surface of the door, where he was smelling. I found that the wood was covered with a network of scratches, crossing and recrossing one another, in inextricable confusion. In addition to this, I noticed that the doorposts, themselves, were gnawed in places. Beyond these, I could find nothing; and so, standing up, I began to make the tour of the house wall.

Pepper, as soon as I walked away, left the door, and ran ahead, still nosing and sniffing as he went along. At times, he stopped to investigate. Here, it would be a bullet-hole in the pathway, or, perhaps, a powder stained wad. Anon, it might be a piece of torn sod, or a disturbed patch of weedy path; but, save for such trifles, he found nothing. I observed him, critically, as he went along, and could discover nothing of uneasiness, in his demeanor, to indicate that he felt the nearness of any of the creatures. By this, I was assured that the gardens were empty, at least for the present, of those hateful Things. Pepper could not be easily deceived, and it was a relief to feel that he would know, and give me timely warning, if there were any danger.

Reaching the place where I had shot that first creature, I stopped, and made a careful scrutiny; but could see nothing. From there, I went on to where the great copingstone had fallen. It lay on its side, apparently just as it had been left when I shot the brute that was moving it. A couple of feet to the right of the nearer end, was a great dent in the ground; showing where it had struck. The other end was still within the indentation—half in, and half out. Going nearer, I looked at the stone, more closely. What a huge piece of masonry it was! And that creature had moved it, single-handed, in its attempt to reach what lay below.

I went 'round to the further end of the stone. Here, I found that it was possible to see under it, for a distance of nearly a couple of feet. Still, I could see nothing of the stricken creatures, and I felt much surprised. I had, as I have before said, guessed that the remains had been removed; yet, I could not conceive that it had been done so thoroughly as not to leave some certain sign, beneath the stone, indicative of their fate. I had seen several of the brutes struck down beneath it, with such force that they must have been literally driven into the earth; and now, not a vestige of them was to be seen—not even a bloodstain.

I felt more puzzled, than ever, as I turned the matter over in my mind; but could think of no plausible explanation; and so, finally, gave it up, as one of the many things that were unexplainable.

From there, I transferred my attention to the study door. I could see, now, even more plainly, the effects of the tremendous strain, to which it had been subjected; and I marveled how, even with the support afforded by the props, it had withstood the attacks, so well. There were no marks of blows—indeed, none had been given—but the door had been literally riven from its hinges, by the application of enormous, silent force. One thing that I observed affected me profoundly—the head of one of the props had been driven right through a panel. This was, of itself, sufficient to show how huge an effort the creatures had made to break down the door, and how nearly they had succeeded.

Leaving, I continued my tour 'round the house, finding little else of interest; save at the back, where I came across the piece of piping I had torn from the wall, lying among the long grass underneath the broken window.

Then, I returned to the house, and, having re-bolted the back door, went up to the tower. Here, I spent the afternoon, reading, and occasionally glancing down into the gardens. I had determined, if the night passed quietly, to go as far as the Pit, on the morrow. Perhaps, I should be able to learn, then, something of what had happened. The day slipped away, and the night came, and went much as the last few nights had gone.

When I rose the morning had broken, fine and clear; and I determined to put my project into action. During breakfast, I considered the matter, carefully; after which, I went to the study for my shotgun. In addition, I loaded, and slipped into my pocket, a small, but heavy, pistol. I quite understood that, if there were any danger, it lay in the direction of the Pit and I intended to be prepared.

Leaving the study, I went down to the back door, followed by Pepper. Once outside, I took a quick survey of the surrounding gardens, and then set off toward the Pit. On the way, I kept a sharp outlook, holding my gun, handily. Pepper was running ahead, I noticed, without any apparent hesitation. From this, I augured that there was no imminent danger to be apprehended, and I stepped out more quickly in his wake. He had reached the top of the Pit, now, and was nosing his way along the edge.

A minute later, I was beside him, looking down into the Pit. For a moment, I could scarcely believe that it was the same place, so greatly was it changed. The dark, wooded ravine of a fortnight ago, with a foliage-hidden stream, running sluggishly, at the bottom, existed no longer. Instead, my eyes showed me a ragged chasm, partly filled with a gloomy lake of turbid water. All one side of the ravine was stripped of underwood, showing the bare rock.

A little to my left, the side of the Pit appeared to have collapsed altogether, forming a deep V-shaped cleft in the face of the rocky cliff. This rift ran, from the upper edge of the ravine, nearly down to the water, and penetrated into the Pit side, to a distance of some forty feet. Its opening was, at least, six yards across; and, from this, it seemed to taper into about two. But, what attracted my attention, more than even the stupendous split itself, was a great hole, some distance down the cleft, and right in the angle of the V. It was clearly defined, and not unlike an arched doorway in shape; though, lying as it did in the shadow, I could not see it very distinctly.

The opposite side of the Pit, still retained its verdure; but so torn in places, and everywhere covered with dust and rubbish, that it was hardly distinguishable as such.

My first impression, that there had been a land slip, was, I began to see, not sufficient, of itself, to account for all the changes I witnessed. And the water—?

I turned, suddenly; for I had become aware that, somewhere to my right, there was a noise of running water. I could see nothing; but, now that my attention had been caught, I distinguished, easily, that it came from somewhere at the East end of the Pit.

Slowly, I made my way in that direction; the sound growing plainer as I advanced, until in a little, I stood right above it. Even then, I could not perceive the cause, until I knelt down, and thrust my head over the cliff. Here, the noise came up to me, plainly; and I saw, below me, a torrent of clear water, issuing from a small fissure in the Pit side, and rushing down the rocks, into the lake beneath. A little further along the cliff, I saw another, and, beyond that again, two smaller ones. These, then, would help to account for the quantity of water in the Pit; and, if the fall of rock and earth had blocked the outlet of the stream at the bottom, there was little doubt but that it was contributing a very large share.

Yet, I puzzled my head to account for the generally shaken appearance of the place—these streamlets, and that huge cleft, further up the ravine! It seemed to me, that more than the landslip was necessary to account for these. I could imagine an earthquake, or a great explosion, creating some such condition of affairs as existed; but, of these, there had been neither. Then, I stood up, quickly, remembering that crash, and the cloud of dust that had followed, directly, rushing high into the air. But I shook my head, unbelievingly. No! It must have been the noise of the falling rocks and earth, I had heard; of course, the dust would fly, naturally. Still, in spite of my reasoning, I had an uneasy feeling, that this theory did not satisfy my sense of the probable; and yet, was any other, that I could suggest, likely to be half so plausible? Pepper had been sitting on the grass, while I conducted my examination. Now, as I turned up the North side of the ravine, he rose and followed.

Slowly, and keeping a careful watch in all directions, I made the circuit of the Pit; but found little else, that I had not already seen. From the West end, I could see the four waterfalls, uninterruptedly. They were some considerable distance up from the surface of the lake—about fifty feet, I calculated.

For a little while longer, I loitered about; keeping my eyes and ears open, but still, without seeing or hearing anything suspicious. The whole place was wonderfully quiet; indeed, save for the continuous murmur of the water, at the top end, no sound, of any description, broke the silence.

All this while, Pepper had shown no signs of uneasiness. This seemed, to me, to indicate that, for the time being, at least, there was none of the Swine-creatures in the vicinity. So far as I could see, his attention appeared to have been taken, chiefly, with scratching and sniffing among the grass at the edge of the Pit. At times, he would leave the edge, and run along toward the house, as though following invisible tracks; but, in all cases, returning after a few minutes. I had little doubt but that he was really tracing out the footsteps of the Swine-things; and the very fact that each one seemed to lead him back to the Pit, appeared to me, a proof that the brutes had all returned whence they came.

At noon, I went home, for dinner. During the afternoon, I made a partial search of the gardens, accompanied by Pepper; but, without coming upon anything to indicate the presence of the creatures.

Once, as we made our way through the shrubberies, Pepper rushed in among some bushes, with a fierce yelp. At that, I jumped back, in sudden fright, and threw my gun forward, in readiness; only to laugh, nervously, as Pepper reappeared, chasing an unfortunate cat. Toward evening, I gave up the search, and returned to the house. All at once, as we were passing a great clump of bushes, on our right, Pepper disappeared, and I could hear him sniffing and growling among them, in a suspicious manner. With my gun barrel, I parted the intervening shrubbery, and looked inside. There was nothing to be seen, save that many of the branches were bent down, and broken; as though some animal had made a lair there, at no very previous date. It was probably, I thought, one of the places occupied by some of the Swine-creatures, on the night of the attack.

Next day, I resumed my search through the gardens; but without result. By evening, I had been right through them, and now, I knew, beyond the possibility of doubt, that there were no longer any of the Things concealed about the place. Indeed, I have often thought since, that I was correct in my earlier surmise, that they had left soon after the attack.

Chapter 12

The Subterranean Pit

Another week came and went, during which I spent a great deal of my time about the Pit mouth. I had come to the conclusion a few days earlier, that the arched hole, in the angle of the great rift, was the place through which the Swine-things had made their exit, from some unholy place in the bowels of the world. How near the probable truth this went, I was to learn later.

It may be easily understood, that I was tremendously curious, though in a frightened way, to know to what infernal place that hole led; though, so far, the idea had not struck me, seriously, of making an investigation. I was far too much imbued with a sense of horror of the Swine-creatures, to think of venturing, willingly, where there was any chance of coming into contact with them.

Gradually, however, as time passed, this feeling grew insensibly less; so that when, a few days later, the thought occurred to me that it might be possible to clamber down and have a look into the hole, I was not so exceedingly averse to it, as might have been imagined. Still, I do not think, even then, that I really intended to try any such foolhardy adventure. For all that I could tell, it might be certain death, to enter that doleful looking opening. And yet, such is the pertinacity of human curiosity, that, at last, my chief desire was but to discover what lay beyond that gloomy entrance.

Slowly, as the days slid by, my fear of the Swine-things became an emotion of the past—more an unpleasant, incredible memory, than aught else.

Thus, a day came, when, throwing thoughts and fancies adrift, I procured a rope from the house, and, having made it fast to a stout tree, at the top of the rift, and some little distance back from the Pit edge, let the other end down into the cleft, until it dangled right across the mouth of the dark hole.

Then, cautiously, and with many misgivings as to whether it was not a mad act that I was attempting, I climbed slowly down, using the rope as a support, until I reached the hole. Here, still holding on to the rope, I stood, and peered in. All was perfectly dark, and not a sound came to me. Yet, a moment later, it seemed that I could hear something. I held my breath, and listened; but all was silent as the grave, and I breathed freely once more. At the same instant, I heard the sound again. It was like a noise of labored breathing—deep and sharp-drawn. For a short second, I stood, petrified; not able to move. But now the sounds had ceased again, and I could hear nothing.

As I stood there, anxiously, my foot dislodged a pebble, which fell inward, into the dark, with a hollow chink. At once, the noise was taken up and repeated a score of times; each succeeding echo being fainter, and seeming to travel away from me, as though into remote distance. Then, as the silence fell again, I heard that stealthy breathing. For each respiration I made, I could hear an answering breath. The sounds appeared to be coming nearer; and then, I heard several others; but fainter and more distant. Why I did not grip the rope, and spring up out of danger, I cannot say. It was as though I had been paralyzed. I broke out into a profuse sweat, and tried to moisten my lips with my tongue. My throat had gone suddenly dry, and I coughed, huskily. It came back to me, in a dozen, horrible, throaty tones, mockingly. I peered, helplessly, into the gloom; but still nothing showed. I had a strange, choky sensation, and again I coughed, dryly. Again the echo took it up, rising and falling, grotesquely, and dying slowly into a muffled silence.

Then, suddenly, a thought came to me, and I held my breath. The other breathing stopped. I breathed again, and, once more, it re-commenced. But now, I no longer feared. I knew that the strange sounds were not made by any lurking Swine-creature; but were simply the echo of my own respirations.

Yet, I had received such a fright, that I was glad to scramble up the rift, and haul up the rope. I was far too shaken and nervous to think of entering that dark hole then, and so returned to the house. I felt more myself next morning; but even then, I could not summon up sufficient courage to explore the place.

All this time, the water in the Pit had been creeping slowly up, and now stood but a little below the opening. At the rate at which it was rising, it would be level with the floor in less than another week; and I realized that, unless I carried out my investigations soon, I should probably never do so at all; as the water would rise and rise, until the opening, itself, was submerged.

It may have been that this thought stirred me to act; but, whatever it was, a couple of days later, saw me standing at the top of the cleft, fully equipped for the task.

This time, I was resolved to conquer my shirking, and go right through with the matter. With this intention, I had brought, in addition to the rope, a bundle of candles, meaning to use them as a torch; also my double-barreled shotgun. In my belt, I had a heavy horse-pistol, loaded with buckshot.

As before, I fastened the rope to the tree. Then, having tied my gun across my shoulders, with a piece of stout cord, I lowered myself over the edge of the Pit. At this movement, Pepper, who had been eyeing my actions, watchfully, rose to his feet, and ran to me, with a half bark, half wail, it seemed to me, of warning. But I was resolved on my enterprise, and bade him lie down. I would much have liked to take him with me; but this was next to impossible, in the existing circumstances. As my face dropped level with the Pit edge, he licked me, right across the mouth; and then, seizing my sleeve between his teeth, began to pull back, strongly. It was very evident that he did not want me to go. Yet, having made up my mind, I had no intention of giving up the attempt; and, with a sharp word to Pepper, to release me, I continued my descent, leaving the poor old fellow at the top, barking and crying like a forsaken pup.

Carefully, I lowered myself from projection to projection. I knew that a slip might mean a wetting.

Reaching the entrance, I let go the rope, and untied the gun from my shoulders. Then, with a last look at the sky—which I noticed was clouding over, rapidly—I went forward a couple of paces, so as to be shielded from the wind, and lit one of the candles. Holding it above my head, and grasping my gun, firmly, I began to move on, slowly, throwing my glances in all directions.

For the first minute, I could hear the melancholy sound of Pepper's howling, coming down to me. Gradually, as I penetrated further into the darkness, it grew fainter; until, in a little while, I could hear nothing. The path tended downward somewhat, and to the left. Thence it kept on, still running to the left, until I found that it was leading me right in the direction of the house.

Very cautiously, I moved onward, stopping, every few steps, to listen. I had gone, perhaps, a hundred yards, when, suddenly, it seemed to me that I caught a faint sound, somewhere along the passage behind. With my heart thudding heavily, I listened. The noise grew plainer, and appeared to be approaching, rapidly. I could hear it distinctly, now. It was the soft padding of running feet. In the first moments of fright, I stood, irresolute; not knowing whether to go forward or backward. Then, with a sudden realization of the best thing to do, I backed up to the rocky wall on my right, and, holding the candle above my head, waited—gun in hand—cursing my foolhardy curiosity, for bringing me into such a strait.

I had not long to wait, but a few seconds, before two eyes reflected back from the gloom, the rays of my candle. I raised my gun, using my right hand only, and aimed quickly. Even as I did so, something leapt out of the darkness, with a blustering bark of joy that woke the echoes, like thunder. It was Pepper.

How he had contrived to scramble down the cleft, I could not conceive. As I brushed my hand, nervously, over his coat, I noticed that he was dripping; and concluded that he must have tried to follow me, and fallen into the water; from which he would not find it very difficult to climb.

Having waited a minute, or so, to steady myself, I proceeded along the way, Pepper following, quietly. I was curiously glad to have the old fellow with me. He was company, and, somehow, with him at my heels, I was less afraid. Also, I knew how quickly his keen ears would detect the presence of any unwelcome creature, should there be such, amid the darkness that wrapped us.

For some minutes we went slowly along; the path still leading straight toward the house. Soon, I concluded, we should be standing right beneath it, did the path but carry far enough. I led the way, cautiously, for another fifty yards, or so. Then, I stopped, and held the light high; and reason enough I had to be thankful that I did so; for there, not three paces forward, the path vanished, and, in place, showed a hollow blackness, that sent sudden fear through me.

Very cautiously, I crept forward, and peered down; but could see nothing. Then, I crossed to the left of the passage, to see whether there might be any continuation of the path. Here, right against the wall, I found that a narrow track, some three feet wide, led onward. Carefully, I stepped on to it; but had not gone far, before I regretted venturing thereon. For, after a few paces, the already narrow way, resolved itself into a mere ledge, with, on the one side the solid, unyielding rock, towering up, in a great wall, to the unseen roof, and, on the other, that yawning chasm. I could not help reflecting how helpless I was, should I be attacked there, with no room to turn, and where even the recoil of my weapon might be sufficient to drive me headlong into the depths below.

To my great relief, a little further on, the track suddenly broadened out again to its original breadth. Gradually, as I went onward, I noticed that the path trended steadily to the right, and so, after some minutes, I discovered that I was not going forward; but simply circling the huge abyss. I had, evidently, come to the end of the great passage.

Five minutes later, I stood on the spot from which I had started; having been completely 'round, what I guessed now to be a vast pit, the mouth of which must be at least a hundred yards across.

For some little time, I stood there, lost in perplexing thought. 'What does it all mean?' was the cry that had begun to reiterate through my brain.

A sudden idea struck me, and I searched 'round for a piece of stone. Presently, I found a bit of rock, about the size of a small loaf. Sticking the candle upright in a crevice of the floor, I went back from the edge, somewhat, and, taking a short run, launched the stone forward into the chasm—my idea being to throw it far enough to keep it clear of the sides. Then, I stooped forward, and listened; but, though I kept perfectly quiet, for at least a full minute, no sound came back to me from out of the dark.

I knew, then, that the depth of the hole must be immense; for the stone, had it struck anything, was large enough to have set the echoes of that weird place, whispering for an indefinite period. Even as it was, the cavern had given back the sounds of my footfalls, multitudinously. The place was awesome, and I would willingly have retraced my steps, and left the mysteries of its solitudes unsolved; only, to do so, meant admitting defeat.

Then, a thought came, to try to get a view of the abyss. It occurred to me that, if I placed my candles 'round the edge of the hole, I should be able to get, at least, some dim sight of the place.

I found, on counting, that I had brought fifteen candles, in the bundle—my first intention having been, as I have already said, to make a torch of the lot. These, I proceeded to place 'round the Pit mouth, with an interval of about twenty yards between each.

Having completed the circle, I stood in the passage, and endeavored to get an idea of how the place looked. But I discovered, immediately, that they were totally insufficient for my purpose. They did little more than make the gloom visible. One thing they did, however, and that was, they confirmed my opinion of the size of the opening; and, although they showed me nothing that I wanted to see; yet the contrast they afforded to the heavy darkness, pleased me, curiously. It was as though fifteen tiny stars shone through the subterranean night.

Then, even as I stood, Pepper gave a sudden howl, that was taken up by the echoes, and repeated with ghastly variations, dying away, slowly. With a quick movement, I held aloft the one candle that I had kept, and glanced down at the dog; at the same moment, I seemed to hear a noise, like a diabolical chuckle, rise up from the hitherto, silent depths of the Pit. I started; then, I recollected that it was, probably, the echo of Pepper's howl.

Pepper had moved away from me, up the passage, a few steps; he was nosing along the rocky floor; and I thought I heard him lapping. I went toward him, holding the candle low. As I moved, I heard my boot go sop, sop; and the light was reflected from something that glistened, and crept past my feet, swiftly toward the Pit. I bent lower, and looked; then gave vent to an expression of surprise. From somewhere, higher up the path, a stream of water was running quickly in the direction of the great opening, and growing in size every second.

Again, Pepper gave vent to that deep-drawn howl, and, running at me, seized my coat, and attempted to drag me up the path toward the entrance. With a nervous gesture, I shook him off, and crossed quickly over to the left-hand wall. If anything were coming, I was going to have the wall at my back.

Then, as I stared anxiously up the pathway, my candle caught a gleam, far up the passage. At the same moment, I became conscious of a murmurous roar, that grew louder, and filled the whole cavern with deafening sound. From the Pit, came a deep, hollow echo, like the sob of a giant. Then, I had sprung to one side, on to the narrow ledge that ran 'round the abyss, and, turning, saw a great wall of foam sweep past me, and leap tumultuously into the waiting chasm. A cloud of spray burst over me, extinguishing my candle, and wetting me to the skin. I still held my gun. The three nearest candles went out; but the further ones gave only a short flicker. After the first rush, the flow of water eased down to a steady stream, maybe a foot in depth; though I could not see this, until I had procured one of the lighted candles, and, with it, started to reconnoiter. Pepper had, fortunately, followed me as I leapt for the ledge, and now, very much subdued, kept close behind.

A short examination showed me that the water reached right across the passage, and was running at a tremendous rate. Already, even as I stood there, it had deepened. I could make only a guess at what had happened. Evidently, the water in the ravine had broken into the passage, by some means. If that were the case, it would go on increasing in volume, until I should find it impossible to leave the place. The thought was frightening. It was evident that I must make my exit as hurriedly as possible.

Taking my gun by the stock, I sounded the water. It was a little under knee-deep. The noise it made, plunging down into the Pit, was deafening. Then, with a call to Pepper, I stepped out into the flood, using the gun as a staff. Instantly, the water boiled up over my knees, and nearly to the tops of my thighs, with the speed at which it was racing. For one short moment, I nearly lost my footing; but the thought of what lay behind, stimulated me to a fierce endeavor, and, step-by-step, I made headway.

Of Pepper, I knew nothing at first. I had all I could do to keep on my legs; and was overjoyed, when he appeared beside me. He was wading manfully along. He is a big dog, with longish thin legs, and I suppose the water had less grasp on them, than upon mine. Anyway, he managed a great deal better than I did; going ahead of me, like a guide, and wittingly—or otherwise—helping, somewhat, to break the force of the water. On we went, step by step, struggling and gasping, until somewhere about a hundred yards had been safely traversed. Then, whether it was because I was taking less care, or that there was a slippery place on the rocky floor, I cannot say; but, suddenly, I slipped, and fell on my face. Instantly, the water leapt over me in a cataract, hurling me down, toward that bottomless hole, at a frightful speed. Frantically I struggled; but it was impossible to get a footing. I was helpless, gasping and drowning. All at once, something gripped my coat, and brought me to a standstill. It was Pepper. Missing me, he must have raced back, through the dark turmoil, to find me, and then caught, and held me, until I was able to get to my feet.

I have a dim recollection of having seen, momentarily, the gleams of several lights; but, of this, I have never been quite sure. If my impressions are correct, I must have been washed down to the very brink of that awful chasm, before Pepper managed to bring me to a standstill. And the lights, of course, could only have been the distant flames of the candles, I had left burning. But, as I have said, I am not by any means sure. My eyes were full of water, and I had been badly shaken.

And there was I, without my helpful gun, without light, and sadly confused, with the water deepening; depending solely upon my old friend Pepper, to help me out of that hellish place.

I was facing the torrent. Naturally, it was the only way in which I could have sustained my position a moment; for even old Pepper could not have held me long against that terrific strain, without assistance, however blind, from me.

Perhaps a minute passed, during which it was touch and go with me; then, gradually I re-commenced my tortuous way up the passage. And so began the grimmest fight with death, from which ever I hope to emerge victorious. Slowly, furiously, almost hopelessly, I strove; and that faithful Pepper led me, dragged me, upward and onward, until, at last, ahead I saw a gleam of blessed light. It was the entrance. Only a few yards further, and I reached the opening, with the water surging and boiling hungrily around my loins.

And now I understood the cause of the catastrophe. It was raining heavily, literally in torrents. The surface of the lake was level with the bottom of the opening—nay! more than level, it was above it. Evidently, the rain had swollen the lake, and caused this premature rise; for, at the rate the ravine had been filling, it would not have reached the entrance for a couple more days.

Luckily, the rope by which I had descended, was streaming into the opening, upon the inrushing waters. Seizing the end, I knotted it securely 'round Pepper's body, then, summoning up the last remnant of my strength, I commenced to swarm up the side of the cliff. I reached the Pit edge, in the last stage of exhaustion. Yet, I had to make one more effort, and haul Pepper into safety.

Slowly and wearily, I hauled on the rope. Once or twice, it seemed that I should have to give up; for Pepper is a weighty dog, and I was utterly done. Yet, to let go, would have meant certain death to the old fellow, and the thought spurred me to greater exertions. I have but a very hazy remembrance of the end. I recall pulling, through moments that lagged strangely. I have also some recollection of seeing Pepper's muzzle, appearing over the Pit edge, after what seemed an indefinite period of time. Then, all grew suddenly dark.

Chapter 13

The Trap in the Great Cellar

I suppose I must have swooned; for, the next thing I remember, I opened my eyes, and all was dusk. I was lying on my back, with one leg doubled under the other, and Pepper was licking my ears. I felt horribly stiff, and my leg was numb, from the knee, downward. For a few minutes, I lay thus, in a dazed condition; then, slowly, I struggled to a sitting position, and looked about me.

It had stopped raining, but the trees still dripped, dismally. From the Pit, came a continuous murmur of running water. I felt cold and shivery. My clothes were sodden, and I ached all over. Very slowly, the life came back into my numbed leg, and, after a little, I essayed to stand up. This, I managed, at the second attempt; but I was very tottery, and peculiarly weak. It seemed to me, that I was going to be ill, and I made shift to stumble my way toward the house. My steps were erratic, and my head confused. At each step that I took, sharp pains shot through my limbs.

I had gone, perhaps, some thirty paces, when a cry from Pepper, drew my attention, and I turned, stiffly, toward him. The old dog was trying to follow me; but could come no further, owing to the rope, with which I had hauled him up, being still tied 'round his body, the other end not having been unfastened from the tree. For a moment, I fumbled with the knots, weakly; but they were wet and hard, and I could do nothing. Then, I remembered my knife, and, in a minute, the rope was cut.

How I reached the house, I scarcely know, and, of the days that followed, I remember still less. Of one thing, I am certain, that, had it not been for my sister's untiring love and nursing, I had not been writing at this moment.

When I recovered my senses, it was to find that I had been in bed for nearly two weeks. Yet another week passed, before I was strong enough to totter out into the gardens. Even then, I was not able to walk so far as the Pit. I would have liked to ask my sister, how high the water had risen; but felt it was wiser not to mention the subject to her. Indeed, since then, I have made a rule never to speak to her about the strange things, that happen in this great, old house.

It was not until a couple of days later, that I managed to get across to the Pit. There, I found that, in my few weeks' absence, there had been wrought a wondrous change. Instead of the three-parts filled ravine, I looked out upon a great lake, whose placid surface, reflected the light, coldly. The water had risen to within half a dozen feet of the Pit edge. Only in one part was the lake disturbed, and that was above the place where, far down under the silent waters, yawned the entrance to the vast, underground Pit. Here, there was a continuous bubbling; and, occasionally, a curious sort of sobbing gurgle would find its way up from the depth. Beyond these, there was nothing to tell of the things that were hidden beneath. As I stood there, it came to me how wonderfully things had worked out. The entrance to the place whence the Swine-creatures had come, was sealed up, by a power that made me feel there was nothing more to fear from them. And yet, with the feeling, there was a sensation that, now, I should never learn anything further, of the place from which those dreadful Things had come. It was completely shut off and concealed from human curiosity forever.

Strange—in the knowledge of that underground hell-hole—how apposite has been the naming of the Pit. One wonders how it originated, and when. Naturally, one concludes that the shape and depth of the ravine would suggest the name 'Pit.' Yet, is it not possible that it has, all along, held a deeper significance, a hint—could one but have guessed—of the greater, more stupendous Pit that lies far down in the earth, beneath this old house? Under this house! Even now, the idea is strange and terrible to me. For I have proved, beyond doubt, that the Pit yawns right below the house, which is evidently supported, somewhere above the center of it, upon a tremendous, arched roof, of solid rock.

It happened in this wise, that, having occasion to go down to the cellars, the thought occurred to me to pay a visit to the great vault, where the trap is situated; and see whether everything was as I had left it.

Reaching the place, I walked slowly up the center, until I came to the trap. There it was, with the stones piled upon it, just as I had seen it last. I had a lantern with me, and the idea came to me, that now would be a good time to investigate whatever lay under the great, oak slab. Placing the lantern on the floor, I tumbled the stones off the trap, and, grasping the ring, pulled the door open. As I did so, the cellar became filled with the sound of a murmurous thunder, that rose from far below. At the same time, a damp wind blew up into my face, bringing with it a load of fine spray. Therewith, I dropped the trap, hurriedly, with a half frightened feeling of wonder.

For a moment, I stood puzzled. I was not particularly afraid. The haunting fear of the Swine-things had left me, long ago; but I was certainly nervous and astonished. Then, a sudden thought possessed me, and I raised the ponderous door, with a feeling of excitement. Leaving it standing upon its end, I seized the lantern, and, kneeling down, thrust it into the opening. As I did so, the moist wind and spray drove in my eyes, making me unable to see, for a few moments. Even when my eyes were clear, I could distinguish nothing below me, save darkness, and whirling spray.

Seeing that it was useless to expect to make out anything, with the light so high, I felt in my pockets for a piece of twine, with which to lower it further into the opening. Even as I fumbled, the lantern slipped from my fingers, and hurtled down into the darkness. For a brief instant, I watched its fall, and saw the light shine on a tumult of white foam, some eighty or a hundred feet below me. Then it was gone. My sudden surmise was correct, and now, I knew the cause of the wet and noise. The great cellar was connected with the Pit, by means of the trap, which opened right above it; and the moisture, was the spray, rising from the water, falling into the depths.

In an instant, I had an explanation of certain things, that had hitherto puzzled me. Now, I could understand why the noises—on the first night of the invasion—had seemed to rise directly from under my feet. And the chuckle that had sounded when first I opened the trap! Evidently, some of the Swine-things must have been right beneath me.

Another thought struck me. Were the creatures all drowned? Would they drown? I remembered how unable I had been to find any traces to show that my shooting had been really fatal. Had they life, as we understand life, or were they ghouls? These thoughts flashed through my brain, as I stood in the dark, searching my pockets for matches. I had the box in my hand now, and, striking a light, I stepped to the trap door, and closed it. Then, I piled the stones back upon it; after which, I made my way out from the cellars.

And so, I suppose the water goes on, thundering down into that bottomless hell-pit. Sometimes, I have an inexplicable desire to go down to the great cellar, open the trap, and gaze into the impenetrable, spray-damp darkness. At times, the desire becomes almost overpowering, in its intensity. It is not mere curiosity, that prompts me; but more as though some unexplained influence were at work. Still, I never go; and intend to fight down the strange longing, and crush it; even as I would the unholy thought of self-destruction.

This idea of some intangible force being exerted, may seem reasonless. Yet, my instinct warns me, that it is not so. In these things, reason seems to me less to be trusted than instinct.

One thought there is, in closing, that impresses itself upon me, with ever growing insistence. It is, that I live in a very strange house; a very awful house. And I have begun to wonder whether I am doing wisely in staying here. Yet, if I left, where could I go, and still obtain the solitude, and the sense of her presence,[1] that alone make my old life bearable?

Chapter 14

The Sea of Sleep

For a considerable period after the last incident which I have narrated in my diary, I had serious thoughts of leaving this house, and might have done so; but for the great and wonderful thing, of which I am about to write.

How well I was advised, in my heart, when I stayed on here—spite of those visions and sights of unknown and unexplainable things; for, had I not stayed, then I had not seen again the face of her I loved. Yes, though few know it, none now save my sister Mary, I have loved and, ah! me—lost.

I would write down the story of those sweet, old days; but it would be like the tearing of old wounds; yet, after that which has happened, what need have I to care? For she has come to me out of the unknown. Strangely, she warned me; warned me passionately against this house; begged me to leave it; but admitted, when I questioned her, that she could not have come to me, had I been elsewhere. Yet, in spite of this, still she warned me, earnestly; telling me that it was a place, long ago given over to evil, and under the power of grim laws, of which none here have knowledge. And I—I just asked her, again, whether she would come to me elsewhere, and she could only stand, silent.

It was thus, that I came to the place of the Sea of Sleep—so she termed it, in her dear speech with me. I had stayed up, in my study, reading; and must have dozed over the book. Suddenly, I awoke and sat upright, with a start. For a moment, I looked 'round, with a puzzled sense of something unusual. There was a misty look about the room, giving a curious softness to each table and chair and furnishing.

Gradually, the mistiness increased; growing, as it were, out of nothing. Then, slowly, a soft, white light began to glow in the room. The flames of the candles shone through it, palely. I looked from side to side, and found that I could still see each piece of furniture; but in a strangely unreal way, more as though the ghost of each table and chair had taken the place of the solid article.

Gradually, as I looked, I saw them fade and fade; until, slowly, they resolved into nothingness. Now, I looked again at the candles. They shone wanly, and, even as I watched, grew more unreal, and so vanished. The room was filled, now, with a soft, yet luminous, white twilight, like a gentle mist of light. Beyond this, I could see nothing. Even the walls had vanished.

Presently, I became conscious that a faint, continuous sound, pulsed through the silence that wrapped me. I listened intently. It grew more distinct, until it appeared to me that I harked to the breathings of some great sea. I cannot tell how long a space passed thus; but, after a while, it seemed that I could see through the mistiness; and, slowly, I became aware that I was standing upon the shore of an immense and silent sea. This shore was smooth and long, vanishing to right and left of me, in extreme distances. In front, swam a still immensity of sleeping ocean. At times, it seemed to me that I caught a faint glimmer of light, under its surface; but of this, I could not be sure. Behind me, rose up, to an extraordinary height, gaunt, black cliffs.

Overhead, the sky was of a uniform cold grey color—the whole place being lit by a stupendous globe of pale fire, that swam a little above the far horizon, and shed a foamlike light above the quiet waters.

Beyond the gentle murmur of the sea, an intense stillness prevailed. For a long while, I stayed there, looking out across its strangeness. Then, as I stared, it seemed that a bubble of white foam floated up out of the depths, and then, even now I know not how it was, I was looking upon, nay, looking into the face of Her—aye! into her face—into her soul; and she looked back at me, with such a commingling of joy and sadness, that I ran toward her, blindly; crying strangely to her, in a very agony of remembrance, of terror, and of hope, to come to me. Yet, spite of my crying, she stayed out there upon the sea, and only shook her head, sorrowfully; but, in her eyes was the old earth-light of tenderness, that I had come to know, before all things, ere we were parted.

"At her perverseness, I grew desperate, and essayed to wade out to her; yet, though I would, I could not. Something, some invisible barrier, held me back, and I was fain to stay where I was, and cry out to her in the fullness of my soul, 'O, my Darling, my Darling—' but could say no more, for very intensity. And, at that, she came over, swiftly, and touched me, and it was as though heaven had opened. Yet, when I reached out my hands to her, she put me from her with tenderly stern hands, and I was abashed—"

THE FRAGMENTS [2]

(The legible portions of the mutilated leaves.)

... through tears ... noise of eternity in my ears, we parted ... She whom I love. O, my God ...!

I was a great time dazed, and then I was alone in the blackness of the night. I knew that I journeyed back, once more, to the known universe. Presently, I emerged from that enormous darkness. I had come among the stars ... vast time ... the sun, far and remote.

I entered into the gulf that separates our system from the outer suns. As I sped across the dividing dark, I watched, steadily, the ever-growing brightness and size of our sun. Once, I glanced back to the stars, and saw them shift, as it were, in my wake, against the mighty background of night, so vast was the speed of my passing spirit.

I drew nigher to our system, and now I could see the shine of Jupiter. Later, I distinguished the cold, blue gleam of the earthlight.... I had a moment of bewilderment. All about the sun there seemed to be bright, objects, moving in rapid orbits. Inward, nigh to the savage glory of the sun, there circled two darting points of light, and, further off, there flew a blue, shining speck, that I knew to be the earth. It circled the sun in a space that seemed to be no more than an earth-minute.

... nearer with great speed. I saw the radiances of Jupiter and Saturn, spinning, with incredible swiftness, in huge orbits. And ever I drew more nigh, and looked out upon this strange sight—the visible circling of the planets about the mother sun. It was as though time had been annihilated for me; so that a year was no more to my unfleshed spirit, than is a moment to an earth-bound soul.

The speed of the planets, appeared to increase; and, presently, I was watching the sun, all ringed about with hairlike circles of different colored fire—the paths of the planets, hurtling at mighty speed, about the central flame....

"... the sun grew vast, as though it leapt to meet me.... And now I was within the circling of the outer planets, and flitting swiftly, toward the place where the earth, glimmering through the blue splendor of its orbit, as though a fiery mist, circled the sun at a monstrous speed...." [3]

Chapter 15

The Noise in the Night

And now, I come to the strangest of all the strange happenings that have befallen me in this house of mysteries. It occurred quite lately—within the month; and I have little doubt but that what I saw was in reality the end of all things. However, to my story.

I do not know how it is; but, up to the present, I have never been able to write these things down, directly they happened. It is as though I have to wait a time, recovering my just balance, and digesting—as it were—the things I have heard or seen. No doubt, this is as it should be; for, by waiting, I see the incidents more truly, and write of them in a calmer and more judicial frame of mind. This by the way.

It is now the end of November. My story relates to what happened in the first week of the month.

It was night, about eleven o'clock. Pepper and I kept one another company in the study—that great, old room of mine, where I read and work. I was reading, curiously enough, the Bible. I have begun, in these later days, to take a growing interest in that great and ancient book. Suddenly, a distinct tremor shook the house, and there came a faint and distant, whirring buzz, that grew rapidly into a far, muffled screaming. It reminded me, in a queer, gigantic way, of the noise that a clock makes, when the catch is released, and it is allowed to run down. The sound appeared to come from some remote height—somewhere up in the night. There was no repetition of the shock. I looked across at Pepper. He was sleeping peacefully.

Gradually, the whirring noise decreased, and there came a long silence.

All at once, a glow lit up the end window, which protrudes far out from the side of the house, so that, from it, one may look both East and West. I felt puzzled, and, after a moment's hesitation, walked across the room, and pulled aside the blind. As I did so, I saw the Sun rise, from behind the horizon. It rose with a steady, perceptible movement. I could see it travel upward. In a minute, it seemed, it had reached the tops of the trees, through which I had watched it. Up, up—It was broad daylight now. Behind me, I was conscious of a sharp, mosquitolike buzzing. I glanced 'round, and knew that it came from the clock. Even as I looked, it marked off an hour. The minute hand was moving 'round the dial, faster than an ordinary second-hand. The hour hand moved quickly from space to space. I had a numb sense of astonishment. A moment later, so it seemed, the two candles went out, almost together. I turned swiftly back to the window; for I had seen the shadow of the window-frames, traveling along the floor toward me, as though a great lamp had been carried up past the window.

I saw now, that the sun had risen high into the heavens, and was still visibly moving. It passed above the house, with an extraordinary sailing kind of motion. As the window came into shadow, I saw another extraordinary thing. The fine-weather clouds were not passing, easily, across the sky—they were scampering, as though a hundred-mile-an-hour wind blew. As they passed, they changed their shapes a thousand times a minute, as though writhing with a strange life; and so were gone. And, presently, others came, and whisked away likewise.

To the West, I saw the sun, drop with an incredible, smooth, swift motion. Eastward, the shadows of every seen thing crept toward the coming greyness. And the movement of the shadows was visible to me—a stealthy, writhing creep of the shadows of the wind-stirred trees. It was a strange sight.

Quickly, the room began to darken. The sun slid down to the horizon, and seemed, as it were, to disappear from my sight, almost with a jerk. Through the greyness of the swift evening, I saw the silver crescent of the moon, falling out of the Southern sky, toward the West. The evening seemed to merge into an almost instant night. Above me, the many constellations passed in a strange, 'noiseless' circling, Westward. The moon fell through that last thousand fathoms of the night-gulf, and there was only the starlight....

About this time, the buzzing in the corner ceased; telling me that the clock had run down. A few minutes passed, and I saw the Eastward sky lighten. A grey, sullen morning spread through all the darkness, and hid the march of the stars. Overhead, there moved, with a heavy, everlasting rolling, a vast, seamless sky of grey clouds—a cloud-sky that would have seemed motionless, through all the length of an ordinary earth-day. The sun was hidden from me; but, from moment to moment, the world would brighten and darken, brighten and darken, beneath waves of subtle light and shadow....

The light shifted ever Westward, and the night fell upon the earth. A vast rain seemed to come with it, and a wind of a most extraordinary loudness— as though the howling of a nightlong gale, were packed into the space of no more than a minute.

This noise passed, almost immediately, and the clouds broke; so that, once more, I could see the sky. The stars were flying Westward, with astounding speed. It came to me now, for the first time, that, though the noise of the wind had passed, yet a constant 'blurred' sound was in my ears. Now that I noticed it, I was aware that it had been with me all the time. It was the world-noise.

And then, even as I grasped at so much comprehension, there came the Eastward light. No more than a few heartbeats, and the sun rose, swiftly. Through the trees, I saw it, and then it was above the trees. Up—up, it soared and all world was light. It passed, with a swift, steady swing to its highest altitude, and fell thence, Westward. I saw the day roll visibly over my head. A few light clouds flittered Northward, and vanished. The sun went down with one swift, clear plunge, and there was about me, for a few seconds, the darker growing grey of the gloaming.

Southward and Westward, the moon was sinking rapidly. The night had come, already. A minute it seemed, and the moon fell those remaining fathoms of dark sky. Another minute, or so, and the Eastward sky glowed with the coming dawn. The sun leapt upon me with a frightening abruptness, and soared ever more swiftly toward the zenith. Then, suddenly, a fresh thing came to my sight. A black thundercloud rushed up out of the South, and seemed to leap all the arc of the sky, in a single instant. As it came, I saw that its advancing edge flapped, like a monstrous black cloth in the heaven, twirling and undulating rapidly, with a horrid suggestiveness. In an instant, all the air was full of rain, and a hundred lightning flashes seemed to flood downward, as it were in one great shower. In the same second of time, the world-noise was drowned in the roar of the wind, and then my ears ached, under the stunning impact of the thunder.

And, in the midst of this storm, the night came; and then, within the space of another minute, the storm had passed, and there was only the constant 'blur' of the world-noise on my hearing. Overhead, the stars were sliding quickly Westward; and something, mayhaps the particular speed to which they had attained, brought home to me, for the first time, a keen realization of the knowledge that it was the world that revolved. I seemed to see, suddenly, the world—a vast, dark mass—revolving visibly against the stars.

The dawn and the sun seemed to come together, so greatly had the speed of the world-revolution increased. The sun drove up, in one long, steady curve; passed its highest point, and swept down into the Western sky, and disappeared. I was scarcely conscious of evening, so brief was it. Then I was watching the flying constellations, and the Westward hastening moon. In but a space of seconds, so it seemed, it was sliding swiftly downward through the night-blue, and then was gone. And, almost directly, came the morning.

And now there seemed to come a strange acceleration. The sun made one clean, clear sweep through the sky, and disappeared behind the Westward horizon, and the night came and went with a like haste.

As the succeeding day, opened and closed upon the world, I was aware of a sweat of snow, suddenly upon the earth. The night came, and, almost immediately, the day. In the brief leap of the sun, I saw that the snow had vanished; and then, once more, it was night.

Thus matters were; and, even after the many incredible things that I have seen, I experienced all the time a most profound awe. To see the sun rise and set, within a space of time to be measured by seconds; to watch (after a little) the moon leap—a pale, and ever growing orb—up into the night sky, and glide, with a strange swiftness, through the vast arc of blue; and, presently, to see the sun follow, springing out of the Eastern sky, as though in chase; and then again the night, with the swift and ghostly passing of starry constellations, was all too much to view believingly. Yet, so it was—the day slipping from dawn to dusk, and the night sliding swiftly into day, ever rapidly and more rapidly.

The last three passages of the sun had shown me a snow-covered earth, which, at night, had seemed, for a few seconds, incredibly weird under the fast-shifting light of the soaring and falling moon. Now, however, for a little space, the sky was hidden, by a sea of swaying, leaden-white clouds, which lightened and blackened, alternately, with the passage of day and night.

The clouds rippled and vanished, and there was once more before me, the vision of the swiftly leaping sun, and nights that came and went like shadows.

Faster and faster, spun the world. And now each day and night was completed within the space of but a few seconds; and still the speed increased.

It was a little later, that I noticed that the sun had begun to have the suspicion of a trail of fire behind it. This was due, evidently, to the speed at which it, apparently, traversed the heavens. And, as the days sped, each one quicker than the last, the sun began to assume the appearance of a vast, flaming comet[4] flaring across the sky at short, periodic intervals. At night, the moon presented, with much greater truth, a cometlike aspect; a pale, and singularly clear, fast traveling shape of fire, trailing streaks of cold flame. The stars showed now, merely as fine hairs of fire against the dark.

Once, I turned from the window, and glanced at Pepper. In the flash of a day, I saw that he slept, quietly, and I moved once more to my watching.

The sun was now bursting up from the Eastern horizon, like a stupendous rocket, seeming to occupy no more than a second or two in hurling from East to West. I could no longer perceive the passage of clouds across the sky, which seemed to have darkened somewhat. The brief nights, appeared to have lost the proper darkness of night; so that the hairlike fire of the flying stars, showed but dimly. As the speed increased, the sun began to sway very slowly in the sky, from South to North, and then, slowly again, from North to South.

So, amid a strange confusion of mind, the hours passed.

All this while had Pepper slept. Presently, feeling lonely and distraught, I called to him, softly; but he took no notice. Again, I called, raising my voice slightly; still he moved not. I walked over to where he lay, and touched him with my foot, to rouse him. At the action, gentle though it was, he fell to pieces. That is what happened; he literally and actually crumbled into a mouldering heap of bones and dust.

For the space of, perhaps a minute, I stared down at the shapeless heap, that had once been Pepper. I stood, feeling stunned. What can have happened? I asked myself; not at once grasping the grim significance of that little hill of ash. Then, as I stirred the heap with my foot, it occurred to me that this could only happen in a great space of time. Years—and years.

Outside, the weaving, fluttering light held the world. Inside, I stood, trying to understand what it meant—what that little pile of dust and dry bones, on the carpet, meant. But I could not think, coherently.

I glanced away, 'round the room, and now, for the first time, noticed how dusty and old the place looked. Dust and dirt everywhere; piled in little heaps in the corners, and spread about upon the furniture. The very carpet, itself, was invisible beneath a coating of the same, all pervading, material. As I walked, little clouds of the stuff rose up from under my footsteps, and assailed my nostrils, with a dry, bitter odor that made me wheeze, huskily.

Suddenly, as my glance fell again upon Pepper's remains, I stood still, and gave voice to my confusion—questioning, aloud, whether the years were, indeed, passing; whether this, which I had taken to be a form of vision, was, in truth, a reality. I paused. A new thought had struck me. Quickly, but with steps which, for the first time, I noticed, tottered, I went across the room to the great pier-glass, and looked in. It was too covered with grime, to give back any reflection, and, with trembling hands, I began to rub off the dirt. Presently, I could see myself. The thought that had come to me, was confirmed. Instead of the great, hale man, who scarcely looked fifty, I was looking at a bent, decrepit man, whose shoulders stooped, and whose face was wrinkled with the years of a century. The hair—which a few short hours ago had been nearly coal black—was now silvery white. Only the eyes were bright. Gradually, I traced, in that ancient man, a faint resemblance to my self of other days.

I turned away, and tottered to the window. I knew, now, that I was old, and the knowledge seemed to confirm my trembling walk. For a little space, I stared moodily out into the blurred vista of changeful landscape. Even in that short time, a year passed, and, with a petulant gesture, I left the window. As I did so, I noticed that my hand shook with the palsy of old age; and a short sob choked its way through my lips.

For a little while, I paced, tremulously, between the window and the table; my gaze wandering hither and thither, uneasily. How dilapidated the room was. Everywhere lay the thick dust—thick, sleepy, and black. The fender was a shape of rust. The chains that held the brass clock-weights, had rusted through long ago, and now the weights lay on the floor beneath; themselves two cones of verdigris.

As I glanced about, it seemed to me that I could see the very furniture of the room rotting and decaying before my eyes. Nor was this fancy, on my part; for, all at once, the bookshelf, along the sidewall, collapsed, with a cracking and rending of rotten wood, precipitating its contents upon the floor, and filling the room with a smother of dusty atoms.

How tired I felt. As I walked, it seemed that I could hear my dry joints, creak and crack at every step. I wondered about my sister. Was she dead, as well as Pepper? All had happened so quickly and suddenly. This must be, indeed, the beginning of the end of all things! It occurred to me, to go to look for her; but I felt too weary. And then, she had been so queer about these happenings, of late. Of late! I repeated the words, and laughed, feebly—mirthlessly, as the realization was borne in upon me that I spoke of a time, half a century gone. Half a century! It might have been twice as long!

I moved slowly to the window, and looked out once more across the world. I can best describe the passage of day and night, at this period, as a sort of gigantic, ponderous flicker. Moment by moment, the acceleration of time continued; so that, at nights now, I saw the moon, only as a swaying trail of palish fire, that varied from a mere line of light to a nebulous path, and then dwindled again, disappearing periodically.

The flicker of the days and nights quickened. The days had grown perceptibly darker, and a queer quality of dusk lay, as it were, in the atmosphere. The nights were so much lighter, that the stars were scarcely to be seen, saving here and there an occasional hairlike line of fire, that seemed to sway a little, with the moon.

Quicker, and ever quicker, ran the flicker of day and night; and, suddenly it seemed, I was aware that the flicker had died out, and, instead, there reigned a comparatively steady light, which was shed upon all the world, from an eternal river of flame that swung up and down, North and South, in stupendous, mighty swings.

The sky was now grown very much darker, and there was in the blue of it a heavy gloom, as though a vast blackness peered through it upon the earth. Yet, there was in it, also, a strange and awful clearness, and emptiness. Periodically, I had glimpses of a ghostly track of fire that swayed thin and darkly toward the sun-stream; vanished and reappeared. It was the scarcely visible moon-stream.

Looking out at the landscape, I was conscious again, of a blurring sort of 'flitter,' that came either from the light of the ponderous-swinging sun-stream, or was the result of the incredibly rapid changes of the earth's surface. And every few moments, so it seemed, the snow would lie suddenly upon the world, and vanish as abruptly, as though an invisible giant 'flitted' a white sheet off and on the earth.

Time fled, and the weariness that was mine, grew insupportable. I turned from the window, and walked once across the room, the heavy dust deadening the sound of my footsteps. Each step that I took, seemed a greater effort than the one before. An intolerable ache, knew me in every joint and limb, as I trod my way, with a weary uncertainty.

By the opposite wall, I came to a weak pause, and wondered, dimly, what was my intent. I looked to my left, and saw my old chair. The thought of sitting in it brought a faint sense of comfort to my bewildered wretchedness. Yet, because I was so weary and old and tired, I would scarcely brace my mind to do anything but stand, and wish myself past those few yards. I rocked, as I stood. The floor, even, seemed a place for rest; but the dust lay so thick and sleepy and black. I turned, with a great effort of will, and made toward my chair. I reached it, with a groan of thankfulness. I sat down.

Everything about me appeared to be growing dim. It was all so strange and unthought of. Last night, I was a comparatively strong, though elderly man; and now, only a few hours later—! I looked at the little dust-heap that had once been Pepper. Hours! and I laughed, a feeble, bitter laugh; a shrill, cackling laugh, that shocked my dimming senses.

For a while, I must have dozed. Then I opened my eyes, with a start. Somewhere across the room, there had been a muffled noise of something falling. I looked, and saw, vaguely, a cloud of dust hovering above a pile of débris. Nearer the door, something else tumbled, with a crash. It was one of the cupboards; but I was tired, and took little notice. I closed my eyes, and sat there in a state of drowsy, semi-unconsciousness. Once or twice—as though coming through thick mists—I heard noises, faintly. Then I must have slept.

Chapter 16

The Awakening

I awoke, with a start. For a moment, I wondered where I was. Then memory came to me....

The room was still lit with that strange light—half-sun, half-moon, light. I felt refreshed, and the tired, weary ache had left me. I went slowly across to the window, and looked out. Overhead, the river of flame drove up and down, North and South, in a dancing semi-circle of fire. As a mighty sleigh in the loom of time it seemed—in a sudden fancy of mine—to be beating home the picks of the years. For, so vastly had the passage of time been accelerated, that there was no longer any sense of the sun passing from East to West. The only apparent movement was the North and South beat of the sun-stream, that had become so swift now, as to be better described as a quiver.

As I peered out, there came to me a sudden, inconsequent memory of that last journey among the Outer worlds. I remembered the sudden vision that had come to me, as I neared the Solar System, of the fast whirling planets about the sun—as though the governing quality of time had been held in abeyance, and the Machine of a Universe allowed to run down an eternity, in a few moments or hours. The memory passed, along with a, but partially comprehended, suggestion that I had been permitted a glimpse into further time spaces. I stared out again, seemingly, at the quake of the sun-stream. The speed seemed to increase, even as I looked. Several lifetimes came and went, as I watched.

Suddenly, it struck me, with a sort of grotesque seriousness, that I was still alive. I thought of Pepper, and wondered how it was that I had not followed his fate. He had reached the time of his dying, and had passed, probably through sheer length of years. And here was I, alive, hundreds of thousands of centuries after my rightful period of years.

For, a time, I mused, absently. 'Yesterday—' I stopped, suddenly. Yesterday! There was no yesterday. The yesterday of which I spoke had been swallowed up in the abyss of years, ages gone. I grew dazed with much thinking.

Presently, I turned from the window, and glanced 'round the room. It seemed different—strangely, utterly different. Then, I knew what it was that made it appear so strange. It was bare: there was not a piece of furniture in the room; not even a solitary fitting of any sort. Gradually, my amazement went, as I remembered, that this was but the inevitable end of that process of decay, which I had witnessed commencing, before my sleep. Thousands of years! Millions of years!

Over the floor was spread a deep layer of dust, that reached half way up to the window-seat. It had grown immeasurably, whilst I slept; and represented the dust of untold ages. Undoubtedly, atoms of the old, decayed furniture helped to swell its bulk; and, somewhere among it all, mouldered the long-ago-dead Pepper.

All at once, it occurred to me, that I had no recollection of wading knee-deep through all that dust, after I awoke. True, an incredible age of years had passed, since I approached the window; but that was evidently as nothing, compared with the countless spaces of time that, I conceived, had vanished whilst I was sleeping. I remembered now, that I had fallen asleep, sitting in my old chair. Had it gone...? I glanced toward where it had stood. Of course, there was no chair to be seen. I could not satisfy myself, whether it had disappeared, after my waking, or before. If it had mouldered under me, surely, I should have been waked by the collapse. Then I remembered that the thick dust, which covered the floor, would have been sufficient to soften my fall; so that it was quite possible, I had slept upon the dust for a million years or more.

As these thoughts wandered through my brain, I glanced again, casually, to where the chair had stood. Then, for the first time, I noticed that there were no marks, in the dust, of my footprints, between it and the window. But then, ages of years had passed, since I had awaked—tens of thousands of years!

My look rested thoughtfully, again upon the place where once had stood my chair. Suddenly, I passed from abstraction to intentness; for there, in its standing place, I made out a long undulation, rounded off with the heavy dust. Yet it was not so much hidden, but that I could tell what had caused it. I knew—and shivered at the knowledge—that it was a human body, ages-dead, lying there, beneath the place where I had slept. It was lying on its right side, its back turned toward me. I could make out and trace each curve and outline, softened, and moulded, as it were, in the black dust. In a vague sort of way, I tried to account for its presence there. Slowly, I began to grow bewildered, as the thought came to me that it lay just about where I must have fallen when the chair collapsed.

Gradually, an idea began to form itself within my brain; a thought that shook my spirit. It seemed hideous and insupportable; yet it grew upon me, steadily, until it became a conviction. The body under that coating, that shroud of dust, was neither more nor less than my own dead shell. I did not attempt to prove it. I knew it now, and wondered I had not known it all along. I was a bodiless thing.

Awhile, I stood, trying to adjust my thoughts to this new problem. In time—how many thousands of years, I know not—I attained to some degree of quietude—sufficient to enable me to pay attention to what was transpiring around me.

Now, I saw that the elongated mound had sunk, collapsed, level with the rest of the spreading dust. And fresh atoms, impalpable, had settled above that mixture of grave-powder, which the aeons had ground. A long while, I stood, turned from the window. Gradually, I grew more collected, while the world slipped across the centuries into the future.

Presently, I began a survey of the room. Now, I saw that time was beginning its destructive work, even on this strange old building. That it had stood through all the years was, it seemed to me, proof that it was something different from any other house. I do not think, somehow, that I had thought of its decaying. Though, why, I could not have said. It was not until I had meditated upon the matter, for some considerable time, that I fully realized that the extraordinary space of time through which it had stood, was sufficient to have utterly pulverized the very stones of which it was built, had they been taken from any earthly quarry. Yes, it was undoubtedly mouldering now. All the plaster had gone from the walls; even as the woodwork of the room had gone, many ages before.

While I stood, in contemplation, a piece of glass, from one of the small, diamond-shaped panes, dropped, with a dull tap, amid the dust upon the sill behind me, and crumbled into a little heap of powder. As I turned from contemplating it, I saw light between a couple of the stones that formed the outer wall. Evidently, the mortar was falling away....

After awhile, I turned once more to the window, and peered out. I discovered, now, that the speed of time had become enormous. The lateral quiver of the sun-stream, had grown so swift as to cause the dancing semi-circle of flame to merge into, and disappear in, a sheet of fire that covered half the Southern sky from East to West.

From the sky, I glanced down to the gardens. They were just a blur of a palish, dirty green. I had a feeling that they stood higher, than in the old days; a feeling that they were nearer my window, as though they had risen, bodily.

Yet, they were still a long way below me; for the rock, over the mouth of the pit, on which this house stands, arches up to a great height.

It was later, that I noticed a change in the constant color of the gardens. The pale, dirty green was growing ever paler and paler, toward white. At last, after a great space, they became greyish-white, and stayed thus for a very long time. Finally, however, the greyness began to fade, even as had the green, into a dead white. And this remained, constant and unchanged. And by this I knew that, at last, snow lay upon all the Northern world.

And so, by millions of years, time winged onward through eternity, to the end—the end, of which, in the old-earth days, I had thought remotely, and in hazily speculative fashion. And now, it was approaching in a manner of which none had ever dreamed.

I recollect that, about this time, I began to have a lively, though morbid, curiosity, as to what would happen when the end came—but I seemed strangely without imaginings.

All this while, the steady process of decay was continuing. The few remaining pieces of glass, had long ago vanished; and, every now and then, a soft thud, and a little cloud of rising dust, would tell of some fragment of fallen mortar or stone.

I looked up again, to the fiery sheet that quaked in the heavens above me and far down into the Southern sky. As I looked, the impression was borne in upon me, that it had lost some of its first brilliancy—that it was duller, deeper hued.

I glanced down, once more, to the blurred white of the worldscape. Sometimes, my look returned to the burning sheet of dulling flame, that was, and yet hid, the sun. At times, I glanced behind me, into the growing dusk of the great, silent room, with its aeon-carpet of sleeping dust....

So, I watched through the fleeting ages, lost in soul-wearing thoughts and wonderings, and possessed with a new weariness.

Chapter 17

The Slowing Rotation

It might have been a million years later, that I perceived, beyond possibility of doubt, that the fiery sheet that lit the world, was indeed darkening.

Another vast space went by, and the whole enormous flame had sunk to a deep, copper color. Gradually, it darkened, from copper to copper-red, and from this, at times, to a deep, heavy, purplish tint, with, in it, a strange loom of blood.

Although the light was decreasing, I could perceive no diminishment in the apparent speed of the sun. It still spread itself in that dazzling veil of speed.

The world, so much of it as I could see, had assumed a dreadful shade of gloom, as though, in very deed, the last day of the worlds approached.

The sun was dying; of that there could be little doubt; and still the earth whirled onward, through space and all the aeons. At this time, I remember, an extraordinary sense of bewilderment took me. I found myself, later, wandering, mentally, amid an odd chaos of fragmentary modern theories and the old Biblical story of the world's ending.

Then, for the first time, there flashed across me, the memory that the sun, with its system of planets, was, and had been, traveling through space at an incredible speed. Abruptly, the question rose—Where? For a very great time, I pondered this matter; but, finally, with a certain sense of the futility of my puzzlings, I let my thoughts wander to other things. I grew to wondering, how much longer the house would stand. Also, I queried, to myself, whether I should be doomed to stay, bodiless, upon the earth, through the dark-time that I knew was coming. From these thoughts, I fell again to speculations upon the possible direction of the sun's journey through space.... And so another great while passed.

Gradually, as time fled, I began to feel the chill of a great winter. Then, I remembered that, with the sun dying, the cold must be, necessarily, extraordinarily intense. Slowly, slowly, as the aeons slipped into eternity, the earth sank into a heavier and redder gloom. The dull flame in the firmament took on a deeper tint, very somber and turbid.

Then, at last, it was borne upon me that there was a change. The fiery, gloomy curtain of flame that hung quaking overhead, and down away into the Southern sky, began to thin and contract; and, in it, as one sees the fast vibrations of a jarred harp-string, I saw once more the sun-stream quivering, giddily, North and South.

Slowly, the likeness to a sheet of fire, disappeared, and I saw, plainly, the slowing beat of the sun-stream. Yet, even then, the speed of its swing was inconceivably swift. And all the time, the brightness of the fiery arc grew ever duller. Underneath, the world loomed dimly—an indistinct, ghostly region.

Overhead, the river of flame swayed slower, and even slower; until, at last, it swung to the North and South in great, ponderous beats, that lasted through seconds. A long space went by, and now each sway of the great belt lasted nigh a minute; so that, after a great while, I ceased to distinguish it as a visible movement; and the streaming fire ran in a steady river of dull flame, across the deadly-looking sky.

An indefinite period passed, and it seemed that the arc of fire became less sharply defined. It appeared to me to grow more attenuated, and I thought blackish streaks showed, occasionally. Presently, as I watched, the smooth onward-flow ceased; and I was able to perceive that there came a momentary, but regular, darkening of the world. This grew until, once more, night descended, in short, but periodic, intervals upon the wearying earth.

Longer and longer became the nights, and the days equaled them; so that, at last, the day and the night grew to the duration of seconds in length, and the sun showed, once more, like an almost invisible, coppery-red colored ball, within the glowing mistiness of its flight. Corresponding to the dark lines, showing at times in its trail, there were now distinctly to be seen on the half-visible sun itself, great, dark belts.

Year after year flashed into the past, and the days and nights spread into minutes. The sun had ceased to have the appearance of a tail; and now rose and set—a tremendous globe of a glowing copper-bronze hue; in parts ringed with blood-red bands; in others, with the dusky ones, that I have already mentioned. These circles—both red and black—were of varying thicknesses. For a time, I was at a loss to account for their presence. Then it occurred to me, that it was scarcely likely that the sun would cool evenly all over; and that these markings were due, probably, to differences in temperature of the various areas; the red representing those parts where the heat was still fervent, and the black those portions which were already comparatively cool.

It struck me, as a peculiar thing, that the sun should cool in evenly defined rings; until I remembered that, possibly, they were but isolated patches, to which the enormous rotatory speed of the sun had imparted a beltlike appearance. The sun, itself, was very much greater than the sun I had known in the old-world days; and, from this, I argued that it was considerably nearer.

At nights, the moon[6] still showed; but small and remote; and the light she reflected was so dull and weak that she seemed little more than the small, dim ghost of the olden moon, that I had known.

Gradually, the days and nights lengthened out, until they equaled a space somewhat less than one of the old-earth hours; the sun rising and setting like a great, ruddy bronze disk, crossed with ink-black bars. About this time, I found myself, able once more, to see the gardens, with clearness. For the world had now grown very still, and changeless. Yet, I am not correct in saying, 'gardens'; for there were no gardens—nothing that I knew or recognized. In place thereof, I looked out upon a vast plain, stretching away into distance. A little to my left, there was a low range of hills. Everywhere, there was a uniform, white covering of snow, in places rising into hummocks and ridges.

It was only now, that I recognized how really great had been the snowfall. In places it was vastly deep, as was witnessed by a great, upleaping, wave-shaped hill, away to my right; though it is not impossible, that this was due, in part, to some rise in the surface of the ground. Strangely enough, the range of low hills to my left—already mentioned—was not entirely covered with the universal snow; instead, I could see their bare, dark sides showing in several places. And everywhere and always there reigned an incredible death-silence and desolation. The immutable, awful quiet of a dying world.

All this time, the days and nights were lengthening, perceptibly. Already, each day occupied, maybe, some two hours from dawn to dusk. At night, I had been surprised to find that there were very few stars overhead, and these small, though of an extraordinary brightness; which I attributed to the peculiar, but clear, blackness of the nighttime.

Away to the North, I could discern a nebulous sort of mistiness; not unlike, in appearance, a small portion of the Milky Way. It might have been an extremely remote star-cluster; or—the thought came to me suddenly—perhaps it was the sidereal universe that I had known, and now left far behind, forever—a small, dimly glowing mist of stars, far in the depths of space.

Still, the days and nights lengthened, slowly. Each time, the sun rose duller than it had set. And the dark belts increased in breadth.

About this time, there happened a fresh thing. The sun, earth, and sky were suddenly darkened, and, apparently, blotted out for a brief space. I had a sense, a certain awareness (I could learn little by sight), that the earth was enduring a very great fall of snow. Then, in an instant, the veil that had obscured everything, vanished, and I looked out, once more. A marvelous sight met my gaze. The hollow in which this house, with its gardens, stands, was brimmed with snow.[7] It lipped over the sill of my window. Everywhere, it lay, a great level stretch of white, which caught and reflected, gloomily, the somber coppery glows of the dying sun. The world had become a shadowless plain, from horizon to horizon.

I glanced up at the sun. It shone with an extraordinary, dull clearness. I saw it, now, as one who, until then, had seen it, only through a partially obscuring medium. All about it, the sky had become black, with a clear, deep blackness, frightful in its nearness, and its unmeasured deep, and its utter unfriendliness. For a great time, I looked into it, newly, and shaken and fearful. It was so near. Had I been a child, I might have expressed some of my sensation and distress, by saying that the sky had lost its roof.

Later, I turned, and peered about me, into the room. Everywhere, it was covered with a thin shroud of the all-pervading white. I could see it but dimly, by reason of the somber light that now lit the world. It appeared to cling to the ruined walls; and the thick, soft dust of the years, that covered the floor knee-deep, was nowhere visible. The snow must have blown in through the open framework of the windows. Yet, in no place had it drifted; but lay everywhere about the great, old room, smooth and level. Moreover, there had been no wind these many thousand years. But there was the snow,[8] as I have told.

And all the earth was silent. And there was a cold, such as no living man can ever have known.

The earth was now illuminated, by day, with a most doleful light, beyond my power to describe. It seemed as though I looked at the great plain, through the medium of a bronze-tinted sea.

It was evident that the earth's rotatory movement was departing, steadily.

The end came, all at once. The night had been the longest yet; and when the dying sun showed, at last, above the world's edge, I had grown so wearied of the dark, that I greeted it as a friend. It rose steadily, until about twenty degrees above the horizon. Then, it stopped suddenly, and, after a strange retrograde movement, hung motionless—a great shield in the sky[9]. Only the circular rim of the sun showed bright—only this, and one thin streak of light near the equator.

Gradually, even this thread of light died out; and now, all that was left of our great and glorious sun, was a vast dead disk, rimmed with a thin circle of bronze-red light.

Chapter 18

The Green Star

The world was held in a savage gloom—cold and intolerable. Outside, all was quiet—quiet! From the dark room behind me, came the occasional, soft thud[10] of falling matter—fragments of rotting stone. So time passed, and night grasped the world, wrapping it in wrappings of impenetrable blackness.

There was no night-sky, as we know it. Even the few straggling stars had vanished, conclusively. I might have been in a shuttered room, without a light; for all that I could see. Only, in the impalpableness of gloom, opposite, burnt that vast, encircling hair of dull fire. Beyond this, there was no ray in all the vastitude of night that surrounded me; save that, far in the North, that soft, mistlike glow still shone.

Silently, years moved on. What period of time passed, I shall never know. It seemed to me, waiting there, that eternities came and went, stealthily; and still I watched. I could see only the glow of the sun's edge, at times; for now, it had commenced to come and go—lighting up a while, and again becoming extinguished.

All at once, during one of these periods of life, a sudden flame cut across the night—a quick glare that lit up the dead earth, shortly; giving me a glimpse of its flat lonesomeness. The light appeared to come from the sun—shooting out from somewhere near its center, diagonally. A moment, I gazed, startled. Then the leaping flame sank, and the gloom fell again. But now it was not so dark; and the sun was belted by a thin line of vivid, white light. I stared, intently. Had a volcano broken out on the sun? Yet, I negatived the thought, as soon as formed. I felt that the light had been far too intensely white, and large, for such a cause.

Another idea there was, that suggested itself to me. It was, that one of the inner planets had fallen into the sun—becoming incandescent, under that impact. This theory appealed to me, as being more plausible, and accounting more satisfactorily for the extraordinary size and brilliance of the blaze, that had lit up the dead world, so unexpectedly.

Full of interest and emotion, I stared, across the darkness, at that line of white fire, cutting the night. One thing it told to me, unmistakably: the sun was yet rotating at an enormous speed.[11] Thus, I knew that the years were still fleeting at an incalculable rate; though so far as the earth was concerned, life, and light, and time, were things belonging to a period lost in the long gone ages.

After that one burst of flame, the light had shown, only as an encircling band of bright fire. Now, however, as I watched, it began slowly to sink into a ruddy tint, and, later, to a dark, copper-red color; much as the sun had done. Presently, it sank to a deeper hue; and, in a still further space of time, it began to fluctuate; having periods of glowing, and anon, dying. Thus, after a great while, it disappeared.

Long before this, the smoldering edge of the sun had deadened into blackness. And so, in that supremely future time, the world, dark and intensely silent, rode on its gloomy orbit around the ponderous mass of the dead sun.

My thoughts, at this period, can be scarcely described. At first, they were chaotic and wanting in coherence. But, later, as the ages came and went, my soul seemed to imbibe the very essence of the oppressive solitude and dreariness, that held the earth.

With this feeling, there came a wonderful clearness of thought, and I realized, despairingly, that the world might wander for ever, through that enormous night. For a while, the unwholesome idea filled me, with a sensation of overbearing desolation; so that I could have cried like a child. In time, however, this feeling grew, almost insensibly, less, and an unreasoning hope possessed me. Patiently, I waited.

From time to time, the noise of dropping particles, behind in the room, came dully to my ears. Once, I heard a loud crash, and turned, instinctively, to look; forgetting, for the moment, the impenetrable night in which every detail was submerged. In a while, my gaze sought the heavens; turning, unconsciously, toward the North. Yes, the nebulous glow still showed. Indeed, I could have almost imagined that it looked somewhat plainer. For a long time, I kept my gaze fixed upon it; feeling, in my lonely soul, that its soft haze was, in some way, a tie with the past. Strange, the trifles from which one can suck comfort! And yet, had I but known—But I shall come to that in its proper time.

For a very long space, I watched, without experiencing any of the desire for sleep, that would so soon have visited me in the old-earth days. How I should have welcomed it; if only to have passed the time, away from my perplexities and thoughts.

Several times, the comfortless sound of some great piece of masonry falling, disturbed my meditations; and, once, it seemed I could hear whispering in the room, behind me. Yet it was utterly useless to try to see anything. Such blackness, as existed, scarcely can be conceived. It was palpable, and hideously brutal to the sense; as though something dead, pressed up against me—something soft, and icily cold.

Under all this, there grew up within my mind, a great and overwhelming distress of uneasiness, that left me, but to drop me into an uncomfortable brooding. I felt that I must fight against it; and, presently, hoping to distract my thoughts, I turned to the window, and looked up toward the North, in search of the nebulous whiteness, which, still, I believed to be the far and misty glowing of the universe we had left. Even as I raised my eyes, I was thrilled with a feeling of wonder; for, now, the hazy light had resolved into a single, great star, of vivid green.

As I stared, astonished, the thought flashed into my mind; that the earth must be traveling toward the star; not away, as I had imagined. Next, that it could not be the universe the earth had left; but, possibly, an outlying star, belonging to some vast star-cluster, hidden in the enormous depths of space. With a sense of commingled awe and curiosity, I watched it, wondering what new thing was to be revealed to me.

For a while, vague thoughts and speculations occupied me, during which my gaze dwelt insatiably upon that one spot of light, in the otherwise pitlike darkness. Hope grew up within me, banishing the oppression of despair, that had seemed to stifle me. Wherever the earth was traveling, it was, at least, going once more toward the realms of light. Light! One must spend an eternity wrapped in soundless night, to understand the full horror of being without it.

Slowly, but surely, the star grew upon my vision, until, in time, it shone as brightly as had the planet Jupiter, in the old-earth days. With increased size, its color became more impressive; reminding me of a huge emerald, scintillating rays of fire across the world.

Years fled away in silence, and the green star grew into a great splash of flame in the sky. A little later, I saw a thing that filled me with amazement. It was the ghostly outline of a vast crescent, in the night; a gigantic new moon, seeming to be growing out of the surrounding gloom. Utterly bemused, I stared at it. It appeared to be quite close—comparatively; and I puzzled to understand how the earth had come so near to it, without my having seen it before.

The light, thrown by the star, grew stronger; and, presently, I was aware that it was possible to see the earthscape again; though indistinctly. Awhile, I stared, trying to make out whether I could distinguish any detail of the world's surface, but I found the light insufficient. In a little, I gave up the attempt, and glanced once more toward the star. Even in the short space, that my attention had been diverted, it had increased considerably, and seemed now, to my bewildered sight, about a quarter of the size of the full moon. The light it threw, was extraordinarily powerful; yet its color was so abominably unfamiliar, that such of the world as I could see, showed unreal; more as though I looked out upon a landscape of shadow, than aught else.

All this time, the great crescent was increasing in brightness, and began, now, to shine with a perceptible shade of green. Steadily, the star increased in size and brilliancy, until it showed, fully as large as half a full moon; and, as it grew greater and brighter, so did the vast crescent throw out more and more light, though of an ever deepening hue of green. Under the combined blaze of their radiances, the wilderness that stretched before me, became steadily more visible. Soon, I seemed able to stare across the whole world, which now appeared, beneath the strange light, terrible in its cold and awful, flat dreariness.

It was a little later, that my attention was drawn to the fact, that the great star of green flame, was slowly sinking out of the North, toward the East. At first, I could scarcely believe that I saw aright; but soon there could be no doubt that it was so. Gradually, it sank, and, as it fell, the vast crescent of glowing green, began to dwindle and dwindle, until it became a mere arc of light, against the livid colored sky. Later it vanished, disappearing in the self-same spot from which I had seen it slowly emerge.

By this time, the star had come to within some thirty degrees of the hidden horizon. In size it could now have rivaled the moon at its full; though, even yet, I could not distinguish its disk. This fact led me to conceive that it was, still, an extraordinary distance away; and, this being so, I knew that its size must be huge, beyond the conception of man to understand or imagine.

Suddenly, as I watched, the lower edge of the star vanished—cut by a straight, dark line. A minute—or a century—passed, and it dipped lower, until the half of it had disappeared from sight. Far away out on the great plain, I saw a monstrous shadow blotting it out, and advancing swiftly. Only a third of the star was visible now. Then, like a flash, the solution of this extraordinary phenomenon revealed itself to me. The star was sinking behind the enormous mass of the dead sun. Or rather, the sun—obedient to its attraction—was rising toward it,[12] with the earth following in its trail. As these thoughts expanded in my mind, the star vanished; being completely hidden by the tremendous bulk of the sun. Over the earth there fell, once more, the brooding night.

With the darkness, came an intolerable feeling of loneliness and dread. For the first time, I thought of the Pit, and its inmates. After that, there rose in my memory the still more terrible Thing, that had haunted the shores of the Sea of Sleep, and lurked in the shadows of this old building. Where were they? I wondered—and shivered with miserable thoughts. For a time, fear held me, and I prayed, wildly and incoherently, for some ray of light with which to dispel the cold blackness that enveloped the world.

How long I waited, it is impossible to say—certainly for a very great period. Then, all at once, I saw a loom of light shine out ahead. Gradually, it became more distinct. Suddenly, a ray of vivid green, flashed across the darkness. At the same moment, I saw a thin line of livid flame, far in the night. An instant, it seemed, and it had grown into a great clot of fire; beneath which, the world lay bathed in a blaze of emerald green light. Steadily it grew, until, presently, the whole of the green star had come into sight again. But now, it could be scarcely called a star; for it had increased to vast proportions, being incomparably greater than the sun had been in the olden time.

"Then, as I stared, I became aware that I could see the edge of the lifeless sun, glowing like a great crescent-moon. Slowly, its lighted surface, broadened out to me, until half of its diameter was visible; and the star began to drop away on my right. Time passed, and the earth moved on, slowly traversing the tremendous face of the dead sun." [13]

Gradually, as the earth traveled forward, the star fell still more to the right; until, at last, it shone on the back of the house, sending a flood of broken rays, in through the skeletonlike walls. Glancing upward, I saw that much of the ceiling had vanished, enabling me to see that the upper storeys were even more decayed. The roof had, evidently, gone entirely; and I could see the green effulgence of the Starlight shining in, slantingly.

Chapter 19

The End of the Solar System

From the abutment, where once had been the windows, through which I had watched that first, fatal dawn, I could see that the sun was hugely greater, than it had been, when first the Star lit the world. So great was it, that its lower edge seemed almost to touch the far horizon. Even as I watched, I imagined that it drew closer. The radiance of green that lit the frozen earth, grew steadily brighter.

Thus, for a long space, things were. Then, on a sudden, I saw that the sun was changing shape, and growing smaller, just as the moon would have done in past time. In a while, only a third of the illuminated part was turned toward the earth. The Star bore away on the left.

Gradually, as the world moved on, the Star shone upon the front of the house, once more; while the sun showed, only as a great bow of green fire. An instant, it seemed, and the sun had vanished. The Star was still fully visible. Then the earth moved into the black shadow of the sun, and all was night—Night, black, starless, and intolerable.

Filled with tumultuous thoughts, I watched across the night—waiting. Years, it may have been, and then, in the dark house behind me, the clotted stillness of the world was broken. I seemed to hear a soft padding of many feet, and a faint, inarticulate whisper of sound, grew on my sense. I looked 'round into the blackness, and saw a multitude of eyes. As I stared, they increased, and appeared to come toward me. For an instant, I stood, unable to move. Then a hideous swine-noise[14] rose up into the night; and, at that, I leapt from the window, out on to the frozen world. I have a confused notion of having run awhile; and, after that, I just waited—waited. Several times, I heard shrieks; but always as though from a distance. Except for these sounds, I had no idea of the whereabouts of the house. Time moved onward. I was conscious of little, save a sensation of cold and hopelessness and fear.

An age, it seemed, and there came a glow, that told of the coming light. It grew, tardily. Then—with a loom of unearthly glory—the first ray from the

Green Star, struck over the edge of the dark sun, and lit the world. It fell upon a great, ruined structure, some two hundred yards away. It was the house. Staring, I saw a fearsome sight—over its walls crawled a legion of unholy things, almost covering the old building, from tottering towers to base. I could see them, plainly; they were the Swine-creatures.

The world moved out into the light of the Star, and I saw that, now, it seemed to stretch across a quarter of the heavens. The glory of its livid light was so tremendous, that it appeared to fill the sky with quivering flames. Then, I saw the sun. It was so close that half of its diameter lay below the horizon; and, as the world circled across its face, it seemed to tower right up into the sky, a stupendous dome of emerald colored fire. From time to time, I glanced toward the house; but the Swine-things seemed unaware of my proximity.

Years appeared to pass, slowly. The earth had almost reached the center of the sun's disk. The light from the Green Sun—as now it must be called—shone through the interstices, that gapped the mouldered walls of the old house, giving them the appearance of being wrapped in green flames. The Swine-creatures still crawled about the walls.

Suddenly, there rose a loud roar of swine-voices, and, up from the center of the roofless house, shot a vast column of blood-red flame. I saw the little, twisted towers and turrets flash into fire; yet still preserving their twisted crookedness. The beams of the Green Sun, beat upon the house, and intermingled with its lurid glows; so that it appeared a blazing furnace of red and green fire.

Fascinated, I watched, until an overwhelming sense of coming danger, drew my attention. I glanced up, and, at once, it was borne upon me, that the sun was closer; so close, in fact, that it seemed to overhang the world. Then—I know not how—I was caught up into strange heights—floating like a bubble in the awful effulgence.

Far below me, I saw the earth, with the burning house leaping into an ever growing mountain of flame, 'round about it, the ground appeared to be glowing; and, in places, heavy wreaths of yellow smoke ascended from the earth. It seemed as though the world were becoming ignited from that one plague-spot of fire. Faintly, I could see the Swine-things. They appeared quite unharmed. Then the ground seemed to cave in, suddenly, and the house, with its load of foul creatures, disappeared into the depths of the earth, sending a strange, blood colored cloud into the heights. I remembered the hell Pit under the house.

In a while, I looked 'round. The huge bulk of the sun, rose high above me. The distance between it and the earth, grew rapidly less. Suddenly, the earth appeared to shoot forward. In a moment, it had traversed the space between it and the sun. I heard no sound; but, out from the sun's face, gushed an ever-growing tongue of dazzling flame. It seemed to leap, almost to the distant Green Sun—shearing through the emerald light, a very cataract of blinding fire. It reached its limit, and sank; and, on the sun, glowed a vast splash of burning white—the grave of the earth.

The sun was very close to me, now. Presently, I found that I was rising higher; until, at last, I rode above it, in the emptiness. The Green Sun was now so huge that its breadth seemed to fill up all the sky, ahead. I looked down, and noted that the sun was passing directly beneath me.

A year may have gone by—or a century—and I was left, suspended, alone. The sun showed far in front—a black, circular mass, against the molten splendor of the great, Green Orb. Near one edge, I observed that a lurid glow had appeared, marking the place where the earth had fallen. By this, I knew that the long-dead sun was still revolving, though with great slowness.

Afar to my right, I seemed to catch, at times, a faint glow of whitish light. For a great time, I was uncertain whether to put this down to fancy or not. Thus, for a while, I stared, with fresh wonderings; until, at last, I knew that it was no imaginary thing; but a reality. It grew brighter; and, presently, there slid out of the green, a pale globe of softest white. It came nearer, and I saw that it was apparently surrounded by a robe of gently glowing clouds. Time passed....

I glanced toward the diminishing sun. It showed, only as a dark blot on the face of the Green Sun. As I watched, I saw it grow smaller, steadily, as though rushing toward the superior orb, at an immense speed. Intently, I stared. What would happen? I was conscious of extraordinary emotions, as I realized that it would strike the Green Sun. It grew no bigger than a pea, and I looked, with my whole soul, to witness the final end of our System— that system which had borne the world through so many aeons, with its multitudinous sorrows and joys; and now—

Suddenly, something crossed my vision, cutting from sight all vestige of the spectacle I watched with such soul-interest. What happened to the dead sun, I did not see; but I have no reason—in the light of that which I saw afterward— to disbelieve that it fell into the strange fire of the Green Sun, and so perished.

And then, suddenly, an extraordinary question rose in my mind, whether this stupendous globe of green fire might not be the vast Central Sun— the great sun, 'round which our universe and countless others revolve. I felt confused. I thought of the probable end of the dead sun, and another suggestion came, dumbly—Do the dead stars make the Green Sun their grave? The idea appealed to me with no sense of grotesqueness; but rather as something both possible and probable.

Chapter 20

The Celestial Globes

For a while, many thoughts crowded my mind, so that I was unable to do aught, save stare, blindly, before me. I seemed whelmed in a sea of doubt and wonder and sorrowful remembrance.

It was later, that I came out of my bewilderment. I looked about, dazedly. Thus, I saw so extraordinary a sight that, for a while, I could scarcely believe I was not still wrapped in the visionary tumult of my own thoughts. Out of the reigning green, had grown a boundless river of softly shimmering globes—each one enfolded in a wondrous fleece of pure cloud. They reached, both above and below me, to an unknown distance; and, not only hid the shining of the Green Sun; but supplied, in place thereof, a tender glow of light, that suffused itself around me, like unto nothing I have ever seen, before or since.

In a little, I noticed that there was about these spheres, a sort of transparency, almost as though they were formed of clouded crystal, within which burned a radiance—gentle and subdued. They moved on, past me, continually, floating onward at no great speed; but rather as though they had eternity before them. A great while, I watched, and could perceive no end to them. At times, I seemed to distinguish faces, amid the cloudiness; but strangely indistinct, as though partly real, and partly formed of the mistiness through which they showed.

For a long time, I waited, passively, with a sense of growing content. I had no longer that feeling of unutterable loneliness; but felt, rather, that I was less alone, than I had been for kalpas of years. This feeling of contentment, increased, so that I would have been satisfied to float in company with those celestial globules, forever.

Ages slipped by, and I saw the shadowy faces, with increased frequency, also with greater plainness. Whether this was due to my soul having become more attuned to its surroundings, I cannot tell—probably it was so. But, however this may be, I am assured now, only of the fact that I became steadily more conscious of a new mystery about me, telling me that I had, indeed, penetrated within the borderland of some unthought-of region—some subtle, intangible place, or form, of existence.

The enormous stream of luminous spheres continued to pass me, at an unvarying rate—countless millions; and still they came, showing no signs of ending, nor even diminishing.

Then, as I was borne, silently, upon the unbuoying ether, I felt a sudden, irresistible, forward movement, toward one of the passing globes. An instant, and I was beside it. Then, I slid through, into the interior, without experiencing the least resistance, of any description. For a short while, I could see nothing; and waited, curiously.

All at once, I became aware that a sound broke the inconceivable stillness. It was like the murmur of a great sea at calm—a sea breathing in its sleep. Gradually, the mist that obscured my sight, began to thin away; and so, in time, my vision dwelt once again upon the silent surface of the Sea of Sleep.

For a little, I gazed, and could scarcely believe I saw aright. I glanced 'round. There was the great globe of pale fire, swimming, as I had seen it before, a short distance above the dim horizon. To my left, far across the sea, I discovered, presently, a faint line, as of thin haze, which I guessed to be the shore, where my Love and I had met, during those wonderful periods of soul-wandering, that had been granted to me in the old earth days.

Another, a troubled, memory came to me—of the Formless Thing that had haunted the shores of the Sea of Sleep. The guardian of that silent, echoless place. These, and other, details, I remembered, and knew, without doubt that I was looking out upon that same sea. With the assurance, I was filled with an overwhelming feeling of surprise, and joy, and shaken expectancy, conceiving it possible that I was about to see my Love, again. Intently, I gazed around; but could catch no sight of her. At that, for a little, I felt hopeless. Fervently, I prayed, and ever peered, anxiously.... How still was the sea!

Down, far beneath me, I could see the many trails of changeful fire, that had drawn my attention, formerly. Vaguely, I wondered what caused them; also, I remembered that I had intended to ask my dear One about them, as well as many other matters—and I had been forced to leave her, before the half that I had wished to say, was said.

My thoughts came back with a leap. I was conscious that something had touched me. I turned quickly. God, Thou wert indeed gracious—it was She! She looked up into my eyes, with an eager longing, and I looked down to her, with all my soul. I should like to have held her; but the glorious purity of her face, kept me afar. Then, out of the winding mist, she put her dear arms.

Her whisper came to me, soft as the rustle of a passing cloud. 'Dearest!' she said. That was all; but I had heard, and, in a moment I held her to me—as I prayed—forever.

In a little, she spoke of many things, and I listened. Willingly, would I have done so through all the ages that are to come. At times, I whispered back, and my whispers brought to her spirit face, once more, an indescribably delicate tint—the bloom of love. Later, I spoke more freely, and to each word she listened, and made answer, delightfully; so that, already, I was in Paradise.

She and I; and nothing, save the silent, spacious void to see us; and only the quiet waters of the Sea of Sleep to hear us.

Long before, the floating multitude of cloud-enfolded spheres had vanished into nothingness. Thus, we looked upon the face of the slumberous deeps, and were alone. Alone, God, I would be thus alone in the hereafter, and yet be never lonely! I had her, and, greater than this, she had me. Aye, aeon-aged me; and on this thought, and some others, I hope to exist through the few remaining years that may yet lie between us.

Chapter 21

The Dark Sun

How long our souls lay in the arms of joy, I cannot say; but, all at once, I was waked from my happiness, by a diminution of the pale and gentle light that lit the Sea of Sleep. I turned toward the huge, white orb, with a premonition of coming trouble. One side of it was curving inward, as though a convex, black shadow were sweeping across it. My memory went back. It was thus, that the darkness had come, before our last parting. I turned toward my Love, inquiringly. With a sudden knowledge of woe, I noticed how wan and unreal she had grown, even in that brief space. Her voice seemed to come to me from a distance. The touch of her hands was no more than the gentle pressure of a summer wind, and grew less perceptible.

Already, quite half of the immense globe was shrouded. A feeling of desperation seized me. Was she about to leave me? Would she have to go, as she had gone before? I questioned her, anxiously, frightenedly; and she, nestling closer, explained, in that strange, faraway voice, that it was imperative she should leave me, before the Sun of Darkness—as she termed it—blotted out the light. At this confirmation of my fears, I was overcome with despair; and could only look, voicelessly, across the quiet plains of the silent sea.

How swiftly the darkness spread across the face of the White Orb. Yet, in reality, the time must have been long, beyond human comprehension.

At last, only a crescent of pale fire, lit the, now dim, Sea of Sleep. All this while, she had held me; but, with so soft a caress, that I had been scarcely conscious of it. We waited there, together, she and I; speechless, for very sorrow. In the dimming light, her face showed, shadowy—blending into the dusky mistiness that encircled us.

Then, when a thin, curved line of soft light was all that lit the sea, she released me—pushing me from her, tenderly. Her voice sounded in my ears, 'I may not stay longer, Dear One.' It ended in a sob.

She seemed to float away from me, and became invisible. Her voice came to me, out of the shadows, faintly; apparently from a great distance:—

'A little while—' It died away, remotely. In a breath, the Sea of Sleep darkened into night. Far to my left, I seemed to see, for a brief instant, a soft glow. It vanished, and, in the same moment, I became aware that I was no longer above the still sea; but once more suspended in infinite space, with the Green Sun—now eclipsed by a vast, dark sphere—before me.

Utterly bewildered, I stared, almost unseeingly, at the ring of green flames, leaping above the dark edge. Even in the chaos of my thoughts, I wondered, dully, at their extraordinary shapes. A multitude of questions assailed me. I thought more of her, I had so lately seen, than of the sight before me. My grief, and thoughts of the future, filled me. Was I doomed to be separated from her, always? Even in the old earth-days, she had been mine, only for a little while; then she had left me, as I thought, forever. Since then, I had seen her but these times, upon the Sea of Sleep.

A feeling of fierce resentment filled me, and miserable questionings. Why could I not have gone with my Love? What reason to keep us apart? Why had I to wait alone, while she slumbered through the years, on the still bosom of the Sea of Sleep? The Sea of Sleep! My thoughts turned, inconsequently, out of their channel of bitterness, to fresh, desperate questionings. Where was it? Where was it? I seemed to have but just parted from my Love, upon its quiet surface, and it had gone, utterly. It could not be far away! And the White Orb which I had seen hidden in the shadow of the Sun of Darkness! My sight dwelt upon the Green Sun—eclipsed. What had eclipsed it? Was there a vast, dead star circling it? Was the Central Sun—as I had come to regard it—a double star? The thought had come, almost unbidden; yet why should it not be so?

My thoughts went back to the White Orb. Strange, that it should have been—I stopped. An idea had come, suddenly. The White Orb and the Green Sun! Were they one and the same? My imagination wandered backward, and I remembered the luminous globe to which I had been so unaccountably attracted. It was curious that I should have forgotten it, even momentarily. Where were the others? I reverted again to the globe I had entered. I thought, for a time, and matters became clearer. I conceived that, by entering that impalpable globule, I had passed, at once, into some further, and, until then, invisible dimension; There, the Green Sun was still visible; but as a stupendous sphere of pale, white light—almost as though its ghost showed, and not its material part.

A long time, I mused on the subject. I remembered how, on entering the sphere, I had, immediately, lost all sight of the others. For a still further period, I continued to revolve the different details in my mind.

In a while, my thoughts turned to other things. I came more into the present, and began to look about me, seeingly. For the first time, I perceived that innumerable rays, of a subtle, violet hue, pierced the strange semi-darkness, in all directions. They radiated from the fiery rim of the Green Sun. They seemed to grow upon my vision, so that, in a little, I saw that they were countless. The night was filled with them—spreading outward from the Green Sun, fan-wise. I concluded that I was enabled to see them, by reason of the Sun's glory being cut off by the eclipse. They reached right out into space, and vanished.

Gradually, as I looked, I became aware that fine points of intensely brilliant light, traversed the rays. Many of them seemed to travel from the Green Sun, into distance. Others came out of the void, toward the Sun; but one and all, each kept strictly to the ray in which it traveled. Their speed was inconceivably great; and it was only when they neared the Green Sun, or as they left it, that I could see them as separate specks of light. Further from the sun, they became thin lines of vivid fire within the violet.

The discovery of these rays, and the moving sparks, interested me, extraordinarily. To where did they lead, in such countless profusion? I thought of the worlds in space.... And those sparks! Messengers! Possibly, the idea was fantastic; but I was not conscious of its being so. Messengers! Messengers from the Central Sun!

An idea evolved itself, slowly. Was the Green Sun the abode of some vast Intelligence? The thought was bewildering. Visions of the Unnamable rose, vaguely. Had I, indeed, come upon the dwelling-place of the Eternal? For a time, I repelled the thought, dumbly. It was too stupendous. Yet....

Huge, vague thoughts had birth within me. I felt, suddenly, terribly naked. And an awful Nearness, shook me.

And Heaven ...! Was that an illusion?

My thoughts came and went, erratically. The Sea of Sleep—and she! Heaven.... I came back, with a bound, to the present. Somewhere, out of the void behind me, there rushed an immense, dark body—huge and silent. It was a dead star, hurling onward to the burying place of the stars. It drove between me and the Central Suns—blotting them out from my vision, and plunging me into an impenetrable night.

An age, and I saw again the violet rays. A great while later—aeons it must have been—a circular glow grew in the sky, ahead, and I saw the edge of the receding star, show darkly against it. Thus, I knew that it was nearing the Central Suns. Presently, I saw the bright ring of the Green Sun, show plainly against the night The star had passed into the shadow of the Dead Sun. After that, I just waited. The strange years went slowly, and ever, I watched, intently.

'The thing I had expected, came at last—suddenly, awfully. A vast flare of dazzling light. A streaming burst of white flame across the dark void. For an indefinite while, it soared outward—a gigantic mushroom of fire. It ceased to grow. Then, as time went by, it began to sink backward, slowly. I saw, now, that it came from a huge, glowing spot near the center of the Dark Sun. Mighty flames, still soared outward from this. Yet, spite of its size, the grave of the star was no more than the shining of Jupiter upon the face of an ocean, when compared with the inconceivable mass of the Dead Sun.

I may remark here, once more, that no words will ever convey to the imagination, the enormous bulk of the two Central Suns.

Chapter 22

The Dark Nebula

Years melted into the past, centuries, aeons. The light of the incandescent star, sank to a furious red.

It was later, that I saw the dark nebula—at first, an impalpable cloud, away to my right. It grew, steadily, to a clot of blackness in the night. How long I watched, it is impossible to say; for time, as we count it, was a thing of the past. It came closer, a shapeless monstrosity of darkness—tremendous. It seemed to slip across the night, sleepily—a very hell-fog. Slowly, it slid nearer, and passed into the void, between me and the Central Suns. It was as though a curtain had been drawn before my vision. A strange tremor of fear took me, and a fresh sense of wonder.

The green twilight that had reigned for so many millions of years, had now given place to impenetrable gloom. Motionless, I peered about me. A century fled, and it seemed to me that I detected occasional dull glows of red, passing me at intervals.

Earnestly, I gazed, and, presently, seemed to see circular masses, that showed muddily red, within the clouded blackness. They appeared to be growing out of the nebulous murk. Awhile, and they became plainer to my accustomed vision. I could see them, now, with a fair amount of distinctness—ruddy-tinged spheres, similar, in size, to the luminous globes that I had seen, so long previously.

They floated past me, continually. Gradually, a peculiar uneasiness seized me. I became aware of a growing feeling of repugnance and dread. It was directed against those passing orbs, and seemed born of intuitive knowledge, rather than of any real cause or reason.

Some of the passing globes were brighter than others; and, it was from one of these, that a face looked, suddenly. A face, human in its outline; but so tortured with woe, that I stared, aghast. I had not thought there was such sorrow, as I saw there. I was conscious of an added sense of pain, on perceiving that the eyes, which glared so wildly, were sightless. A while longer, I saw it; then it had passed on, into the surrounding gloom. After this, I saw others—all wearing that look of hopeless sorrow; and blind.

A long time went by, and I became aware that I was nearer to the orbs, than I had been. At this, I grew uneasy; though I was less in fear of those strange globules, than I had been, before seeing their sorrowful inhabitants; for sympathy had tempered my fear.

Later, there was no doubt but that I was being carried closer to the red spheres, and, presently, I floated among them. In awhile, I perceived one bearing down upon me. I was helpless to move from its path. In a minute, it seemed, it was upon me, and I was submerged in a deep red mist. This cleared, and I stared, confusedly, across the immense breadth of the Plain of Silence. It appeared just as I had first seen it. I was moving forward, steadily, across its surface. Away ahead, shone the vast, blood-red ring[15] that lit the place. All around, was spread the extraordinary desolation of stillness, that had so impressed me during my previous wanderings across its starkness.

Presently, I saw, rising up into the ruddy gloom, the distant peaks of the mighty amphitheatre of mountains, where, untold ages before, I had been shown my first glimpse of the terrors that underlie many things; and where, vast and silent, watched by a thousand mute gods, stands the replica of this house of mysteries—this house that I had seen swallowed up in that hell-fire, ere the earth had kissed the sun, and vanished for ever.

Though I could see the crests of the mountain-amphitheatre, yet it was a great while before their lower portions became visible. Possibly, this was due to the strange, ruddy haze, that seemed to cling to the surface of the Plain. However, be this as it may, I saw them at last.

In a still further space of time, I had come so close to the mountains, that they appeared to overhang me. Presently, I saw the great rift, open before me, and I drifted into it; without volition on my part.

Later, I came out upon the breadth of the enormous arena. There, at an apparent distance of some five miles, stood the House, huge, monstrous and silent—lying in the very center of that stupendous amphitheatre. So far as I could see, it had not altered in any way; but looked as though it were only yesterday that I had seen it. Around, the grim, dark mountains frowned down upon me from their lofty silences.

Far to my right, away up among inaccessible peaks, loomed the enormous bulk of the great Beast-god. Higher, I saw the hideous form of the dread goddess, rising up through the red gloom, thousands of fathoms above me. To the left, I made out the monstrous Eyeless-Thing, grey and inscrutable. Further off, reclining on its lofty ledge, the livid Ghoul-Shape showed—a splash of sinister color, among the dark mountains.

Slowly, I moved out across the great arena—floating. As I went, I made out the dim forms of many of the other lurking Horrors that peopled those supreme heights.

Gradually, I neared the House, and my thoughts flashed back across the abyss of years. I remembered the dread Specter of the Place. A short while passed, and I saw that I was being wafted directly toward the enormous mass of that silent building.

About this time, I became aware, in an indifferent sort of way, of a growing sense of numbness, that robbed me of the fear, which I should otherwise have felt, on approaching that awesome Pile. As it was, I viewed it, calmly—much as a man views calamity through the haze of his tobacco smoke.

In a little while, I had come so close to the House, as to be able to distinguish many of the details about it. The longer I looked, the more was I confirmed in my long-ago impressions of its entire similitude to this strange house. Save in its enormous size, I could find nothing unlike.

Suddenly, as I stared, a great feeling of amazement filled me. I had come opposite to that part, where the outer door, leading into the study, is situated. There, lying right across the threshold, lay a great length of coping stone, identical—save in size and color—with the piece I had dislodged in my fight with the Pit-creatures.

I floated nearer, and my astonishment increased, as I noted that the door was broken partly from its hinges, precisely in the manner that my study door had been forced inward, by the assaults of the Swine-things. The sight started a train of thoughts, and I began to trace, dimly, that the attack on this house, might have a far deeper significance than I had, hitherto, imagined. I remembered how, long ago, in the old earth-days, I had half suspected that, in some unexplainable manner, this house, in which I live, was en rapport—to use a recognized term—with that other tremendous structure, away in the midst of that incomparable Plain.

Now, however, it began to be borne upon me, that I had but vaguely conceived what the realization of my suspicion meant. I began to understand, with a more than human clearness, that the attack I had repelled, was, in some extraordinary manner, connected with an attack upon that strange edifice.

With a curious inconsequence, my thoughts abruptly left the matter; to dwell, wonderingly, upon the peculiar material, out of which the House was constructed. It was—as I have mentioned, earlier—of a deep, green color. Yet, now that I had come so close to it, I perceived that it fluctuated at times, though slightly—glowing and fading, much as do the fumes of phosphorus, when rubbed upon the hand, in the dark.

Presently, my attention was distracted from this, by coming to the great entrance. Here, for the first time, I was afraid; for, all in a moment, the huge doors swung back, and I drifted in between them, helplessly. Inside, all was blackness, impalpable. In an instant, I had crossed the threshold, and the great doors closed, silently, shutting me in that lightless place.

For a while, I seemed to hang, motionless; suspended amid the darkness. Then, I became conscious that I was moving again; where, I could not tell. Suddenly, far down beneath me, I seemed to hear a murmurous noise of Swine-laughter. It sank away, and the succeeding silence appeared clogged with horror.

Then a door opened somewhere ahead; a white haze of light filtered through, and I floated slowly into a room, that seemed strangely familiar. All at once, there came a bewildering, screaming noise, that deafened me. I saw a blurred vista of visions, flaming before my sight. My senses were dazed, through the space of an eternal moment. Then, my power of seeing, came back to me. The dizzy, hazy feeling passed, and I saw, clearly.

Chapter 23

Pepper

I was seated in my chair, back again in this old study. My glance wandered 'round the room. For a minute, it had a strange, quivery appearance—unreal and unsubstantial. This disappeared, and I saw that nothing was altered in any way. I looked toward the end window—the blind was up.

I rose to my feet, shakily. As I did so, a slight noise, in the direction of the door, attracted my attention. I glanced toward it. For a short instant, it appeared to me that it was being closed, gently. I stared, and saw that I must have been mistaken—it seemed closely shut.

With a succession of efforts, I trod my way to the window, and looked out. The sun was just rising, lighting up the tangled wilderness of gardens. For, perhaps, a minute, I stood, and stared. I passed my hand, confusedly, across my forehead.

Presently, amid the chaos of my senses, a sudden thought came to me; I turned, quickly, and called to Pepper. There was no answer, and I stumbled across the room, in a quick access of fear. As I went, I tried to frame his name; but my lips were numb. I reached the table, and stooped down to him, with a catching at my heart. He was lying in the shadow of the table, and I had not been able to see him, distinctly, from the window. Now, as I stooped, I took my breath, shortly. There was no Pepper; instead, I was reaching toward an elongated, little heap of grey, ashlike dust....

I must have remained, in that half-stooped position, for some minutes. I was dazed—stunned. Pepper had really passed into the land of shadows.

Chapter 24

The Footsteps of Children

Pepper is dead! Even now, at times, I seem scarcely able to realize that this is so. It is many weeks, since I came back from that strange and terrible journey through space and time. Sometimes, in my sleep, I dream about it, and go through, in imagination, the whole of that fearsome happening. When I wake, my thoughts dwell upon it. That Sun—those Suns, were they indeed the great Central Suns, 'round which the whole universe, of the unknown heavens, revolves? Who shall say? And the bright globules, floating forever in the light of the Green Sun! And the Sea of Sleep on which they float! How unbelievable it all is. If it were not for Pepper, I should, even after the many extraordinary things that I have witnessed, be inclined to imagine that it was but a gigantic dream. Then, there is that dreadful, dark nebula (with its multitudes of red spheres) moving always within the shadow of the Dark Sun, sweeping along on its stupendous orbit, wrapped eternally in gloom. And the faces that peered out at me! God, do they, and does such a thing really exist? ... There is still that little heap of grey ash, on my study floor. I will not have it touched.

At times, when I am calmer, I have wondered what became of the outer planets of the Solar System. It has occurred to me, that they may have broken loose from the sun's attraction, and whirled away into space. This is, of course, only a surmise. There are so many things, about which I wonder.

Now that I am writing, let me record that I am certain, there is something horrible about to happen. Last night, a thing occurred, which has filled me with an even greater terror, than did the Pit fear. I will write it down now, and, if anything more happens, endeavor to make a note of it, at once. I have a feeling, that there is more in this last affair, than in all those others. I am shaky and nervous, even now, as I write. Somehow, I think death is not very far away. Not that I fear death—as death is understood. Yet, there is that in the air, which bids me fear—an intangible, cold horror. I felt it last night. It was thus:—

Last night, I was sitting here in my study, writing. The door, leading into the garden, was half open. At times, the metallic rattle of a dog's chain, sounded faintly. It belongs to the dog I have bought, since Pepper's death. I will not have him in the house—not after Pepper. Still, I have felt it better to have a dog about the place. They are wonderful creatures.

I was much engrossed in my work, and the time passed, quickly. Suddenly, I heard a soft noise on the path, outside in the garden—pad, pad, pad, it went, with a stealthy, curious sound. I sat upright, with a quick movement, and looked out through the opened door. Again the noise came—pad, pad, pad. It appeared to be approaching. With a slight feeling of nervousness, I stared into the gardens; but the night hid everything.

Then the dog gave a long howl, and I started. For a minute, perhaps, I peered, intently; but could hear nothing. After a little, I picked up the pen, which I had laid down, and recommenced my work. The nervous feeling had gone; for I imagined that the sound I had heard, was nothing more than the dog walking 'round his kennel, at the length of his chain.

A quarter of an hour may have passed; then, all at once, the dog howled again, and with such a plaintively sorrowful note, that I jumped to my feet, dropping my pen, and inking the page on which I was at work.

'Curse that dog!' I muttered, noting what I had done. Then, even as I said the words, there sounded again that queer—pad, pad, pad. It was horribly close—almost by the door, I thought. I knew, now, that it could not be the dog; his chain would not allow him to come so near.

The dog's growl came again, and I noted, subconsciously, the taint of fear in it.

Outside, on the windowsill, I could see Tip, my sister's pet cat. As I looked, it sprang to its feet, its tail swelling, visibly. For an instant it stood thus; seeming to stare, fixedly, at something, in the direction of the door. Then, quickly, it began to back along the sill; until, reaching the wall at the end, it could go no further. There it stood, rigid, as though frozen in an attitude of extraordinary terror.

Frightened, and puzzled, I seized a stick from the corner, and went toward the door, silently; taking one of the candles with me. I had come to within a few paces of it, when, suddenly, a peculiar sense of fear thrilled through me—a fear, palpitant and real; whence, I knew not, nor why. So great was the feeling of terror, that I wasted no time; but retreated straight-way—walking backward, and keeping my gaze, fearfully, on the door. I would have given much, to rush at it, fling it to, and shoot the bolts; for I have had it repaired and strengthened, so that, now, it is far stronger than ever it has been. Like Tip, I continued my, almost unconscious, progress backward, until the wall brought me up. At that, I started, nervously, and glanced 'round, apprehensively. As I did so, my eyes dwelt, momentarily, on the rack of firearms, and I took a step toward them; but stopped, with a curious feeling that they would be needless. Outside, in the gardens, the dog moaned, strangely.

Suddenly, from the cat, there came a fierce, long screech. I glanced, jerkily, in its direction—Something, luminous and ghostly, encircled it, and grew upon my vision. It resolved into a glowing hand, transparent, with a lambent, greenish flame flickering over it. The cat gave a last, awful caterwaul, and I saw it smoke and blaze. My breath came with a gasp, and I leant against the wall. Over that part of the window there spread a smudge, green and fantastic. It hid the thing from me, though the glare of fire shone through, dully. A stench of burning, stole into the room.

Pad, pad, pad—Something passed down the garden path, and a faint, mouldy odor seemed to come in through the open door, and mingle with the burnt smell.

The dog had been silent for a few moments. Now, I heard him yowl, sharply, as though in pain. Then, he was quiet, save for an occasional, subdued whimper of fear.

A minute went by; then the gate on the West side of the gardens, slammed, distantly. After that, nothing; not even the dog's whine.

I must have stood there some minutes. Then a fragment of courage stole into my heart, and I made a frightened rush at the door, dashed it to, and bolted it. After that, for a full half-hour, I sat, helpless—staring before me, rigidly.

Slowly, my life came back into me, and I made my way, shakily, up-stairs to bed.

That is all.

Chapter 25

The Thing from the Arena

This morning, early, I went through the gardens; but found everything as usual. Near the door, I examined the path, for footprints; yet, here again, there was nothing to tell me whether, or not, I dreamed last night.

It was only when I came to speak to the dog, that I discovered tangible proof, that something did happen. When I went to his kennel, he kept inside, crouching up in one corner, and I had to coax him, to get him out. When, finally, he consented to come, it was in a strangely cowed and subdued manner. As I patted him, my attention was attracted to a greenish patch, on his left flank. On examining it, I found, that the fur and skin had been apparently, burnt off; for the flesh showed, raw and scorched. The shape of the mark was curious, reminding me of the imprint of a large talon or hand.

I stood up, thoughtful. My gaze wandered toward the study window. The rays of the rising sun, shimmered on the smoky patch in the lower corner, causing it to fluctuate from green to red, oddly. Ah! that was undoubtedly another proof; and, suddenly, the horrible Thing I saw last night, rose in my mind. I looked at the dog, again. I knew the cause, now, of that hateful looking wound on his side—I knew, also, that, what I had seen last night, had been a real happening. And a great discomfort filled me. Pepper! Tip! And now this poor animal ...! I glanced at the dog again, and noticed that he was licking at his wound.

'Poor brute!' I muttered, and bent to pat his head. At that, he got upon his feet, nosing and licking my hand, wistfully.

Presently, I left him, having other matters to which to attend.

After dinner, I went to see him, again. He seemed quiet, and disinclined to leave his kennel. From my sister, I have learnt that he has refused all food today. She appeared a little puzzled, when she told me; though quite unsuspicious of anything of which to be afraid.

The day has passed, uneventfully enough. After tea, I went, again, to have a look at the dog. He seemed moody, and somewhat restless; yet persisted in remaining in his kennel. Before locking up, for the night, I moved his kennel out, away from the wall, so that I shall be able to watch it from the small window, tonight. The thought came to me, to bring him into the house for the night; but consideration has decided me, to let him remain out. I cannot say that the house is, in any degree, less to be feared than the gardens. Pepper was in the house, and yet....

It is now two o'clock. Since eight, I have watched the kennel, from the small, side window in my study. Yet, nothing has occurred, and I am too tired to watch longer. I will go to bed....

During the night, I was restless. This is unusual for me; but, toward morning, I obtained a few hours' sleep.

I rose early, and, after breakfast, visited the dog. He was quiet; but morose, and refused to leave his kennel. I wish there was some horse doctor near here; I would have the poor brute looked to. All day, he has taken no food; but has shown an evident desire for water—lapping it up, greedily. I was relieved to observe this.

The evening has come, and I am in my study. I intend to follow my plan of last night, and watch the kennel. The door, leading into the garden, is bolted, securely. I am consciously glad there are bars to the windows....

Night:—Midnight has gone. The dog has been silent, up to the present. Through the side window, on my left, I can make out, dimly, the outlines of the kennel. For the first time, the dog moves, and I hear the rattle of his chain. I look out, quickly. As I stare, the dog moves again, restlessly, and I see a small patch of luminous light, shine from the interior of the kennel. It vanishes; then the dog stirs again, and, once more, the gleam comes. I am puzzled. The dog is quiet, and I can see the luminous thing, plainly. It shows distinctly. There is something familiar about the shape of it. For a moment, I wonder; then it comes to me, that it is not unlike the four fingers and thumb of a hand. Like a hand! And I remember the contour of that fearsome wound on the dog's side. It must be the wound I see. It is luminous at night—Why? The minutes pass. My mind is filled with this fresh thing....

Suddenly, I hear a sound, out in the gardens. How it thrills through me. It is approaching. Pad, pad, pad. A prickly sensation traverses my spine, and seems to creep across my scalp. The dog moves in his kennel, and whimpers, frightenedly. He must have turned 'round; for, now, I can no longer see the outline of his shining wound.

Outside, the gardens are silent, once more, and I listen, fearfully. A minute passes, and another; then I hear the padding sound, again. It is quite close, and appears to be coming down the graveled path. The noise is curiously measured and deliberate. It ceases outside the door; and I rise to my feet, and stand motionless. From the door, comes a slight sound—the latch is being slowly raised. A singing noise is in my ears, and I have a sense of pressure about the head—

The latch drops, with a sharp click, into the catch. The noise startles me afresh; jarring, horribly, on my tense nerves. After that, I stand, for a long while, amid an ever-growing quietness. All at once, my knees begin to tremble, and I have to sit, quickly.

An uncertain period of time passes, and, gradually, I begin to shake off the feeling of terror, that has possessed me. Yet, still I sit. I seem to have lost the power of movement. I am strangely tired, and inclined to doze. My eyes open and close, and, presently, I find myself falling asleep, and waking, in fits and starts.

It is some time later, that I am sleepily aware that one of the candles is guttering. When I wake again, it has gone out, and the room is very dim, under the light of the one remaining flame. The semi-darkness troubles me little. I have lost that awful sense of dread, and my only desire seems to be to sleep—sleep.

Suddenly, although there is no noise, I am awake—wide awake. I am acutely conscious of the nearness of some mystery, of some overwhelming Presence. The very air seems pregnant with terror. I sit huddled, and just listen, intently. Still, there is no sound. Nature, herself, seems dead. Then, the oppressive stillness is broken by a little eldritch scream of wind, that sweeps 'round the house, and dies away, remotely.

I let my gaze wander across the half-lighted room. By the great clock in the far corner, is a dark, tall shadow. For a short instant, I stare, frightenedly. Then, I see that it is nothing, and am, momentarily, relieved.

In the time that follows, the thought flashes through my brain, why not leave this house—this house of mystery and terror? Then, as though in answer, there sweeps up, across my sight, a vision of the wondrous Sea of Sleep,—the Sea of Sleep where she and I have been allowed to meet, after the years of separation and sorrow; and I know that I shall stay on here, whatever happens.

Through the side window, I note the somber blackness of the night. My glance wanders away, and 'round the room; resting on one shadowy object and another. Suddenly, I turn, and look at the window on my right; as I do so, I breathe quickly, and bend forward, with a frightened gaze at something outside the window, but close to the bars. I am looking at a vast, misty swine-face, over which fluctuates a flamboyant flame, of a greenish hue. It is the Thing from the arena. The quivering mouth seems to drip with a continual, phosphorescent slaver. The eyes are staring straight into the room, with an inscrutable expression. Thus, I sit rigidly—frozen.

The Thing has begun to move. It is turning, slowly, in my direction. Its face is coming 'round toward me. It sees me. Two huge, inhumanly human, eyes are looking through the dimness at me. I am cold with fear; yet, even now, I am keenly conscious, and note, in an irrelevant way, that the distant stars are blotted out by the mass of the giant face.

A fresh horror has come to me. I am rising from my chair, without the least intention. I am on my feet, and something is impelling me toward the door that leads out into the gardens. I wish to stop; but cannot. Some immutable power is opposed to my will, and I go slowly forward, unwilling and resistant. My glance flies 'round the room, helplessly, and stops at the window. The great swine-face has disappeared, and I hear, again, that stealthy pad, pad, pad. It stops outside the door—the door toward which I am being compelled....

There succeeds a short, intense silence; then there comes a sound. It is the rattle of the latch, being slowly lifted. At that, I am filled with desperation. I will not go forward another step. I make a vast effort to return; but it is, as though I press back, upon an invisible wall. I groan out loud, in the agony of my fear, and the sound of my voice is frightening. Again comes that rattle, and I shiver, clammily. I try—aye, fight and struggle, to hold back, back; but it is no use....

I am at the door, and, in a mechanical way, I watch my hand go forward, to undo the topmost bolt. It does so, entirely without my volition. Even as I reach up toward the bolt, the door is violently shaken, and I get a sickly whiff of mouldy air, which seems to drive in through the interstices of the doorway. I draw the bolt back, slowly, fighting, dumbly, the while. It comes out of its socket, with a click, and I begin to shake, aguishly. There are two more; one at the bottom of the door; the other, a massive affair, is placed about the middle.

For, perhaps a minute, I stand, with my arms hanging slackly, by my sides. The influence to meddle with the fastenings of the door, seems to have gone. All at once, there comes the sudden rattle of iron, at my feet. I glance down, quickly, and realize, with an unspeakable terror, that my foot is pushing back the lower bolt. An awful sense of helplessness assails me.... The bolt comes out of its hold, with a slight, ringing sound and I stagger on my feet, grasping at the great, central bolt, for support. A minute passes, an eternity; then another—My God, help me! I am being forced to work upon the last fastening. I will not! Better to die, than open to the Terror, that is on the other side of the door. Is there no escape ...? God help me, I have jerked the bolt half out of its socket! My lips emit a hoarse scream of terror, the bolt is three parts drawn, now, and still my unconscious hands work toward my doom. Only a fraction of steel, between my soul and That. Twice, I scream out in the supreme agony of my fear; then, with a mad effort, I tear my hands away. My eyes seem blinded. A great blackness is falling upon me. Nature has come to my rescue. I feel my knees giving. There is a loud, quick thudding upon the door, and I am falling, falling....

I must have lain there, at least a couple of hours. As I recover, I am aware that the other candle has burnt out, and the room is in an almost total darkness. I cannot rise to my feet, for I am cold, and filled with a terrible cramp. Yet my brain is clear, and there is no longer the strain of that unholy influence.

Cautiously, I get upon my knees, and feel for the central bolt. I find it, and push it securely back into its socket; then the one at the bottom of the door. By this time, I am able to rise to my feet, and so manage to secure the fastening at the top. After that, I go down upon my knees, again, and creep away among the furniture, in the direction of the stairs. By doing this, I am safe from observation from the window.

I reach the opposite door, and, as I leave the study, cast one nervous glance over my shoulder, toward the window. Out in the night, I seem to catch a glimpse of something impalpable; but it may be only a fancy. Then, I am in the passage, and on the stairs.

Reaching my bedroom, I clamber into bed, all clothed as I am, and pull the bedclothes over me. There, after awhile, I begin to regain a little confidence. It is impossible to sleep; but I am grateful for the added warmth of the bedclothes. Presently, I try to think over the happenings of the past night; but, though I cannot sleep, I find that it is useless, to attempt consecutive thought. My brain seems curiously blank.

Toward morning, I begin to toss, uneasily. I cannot rest, and, after awhile, I get out of bed, and pace the floor. The wintry dawn is beginning to creep through the windows, and shows the bare discomfort of the old room. Strange, that, through all these years, it has never occurred to me how dismal the place really is. And so a time passes.

From somewhere down stairs, a sound comes up to me. I go to the bedroom door, and listen. It is Mary, bustling about the great, old kitchen, getting the breakfast ready. I feel little interest. I am not hungry. My thoughts, however; continue to dwell upon her. How little the weird happenings in this house seem to trouble her. Except in the incident of the Pit creatures, she has seemed unconscious of anything unusual occurring. She is old, like myself; yet how little we have to do with one another. Is it because we have nothing in common; or only that, being old, we care less for society, than quietness? These and other matters pass through my mind, as I meditate; and help to distract my attention, for a while, from the oppressive thoughts of the night.

After a time, I go to the window, and, opening it, look out. The sun is now above the horizon, and the air, though cold, is sweet and crisp. Gradually, my brain clears, and a sense of security, for the time being, comes to me. Somewhat happier, I go down stairs, and out into the garden, to have a look at the dog.

As I approach the kennel, I am greeted by the same mouldy stench that assailed me at the door last night. Shaking off a momentary sense of fear, I call to the dog; but he takes no heed, and, after calling once more, I throw a small stone into the kennel. At this, he moves, uneasily, and I shout his name, again; but do not go closer. Presently, my sister comes out, and joins me, in trying to coax him from the kennel.

In a little the poor beast rises, and shambles out lurching queerly. In the daylight he stands swaying from side to side, and blinking stupidly. I look and note that the horrid wound is larger, much larger, and seems to have a whitish, fungoid appearance. My sister moves to fondle him; but I detain her, and explain that I think it will be better not to go too near him for a few days; as it is impossible to tell what may be the matter with him; and it is well to be cautious.

A minute later, she leaves me; coming back with a basin of odd scraps of food. This she places on the ground, near the dog, and I push it into his reach, with the aid of a branch, broken from one of the shrubs. Yet, though the meat should be tempting, he takes no notice of it; but retires to his kennel. There is still water in his drinking vessel, so, after a few moments' talk, we go back to the house. I can see that my sister is much puzzled as to what is the matter with the animal; yet it would be madness, even to hint the truth to her.

The day slips away, uneventfully; and night comes on. I have determined to repeat my experiment of last night. I cannot say that it is wisdom; yet my mind is made up. Still, however, I have taken precautions; for I have driven stout nails in at the back of each of the three bolts, that secure the door, opening from the study into the gardens. This will, at least, prevent a recurrence of the danger I ran last night.

From ten to about two-thirty, I watch; but nothing occurs; and, finally, I stumble off to bed, where I am soon asleep.

Chapter 26

The Luminous Peak

I awake suddenly. It is still dark. I turn over, once or twice, in my endeavors to sleep again; but I cannot sleep. My head is aching, slightly; and, by turns I am hot and cold. In a little, I give up the attempt, and stretch out my hand, for the matches. I will light my candle, and read, awhile; perhaps, I shall be able to sleep, after a time. For a few moments, I grope; then my hand touches the box; but, as I open it, I am startled, to see a phosphorescent speck of fire, shining amid the darkness. I put out my other hand, and touch it. It is on my wrist. With a feeling of vague alarm, I strike a light, hurriedly, and look; but can see nothing, save a tiny scratch.

'Fancy!' I mutter, with a half sigh of relief. Then the match burns my finger, and I drop it, quickly. As I fumble for another, the thing shines out again. I know, now, that it is no fancy. This time, I light the candle, and examine the place, more closely. There is a slight, greenish discoloration 'round the scratch. I am puzzled and worried. Then a thought comes to me. I remember the morning after the Thing appeared. I remember that the dog licked my hand. It was this one, with the scratch on it; though I have not been even conscious of the abasement, until now. A horrible fear has come to me. It creeps into my brain—the dog's wound, shines at night. With a dazed feeling, I sit down on the side of the bed, and try to think; but cannot. My brain seems numbed with the sheer horror of this new fear.

Time moves on, unheeded. Once, I rouse up, and try to persuade myself that I am mistaken; but it is no use. In my heart, I have no doubt.

Hour after hour, I sit in the darkness and silence, and shiver, hopelessly....

The day has come and gone, and it is night again.

This morning, early, I shot the dog, and buried it, away among the bushes. My sister is startled and frightened; but I am desperate. Besides, it is better so. The foul growth had almost hidden its left side. And I—the place on my wrist has enlarged, perceptibly. Several times, I have caught myself muttering prayers—little things learnt as a child. God, Almighty God, help me! I shall go mad.

Six days, and I have eaten nothing. It is night. I am sitting in my chair. Ah, God! I wonder have any ever felt the horror of life that I have come to know? I am swathed in terror. I feel ever the burning of this dread growth. It has covered all my right arm and side, and is beginning to creep up my neck. Tomorrow, it will eat into my face. I shall become a terrible mass of living corruption. There is no escape. Yet, a thought has come to me, born of a sight of the gun-rack, on the other side of the room. I have looked again—with the strangest of feelings. The thought grows upon me. God, Thou knowest, Thou must know, that death is better, aye, better a thousand times than This. This! Jesus, forgive me, but I cannot live, cannot, cannot! I dare not! I am beyond all help—there is nothing else left. It will, at least, spare me that final horror....

I think I must have been dozing. I am very weak, and oh! so miserable, so miserable and tired—tired. The rustle of the paper, tries my brain. My hearing seems preternaturally sharp. I will sit awhile and think....

"Hush! I hear something, down—down in the cellars. It is a creaking sound. My God, it is the opening of the great, oak trap. What can be doing that? The scratching of my pen deafens me ... I must listen.... There are steps on the stairs; strange padding steps, that come up and nearer.... Jesus, be merciful to me, an old man. There is something fumbling at the door-handle. O God, help me now! Jesus—The door is opening—slowly. Somethi—"

That is all.[16]

Chapter 27

Conclusion

I put down the Manuscript, and glanced across at Tonnison: he was sitting, staring out into the dark. I waited a minute; then I spoke.

"Well?" I said.

He turned, slowly, and looked at me. His thoughts seemed to have gone out of him into a great distance.

"Was he mad?" I asked, and indicated the MS., with a half nod.

Tonnison stared at me, unseeingly, a moment; then, his wits came back to him, and, suddenly, he comprehended my question.

"No!" he said.

I opened my lips, to offer a contradictory opinion; for my sense of the saneness of things, would not allow me to take the story literally; then I shut them again, without saying anything. Somehow, the certainty in Tonnison's voice affected my doubts. I felt, all at once, less assured; though I was by no means convinced as yet.

After a few moments' silence, Tonnison rose, stiffly, and began to undress. He seemed disinclined to talk; so I said nothing; but followed his example. I was weary; though still full of the story I had just read.

Somehow, as I rolled into my blankets, there crept into my mind a memory of the old gardens, as we had seen them. I remembered the odd fear that the place had conjured up in our hearts; and it grew upon me, with conviction, that Tonnison was right.

It was very late when we rose—nearly midday; for the greater part of the night had been spent in reading the MS.

Tonnison was grumpy, and I felt out of sorts. It was a somewhat dismal day, and there was a touch of chilliness in the air. There was no mention of going out fishing on either of our parts. We got dinner, and, after that, just sat and smoked in silence.

Presently, Tonnison asked for the Manuscript: I handed it to him, and he spent most of the afternoon in reading it through by himself.

It was while he was thus employed, that a thought came to me:—

"What do you say to having another look at—?" I nodded my head down stream.

Tonnison looked up. "Nothing!" he said, abruptly; and, somehow, I was less annoyed, than relieved, at his answer.

After that, I left him alone.

A little before teatime, he looked up at me, curiously.

"Sorry, old chap, if I was a bit short with you just now;" (just now, indeed! he had not spoken for the last three hours) "but I would not go there again," and he indicated with his head, "for anything that you could offer me. Ugh!" and he put down that history of a man's terror and hope and despair.

The next morning, we rose early, and went for our accustomed swim: we had partly shaken off the depression of the previous day; and so, took our rods when we had finished breakfast, and spent the day at our favorite sport.

After that day, we enjoyed our holiday to the utmost; though both of us looked forward to the time when our driver should come; for we were tremendously anxious to inquire of him, and through him among the people of the tiny hamlet, whether any of them could give us information about that strange garden, lying away by itself in the heart of an almost unknown tract of country.

At last, the day came, on which we expected the driver to come across for us. He arrived early, while we were still abed; and, the first thing we knew, he was at the opening of the tent, inquiring whether we had had good sport. We replied in the affirmative; and then, both together, almost in the same breath, we asked the question that was uppermost in our minds:—Did he know anything about an old garden, and a great pit, and a lake, situated some miles away, down the river; also, had he ever heard of a great house thereabouts?

No, he did not, and had not; yet, stay, he had heard a rumor, once upon a time, of a great, old house standing alone out in the wilderness; but, if he remembered rightly it was a place given over to the fairies; or, if that had not been so, he was certain that there had been something "quare" about it; and, anyway, he had heard nothing of it for a very long while—not since he was quite a gossoon. No, he could not remember anything particular about it; indeed, he did not know he remembered anything "at all, at all" until we questioned him.

"Look here," said Tonnison, finding that this was about all that he could tell us, "just take a walk 'round the village, while we dress, and find out something, if you can."

With a nondescript salute, the man departed on his errand; while we made haste to get into our clothes; after which, we began to prepare breakfast.

We were just sitting down to it, when he returned.

"It's all in bed the lazy divvils is, sor," he said, with a repetition of the salute, and an appreciative eye to the good things spread out on our provision chest, which we utilized as a table.

"Oh, well, sit down," replied my friend, "and have something to eat with us." Which the man did without delay.

After breakfast, Tonnison sent him off again on the same errand, while we sat and smoked. He was away some three-quarters of an hour, and, when he returned, it was evident that he had found out something. It appeared that he had got into conversation with an ancient man of the village, who, probably, knew more—though it was little enough—of the strange house, than any other person living.

The substance of this knowledge was, that, in the "ancient man's" youth—and goodness knows how long back that was—there had stood a great house in the center of the gardens, where now was left only that fragment of ruin. This house had been empty for a great while; years before his—the ancient man's—birth. It was a place shunned by the people of the village, as it had been shunned by their fathers before them. There were many things said about it, and all were of evil. No one ever went near it, either by day or night. In the village it was a synonym of all that is unholy and dreadful.

And then, one day, a man, a stranger, had ridden through the village, and turned off down the river, in the direction of the House, as it was always termed by the villagers. Some hours afterward, he had ridden back, taking the track by which he had come, toward Ardrahan. Then, for three months or so, nothing was heard. At the end of that time, he reappeared; but now, he was accompanied by an elderly woman, and a large number of donkeys, laden with various articles. They had passed through the village without stopping, and gone straight down the bank of the river, in the direction of the House.

Since that time, no one, save the man whom they had chartered to bring over monthly supplies of necessaries from Ardrahan, had ever seen either of them: and him, none had ever induced to talk; evidently, he had been well paid for his trouble.

The years had moved onward, uneventfully enough, in that little hamlet; the man making his monthly journeys, regularly.

One day, he had appeared as usual on his customary errand. He had passed through the village without exchanging more than a surly nod with the inhabitants and gone on toward the House. Usually, it was evening before he made the return journey. On this occasion, however, he had reappeared in the village, a few hours later, in an extraordinary state of excitement, and with the astounding information, that the House had disappeared bodily, and that a stupendous pit now yawned in the place where it had stood.

This news, it appears, so excited the curiosity of the villagers, that they overcame their fears, and marched en masse to the place. There, they found everything, just as described by the carrier.

This was all that we could learn. Of the author of the MS., who he was, and whence he came, we shall never know.

His identity is, as he seems to have desired, buried forever.

That same day, we left the lonely village of Kraighten. We have never been there since.

Sometimes, in my dreams, I see that enormous pit, surrounded, as it is, on all sides by wild trees and bushes. And the noise of the water rises upward, and blends—in my sleep—with other and lower noises; while, over all, hangs the eternal shroud of spray.

GRIEF[17]

Fierce hunger reigns within my breast, I had not dreamt that this whole world,
Crushed in the hand of God, could yield
Such bitter essence of unrest, Such pain as Sorrow now hath hurled
Out of its dreadful heart, unsealed!
Each sobbing breath is but a cry, My heart-strokes knells of agony,
And my whole brain has but one thought
That nevermore through life shall I (Save in the ache of memory)
Touch hands with thee, who now art naught!
Through the whole void of night I search, So dumbly crying out to thee;
But thou are not; and night's vast throne
Becomes an all stupendous church With star-bells knelling unto me
Who in all space am most alone!
An hungered, to the shore I creep, Perchance some comfort waits on me
From the old Sea's eternal heart;
But lo! from all the solemn deep, Far voices out of mystery
Seem questioning why we are apart!
"Where'er I go I am alone Who once, through thee, had all the world.
My breast is one whole raging pain
For that which was, and now is flown Into the Blank where life is hurled
Where all is not, nor is again!"

Footnotes

[1] An apparently unmeaning interpolation. I can find no previous reference in the MS. to this matter. It becomes clearer, however, in the light of succeeding incidents.—Ed.

[2] Here, the writing becomes undecipherable, owing to the damaged condition of this part of the MS. Below I print such fragments as are legible.—Ed.

[3] The severest scrutiny has not enabled me to decipher more of the damaged portion of the MS. It commences to be legible again with the chapter entitled "The Noise in the Night."—Ed.

[4] The Recluse uses this as an illustration, evidently in the sense of the popular conception of a comet.—Ed.

[5] Evidently referring to something set forth in the missing and mutilated pages. See Fragments, Chapter 14—Ed.

[6] No further mention is made of the moon. From what is said here, it is evident that our satellite had greatly increased its distance from the earth. Possibly, at a later age it may even have broken loose from our attraction. I cannot but regret that no light is shed on this point.—Ed.

[7] Conceivably, frozen air.—Ed.

[8] See previous footnote. This would explain the snow (?) within the room.—Ed.

[9] I am confounded that neither here, nor later on, does the Recluse make any further mention of the continued north and south movement (apparent, of course,) of the sun from solstice to solstice.—Ed.

[10] At this time the sound-carrying atmosphere must have been either incredibly attenuated, or—more probably—nonexistent. In the light of this, it cannot be supposed that these, or any other, noises would have been apparent to living ears—to hearing, as we, in the material body, understand that sense.—Ed.

[11] I can only suppose that the time of the earth's yearly journey had ceased to bear its present relative proportion to the period of the sun's rotation.—Ed.

[12] A careful reading of the MS. suggests that, either the sun is traveling on

an orbit of great eccentricity, or else that it was approaching the green star on a lessening orbit. And at this moment, I conceive it to be finally torn directly from its oblique course, by the gravitational pull of the immense star.—Ed.

[13] It will be noticed here that the earth was "slowly traversing the tremendous face of the dead sun." No explanation is given of this, and we must conclude, either that the speed of time had slowed, or else that the earth was actually progressing on its orbit at a rate, slow, when measured by existing standards. A careful study of the MS. however, leads me to conclude that the speed of time had been steadily decreasing for a very considerable period.—Ed.

[14] See first footnote, Chapter 18.

[15] Without doubt, the flame-edged mass of the Dead Central Sun, seen from another dimension.—Ed.

[16] From the unfinished word, it is possible, on the MS., to trace a faint line of ink, which suggests that the pen has trailed away over the paper; possibly, through fright and weakness.—Ed.

[17] These stanzas I found, in pencil, upon a piece of foolscap gummed in behind the fly-leaf of the MS. They have all the appearance of having been written at an earlier date than the Manuscript.--Ed.

FANTASTIC TALES

From the Tideless Sea

William Hope Hodgson

The Captain of the schooner leant over the rail, and stared for a moment, intently.

"Pass us them glasses, Jock," he said, reaching a hand behind him.

Jock left the wheel for an instant, and ran into the little companionway. He emerged immediately with a pair of marine-glasses, which he pushed into the waiting hand.

For a little, the Captain inspected the object through the binoculars. Then he lowered them, and polished the object glasses.

"Seems like er water-logged barr'l as sumone's been doin' fancy paintin' on," he remarked after a further stare. "Shove ther 'elm down er bit, Jock, an' we'll 'ave er closer look at it."

Jock obeyed, and soon the schooner bore almost straight for the object which held the Captain's attention. Presently, it was within some fifty feet, and the Captain sung out to the boy in the caboose to pass along the boathook.

Very slowly, the schooner drew nearer, for the wind was no more than breathing gently. At last the cask was within reach, and the Captain grappled at it with the boathook. It bobbed in the calm water, under his ministrations; and, for a moment, the thing seemed likely to elude him. Then he had the hook fast in a bit of rotten-looking rope which was attached to it. He did not attempt to lift it by the rope; but sung out to the boy to get a bowline round it. This was done, and the two of them hove it up on to the deck.

The Captain could see now, that the thing was a small water-breaker, the upper part of which was ornamented with the remains of a painted name.

"H—M—E—B—" spelt out the Captain with difficulty, and scratched his head. "'ave er look at this 'ere, Jock. See wot you makes of it."

Jock bent over from the wheel, expectorated, and then stared at the breaker. For nearly a minute he looked at it in silence.

"I'm thinkin' some of the letterin's washed awa'," he said at last, with considerable deliberation. "I have ma doots if he'll be able to read it."

"Hadn't ye no better knock in the end?" he suggested, after a further period of pondering. "I'm thinkin' ye'll be lang comin' at them contents otherwise."

"It's been in ther water er thunderin' long time," remarked the Captain, turning the bottom side upwards. "Look at them barnacles!"

Then, to the boy:—

"Pass erlong ther 'atchet outer ther locker."

Whilst the boy was away, the Captain stood the little barrel on end, and kicked away some of the barnacles from the underside. With them, came away a great shell of pitch. He bent, and inspected it.

"Blest if ther thing ain't been pitched!" he said. "This 'ere's been put afloat er purpose, an' they've been, mighty anxious as ther stuff in it shouldn't be 'armed."

He kicked away another mass of the barnacle-studded pitch. Then, with a sudden impulse, he picked up the whole thing and shook it violently. It gave out a light, dull, thudding sound, as though something soft and small were within. Then the boy came with the hatchet.

"Stan' clear!" said the Captain, and raised the implement. The next instant, he had driven in one end of the barrel. Eagerly, he stooped forward. He dived his hand down and brought out a little bundle stitched up in oilskin.

"I don' spect as it's anythin' of valley," he remarked. "But I guess as there's sumthin' 'ere as 'll be worth tellin' 'bout w'en we gets 'ome."

He slit up the oilskin as he spoke. Underneath, there was another covering of the same material, and under that a third. Then a longish bundle done up in tarred canvas. This was removed, and a black, cylindrical shaped case disclosed to view. It proved to be a tin canister, pitched over. Inside of it, neatly wrapped within a last strip of oilskin, was a roll of papers, which, on opening, the Captain found to be covered with writing. The Captain shook out the various wrappings; but found nothing further. He handed the MS. across to Jock.

"More 'n your line 'n mine, I guess," he remarked. "Jest you read it up, an' I'll listen."

He turned to the boy.

"Fetch thef dinner erlong 'ere. Me an' ther Mate 'll 'ave it comfortable up 'ere, an' you can take ther wheel.... Now then, Jock!"

And, presently, Jock began to read.

"The Losing of the Homebird"

"The 'Omebird!" exclaimed the Captain. "Why, she were lost w'en I wer' quite a young feller. Let me see—seventy-three. That were it. Tail end er seventy-three w'en she left 'ome, an' never 'eard of since; not as I knows. Go a'ead with ther yarn, Jock."

"It is Christmas eve. Two years ago to-day, we became lost to the world. Two years! It seems like twenty since I had my last Christmas in England. Now, I suppose, we are already forgotten—and this ship is but one more among the missing! My God! to think upon our loneliness gives me a choking feeling, a tightness across the chest!

"I am writing this in the saloon of the sailing ship, Homebird, and writing with but little hope of human eye ever seeing that which I write; for we are in the heart of the dread Sargasso Sea—the Tideless Sea of the North Atlantic.

From the stump of our mizzen mast, one may see, spread out to the far horizon, an interminable waste of weed—a treacherous, silent vastitude of slime and hideousness!

"On our port side, distant some seven or eight miles, there is a great, shapeless, discoloured mass. No one, seeing it for the first time, would suppose it to be the hull of a long lost vessel. It bears but little resemblance to a sea-going craft, because of a strange superstructure which has been built upon it. An examination of the vessel herself, through a telescope, tells one that she is unmistakably ancient. Probably a hundred, possibly two hundred, years. Think of it! Two hundred years in the midst of this desolation! It is an eternity.

"At first we wondered at that extraordinary superstructure. Later, we were to learn its use—and profit by the teaching of hands long withered. It is inordinately strange that we should have come upon this sight for the dead! Yet, thought suggests, that there may be many such, which have lain here through the centuries in this World of Desolation. I had not imagined that the earth contained so much loneliness, as is held within the circle, seen from the stump of our shattered mast. Then comes the thought that I might wander a hundred miles in any direction—and still be lost.

"And that craft yonder, that one break in the monotony, that monument of a few men's misery, serves only to make the solitude the more atrocious; for she is a very effigy of terror, telling of tragedies in the past, and to come!

"And now to get back to the beginnings of it. I joined the Homebird, as a passenger, in the early part of November. My health was not quite the thing, and I hoped the voyage would help to set me up. We had a lot of dirty weather for the first couple of weeks out, the wind dead ahead. Then we got a Southerly slant, that carried us down through the forties; but a good deal more to the Westward than we desired. Here we ran right into a tremendous cyclonic storm. All hands were called to shorten sail, and so urgent seemed our need, that the very officers went aloft to help make up the sails, leaving only the Captain (who had taken the wheel) and myself upon the poop. On the maindeck; the cook was busy letting go such ropes as the Mates desired.

"Abruptly, some distance ahead, through the vague sea-mist, but rather on the port bow, I saw loom up a great black wall of cloud.

"'Look, Captain!' I exclaimed; but it had vanished before I had finished speaking. A minute later it came again, and this time the Captain saw it.

"'O, my God!' he cried, and dropped his hands from the wheel. He leapt into the companionway, and seized a speaking trumpet. Then out on deck. He put it to his lips.

"Come down from aloft! Come down! Come down!' he shouted. And suddenly I lost his voice in a terrific mutter of sound from somewhere to port. It was the voice of the storm—shouting. My God! I had never heard anything like it! It ceased as suddenly as it had begun, and, in the succeeding quietness, I heard the whining of the kicking-tackles through the blocks. Then came a quick clang of brass upon the deck, and I turned quickly. The Captain had thrown down the trumpet, and sprung back to the wheel. I glanced aloft, and saw that many of the men were already in the rigging, and racing down like cats.

"I heard the Captain draw his breath with a quick gasp.

"Hold on for your lives!' he shouted, in a hoarse, unnatural voice.

"I looked at him. He was staring to windward with a fixed stare of painful intentness, and my gaze followed his. I saw, not four hundred yards distant, an enormous mass of foam and water coming down upon us. In the same instant, I caught the hiss of it, and immediately it was a shriek, so intense and awful, that I cringed impotently with sheer terror.

"The smother of water and foam took the ship a little fore-side of the beam, and the wind was with it. Immediately, the vessel rolled over on to her side, the sea-froth flying over her in tremendous cataracts.

"It seemed as though nothing could save us. Over, over we went, until I was swinging against the deck, almost as against the side of a house; for I had grasped the weather rail at the Captain's warning. As I swung there, I saw a strange thing. Before me was the port quarter boat. Abruptly, the canvas cover was flipped clean off it, as though by a vast, invisible hand.

"The next instant, a flurry of oars, boats' masts and odd gear flittered up into the air, like so many feathers, and blew to leeward and was lost in the roaring chaos of foam. The boat, herself, lifted in her chocks, and suddenly was blown clean down on to the maindeck, where she lay all in a ruin of white-painted timbers.

"A minute of the most intense suspense passed; then, suddenly, the ship righted, and I saw that the three masts had carried away. Yet, so hugely loud was the crying of the storm, that no sound of their breaking had reached me.

"I looked towards the wheel; but no one was there. Then I made out something crumpled up against the lee rail. I struggled across to it, and found that it was the Captain. He was insensible, and queerly limp in his right arm and leg. I looked round. Several of the men were crawling aft along the poop. I beckoned to them, and pointed to the wheel, and then to the Captain. A couple of them came towards me, and one went to the wheel. Then I made out through the spray the form of the Second Mate. He had several more of the men with him, and they had a coil of rope, which they took forrard. I learnt afterwards that they were hastening to get out a sea-anchor, so as to keep the ship's head towards the wind.

"We got the Captain below, and into his bunk. There, I left him in the hands of his daughter and the steward, and returned on deck.

"Presently, the Second Mate came back, and with him the remainder of the men. I found then that only seven had been saved in all. The rest had gone.

"The day passed terribly—the wind getting stronger hourly; though, at its worst, it was nothing like so tremendous as that first burst.

"The night came—a night of terror, with the thunder and hiss of the giant seas in the air above us, and the wind bellowing like some vast Elemental beast.

"Then, just before the dawn, the wind lulled, almost in a moment; the ship rolling and wallowing fearfully, and the water coming aboard—hundreds of tons at a time. Immediately afterwards it caught us again; but more on the beam, and bearing the vessel over on to her side, and this only by the pressure of the element upon the stark hull. As we came head to wind again, we righted, and rode, as we had for hours, amid a thousand fantastic hills of phosphorescent flame.

"Again the wind died—coming again after a longer pause, and then, all at once, leaving us. And so, for the space of a terrible half hour, the ship lived through the most awful, windless sea that can be imagined. There was no doubting but that we had driven right into the calm centre of the cyclone—calm only so far as lack of wind, and yet more dangerous a thousand times than the most furious hurricane that ever blew.

"For now we were beset by the stupendous Pyramidal Sea; a sea once witnessed, never forgotten; a sea in which the whole bosom of the ocean is projected towards heaven in monstrous hills of water; not leaping forward, as would be the case if there were wind; but hurling upwards in jets and peaks of living brine, and falling back in a continuous thunder of foam.

"Imagine this, if you can, and then have the clouds break away suddenly overhead, and the moon shine down upon that hellish turmoil, and you will have such a sight as has been given to mortals but seldom, save with death. And this is what we saw, and to my mind there is nothing within the knowledge of man to which I can liken it.

"Yet we lived through it, and through the wind that came later. But two more complete days and nights had passed, before the storm ceased to be a terror to us, and then, only because it had carried us into the seaweed laden waters of the vast Sargasso Sea.

"Here, the great billows first became foamless; and dwindled gradually in size as we drifted further among the floating masses of weed. Yet the wind was still furious, so that the ship drove on steadily, sometimes between banks, and other times over them.

"For a day and a night we drifted thus; and then astern I made out a great bank of weed, vastly greater than any which hitherto we had encountered. Upon this, the wind drove us stern foremost, so that we over-rode it. We had been forced some distance across it, when it occurred to me that our speed was slackening. I guessed presently that the sea-anchor, ahead, had caught in the weed, and was holding. Even as I surmised this, I heard from beyond the bows a faint, droning, twanging sound, blending with the roar of the wind. There came an indistinct report, and the ship lurched backwards through the weed. The hawser, connecting us with the sea-anchor, had parted.

"I saw the Second Mate run forrard with several men. They hauled in upon the hawser, until the broken end was aboard. In the meantime, the ship, having nothing ahead to keep her "bows on," began to slew broadside towards the wind. I saw the men attach a chain to the end of the broken hawser; then they paid it out again, and the ship's head came back to the gale.

"When the Second Mate came aft, I asked him why this had been done, and he explained that so long as the vessel was end-on, she would travel over the weed. I inquired why he wished her to go over the weed, and he told me that one of the men had made out what appeared to be clear water astern, and that—could we gain it—we might win free.

"Through the whole of that day, we moved rearwards across the great bank; yet, so far from the weed appearing to show signs of thinning, it grew steadily thicker, and, as it became denser, so did our speed slacken, until the ship was barely moving. And so the night found us.

"The following morning discovered to us that we were within a quarter of a mile of a great expanse of clear water—apparently the open sea; but unfortunately the wind had dropped to a moderate breeze, and the vessel was motionless, deep sunk in the weed; great tufts of which rose up on all sides, to within a few feet of the level of our maindeck.

"A man was sent up the stump of the mizzen, to take a look round. From there, he reported that he could see something, that might be weed, across the water; but it was too far distant for him to be in any way certain. Immediately afterwards, he called out that there was something, away on our port beam; but what it was, he could not say, and it was not until a telescope was brought to bear, that we made it out to be the hull of the ancient vessel I have previously mentioned.

"And now, the Second Mate began to cast about for some means by which he could bring the ship to the clear water astern. The first thing which he did, was to bend a sail to a spare yard, and hoist it to the top of the mizzen stump. By this means, he was able to dispense with the cable towing over the bows, which, of course, helped to prevent the ship from moving. In addition, the sail would prove helpful to force the vessel across the weed. Then he routed out a couple of kedges. These, he bent on to the ends of a short piece of cable, and, to the bight of this, the end of a long coil of strong rope.

"After that, he had the starboard quarter boat lowered into the weed, and in it he placed the two kedge anchors. The end of another length of rope, he made fast to the boat's painter. This done, he took four of the men with him, telling them to bring chain-hooks, in addition to the oars—his intention being to force the boat through the weed, until he reached the clear water. There, in the marge of the weed, he would plant the two anchors in the thickest clumps of the growth; after which we were to haul the boat back to the ship, by means of the rope attached to the painter.

"'Then,' as he put it, 'we'll take the kedge-rope to the capstan, and heave her out of this blessed cabbage heap!'

"The weed proved a greater obstacle to the progress of the boat, than, I think, he had anticipated. After half an hour's work, they had gone scarcely more than some two hundred feet from the vessel; yet, so thick was the stuff, that no sign could we see of them, save the movement they made among the weed, as they forced the boat along.

"Another quarter of an hour passed away, during which the three men left upon the poop, paid out the ropes as the boat forged slowly ahead. All at once, I heard my name called. Turning, I saw the Captain's daughter in the companionway, beckoning to me. I walked across to her.

"'My father has sent me up to know, Mr. Philips, how they are getting on?'

"'Very slowly, Miss Knowles,' I replied. 'Very slowly indeed. The weed is so extraordinarily thick.'

"She nodded intelligently, and turned to descend; but I detained her a moment.

"'Your father, how is he?' I asked.

"She drew her breath swiftly.

"'Quite himself,' she said; 'but so dreadfully weak. He—'

"An outcry from one of the men, broke across her speech:—

"'Lord 'elp us, mates! wot were that!'

"I turned sharply. The three of them were staring over the taffrail. I ran towards them, and Miss Knowles followed.

"'Hush!' she said, abruptly. 'Listen!'

"I stared astern to where I knew the boat to be. The weed all about it was quaking queerly—the movement extending far beyond the radius of their hooks and oars. Suddenly, I heard the Second Mate's voice:

"'Look out, lads! My God, look out!'

"And close upon this, blending almost with it, came the hoarse scream of a man in sudden agony.

"I saw an oar come up into view, and descend violently, as though someone struck at something with it. Then the Second Mate's voice, shouting:—

"'Aboard there! Aboard there! Haul in on the rope! Haul in on the rope—!' It broke off into a sharp cry.

"As we seized hold of the rope, I saw the weed hurled in all directions, and a great crying and choking swept to us over the brown hideousness around.

"'Pull!' I yelled, and we pulled. The rope tautened; but the boat never moved.

"'Tek it ter ther capsting!' gasped one of the men.

"Even as he spoke, the rope slackened. 'It's coming!' cried Miss Knowles. 'Pull! Oh! Pull!'

"She had hold of the rope along with us, and together we hauled, the boat yielding to our strength with surprising ease.

"'There it is!' I shouted, and then I let go of the rope. There was no one in the boat.

"'For the half of a minute, we stared, dumfoundered. Then my gaze wandered astern to the place from which we had plucked it. There was a heaving movement among the great weed masses. I saw something waver up aimlessly against the sky; it was sinuous, and it flickered once or twice from side to side; then sank back among the growth, before I could concentrate my attention upon it.

"I was recalled to myself by a sound of dry sobbing. Miss Knowles was kneeling upon the deck, her hands clasped round one of the iron uprights of the rail. She seemed momentarily all to pieces.

"'Come! Miss Knowles,' I said, gently. 'You must be brave. We cannot let your father know of this in his present state.'

"She allowed me to help her to her feet. I could feel that she was trembling badly. Then, even as I sought for words with which to reassure her, there came a dull thud from the direction of the companionway. We looked round. On the deck, face downward, lying half in and half out of the scuttle, was the Captain. Evidently, he had witnessed everything. Miss Knowles gave out a wild cry, and ran to her father. I beckoned to one of the men to help me, and, together, we carried him back to his bunk. An hour later, he recovered from his swoon. He was quite calm, though very weak, and evidently in considerable pain.

"Through his daughter, he made known to me that he wished me to take the reins of authority in his place. This, after a slight demur, I decided to do; for, as I reassured myself, there were no duties required of me, needing any special knowledge of shipcraft. The vessel was fast; so far as I could see, irrevocably fast. It would be time to talk of freeing her, when the Captain was well enough to take charge once more.

"I returned on deck, and made known to the men the Captain's wishes. Then I chose one to act as a sort of bo'sun over the other two, and to him I gave orders that everything should be put to rights before the night came. I had sufficient sense to leave him to manage matters in his own way; for, whereas my knowledge of what was needful, was fragmentary, his was complete.

"By this time, it was near to sunsetting, and it was with melancholy feelings that I watched the great hull of the sun plunge lower. For awhile, I paced the poop, stopping ever and anon to stare over the dreary waste by which we were surrounded. The more I looked about, the more a sense of lonesomeness and depression and fear assailed me. I had pondered much upon the dread happening of the day, and all my ponderings led to a vital questioning:— What was there among all that quiet weed, which had come upon the crew of the boat, and destroyed them? And I could not make answer, and the weed was silent—dreadly silent!

"The sun had drawn very near to the dim horizon, and I watched it, moodily, as it splashed great clots of red fire across the water that lay stretched into the distance across our stern. Abruptly, as I gazed, its perfect lower edge was marred by an irregular shape. For a moment, I stared, puzzled. Then I fetched a pair of glasses from the holdfast in the companion. A glance through these, and I knew the extent of our fate. That line, blotching the round of the sun, was the conformation of another enormous weed bank.

"I remembered that the man had reported something as showing across the water, when he was sent up to the top of the mizzen stump in the morning; but, what it was, he had been unable to say. The thought flashed into my mind that it had been only just visible from aloft in the morning, and now it was in sight from the deck. It occurred to me that the wind might be compacting the weed, and driving the bank which surrounded the ship, down upon a larger portion. Possibly, the clear stretch of water had been but a temporary rift within the heart of the Sargasso Sea. It seemed only too probable.

"Thus it was that I meditated, and so, presently, the night found me. For some hours further, I paced the deck in the darkness, striving to understand the incomprehensible; yet with no better result than to weary myself to death. Then, somewhere about midnight, I went below to sleep.

"The following morning, on going on deck, I found that the stretch of clear water had disappeared entirely, during the night, and now, so far as the eye could reach, there was nothing but a stupendous desolation of weed.

"The wind had dropped completely, and no sound came from all that weed-ridden immensity. We had, in truth, reached the Cemetery of the Ocean!

"The day passed uneventfully enough. It was only when I served out some food to the men, and one of them asked whether they could have a few raisins, that I remembered, with a pang of sudden misery, that it was Christmas day. I gave them the fruit, as they desired, and they spent the morning in the galley, cooking their dinner. Their stolid indifference to the late terrible happenings, appalled me somewhat, until I remembered what their lives were, and had been. Poor fellows! One of them ventured aft at dinner time, and offered me a slice of what he called 'plum duff.' He brought it on a plate which he had found in the galley and scoured thoroughly with sand and water. He tendered it shyly enough, and I took it, so graciously as I could, for I would not hurt his feelings; though the very smell of the stuff was an abomination.

"During the afternoon, I brought out the Captain's telescope, and made a thorough examination of the ancient hulk on our port beam. Particularly did I study the extraordinary superstructure around her sides; but could not, as I have said before, conceive of its use.

"The evening, I spent upon the poop, my eyes searching wearily across that vile quietness, and so, in a little, the night came—Christmas night, sacred to a thousand happy memories. I found myself dreaming of the night a year previous, and, for a little while, I forgot what was before me. I was recalled suddenly—terribly. A voice rose out of the dark which hid the maindeck. For the fraction of an instant, it expressed surprise; then pain and terror leapt into it. Abruptly, it seemed to come from above, and then from somewhere beyond the ship, and so in a moment there was silence, save for a rush of feet and the bang of a door forrard.

"I leapt down the poop ladder, and ran along the maindeck, towards the fo'cas'le. As I ran, something knocked off my cap. I scarcely noticed it then. I reached the fo'cas'le, and caught at the latch of the port door. I lifted it and pushed; but the door was fastened.

"'Inside there!' I cried, and banged upon the panels with my clenched fist.

"A man's voice came, incoherently.

"'Open the door!' I shouted. 'Open the door!'

"'Yes, Sir—I'm com—ming, Sir,' said one of them, jerkily.

"I heard footsteps stumble across the planking. Then a hand fumbled at the fastening, and the door flew open under my weight.

"The man who had opened to me, started back. He held a flaring slush-lamp above his head, and, as I entered, he thrust it forward. His hand was trembling visibly, and, behind him, I made out the face of one of his mates, the brow and dirty, clean-shaven upper lip drenched with sweat. The man who held the lamp, opened his mouth, and gabbered at me; but, for a moment, no sound came.

"'Wot—wot were it? Wot we-ere it?' he brought out at last, with a gasp.

"The man behind, came to his side, and gesticulated.

"'What was what?' I asked sharply, and looking from one to the other. 'Where's the other man? What was that screaming?'

"The second man drew the palm of his hand across his brow; then flirted his fingers deckwards.

"'We don't know, Sir! We don't know! It were Jessop! Somethin's took 'im just as we was comin' forrid! We—we—He-he-HARK!'

"His head came forward with a jerk as he spoke, and then, for a space, no one stirred. A minute passed, and I was about to speak, when, suddenly, from somewhere out upon the deserted maindeck, there came a queer, subdued noise, as though something moved stealthily hither and thither. The man with the lamp caught me by the sleeve, and then, with an abrupt movement, slammed the door and fastened it.

"'That's IT, Sir!' he exclaimed, with a note of terror and conviction in his voice.

"I bade him be silent, while I listened; but no sound came to us through the door, and so I turned to the men and told them to let me have all they knew.

"It was little enough. They had been sitting in the galley, yarning, until, feeling tired, they had decided to go forrard and turn-in. They extinguished the light, and came out upon the deck, closing the door behind them. Then, just as they turned to go forrard, Jessop gave out a yell. The next instant they heard him screaming in the air above their heads, and, realising that some terrible thing was upon them, they took forthwith to their heels, and ran for the security of the fo'cas'le.

"Then I had come.

"As the men made an end of telling me, I thought I heard something outside, and held up my hand for silence. I caught the sound again. Someone was calling my name. It was Miss Knowles. Likely enough she was calling me to supper—and she had no knowledge of the dread thing which had happened. I sprang to the door. She might be coming along the maindeck in search of me. And there was Something out there, of which I had no conception—something unseen, but deadly tangible!

"'Stop, Sir!' shouted the men, together; but I had the door open.

"'Mr. Philips!' came the girl's voice at no great distance. 'Mr. Philips!'

"'Coming, Miss Knowles!' I shouted, and snatched the lamp from the man's hand.

"'The next instant, I was running aft, holding the lamp high, and glancing fearfully from side to side. I reached the place where the mainmast had been, and spied the girl coming towards me.

"'Go back!' I shouted. 'Go back!'

"She turned at my shout, and ran for the poop ladder. I came up with her, and followed close at her heels. On the poop, she turned and faced me.

"'What is it, Mr. Philips?'

"I hesitated. Then:—

"'I don't know!' I said.

"'My father heard something,' she began. 'He sent me. He—'

"I put up my hand. It seemed to me that I had caught again the sound of something stirring on the maindeck.

"'Quick!' I said sharply. 'Down into the cabin!.' And she, being a sensible girl, turned and ran down without waste of time. I followed, closing and fastening the companion-doors behind me.

"In the saloon, we had a whispered talk, and I told her everything. She bore up bravely, and said nothing; though her eyes were very wide, and her face pale. Then the Captain's voice came to us from the adjoining cabin.

"'Is Mr. Philips there, Mary?'

"'Yes, father.'

"'Bring him in.'

"I went in.

"'What was it, Mr. Philips?' he asked, collectedly.

"I hesitated; for I was willing to spare him the ill news; but he looked at me with calm eyes for a moment, and I knew that it was useless attempting to deceive him.

"'Something has happened, Mr. Philips,' he said, quietly. 'You need not be afraid to tell me.'

"At that, I told him so much as I knew, he listening, and nodding his comprehension of the story.

"'It must be something big,' he remarked, when I had made an end. 'And yet you saw nothing when you came aft?'

"'No,' I replied.

"'It is something in the weed,' he went on. 'You will have to keep off the deck at night.'

"After a little further talk, in which he displayed a calmness that amazed me, I left him, and went presently to my berth.

"The following day, I took the two men, and, together, we made a thorough search through the ship; but found nothing. It was evident to me that the Captain was right. There was some dread Thing hidden within the weed. I went to the side and looked down. The two men followed me. Suddenly, one of them pointed.

"'Look, Sir!' he exclaimed. 'Right below you, Sir! Two eyes like blessed great saucers! Look!'

"I stared; but could see nothing. The man left my side, and ran into the galley. In a moment, he was back with a great lump of coal.

"'Just there, Sir,' he said, and hove it down into the weed immediately beneath where we stood.

"Too late, I saw the thing at which he aimed—two immense eyes, some little distance below the surface of the weed. I knew instantly to what they belonged; for I had seen large specimens of the octopus some years previously, during a cruise in Australasian waters.

"'Look out, man!' I shouted, and caught him by the arm. 'It's an octopus! Jump back!' I sprang down on to the deck. In the same instant, huge masses of weed were hurled in all directions, and half a dozen immense tentacles whirled up into the air. One lapped itself about his neck. I caught his leg; but he was torn from my grasp, and I tumbled backwards on to the deck. I heard a scream from the other man as I scrambled to my feet. I looked to where he had been; but of him there was no sign. Regardless of the danger, in my great agitation, I leapt upon the rail, and gazed down with frightened eyes. Yet, neither of him nor his mate, nor the monster, could I perceive a vestige.

"How long I stood there staring down bewilderedly, I cannot say; certainly some minutes. I was so bemazed that I seemed incapable of movement. Then, all at once, I became aware that a light quiver ran across the weed, and the next instant, something stole up out of the depths with a deadly celerity.

"Well it was for me that I had seen it in time, else should I have shared the fate of those two—and the others. As it was, I saved myself only by leaping backwards on to the deck. For a moment, I saw the feeler wave above the rail with a certain apparent aimlessness; then it sank out of sight, and I was alone.

"An hour passed before I could summon a sufficiency of courage to break the news of this last tragedy to the Captain and his daughter, and when I had made an end, I returned to the solitude of the poop; there to brood upon the hopelessness of our position.

"As I paced up and down, I caught myself glancing continuously at the nearer weed tufts. The happenings of the past two days had shattered my nerves, and I feared every moment to see some slender death-grapple searching over the rail for me. Yet, the poop, being very much higher out of the weed than the maindeck, was comparatively safe; though only comparatively.

"Presently, as I meandered up and down, my gaze fell upon the hulk of the ancient ship, and, in a flash, the reason for that great superstructure was borne upon me. It was intended as a protection against the dread creatures which inhabited the weed. The thought came to me that I would attempt some similar means of protection; for the feeling that, at any moment, I might be caught and lifted out into that slimy wilderness, was not to be borne. In addition, the work would serve to occupy my mind, and help me to bear up against the intolerable sense of loneliness which assailed me.

"I resolved that I would lose no time, and so, after some thought as to the manner in which I should proceed, I routed out some coils of rope and several sails. Then I went down on to the maindeck and brought up an armful of capstan bars. These I lashed vertically to the rail all round the poop. Then I knotted the rope to each, stretching it tightly between them, and over this framework stretched the sails, sewing the stout canvas to the rope, by means of twine and some great needles which I found in the Mate's room.

"It is not to be supposed that this piece of work was accomplished immediately. Indeed, it was only after three days of hard labour that I got the poop completed. Then I commenced work upon the maindeck. This was a tremendous undertaking, and a whole fortnight passed before I had the entire length of it enclosed; for I had to be continually on the watch against the hidden enemy. Once, I was very nearly surprised, and saved myself only by a quick leap. Thereafter, for the rest of that day, I did no more work; being too greatly shaken in spirit. Yet, on the following morning, I recommenced, and from thence, until the end, I was not molested.

"Once the work was roughly completed, I felt at ease to begin and perfect it. This I did, by tarring the whole of the sails with Stockholm tar; thereby making them stiff, and capable of resisting the weather. After that, I added many fresh uprights, and much strengthening ropework, and finally doubled the sailcloth with additional sails, liberally smeared with the tar.

"In this manner, the whole of January passed away, and a part of February. Then, it would be on the last day of the month, the Captain sent for me, and told me, without any preliminary talk, that he was dying. I looked at him; but said nothing; for I had known long that it was so. In return, he stared back with a strange intentness, as though he would read my inmost thoughts, and this for the space of perhaps two minutes.

"'Mr. Philips,' he said at last, 'I may be dead by this time to-morrow. Has it ever occurred to you that my daughter will be alone with you ?'

"'Yes, Captain Knowles,' I replied, quietly, and waited.

"For a few seconds, he remained silent; though, from the changing expressions of his face, I knew that he was pondering how best to bring forward the thing which it was in his mind to say.

"'You are a gentleman—' he began, at last.

"'I will marry her,' I said, ending the sentence for him.

"A slight flush of surprise crept into his face.

"'You—you have thought seriously about it?'

"'I have thought very seriously,' I explained.

"'Ah!' he said, as one who comprehends. And then, for a little, he lay there quietly. It was plain to me that memories of past days were with him. Presently, he came out of his dreams, and spoke, evidently referring to my marriage with his daughter.

"'It is the only thing,' he said, in a level voice.

"I bowed, and after that, he was silent again for a space. In a little, however, he turned once more to me:—

"'Do you—do you love her?'

"His tone was keenly wistful, and a sense of trouble lurked in his eyes.

"'She will be my wife,' I said, simply; and he nodded.

"'God has dealt strangely with us,' he murmured presently, as though to himself.

"Abruptly, he bade me tell her to come in.

"And then he married us.

"Three days later, he was dead, and we were alone.

"For a while, my wife was a sad woman; but gradually time eased her of the bitterness of her grief.

"Then, some eight months after our marriage, a new interest stole into her life. She whispered it to me, and we, who had borne our loneliness uncomplainingly, had now this new thing to which to look forward. It became a bond between us, and bore promise of some companionship as we grew old. Old! At the idea of age, a sudden flash of thought darted like lightning across the sky of my mind:—FOOD! Hitherto, I had thought of myself, almost as of one already dead, and had cared naught for anything beyond the immediate troubles which each day forced upon me. The loneliness of the vast Weed World had become an assurance of doom to me, which had clouded and dulled my faculties, so that I had grown apathetic. Yet, immediately, as it seemed, at the shy whispering of my wife, was all this changed.

"That very hour, I began a systematic search through the ship. Among the cargo, which was of a 'general' nature, I discovered large quantities of preserved and tinned provisions, all of which I put carefully on one side. I continued my examination until I had ransacked the whole vessel. The business took me near upon six months to complete, and when it was finished, I seized paper, and made calculations, which led me to the conclusion that we had sufficient food in the ship to preserve life in three people for some fifteen to seventeen years. I could not come nearer to it than this; for I had no means of computing the quantity the child would need year by year. Yet it is sufficient to show me that seventeen years must be the limit. Seventeen years! And then—

"Concerning water, I am not troubled; for I have rigged a great sailcloth tun-dish, with a canvas pipe into the tanks; and from every rain, I draw a supply, which has never run short.

"The child was born nearly five months ago. She is a fine little girl, and her mother seems perfectly happy. I believe I could be quietly happy with them, were it not that I have ever in mind the end of those seventeen years. True! we may be dead long before then; but, if not, our little girl will be in her teens—and it is a hungry age.

"If one of us died—but no! Much may happen in seventeen years. I will wait.

"My method of sending this clear of the weed is likely to succeed. I have constructed a small fire-balloon, and this missive, safely enclosed in a little barrel, will be attached. The wind will carry it swiftly hence.

"Should this ever reach civilised beings, will they see that it is forwarded to:—"

(Here followed an address, which, for some reason, had been roughly obliterated. Then came the signature of the writer)

"Arthur Samuel Philips."

The captain of the schooner looked over at Jock, as the man made an end of his reading.

"Seventeen years pervisions," he muttered thoughtfully. "An' this 'ere were written sumthin' like twenty-nine years ago!" He nodded his head several times. "Poor creatures!" he exclaimed. "It'd be er long while, Jock—a long while!"

Further News of the 'Homebird'

(From the Tideless Sea, Part 2)

In the August of 1902, Captain Bateman, of the schooner Agnes, picked up a small barrel, upon which was painted a half obliterated word; which, finally, he succeeded in deciphering as "Homebird," the name of a full-rigged ship, which left London in the November of 1873, and from thenceforth was heard of no more by any man.

Captain Bateman opened the barrel, and discovered a packet of Manuscript, wrapped in oilskin. This, on examination, proved to be an account of the losing of the Homebird amid the desolate wastes of the Sargasso Sea. The papers were written by one, Arthur Samuel Philips, a passenger in the ship; and, from them, Captain Bateman was enabled to gather that the ship, mastless, lay in the very heart of the dreaded Sargasso; and that all of the crew had been lost—some in the storm which drove them thither, and some in attempts to free the ship from the weed, which locked them in on all sides.

Only Mr. Philips and the Captain's daughter had been left alive, and they two, the dying Captain had married. To them had been born a daughter, and the papers ended with a brief but touching allusion to their fear that, eventually, they must run short of food.

There is need to say but little more. The account was copied into most of the papers of the day, and caused widespread comment. There was even some talk of fitting out a rescue expedition; but this fell through, owing chiefly to lack of knowledge of the whereabouts of the ship in all the vastness of the immense Sargasso Sea. And so, gradually, the matter has slipped into the background of the Public's memory.

Now, however, interest will be once more excited in the lonesome fate of this lost trio; for a second barrel, identical, it would seem, with that found by Captain Bateman, has been picked up by a Mr. Bolton, of Baltimore, master of a small brig, engaged in the South American coast-trade. In this barrel was enclosed a further message from Mr. Philips—the fifth that he has sent abroad to the world; but the second, third and fourth, up to this time, have not been discovered.

This "fifth message" contains a vital and striking account of their lives during the year 1879, and stands unique as a document informed with human lonesomeness and longing. I have seen it, and read it through, with the most intense and painful interest. The writing, though faint, is very legible; and the whole manuscript bears the impress of the same hand and mind that wrote the piteous account of the losing of the Homebird, of which I have already made mention, and with which, no doubt, many are well acquainted.

In closing this little explanatory note, I am stimulated to wonder whether, somewhere, at some time, those three missing messages ever shall be found. And then there may be others. What stories of human, strenuous fighting with Fate may they not contain.

We can but wait and wonder. Nothing more may we ever learn; for what is this one little tragedy among the uncounted millions that the silence of the sea holds so remorselessly. And yet, again, news may come to us out of the Unknown—out of the lonesome silences of the dread Sargasso Sea—the loneliest and the most inaccessible place of all the lonesome and inaccessible places of this earth.

And so I say, let us wait.

W. H. H.

The Fifth Message

"This is the fifth message that I have sent abroad over the loathsome surface of this vast Weed-World, praying that it may come to the open sea, ere the lifting power of my fire-balloon be gone, and yet, if it come there—the which I could now doubt—how shall I be the better for it! Yet write I must, or go mad, and so I choose to write, though feeling as I write that no living creature, save it be the giant octopi that live in the weed about me, will ever see the thing I write.

"My first message I sent out on Christmas Eve, 1875, and since then, each eve of the birth of Christ has seen a message go skywards upon the winds, towards the open sea. It is as though this approaching time, of festivity and the meeting of parted loved ones, overwhelms me, and drives away the half apathetic peace that has been mine through spaces of these years of lonesomeness; so that I seclude myself from my wife and the little one, and with ink, pen, and paper, try to ease my heart of the pent emotions that seem at times to threaten to burst it.

"It is now six completed years since the Weed-World claimed us from the World of the Living—six years away from our brothers and sisters of the human and living world—It has been six years of living in a grave! And there are all the years ahead! Oh! My God! My God! I dare not think upon them! I must control myself—

"And then there is the little one, she is nearly four and a half now, and growing wonderfully, out among these wilds. Four and a half years, and the little woman has never seen a human face besides ours—think of it! And yet, if she lives four and forty years, she will never see another.... Four and forty years! It is foolishness to trouble about such a space of time; for the future, for us, ends in ten years—eleven at the utmost. Our food will last no longer than that.... My wife does not know; for it seems to me a wicked thing to add unnecessarily to her punishment. She does but know that we must waste no ounce of food-stuff, and for the rest she imagines that the most of the cargo is of an edible nature. Perhaps, I have nurtured this belief. If anything happened to me, the food would last a few extra years; but my wife would have to imagine it an accident, else would each bite she took sicken her.

"I have thought often and long upon this matter, yet I fear to leave them; for who knows but that their very lives might at any time depend upon my strength, more pitifully, perhaps, than upon the food which they must come at last to lack. No, I must not bring upon them, and myself, a near and certain calamity, to defer one that, though it seems to have but little less certainty, is yet at a further distance.

"Until lately, nothing has happened to us in the past four years, if I except the adventures that attended my mad attempt to cut a way through the surrounding weed to freedom, and from which it pleased God that I and those with me should be preserved. Yet, in the latter part of this year, an adventure, much touched with grimness, came to us most unexpectedly, in a fashion quite unthought of—an adventure that has brought into our lives a fresh and more active peril; for now I have learned that the weed holds other terrors besides that of the giant octopi.

"Indeed, I have grown to believe this world of desolation capable of holding any horror, as well it might. Think of it—an interminable stretch of dank, brown loneliness in all directions, to the distant horizon; a place where monsters of the deep and the weed have undisputed reign; where never an enemy may fall upon them; but from which they may strike with sudden deadliness! No human can ever bring an engine of destruction to bear upon them, and the humans whose fate it is to have sight of them, do so only from the decks of lonesome derelicts, whence they stare lonely with fear, and without ability to harm.

"I cannot describe it, nor can any hope ever to imagine it! When the wind falls, a vast silence holds us girt, from horizon to horizon, yet it is a silence through which one seems to feel the pulse of hidden things all about us, watching and waiting—waiting and watching; waiting but for the chance to reach forth a huge and sudden death-grapple.... It is no use! I cannot bring it home to any; nor shall I be better able to convey the frightening sound of the wind, sweeping across these vast, quaking plains—the shrill whispering of the weed-fronds, under the stirring of the winds. To hear it from beyond our canvas screen, is like listening to the uncounted dead of the mighty Sargasso wailing their own requiems. Or again, my fancy, diseased with much loneliness and brooding, likens it to the advancing rustle of armies of the great monsters that are always about us—waiting.

"And so to the coming of this new terror:—

"It was in the latter end of October that we first had knowledge of it—a tapping in the night time against the side of the vessel, below the water-line; a noise that came distinct, yet with a ghostly strangeness in the quietness of the night. It was on a Monday night when first I heard it. I was down in the lazarette, overhauling our stores, and suddenly I heard it—tap—tap—tap—against the outside of the vessel upon the starboard side, and below the water line. I stood for awhile listening; but could not discover what it was that should come a-tapping against our side, away out here in this lonesome world of weed and slime. And then, as I stood there listening, the tapping ceased, and so I waited, wondering, and with a hateful sense of fear, weakening my manhood, and taking the courage out of my heart....

"Abruptly, it recommenced; but now upon the opposite side of the vessel, and as it continued, I fell into a little sweat; for it seemed to me that some foul thing out in the night was tapping for admittance. Tap—tap—tap—it went, and continued, and there I stood listening, and so gripped about with frightened thoughts, that I seemed without power to stir myself; for the spell of the Weed-World, and the fear bred of its hidden terrors and the weight and dreeness of its loneliness have entered into my marrow, so that I could, then and now, believe in the likelihood of matters which, ashore and in the midst of my fellows, I might laugh at in contempt. It is the dire lonesomeness of this strange world into which I have entered, that serves so to take the heart out of a man.

"And so, as I have said, I stood there listening, and full of frightened, but undefined, thoughts; and all the while the tapping continued, sometimes with a regular insistence, and anon with a quick spasmodic tap, tap, tap-a-tap, as though some Thing, having Intelligence, signalled to me.

"Presently, however, I shook off something of the foolish fright that had taken me, and moved over to the place from which the tapping seemed to sound. Coming near to it, I bent my head down, close to the side of the vessel, and listened. Thus, I heard the noises with greater plainness, and could distinguish easily, now, that something knocked with a hard object upon the outside of the ship, as though someone had been striking her iron side with a small hammer.

"Then, even as I listened, came a thunderous blow close to my ear, so loud and astonishing, that I leaped sideways in sheer fright. Directly afterwards there came a second heavy blow, and then a third, as though someone had struck the ship's side with a heavy sledge-hammer, and after that, a space of silence, in which I heard my wife's voice at the trap of the lazarette, calling down to me to know what had happened to cause so great a noise.

"'Hush, My Dear!' I whispered; for it seemed to me that the thing outside might hear her; though this could not have been possible, and I do but mention it as showing how the noises had set me off my natural balance.

"At my whispered command, my wife turned her about and came down the ladder into the semi-darkness of the place.

"'What is it, Arthur?' she asked, coming across to me, and slipping her hand between my arm and side.

"As though in reply to her query, there came against the outside of the ship, a fourth tremendous blow, filling the whole of the lazarette with a dull thunder.

"My wife gave out a frightened cry, and sprang away from me; but the next instant, she was back, and gripping hard at my arm.

"'What is it, Arthur? What is it?' she asked me; her voice, though no more than a frightened whisper, easily heard in the succeeding silence.

"'I don't know, Mary,' I replied, trying to speak in a level tone. 'It's—'

"'There's something again,' she interrupted, as the minor tapping noises recommenced.

"For about a minute, we stood silent, listening to those eerie taps. Then my wife turned to me:—

"'Is it anything dangerous, Arthur—tell me? I promise you I shall be brave.'

"'I can't possibly say, Mary,' I answered. 'I can't say; but I'm going up on deck to listen.... Perhaps,' I paused a moment to think; but a fifth tremendous blow against the ship's side, drove whatever I was going to say, clean from me, and I could do no more than stand there, frightened and bewildered, listening for further sounds. After a short pause, there came a sixth blow. Then my wife caught me by the arm, and commenced to drag me towards the ladder.

"'Come up out of this dark place, Arthur,' she said. 'I shall be ill if we stay here any longer. Perhaps the—the thing outside can hear us, and it may stop if we go upstairs.'

"By this, my wife was all of a shake, and I but little better, so that I was glad to follow her up the ladder. At the top, we paused for a while to listen, bending down over the open hatchway. A space of, maybe, some five minutes passed away in silence; then there commenced again the tapping noises, the sounds coming clearly up to us where we crouched. Presently, they ceased once more, and after that, though we listened for a further space of some ten minutes, they were not repeated. Neither were there any more of the great bangs.

"In a little, I led my wife away from the hatch, to a seat in the saloon; for the hatch is situated under the saloon table. After that, I returned to the opening, and replaced the cover. Then I went into our cabin—the one which had been the Captain's, her father,—and brought from there a revolver, of which we have several. This, I loaded with care, and afterwards placed in my side pocket.

"Having done this, I fetched from the pantry, where I have made it my use to keep such things at hand, a bull's-eye lantern, the same having been used on dark nights when clearing up the ropes from the decks. This, I lit, and afterwards turned the dark-slide to cover the light. Next, I slipped off my boots; and then, as an afterthought, I reached down one of the long-handled American axes from the rack about the mizzenmast—these being keen and very formidable weapons.

"After that, I had to calm my wife and assure her that I would run no unnecessary risks, if, indeed, there were any risks to run; though, as may be imagined, I could not say what new peril might not be upon us. And then, picking up the lantern, I made my way silently on stockinged feet, up the companionway. I had reached the top, and was just stepping out on to the deck, when something caught my arm. I turned swiftly, and perceived that my wife had followed me up the steps, and from the shaking of her hand upon my arm, I gathered that she was very much agitated.

"'Oh, My Dear, My Dear, don't go! don't go!' she whispered, eagerly. 'Wait until it is daylight. Stay below to-night. You don't know what may be about in this horrible place.'

"I put the lantern and the axe upon the deck beside the companion; then bent towards the opening, and took her into my arms, soothing her, and stroking her hair; yet with ever an alert glance to and fro along the indistinct decks. Presently, she was more like her usual self, and listened to my reasoning, that she would do better to stay below, and so, in a little, left me, having made me promise afresh that I would be very wary of danger.

"When she had gone, I picked up the lantern and the axe, and made my way cautiously to the side of the vessel. Here, I paused and listened very carefully, being just above that spot upon the port side where I had heard the greater part of the tapping, and all of the heavy bangs; yet, though I listened, as I have said, with much attention, there was no repetition of the sounds.

"Presently, I rose and made my way forrard to the break of the poop. Here, bending over the rail which ran across, I listened, peering along the dim maindecks; but could neither see nor hear anything; not that, indeed, I had any reason for expecting to see or hear ought unusual aboard of the vessel; for all of the noises had come from over the side, and, more than that, from beneath the water-line. Yet in the state of mind in which I was, I had less use for reason than fancy; for that strange thudding and tapping, out here in the midst of this world of loneliness, had set me vaguely imagining unknowable terrors, stealing upon me from every shadow that lay upon the dimly-seen decks.

"Then, as still I listened, hesitating to go down on to the maindeck, yet too dissatisfied with the result of my peerings, to cease from my search, I heard, faint yet clear in the stillness of the night, the tapping noises recommence.

"I took my weight from off the rail, and listened; but I could no longer hear them, and at that, I leant forward again over the rail, and peered down on to the maindeck. Immediately, the sounds came once more to me, and I knew now, that they were borne to me by the medium of the rail, which conducted them to me through the iron stanchions by which it is fixed to the vessel.

"At that, I turned and went aft along the poop deck, moving very warily and with quietness. I stopped over the place where first I had heard the louder noises, and stooped, putting my ear against the rail. Here, the sounds came to me with great distinctness.

"For a little, I listened; then stood up, and slid away that part of the tarred canvas-screen which covers the port opening through which we dump our refuse; they being made here for convenience, one upon each side of the vessel. This, I did very silently; then, leaning forward through the opening, I peered down into the dimness of the weed. Even as I did so, I heard plainly below me a heavy thud, muffled and dull by reason of the intervening water, against the iron side of the ship. It seemed to me that there was some disturbance amid the dark, shadowy masses of the weed. Then I had opened the dark-slide of my lantern, and sent a clear beam of light down into the blackness. For a brief instant, I thought I perceived a multitude of things moving. Yet, beyond that they were oval in shape, and showed white through the weed fronds, I had no clear conception of anything; for with the flash of the light, they vanished, and there lay beneath me only the dark, brown masses of the weed—demurely quiet.

"But an impression they did leave upon my over excited imagination—an impression that might have been due to morbidity, bred of too much loneliness; but nevertheless it seemed to me that I had seen momentarily a multitude of dead white faces, upturned towards me among the meshes of the weed.

"For a little, I leant there, staring down at the circle of illumined weed; yet with my thoughts in such a turmoil of frightened doubts and conjectures, that my physical eyes did but poor work, compared with the orb that looks inward. And through all the chaos of my mind there rose up weird and creepy memories—ghouls, the un-dead. There seemed nothing improbable, in that moment, in associating the terms with the fears that were besetting me. For no man may dare to say what terrors this world holds, until he has become lost to his brother men, amid the unspeakable desolation of the vast and slimy weed-plains of the Sargasso Sea.

"And then, as I leaned there, so foolishly exposing myself to those dangers which I had learnt did truly exist, my eyes caught and subconsciously noted the strange and subtle undulation which always foretells the approach of one of the giant octopi. Instantly, I leapt back, and whipped the tarred canvas-cover across the opening, and so stood alone there in the night, glancing frightenedly before and behind me, the beam from my lamp casting wavering splashes of light to and fro about the decks. And all the time, I was listening—listening; for it seemed to me that some Terror was brooding in the night, that might come upon us at any moment and in some unimagined form.

"Then, across the silence, stole a whisper, and I turned swiftly towards the companionway. My wife was there, and she reached out her arms to me, begging me to come below into safety. As the light from my lantern flashed upon her, I saw that she had a revolver in her right hand, and at that, I asked her what she had it for; whereupon she informed me that she had been watching over me, through the whole of the time that I had been on deck, save for the little while that it had taken her to get and load the weapon.

"At that, as may be imagined, I went and embraced her very heartily, kissing her for the love that had prompted her actions; and then, after that, we spoke a little together in low tones—she asking that I should come down and fasten up the companion-doors, and I demurring, telling her that I felt too unsettled to sleep; but would rather keep watch about the poop for a while longer.

"Then, even as we discussed the matter, I motioned to her for quietness. In the succeeding silence, she heard it, as well as I, a slow—tap! tap! tap! coming steadily along the dark maindecks. I felt a swift vile fear, and my wife's hold upon me became very tense, despite that she trembled a little. I released her grip from my arm, and made to go towards the break of the poop; but she was after me instantly, praying me at least to stay where I was, if I would not go below.

"Upon that, I bade her very sternly to release me, and go down into the cabin; though all the while I loved her for her very solicitude. But she disobeyed me, asserting very stoutly, though in a whisper, that if I went into danger, she would go with me; and at that I hesitated; but decided, after a moment, to go no further than the break of the poop, and not to venture on to the maindeck.

"I went very silently to the break, and my wife followed me. From the rail across the break, I shone the light of the lantern; but could neither see nor hear anything; for the tapping noise had ceased. Then it recommenced, seeming to have come near to the port side of the stump of the mainmast. I turned the lantern towards it, and, for one brief instant, it seemed to me that I saw something pale, just beyond the brightness of my light. At that, I raised my pistol and fired, and my wife did the same, though without any telling on my part. The noise of the double explosion went very loud and hollow sounding along the decks, and after the echoes had died away, we both of us thought we heard the tapping going away forrard again.

"After that, we stayed awhile, listening and watching; but all was quiet, and, presently, I consented to go below and bar up the companion, as my wife desired; for, indeed, there was much sense in her plea of the futility of my staying up upon the decks.

"The night passed quietly enough, and on the following morning, I made a very careful inspection of the vessel, examining the decks, the weed outside of the ship, and the sides of her. After that, I removed the hatches, and went down into the holds; but could nowhere find anything of an unusual nature.

"That night, just as we were making an end of our supper, we heard three tremendous blows given against the starboard side of the ship, whereat, I sprang to my feet, seized and lit the dark-lantern, which I had kept handy, and ran quickly and silently up on to the deck. My pistol, I had already in my pocket, and as I had soft slippers upon my feet, I needed not to pause to remove my footgear. In the companionway, I had left the axe, and this I seized as I went up the steps.

"Reaching the deck, I moved over quietly to the side, and slid back the canvas door; then I leant out and opened the slide of the lantern, letting its light play upon the weed in the direction from which the bangs had seemed to proceed; but nowhere could I perceive anything out of the ordinary, the weed seeming undisturbed. And so, after a little, I drew in my head, and slid-to the door in the canvas screen; for it was but wanton folly to stand long exposed to any of the giant octopi that might chance to be prowling near, beneath the curtain of the weed.

"From then, until midnight, I stayed upon the poop, talking much in a quiet voice to my wife, who had followed me up into the companion. At times, we could hear the knocking, sometimes against one side of the ship, and again upon the other. And, between the louder knocks, and accompanying them, would sound the minor tap, tap, tap-a-tap, that I had first heard.

"About midnight, feeling that I could do nothing, and no harm appearing to result to us from the unseen things that seemed to be encircling us my wife and I made our way below to rest, securely barring the companion-doors behind us.

"It would be, I should imagine, about two o'clock in the morning, that I was aroused from a somewhat troubled sleep, by the agonised screaming of our great boar, away forrard. I leant up upon my elbow, and listened, and so grew speedily wide awake. I sat up, and slid from my bunk to the floor. My wife, as I could tell from her breathing, was sleeping peacefully, so that I was able to draw on a few clothes without disturbing her.

"Then, having lit the dark-lantern, and turned the slide over the light, I took the axe in my other hand, and hastened towards the door that gives out of the forrard end of the saloon, on to the maindeck, beneath the shelter of the break of the poop. This door, I had locked before turning-in, and now, very noiselessly, I unlocked it, and turned the handle, opening the door with much caution. I peered out along the dim stretch of the maindeck; but could see nothing; then I turned on the slide of the lamp, and let the light play along the decks; but still nothing unusual was revealed to me.

"Away forrard, the shrieking of the pig had been succeeded by an absolute silence, and there was nowhere any noise, if I except an occasional odd tap-a-tap, which seemed to come from the side of the ship. And so, taking hold of my courage, I stepped out on to the maindeck, and proceeded slowly forrard, throwing the beam of light to and fro continuously, as I walked.

"Abruptly, I heard away in the bows of the ship a sudden multitudinous tapping and scraping and slithering; and so loud and near did it sound, that I was brought up all of a round-turn, as the saying is.

For, perhaps, a whole minute, I stood there hesitating, and playing the light all about me, not knowing but that some hateful thing might leap upon me from out of the shadows.

"And then, suddenly, I remembered that I had left the door open behind me, that led into the saloon, so that, were there any deadly thing about the decks, it might chance to get in upon my wife and child as they slept. At the thought, I turned and ran swiftly aft again, and in through the door to my cabin. Here, I made sure that all was right with the two sleepers, and after that, I returned to the deck, shutting the door, and locking it behind me.

"And now, feeling very lonesome out there upon the dark decks, and cut off in a way from a retreat, I had need of all my manhood to aid me forrard to learn the wherefore of the pig's crying, and the cause of that manifold tapping. Yet go I did, and have some right to be proud of the act; for the dreeness and lonesomeness and the cold fear of the Weed-World, squeeze the pluck out of one in a very woeful manner.

"As I approached the empty fo'cas'le, I moved with all wariness, swinging the light to and fro, and holding my axe very handily, and the heart within my breast like a shape of water, so in fear was I. Yet, I came at last to the pigsty, and so discovered a dreadful sight. The pig, a huge boar of twenty-score pounds, had been dragged out on to the deck, and lay before the sty with all his belly ripped up, and stone dead. The iron bars of the sty—great bars they are too—had been torn apart, as though they had been so many straws; and, for the rest, there was a deal of blood both within the sty and upon the decks.

"Yet, I did not stay then to see more; for, all of a sudden, the realisation was borne upon me that this was the work of some monstrous thing, which even at that moment might be stealing upon me; and, with the thought, an overwhelming fear leapt upon me, overbearing my courage; so that I turned and ran for the shelter of the saloon, and never stopped until the stout door was locked between me and that which had wrought such destruction upon the pig. And as I stood there, quivering a little with very fright, I kept questioning dumbly as to what manner of wild-beast thing it was that could burst asunder iron bars, and rip the life out of a great boar, as though it were of no more account than a kitten. And then more vital questions:—How did it get aboard, and where had it hidden? And again:—What was it? And so in this fashion for a good while, until I had grown something more calmed.

"But through all the remainder of that night, I slept not so much as a wink.

"Then in the morning when my wife awoke, I told her of the happenings of the night; whereat she turned very white, and fell to reproaching me for going out at all on to the deck, declaring that I had run needlessly into danger, and that, at least, I should not have left her alone, sleeping in ignorance of what was towards. And after that, she fell into a fit of crying, so that I had some to-do comforting her. Yet, when she had come back to calmness, she was all for accompanying me about the decks, to see by daylight what had indeed befallen in the night-time. And from this decision, I could not turn her; though I assured her I should have told her nothing, had it not been that I wished to warn her from going to and fro between the saloon and the galley, until I had made a thorough search about the decks. Yet, as I have remarked, I could not turn her from her purpose of accompanying me, and so was forced to let her come, though against my desire.

"We made our way on deck through the door that opens under the break of the poop, my wife carrying her loaded revolver half-clumsily in both hands, whilst I had mine held in my left, and the long-handled axe in my right—holding it very readily.

"On stepping out on to the deck, we closed the door behind us, locking it and removing the key; for we had in mind our sleeping child. Then we went slowly forrard along the decks, glancing about warily. As we came fore-side of the pigsty, and my wife saw that which lay beyond it, she let out a little exclamation of horror, shuddering at the sight of the mutilated pig, as, indeed, well she might.

"For my part, I said nothing; but glanced with much apprehension about us; feeling a fresh access of fright; for it was very plain to me that the boar had been molested since I had seen it—the head having been torn, with awful might, from the body; and there were, besides, other new and ferocious wounds, one of which had come nigh to severing the poor brute's body in half. All of which was so much additional evidence of the formidable character of the monster, or Monstrosity, that had attacked the animal.

"I did not delay by the pig, nor attempt to touch it; but beckoned my wife to follow me up on to the fo'cas'le head. Here, I removed the canvas cover from the small skylight which lights the fo'cas'le beneath; and, after that, I lifted off the heavy top, letting a flood of light down into the gloomy place. Then I leant down into the opening, and peered about; but could discover no signs of any lurking thing, and so returned to the maindeck, and made an entrance into the fo'cas'le through the starboard doorway. And now I made a more minute search; but discovered nothing, beyond the mournful array of sea-chests that had belonged to our dead crew.

"My search concluded, I hastened out from the doleful place, into the daylight, and after that made fast the door again, and saw to it that the one upon the port side was also securely locked. Then I went up again on to the fo'cas'le head, and replaced the skylight-top and the canvas cover, battening the whole down very thoroughly.

"And in this wise, and with an incredible care, did I make my search through the ship, fastening up each place behind me, so that I should be certain that no Thing was playing some dread game of hide and seek with me.

"Yet I found nothing, and had it not been for the grim evidence of the dead and mutilated boar, I had been like to have thought nothing more dreadful than an over vivid Imagination had roamed the decks in the darkness of the past night.

"That I had reason to feel puzzled, may be the better understood, when I explain that I had examined the whole of the great, tarred-canvas screen, which I have built about the ship as a protection against the sudden tentacles of any of the roaming giant octopi, without discovering any torn place such as must have been made if any conceivable monster had climbed aboard out of the weed. Also, it must be borne in mind that the ship stands many feet out of the weed, presenting only her smooth iron sides to anything that desires to climb aboard.

"And yet there was the dead pig, lying brutally torn before its empty sty! An undeniable proof that, to go out upon the decks after dark, was to run the risk of meeting a horrible and mysterious death!

"Through all that day, I pondered over this new fear that had come upon us, and particularly upon the monstrous and unearthly power that had torn apart the stout iron bars of the sty, and so ferociously wrenched off the head of the boar. The result of my pondering was that I removed our sleeping belongings that evening from the cabin to the iron half-deck—a little, four-bunked house, standing fore-side of the stump of the main mast, and built entirely of iron, even to the single door, which opens out of the after end.

"Along with our sleeping matters, I carried forrard to our new lodgings, a lamp, and oil, also the dark-lantern, a couple of the axes, two rifles, and all of the revolvers, as well as a good supply of ammunition. Then I bade my wife forage out sufficient provisions to last us for a week, if need be, and whilst she was so busied, I cleaned out and filled the water breaker which belonged to the half-deck.

"At half-past six, I sent my wife forrard to the little iron house, with the baby, and then I locked up the saloon and all of the cabin doors, finally locking after me the heavy, teak door that opened out under the break of the poop.

"Then I went forrard to my wife and child, and shut and bolted the iron door of the half-deck for the night. After that, I went round and saw to it that all of the iron storm-doors, that shut over the eight ports of the house, were in good working order, and so we sat down, as it were, to await the night.

"By eight o'clock, the dusk was upon us, and before half-past, the night hid the decks from my sight. Then I shut down all the iron port-flaps, and screwed them up securely, and after that, I lit the lamp.

"And so a space of waiting ensued, during which I whispered reassuringly to my wife, from time to time, as she looked across at me from her seat beside the sleeping child, with frightened eyes, and a very white face; for somehow there had come upon us within the last hour, a sense of chilly fright, that went straight to one's heart, robbing one vilely of pluck.

"A little later, a sudden sound broke the impressive silence—a sudden dull thud against the side of the ship; and, after that, there came a succession of heavy blows, seeming to be struck all at once upon every side of the vessel; after which there was quietness for maybe a quarter of an hour.

"Then, suddenly, I heard, away forrard, a tap, tap, tap, and then a loud rattling, slurring noise, and a loud crash. After that, I heard many other sounds, and always that tap, tap, tap, repeated a hundred times, as though an army of wooden-legged men were busied all about the decks at the fore end of the ship.

"Presently, there came to me the sound of something coming down the deck, tap, tap, tap, it came. It drew near to the house, paused for nigh a minute; then continued away aft towards the saloon:—tap, tap, tap. I shivered a little, and then, fell half consciously to thanking God that I had been given wisdom to bring my wife and child forrard to the security of the iron deck-house.

"About a minute later, I heard the sound of a heavy blow struck somewhere away aft; and after that a second, and then a third, and seeming by the sounds to have been against iron—the iron of the bulkshead that runs across the break of the poop. There came the noise of a fourth blow, and it blended into the crash of broken woodwork. And therewith, I had a little tense quivering inside me; for the little one and my wife might have been sleeping aft there at that very moment, had it not been for the Providential thought which had sent us forrard to the half-deck.

"With the crash of the broken door, away aft, there came, from forrard of us, a great tumult of noises; and, directly, it sounded as though a multitude of wooden-legged men were coming down the decks from forrard. Tap, tap, tap; tap-a-tap, the noises came, and drew abreast of where we sat in the house, crouched and holding our breaths, for fear that we should make some noise to attract *that* which was without. The sounds passed us, and went tapping away aft, and I let out a little breath of sheer easement. Then, as a sudden thought came to me, I rose and turned down the lamp, fearing that some ray from it might be seen from beneath the door. And so, for the space of an hour, we sat wordless, listening to the sounds which came from away aft, the thud of heavy blows, the occasional crash of wood, and, presently, the tap, tap, tap, again, coming forrard towards us.

"The sounds came to a stop, opposite the starboard side of the house, and, for a full minute, there was quietness. Then suddenly, 'Boom!' a tremendous blow had been struck against the side of the house. My wife gave out a little gasping cry, and there came a second blow; and, at that, the child awoke and began to wail, and my wife was put to it, with trying to soothe her into immediate silence.

"A third blow was struck, filling the little house with a dull thunder of sound, and then I heard the tap, tap, tap, move round to the after end of the house. There came a pause, and then a great blow right upon the door. I grasped the rifle, which I had leant against my chair, and stood up; for I did not know but that the thing might be upon us in a moment, so prodigious was the force of the blows it struck. Once again it struck the door, and after that went tap, tap, tap, round to the port side of the house, and there struck the house again; but now I had more ease of mind; for it was its direct attack upon the door, that had put such horrid dread into my heart.

"After the blows upon the port side of the house, there came a long spell of silence, as though the thing outside were listening; but, by the mercy of God, my wife had been able to soothe the child, so that no sound from us, told of our presence.

"Then, at last, there came again the sounds:—tap, tap, tap, as the voiceless thing moved away forrard. Presently, I heard the noises cease aft; and, after that, there came a multitudinous tap-a-tapping, coming along the decks. It passed the house without so much as a pause, and receded away forrard.

"For a space of over two hours, there was an absolute silence; so that I judged that we were now no longer in danger of being molested. An hour later, I whispered to my wife; but, getting no reply, knew that she had fallen into a doze, and so I sat on, listening tensely; yet making no sort of noise that might attract attention.

"Presently, by the thin line of light from beneath the door, I saw that the day was breaking; and, at that, I rose stiffly, and commenced to unscrew the iron port-covers. I unscrewed the forrard ones first, and looked out into the wan dawn; but could discover nothing unusual about so much of the decks as I could see from there.

"After that, I went round and opened each, as I came to it, in its turn; but it was not until I had uncovered the port which gave me a view of the port side of the after maindeck, that I discovered any thing extraordinary. Then I saw, at first dimly, but more clearly as the day brightened, that the door, leading from beneath the break of the poop into the saloon, had been broken to flinders, some of which lay scattered upon the deck, and some of which still hung from the bent hinges; whilst more, no doubt, were strewed in the passage beyond my sight.

"Turning from the port, I glanced towards my wife, and saw that she lay half in and half out of the baby's bunk, sleeping with her head beside the child's, both upon one pillow. At the sight, a great wave of holy thankfulness took me, that we had been so wonderfully spared from the terrible and mysterious danger that had stalked the decks in the darkness of the preceding night. Feeling thus, I stole across the floor of the house, and kissed them both very gently, being full of tenderness, yet not minded to waken them. And, after that, I lay down in one of the bunks, and slept until the sun was high in the heaven.

"When I awoke, my wife was about and had tended to the child and prepared our breakfast, so that I had naught to do but tumble out and set to, the which I did with a certain keenness of appetite, induced, I doubt not, by the stress of the night. Whilst we ate, we discussed the peril through which we had just passed; but without coming any the nearer to a solution of the weird mystery of the Terror.

"Breakfast over, we took a long and final survey of the decks, from the various ports, and then prepared to sally out. This we did with instinctive caution and quietness, both of us armed as on the previous day. The door of the half-deck we closed and locked behind us, thereby ensuring that the child was open to no danger whilst we were in other parts of the ship.

"After a quick look about us, we proceeded aft towards the shattered door beneath the break of the poop. At the doorway, we stopped, not so much with the intent to examine the broken door, as because of an instinctive and natural hesitation to go forward into the saloon, which but a few hours previous had been visited by some incredible monster or monsters. Finally, we decided to go up upon the poop and peer down through the skylight. This we did, lifting the sides of the dome for that purpose; yet though we peered long and earnestly, we could perceive no signs of any lurking thing. But broken woodwork there appeared to be in plenty, to judge by the scattered pieces.

"After that, I unlocked the companion, and pushed back the big, over-arching slide. Then, silently, we stole down the steps and into the saloon. Here, being now able to see the big cabin through all its length, we discovered a most extraordinary scene; the whole place appeared to be wrecked from end to end; the six cabins that line each side had their bulksheading driven into shards and slivers of broken wood in places. Here, a door would be standing untouched, whilst the bulkshead beside it was in a mass of flinders—There a door would be driven completely from its hinges, whilst the surrounding woodwork was untouched. And so it was, wherever we looked.

"My wife made to go towards our cabin; but I pulled her back, and went forward myself. Here the desolation was almost as great. My wife's bunk-board had been ripped out, whilst the supporting side-batten of mine had been plucked forth, so that all the bottom-boards of the bunk had descended to the floor in a cascade.

"But it was neither of these things that touched us so sharply, as the fact that the child's little swing cot had been wrenched from its standards, and flung in a tangled mass of white-painted iron-work across the cabin. At the sight of that, I glanced across at my wife, and she at me, her face grown very white. Then down she slid to her knees, and fell to crying and thanking God together, so that I found myself beside her in a moment, with a very humble and thankful heart.

"Presently, when we were more controlled, we left the cabin, and finished our search. The pantry, we discovered to be entirely untouched, which, somehow, I do not think was then a matter of great surprise to me; for I had ever a feeling that the things which had broken a way into our sleeping cabin, had been looking for us.

"In a little while, we left the wrecked saloon and cabins, and made our way forrard to the pigsty; for I was anxious to see whether the carcass of the pig had been touched. As we came round the corner of the sty, I uttered a great cry; for there, lying upon the deck, on its back, was a gigantic crab, so vast in size that I had not conceived so huge a monster existed. Brown it was in colour, save for the belly part, which was of a light yellow.

"One of its pincer-claws, or mandibles, had been torn off in the fight in which it must have been slain (for it was all disembowelled). And this one claw weighed so heavy that I had some to-do to lift it from the deck; and by this you may have some idea of the size and formidableness of the creature itself.

"Around the great crab, lay half a dozen smaller ones, no more than from seven or eight to twenty inches across, and all white in colour, save for an occasional mottling of brown. These had all been killed by a single nip of an enormous mandible, which had in every case smashed them almost into two halves. Of the carcass of the great boar, not a fragment remained.

"And so was the mystery solved; and, with the solution, departed the superstitious terror which had suffocated me through those three nights, since the tapping had commenced. We had been attacked by a wandering shoal of giant crabs, which, it is quite possible, roam across the weed from place to place, devouring aught that comes in their path.

"Whether they had ever boarded a ship before, and so, perhaps, developed a monstrous lust for human flesh, or whether their attack had been prompted by curiosity, I cannot possibly say. It may be that, at first, they mistook the hull of the vessel for the body of some dead marine monster, and hence their blows upon her sides, by which, possibly, they were endeavouring to pierce through our somewhat unusually tough hide!

"Or, again, it may be that they have some power of scent, by means of which they were able to smell our presence aboard the ship; but this (as they made no general attack upon us in the deck-house) I feel disinclined to regard as probable. And yet—I do not know. Why their attack upon the saloon, and our sleeping-cabin? As I say, I cannot tell, and so must leave it there.

"The way in which they came aboard, I discovered that same day; for, having learned what manner of creature it was that had attacked us, I made a more intelligent survey of the sides of the ship; but it was not until I came to the extreme bows, that I saw how they had managed. Here, I found that some of the gear of the broken bowsprit and jibboom, trailed down on to the weed, and as I had not extended the canvas-screen across the heel of the bowsprit, the monsters had been able to climb up the gear, and thence aboard, without the least obstruction being opposed to their progress.

"This state of affairs, I very speedily remedied; for, with a few strokes of my axe, I cut through the gear, allowing it to drop down among the weed; and after that, I built a temporary breastwork of wood across the gap, between the two ends of the screen; later on making it more permanent.

"Since that time, we have been no more molested by the giant crabs; though for several nights afterwards, we heard them knocking strangely against our sides. Maybe, they are attracted by such refuse as we are forced to dump overboard, and this would explain their first tappings being aft, opposite to the lazarette; for it is from the openings in this part of the canvas-screen that we cast our rubbish.

"Yet, it is weeks now since we heard aught of them, so that I have reason to believe that they have betaken themselves elsewhere, maybe to attack some other lonely humans, living out their short span of life aboard some lone derelict, lost even to memory in the depth of this vast sea of weed and deadly creatures.

"I shall send this message forth on its journey, as I have sent the other four, within a well-pitched barrel, attached to a small fire balloon. The shell of the severed claw of the monster crab, I shall enclose, as evidence of the terrors that beset us in this dreadful place. Should this message, and the claw, ever fall into human hands, let them, contemplating this vast mandible, try to imagine the size of the other crab or crabs that could destroy so formidable a creature as the one to which this claw belonged.

"What other terrors does this hideous world hold for us?

"I had thought of inclosing, along with the claw, the shell of one of the white smaller crabs. It must have been some of these moving in the weed that night, that set my disordered fancy to imagining of ghouls and the Un-Dead. But, on thinking it over, I shall not; for to do so would be to illustrate nothing that needs illustration, and it would but increase needlessly the weight which the balloon will have to lift.

"And so I grow wearied of writing. The night is drawing near, and I have little more to tell. I am writing this in the saloon, and, though I have mended and carpentered so well as I am able, nothing

I can do will hide the traces of that night when the vast crabs raided through these cabins, searching for—*what?*

"There is nothing more to say. In health, I am well, and so is my wife and the little one, but....

"I must have myself under control, and be patient. We are beyond all help, and must bear that which is before us, with such bravery as we are able. And with this, I end; for my last word shall not be one of complaint.

"Arthur Samuel Philips."

"Christmas Eve, 1879."

The Voice in the Night

William Hope Hodgson

It was a dark, starless night. We were becalmed in the northern Pacific. Our exact position I do not know; for the sun had been hidden during the course of a weary, breathless week by a thin haze which had seemed to float above us, about the height of our mastheads, at whiles descending and shrouding the surrounding sea.

With there being no wind, we had steadied the tiller, and I was the only man on deck. The crew, consisting of two men and a boy, were sleeping forward in their den, while Will—my friend, and the master of our little craft—was aft in his bunk on the port side of the little cabin.

Suddenly, from out of the surrounding darkness, there came a hail:

"Schooner, ahoy!"

The cry was so unexpected that I gave no immediate answer, because of my surprise.

It came again—a voice curiously throaty and inhuman, calling from somewhere upon the dark sea away on our port broadside:

"Schooner, ahoy!"

"Hullo!" I sang out, having gathered my wits somewhat. "What are you? What do you want?"

"You need not be afraid," answered the queer voice, having probably noticed some trace of confusion in my tone. "I am only an old—man."

The pause sounded odd, but it was only afterward that it came back to me with any significance.

"Why don't you come alongside, then?" I queried somewhat snappishly, for I liked not his hinting at my having been a trifle shaken.

"I—I—can't. It wouldn't be safe. I—" The voice broke off, and there was silence.

"What do you mean?" I asked, growing more and more astonished. "What's not safe? Where are you?"

I listened for a moment, but there came no answer. And then, a sudden indefinite suspicion, of I knew not what, coming to me, I stepped swiftly to the binnacle and took out the lighted lamp. At the same time, I knocked on the deck with my heel to waken Will. Then I was back at the side, throwing the yellow funnel of light out into the silent immensity beyond our rail. As I did so, I heard a slight muffled cry, and then the sound of a splash, as though someone had dipped oars abruptly. Yet I cannot say with certainty that I saw anything; save, it seemed to me, that with the first flash of the light there had been something upon the waters, where now there was nothing.

"Hullo, there!" I called. "What foolery is this?"

But there came only the indistinct sounds of a boat being pulled away into the night.

Then I heard Will's voice from the direction of the after scuttle:

"What's up, George?"

"Come here, Will!" I said.

"What is it?" he asked, coming across the deck.

I told him the queer thing that had happened. He put several questions; then, after a moment's silence, he raised his hands to his lips and hailed:

"Boat, ahoy!"

From a long distance away there came back to us a faint reply, and my companion repeated his call. Presently, after a short period of silence, there grew on our hearing the muffled sound of oars, at which Will hailed again.

This time there was a reply: "Put away the light."

"I'm damned if I will," I muttered; but Will told me to do as the voice bade, and I shoved it down under the bulwarks.

"Come nearer," he said, and the oar strokes continued. Then, when apparently some half dozen fathoms distant, they again ceased.

"Come alongside!" exclaimed Will. "There's nothing to be frightened of aboard here."

"Promise that you will not show the light?"

"What's to do with you," I burst out, "that you're so infernally afraid of the light?"

"Because—" began the voice, and stopped short.

"Because what?" I asked quickly.

Will put his hand on my shoulder. "Shut up a minute, old man," he said in a low voice. "Let me tackle him."

He leaned more over the rail. "See here, mister," he said, "this is a pretty queer business, you coming upon us like this, right out in the middle of the blessed Pacific. How are we to know what sort of a hanky-panky trick you're up to? You say there's only one of you. How are we to know, unless we get a squint at you—eh? What's your objection to the light, anyway?"

As he finished, I heard the noise of the oars again, and then the voice came; but now from a greater distance, and sounding extremely hopeless and pathetic.

"I am sorry—sorry! I would not have troubled you, only I am hungry, and—so is she."

The voice died away, and the sound of the oars, dipping irregularly, was borne to us.

"Stop!" sang out Will. "I don't want to drive you away. Come back! We'll keep the light hidden if you don't like it."

He turned to me. "It's a damned queer rig, this; but I think there's nothing to be afraid of?"

There was a question in his tone, and I replied, "No, I think the poor devil's been wrecked around here, and gone crazy."

The sound of the oars drew nearer.

"Shove that lamp back in the binnacle," said Will; then he leaned over the rail and listened. I replaced the lamp and came back to his side. The dipping of the oars ceased some dozen yards distant.

"Won't you come alongside now?" asked Will in an even voice. "I have had the lamp put back in the binnacle."

"I—I cannot," replied the voice. "I dare not come nearer. I dare not even pay you for the— the provisions."

"That's all right," said Will, and hesitated. "You're welcome to as much grub as you can take—" Again he hesitated.

"You are very good!" exclaimed the voice. "May God, who understands everything, reward you—" It broke off huskily.

"The—the lady?" said Will abruptly. "Is she—"

"I have left her behind upon the island," came the voice.

"What island?" I cut in.

"I know not its name," returned the voice. "I would to God—" it began, and checked itself as suddenly.

"Could we not send a boat for her?" asked Will at this point.

"No!" said the voice, with extraordinary emphasis. "My God! No!" There was a moment's pause; then it added, in a tone which seemed a merited reproach, "It was because of our want I ventured—because her agony tortured me."

"I am a forgetful brute!" exclaimed Will. "Just wait a minute, whoever you are, and I will bring you up something at once."

In a couple of minutes he was back again, and his arms were full of various edibles. He paused at the rail.

"Can't you come alongside for them?" he asked.

"No—I dare not," replied the voice, and it seemed to me that in its tones I detected a note of stifled craving, as though the owner hushed a mortal desire. It came to me then in a flash that the poor old creature out there in the darkness was suffering for actual need for that which Will held in his arms; and yet, because of some unintelligible dread, refraining from dashing to the side of our schooner and receiving it. And with the lightninglike conviction there came the knowledge that the Invisible was not mad, but sanely facing some intolerable horror.

"Damn it, Will!" I said, full of many feelings, over which predominated a vast sympathy. "Get a box. We must float off the stuff to him in it."

This we did, propelling it away from the vessel, out into the darkness, by means of a boat hook.

In a minute a slight cry from the Invisible came to us, and we knew that he had secured the box.

A little later he called out a farewell to us, and so heartful a blessing that I am sure we were the better for it. Then, without more ado, we heard the ply of oars across the darkness.

"Pretty soon off," remarked Will, with perhaps just a little sense of injury.

"Wait," I replied. "I think somehow he'll come back. He must have been badly needing that food."

"And the lady," said Will. For a moment he was silent; then he continued, "It's the queerest thing ever I've tumbled across since I've been fishing."

"Yes," I said, and fell to pondering.

And so the time slipped away—an hour, another, and still Will stayed with me; for the queer adventure had knocked all desire for sleep out of him.

The third hour was three parts through when we heard again the sound of oars across the silent ocean.

"Listen!" said Will, a low note of excitement in his voice.

"He's coming, just as I thought," I muttered.

The dipping of the oars grew nearer, and I noted that the strokes were firmer and longer. The food had been needed.

They came to a stop a little distance off the broadside, and the queer voice came again to us through the darkness:

"Schooner, ahoy!"

"That you?" asked Will.

"Yes," replied the voice. "I left you suddenly, but—but there was great need."

"The lady?" questioned Will.

"The—lady is grateful now on earth. She will be more grateful soon in—in heaven."

Will began to make some reply, in a puzzled voice, but became confused and broke off. I said nothing. I was wondering at the curious pauses, and apart from my wonder, I was full of a great sympathy.

The voice continued, "We—she and I, have talked, as we shared the result of God's tenderness and yours—"

Will interposed, but without coherence

"I beg of you not to—to belittle your deed of Christian charity this night," said the voice. "Be sure that it has not escaped His notice."

It stopped, and there was a full minute's silence. Then it came again. "We have spoken together upon that which—which has befallen us. We had thought to go out, without telling anyone of the terror which has come into our—lives. She is with me in believing that tonight's happenings are under a special ruling, and that it is God's wish that we should tell to you all that we have suffered since—since—"

"Yes?" said Will softly.

"Since the sinking of the Albatross."

"Ah!" I exclaimed involuntarily. "She left Newcastle for 'Frisco some six months ago, and hasn't been heard of since."

"Yes" answered the voice. "But some few degrees to the north of the line, she was caught in a terrible storm and dismasted. When the calm came, it was found that she was leaking badly, and presently, it falling to a calm, the sailors took to the boats, leaving—leaving a young lady—my fiancée—and myself upon the wreck.

"We were below, gathering together a few of our belongings, when they left. They were entirely callous, through fear, and when we came up upon the decks, we saw them only as small shapes afar off upon the horizon. Yet we did not despair, but set to work and constructed a small raft. Upon this we put such few matters as it would hold, including a quantity of water and some ship's biscuit. Then, the vessel being very deep in the water, we got ourselves onto the raft and pushed off.

"It was later that I observed we seemed to be in the way of some tide or current, which bore us from the ship at an angle, so that in the course of three hours, by my watch, her hull became invisible to our sight, her broken masts remaining in view for a somewhat longer period. Then, toward evening, it grew misty, and so through the night. The next day we were still encompassed by the mist, the weather remaining quiet.

"For four days we drifted through this strange haze, until, on the evening of the fourth day, there grew upon our ears the murmur of breakers at a distance. Gradually it became plainer, and somewhat after midnight, it appeared to sound upon either hand at no very great space. The raft was raised upon a swell several times, and then we were in smooth water, and the noise of the breakers was behind.

"When the morning came, we found that we were in a sort of great lagoon, but of this we noticed little at the time; for close before us, through the enshrouding mist, loomed the hull of a large sailing vessel. With one accord we fell upon our knees and thanked God, for we thought that here was an end to our perils. We had much to learn.

"The raft drew near to the ship, and we shouted on them to take us aboard; but none answered. Presently the raft touched against the side of the vessel, and seeing a rope hanging downward, I seized it and began to climb. Yet I had much ado to make my way up, because of a kind of gray, lichenous fungus that had seized upon the rope and blotched the side of the ship lividly.

"I reached the rail and clambered over it, onto the deck. Here I saw that the decks were covered in great patches with the gray masses, some of them rising into nodules several feet in height; but at the time I thought less of this matter than of the possibility of there being people aboard the ship. I shouted, but none answered. Then I went to the door below the poop deck. I opened it and peered in. There was a great smell of staleness, so that I knew in a moment that nothing living was within, and with the knowledge, I shut the door quickly, for I felt suddenly lonely.

"I went back to the side where I had scrambled up. My—my sweetheart was still sitting quietly upon the raft. Seeing me look down, she called up to know whether there were any aboard the ship. I replied that the vessel had the appearance of having been long deserted, but that if she would wait a little, I would see whether there was anything in the shape of a ladder by which she could ascend to the deck. Then we would make a search through the vessel together. A little later, on the opposite side of the decks, I found a rope side ladder. This I carried across, and a minute afterward she was beside me.

"Together we explored the cabins and apartments in the afterpart of the ship, but nowhere was there any sign of life. Here and there, within the cabins themselves, we came across odd patches of that queer fungus; but this, as my sweetheart said, could be cleansed away.

"In the end, having assured ourselves that the after portion of the vessel was empty, we picked our ways to the bows, between the ugly gray nodules of that strange growth; and here we made a further search, which told us that there was indeed none aboard but ourselves. "This being now beyond any doubt, we returned to the stern of the ship and proceeded to make ourselves as comfortable as possible. Together we cleared out and cleaned two of the cabins, and after that I made examination whether there was anything eatable in the ship. This I soon found was so, and thanked God for His goodness. In addition to this I discovered a fresh-water pump, and having fixed it, I found the water drinkable, though somewhat unpleasant to the taste.

"For several days we stayed aboard the ship without attempting to get to the shore. We were busily engaged in making the place habitable. Yet even thus early we became aware that our lot was even less to be desired than might have been imagined; for though, as a first step, we scraped away the odd patches of growth that studded the floors and walls of the cabins and saloon, yet they returned almost to their original size within the space of twenty-four hours, which not only discouraged us but gave us a feeling of vague unease.

"Still we would nor admit ourselves beaten, so set to work afresh, and not only scraped away the fungus but soaked the places where it had been with carbolic, a canful of which I had found in the pantry. Yet by the end of the week the growth had returned in full strength, and in addition it had spread to other places, as though our touching it had allowed germs from it to travel elsewhere.

"On the seventh morning, my sweetheart woke to find a small patch of it growing on her pillow, close to her face. At that, she came to me, as soon as she could get her garments upon her. I was in the galley at the time, lighting the fire for breakfast."

'Come here, John,' she said, and led me aft. When I saw the thing upon her pillow I shuddered, and then and there we agreed to go right out of the ship and see whether we could not fare to make ourselves more comfortable ashore.

"Hurriedly we gathered together our few belongings, and even among these I found that the fungus had been at work, for one of her shawls had a little lump of it growing near one edge. I threw the whole thing over the side without saying anything to her.

"The raft was still alongside, but it was too clumsy to guide, and I lowered down a small boat that hung across the stern, and in this we made our way to the shore. Yet as we drew near to it, I became gradually aware that here the vile fungus, which had driven us from the ship, was growing riot. In places it rose into horrible, fantastic mounds, which seemed almost to quiver, as with a quiet life, when the wind blew across them. Here and there it took on the forms of vast fingers, and in others it just spread out flat and smooth and treacherous. Odd places, it appeared as grotesque stunted trees, extraordinarily kinked and gnarled—the whole quaking vilely at times.

"At first it seemed to us that there was no single portion of the surrounding shore which was not hidden beneath the masses of the hideous lichen; yet in this I found we were mistaken, for somewhat later, coasting along the shore at a little distance, we descried a smooth white patch of what appeared to be fine sand, and there we landed. It was not sand. What it was I do not know.

All that I have observed is that upon it the fungus will not grow; while everywhere else, save where the sandlike earth wanders oddly, pathwise, amid the gray desolation of the lichen, there is nothing but that loathsome grayness.

"It is difficult to make you understand how cheered we were to find one place that was absolutely free from the growth, and here we deposited our belongings. Then we went back to the ship for such things as it seemed to us we should need. Among other matters, I managed to bring ashore with me one of the ship's sails. With it I constructed two small tents, which, though exceedingly rough-shaped, served the purposes for which they were intended. In these we lived and stored our various necessities, and thus for a matter of some four weeks all went smoothly and without particular unhappiness. Indeed, I may say with much happiness—for—we were together.

"It was on the thumb of her right hand that the growth first showed. It was only a small circular spot, much like a little gray mole My God! How the fear leaped to my heart when she showed me the place. We cleansed it, between us, washing it with carbolic and water. In the morning of the following day she showed her hand to me again. The gray warty thing had returned. For a little while we looked at one another in silence. Then, still wordless, we started again to remove it. In the midst of the operation she spoke suddenly."

'What's that on the side of your face, dear?' Her voice was sharp with anxiety. I put my hand up to feel."

'There! Under the hair by your ear. A little to the front a bit.' My finger rested upon the place, and then I knew."

'Let us get your thumb done first,' I said. And she submitted, only because she was afraid to touch me until it was cleansed. I finished washing and disinfecting her thumb, and then she turned to my face. After it was finished we sat together and talked awhile of many things; for there had come into our lives sudden, very terrible thoughts. We were, all at once, afraid of something worse than death. We spoke of loading the boat with provisions and water and making our way out onto the sea; yet we were helpless, for many causes, and—and the growth had attacked us already. We decided to stay. God would do with us what was His will. We would wait.

"A month, two months, three months passed and the places grew somewhat, and there had come others. Yet we fought so strenuously with the fear that its headway was but slow, comparatively speaking.

"Occasionally we ventured off to the ship for such stores as we needed. There we found that the fungus grew persistently. One of the nodules on the main deck soon became as high as my head.

"We had now given up all thought or hope of leaving the island. We had realized that it would be unallowable to go among healthy humans with the thing from which we were suffering.

"With this determination and knowledge in our minds we knew that we should have to husband our food and water; for we did not know, at that time, but that we should possibly live for many years.

"This reminds me that I have told you that I am an old man. Judged by years this is not so. But—but—"

He broke off, then continued somewhat abruptly, "As I was saying, we knew that we should have to use care in the matter of food. But we had no idea then how little food there was left of which to take care. It n was a week later that I made the discovery that all the other bread tanks—which I had supposed full—were empty, and that (beyond odd tins of vegetables and meat, and some other matters) we had nothing on which to depend but the bread in the tank which I had already opened.

"After learning this I bestirred myself to do what I could, and set to work at fishing in the lagoon; but with no success. At this I was somewhat inclined to feel desperate, until the thought came to me to try outside the lagoon, in the open sea.

"Here, at times, I caught odd fish, but so infrequently that they proved of but little help in keeping us from the hunger which threatened. It seemed to me that our deaths were likely to come by hunger, and not by the growth of the thing which had seized upon our bodies. We were in this state of mind when the fourth month wore out. Then I made a very horrible discovery. One morning, a little before midday, I came off from the ship with a portion of the biscuits which were left. In the mouth of her tent I saw my sweetheart sitting, eating something. 'What is it, my dear?' I called out as I leaped ashore. Yet, on hearing my voice, she seemed confused, and turning, slyly threw something toward the edge of the little clearing. It fell short, and a vague suspicion having arisen within me, I walked across and picked it up. It was a piece of the gray fungus.

"As I went to her with it in my hand, she turned deadly pale; then a rose red.

"I felt strangely dazed and frightened.

" 'My dear! My dear!' I said, and could say no more. Yet at my words she broke down and cried bitterly. Gradually, as she calmed, I got from her the news that she had tried it the preceding day, and—and liked it. I got her to promise on her knees not to touch it again, however great our hunger. After she had promised, she told me that the desire for it had come suddenly, and that until the moment of desire, she had experienced nothing toward it but the most extreme repulsion.

"Later in the day, feeling strangely restless and much shaken with the thing which I had discovered, I made my way along one of the twisted paths—formed by the white, sandlike substance—which led among the fungoid growth. I had, once before, ventured along there, but not to any great distance. This time, being involved in perplexing thought, I went much farther than hitherto.

"Suddenly I was called to myself by a queer hoarse sound on my left. Turning quickly, I saw that there was movement among an extraordinarily shaped mass of fungus close to my elbow. It was swaying uneasily, as though it possessed life of its own. Abruptly, as I stared, the thought came to me that the thing had a grotesque resemblance to the figure of a distorted human creature. Even as the fancy flashed into my brain, there was a slight, sickening noise of tearing, and I saw that one of the branchlike arms was detaching itself from the surrounding masses, and coming toward me. The head of the thing, a shapeless gray ball, inclined in my direction. I stood stupidly, and the vile arm brushed across my face. I gave out a frightened cry and ran back a few paces. There was a sweetish taste upon my lips where the thing had touched me. I licked them, and was immediately filled with an inhuman desire. I turned and seized a mass of the fungus.

Then more, and—more. I was insatiable. In the midst of devouring, the remembrance of the morning's discovery swept into my amazed brain. It was sent by God. I dashed the fragment I held to the ground. Then, utterly wretched and feeling a dreadful guiltiness, I made my way back to the encampment.

"I think she knew, by some marvelous intuition which love must have given, so soon as she set eyes on me. Her quiet sympathy made it easier for me, and I told her of my sudden weakness, yet omitted to mention the extraordinary thing which had gone before. I desired to spare her all unnecessary terror.

"But for myself I had added an intolerable knowledge, to breed an incessant terror in my brain; for I doubted not that I had seen the end of one of these men who had come to the island in the ship in the lagoon; and in that monstrous ending I had seen our own.

"Thereafter we kept from the abominable food, though the desire for it had entered into our blood. Yet our dreary punishment was upon us; for day by day, with monstrous rapidity, the fungoid growth took hold of our poor bodies. Nothing we could do would check it materially, and so—and so—we who had been human became—Well, it matters less each day. Only—only we had been man and maid!

"And day by day the fight is more dreadful to withstand the hunger-lust for the terrible lichen.

"A week ago we ate the last of the biscuit, and since that time I have caught three fish. I was out here fishing tonight when your schooner drifted upon me out of the mist. I hailed you. You know the rest, and may God, out of His great heart, bless you for your goodness to a—a couple of poor outcast souls."

There was the dip of an oar—another. Then the voice came again, and for the last time, sounding through the slight surrounding mist, ghostly and mournful.

"God bless you! Good-by!"

"Good-by," we shouted together hoarsely, our hearts full of many emotions I glanced about me. I became aware that the dawn was upon us.

The sun flung a stray beam across the hidden sea, pierced the mist dully, and lit up the receding boat with a gloomy fire. Indistinctly I saw something nodding between the oars. I thought of a sponge—a great, gray nodding sponge. The oars continued to ply. They were gray—as was the boat—and my eyes searched a moment vainly for the conjunction of hand and oar. My gaze flashed back to the—head. It nodded forward as the oars went backward for the stroke. Then the oars were dipped, the boat shot out of the patch of light, and the—the thing went nodding into the mist.

The Mystery of the Derelict

William Hope Hodgson

All the night had the four-masted ship, Tarawak, lain motionless in the drift of the Gulf Stream; for she had run into a "calm patch"—into a stark calm which had lasted now for two days and nights.

On every side, had it been light, might have been seen dense masses of floating gulf-weed, studding the ocean even to the distant horizon. In places, so large were the weed-masses that they formed long, low banks, that by daylight, might have been mistaken for low-lying land.

Upon the lee side of the poop, Duthie, one of the 'prentices, leaned with his elbows upon the rail, and stared out across the hidden sea, to where in the Eastern horizon showed the first pink and lemon streamers of the dawn—faint, delicate streaks and washes of colour.

A period of time passed, and the surface of the leeward sea began to show—a great expanse of grey, touched with odd, wavering belts of silver. And everywhere the black specks and islets of the weed.

Presently, the red dome of the sun protruded itself into sight above the dark rim of the horizon; and, abruptly, the watching Duthie saw something—a great, shapeless bulk that lay some miles away to starboard, and showed black and distinct against the gloomy red mass of the rising sun.

"Something in sight to looard, Sir," he informed the Mate, who was leaning, smoking, over the rail that ran across the break of the poop. "I can't just make out what it is."

The Mate rose from his easy position, stretched himself, yawned, and came across to the boy.

"Whereabouts, Toby?" he asked, wearily, and yawning again.

"There, Sir," said Duthie—alias Toby—"broad away on the beam, and right in the track of the sun. It looks something like a big houseboat, or a hay-stack."

The Mate stared in the direction indicated, and saw the thing which puzzled the boy, and immediately the tiredness went out of his eyes and face.

"Pass me the glasses off the skylight, Toby," he commanded, and the youth obeyed.

After the Mate had examined the strange object through his binoculars for, maybe, a minute, he passed them to Toby, telling him to take a "squint," and say what he made of it.

"Looks like an old powder-hulk, Sir," exclaimed the lad, after awhile, and to this description the Mate nodded agreement.

Later, when the sun had risen somewhat, they were able to study the derelict with more exactness. She appeared to be a vessel of an exceedingly old type, mastless, and upon the hull of which had been built a roof-like superstructure; the use of which they could not determine. She was lying just within the borders of one of the weed-banks, and all her side was splotched with a greenish growth.

It was her position, within the borders of the weed, that suggested to the puzzled Mate, how so strange and unseaworthy looking a craft had come so far abroad into the greatness of the ocean. For, suddenly, it occurred to him that she was neither more nor less than a derelict from the vast Sargasso Sea—a vessel that had, possibly, been lost to the world, scores and scores of years gone, perhaps hundreds. The suggestion touched the Mate's thoughts with solemnity, and he fell to examining the ancient hulk with an even greater interest, and pondering on all the lonesome and awful years that must have passed over her, as she had lain desolate and forgotten in that grim cemetery of the ocean.

Through all that day, the derelict was an object of the most intense interest to those aboard the Tarawak, every glass in the ship being brought into use to examine her. Yet, though within no more than some six or seven miles of her, the Captain refused to listen to the Mate's suggestions that they should put a boat into the water, and pay the stranger a visit; for he was a cautious man, and the glass warned him that a sudden change might be expected in the weather; so that he would have no one leave the ship on any unnecessary business. But, for all that he had caution, curiosity was by no means lacking in him, and his telescope, at intervals, was turned on the ancient hulk through all the day.

Then, it would be about six bells in the second dog watch, a sail was sighted astern, coming up steadily but slowly. By eight bells they were able to make out that a small barque was bringing the wind with her; her yards squared, and every stitch set. Yet the night had advanced apace, and it was nigh to eleven o'clock before the wind reached those aboard the Tarawak. When at last it arrived, there was a slight rustling and quaking of canvas, and odd creaks here and there in the darkness amid the gear, as each portion of the running and standing rigging took up the strain.

Beneath the bows, and alongside, there came gentle rippling noises, as the vessel gathered way; and so, for the better part of the next hour, they slid through the water at something less than a couple of knots in the sixty minutes.

To starboard of them, they could see the red light of the little barque, which had brought up the wind with her, and was now forging slowly ahead, being better able evidently than the big, heavy Tarawak to take advantage of so slight a breeze.

About a quarter to twelve, just after the relieving watch had been roused, lights were observed to be moving to and fro upon the small barque, and by midnight it was palpable that, through some cause or other, she was dropping astern.

When the Mate arrived on deck to relieve the Second, the latter officer informed him of the possibility that something unusual had occurred aboard the barque, telling of the lights about her decks, and how that, in the last quarter of an hour, she had begun to drop astern.

On hearing the Second Mate's account, the First sent one of the 'prentices for his night-glasses, and, when they were brought, studied the other vessel intently, that is, so well as he was able through the darkness; for, even through the night-glasses, she showed only as a vague shape, surmounted by the three dim towers of her masts and sails.

Suddenly, the Mate gave out a sharp exclamation; for, beyond the barque, there was something else shown dimly in the field of vision. He studied it with great intentness, ignoring for the instant, the Second's queries as to what it was that had caused him to exclaim.

All at once, he said, with a little note of excitement in his voice:—

"The derelict! The barque's run into the weed around that old hooker!"

The Second Mate gave a mutter of surprised assent, and slapped the rail.

"That's it!" he said. "That's why we're passing her. And that explains the lights. If they're not fast in the weed, they've probably run slap into the blessed derelict!"

"One thing," said the Mate, lowering his glasses, and beginning to fumble for his pipe, "she won't have had enough way on her to do much damage."

The Second Mate, who was still peering through his binoculars, murmured an absent agreement, and continued to peer. The Mate, for his part, filled and lit his pipe, remarking meanwhile to the unhearing Second, that the light breeze was dropping.

Abruptly, the Second Mate called his superior's attention, and in the same instant, so it seemed, the failing wind died entirely away, the sails settling down into runkles, with little rustles and flutters of sagging canvas.

"What's up?" asked the Mate, and raised his glasses.

"There's something queer going on over yonder," said the Second. "Look at the lights moving about, and—Did you see that?"

The last portion of his remark came out swiftly, with a sharp accentuation of the last word.

"What?" asked the Mate, staring hard.

"They're shooting," replied the Second. "Look! There again!"

"Rubbish!" said the Mate, a mixture of unbelief and doubt in his voice.

With the falling of the wind, there had come a great silence upon the sea. And, abruptly, from far across the water, sounded the distant, dullish thud of a gun, followed almost instantly by several minute, but sharply defined, reports, like the cracking of a whip out in the darkness.

"Jove!" cried the Mate, "I believe you're right." He paused and stared. "There!" he said. "I saw the flashes then. They're firing from the poop, I believe.... I must call the Old Man."

He turned and ran hastily down into the saloon, knocked on the door of the Captain's cabin, and entered. He turned up the lamp, and, shaking his superior into wakefulness, told him of the thing he believed to be happening aboard the barque:—

"It's mutiny, Sir; they're shooting from the poop. We ought to do something—" The Mate said many things, breathlessly; for he was a young man; but the Captain stopped him, with a quietly lifted hand.

"I'll be up with you in a minute, Mr. Johnson," he said, and the Mate took the hint, and ran up on deck.

Before the minute had passed, the Skipper was on the poop, and staring through his night-glasses at the barque and the derelict. Yet now, aboard of the barque, the lights had vanished, and there showed no more the flashes of discharging weapons—only there remained the dull, steady red glow of the port sidelight; and, behind it, the night-glasses showed the shadowy outline of the vessel.

The Captain put questions to the Mates, asking for further details.

"It all stopped while the Mate was calling you, Sir," explained the Second. "We could hear the shots quite plainly."

"They seemed to be using a gun as well as their revolvers," interjected the Mate, without ceasing to stare into the darkness.

For awhile the three of them continued to discuss the matter, whilst down on the maindeck the two watches clustered along the starboard rail, and a low hum of talk rose, fore and aft.

Presently, the Captain and the Mates came to a decision. If there had been a mutiny, it had been brought to its conclusion, whatever that conclusion might be, and no interference from those aboard the Tarawak, at that period, would be likely to do good. They were utterly in the dark—in more ways than one—and, for all they knew, there might not even have been any mutiny. If there had been a mutiny, and the mutineers had won, then they had done their worst; whilst if the officers had won well and good. They had managed to do so without help. Of course, if the Tarawak had been a man-of-war with a large crew, capable of mastering any situation, it would have been a simple matter to send a powerful, armed boat's crew to inquire; but as she was merely a merchant vessel, under-manned, as is the modern fashion, they must go warily. They would wait for the morning, and signal. In a couple of hours it would be light. Then they would be guided by circumstances.

The Mate walked to the break of the poop, and sang out to the men:—

"Now then, my lads, you'd better turn in, the watch below, and have a sleep; we may be wanting you by five bells."

There was a muttered chorus of "i, i, Sir," and some of the men began to go forrard to the fo'cas'le; but others of the watch below remained, their curiosity overmastering their desire for sleep.

On the poop, the three officers leaned over the starboard rail, chatting in a desultory fashion, as they waited for the dawn. At some little distance hovered Duthie, who, as eldest 'prentice just out of his time, had been given the post of acting Third Mate.

Presently, the sky to starboard began to lighten with the solemn coming of the dawn. The light grew and strengthened, and the eyes of those in the Tarawak scanned with growing intentness that portion of the horizon where showed the red and dwindling glow of the barque's sidelight.

Then, it was in that moment when all the world is full of the silence of the dawn, something passed over the quiet sea, coming out of the East—a very faint, long-drawn-out, screaming, piping noise. It might almost have been the cry of a little wind wandering out of the dawn across the sea—a ghostly, piping skirl, so attenuated and elusive was it; but there was in it a weird, almost threatening note, that told the three on the poop it was no wind that made so dree and inhuman a sound.

The noise ceased, dying out in an indefinite, mosquito-like shrilling, far and vague and minutely shrill. And so came the silence again.

"I heard that, last night, when they were shooting," said the Second Mate, speaking very slowly, and looking first at the Skipper and then at the Mate. "It was when you were below, calling the Captain," he added.

"Ssh!" said the Mate, and held up a warning hand; but though they listened, there came no further sound; and so they fell to disjointed questionings, and guessed their answers, as puzzled men will. And ever and anon, they examined the barque through their glasses; but without discovering anything of note, save that, when the light grew stronger, they perceived that her jibboom had struck through the superstructure of the derelict, tearing a considerable gap therein.

Presently, when the day had sufficiently advanced, the Mate sung out to the Third, to take a couple of the 'prentices, and pass up the signal flags and the code book. This was done, and a "hoist" made; but those in the barque took not the slightest heed; so that finally the Captain bade them make up the flags and return them to the locker.

After that, he went down to consult the glass, and when he reappeared, he and the Mates had a short discussion, after which, orders were given to hoist out the starboard life-boat. This, in the course of half an hour, they managed; and, after that, six of the men and two of the 'prentices were ordered into her.

Then half a dozen rifles were passed down, with ammunition, and the same number of cutlasses. These were all apportioned among the men, much to the disgust of the two apprentices, who were aggrieved that they should be passed over; but their feelings altered when the Mate descended into the boat, and handed them each a loaded revolver, warning them, however, to play no "monkey tricks" with the weapons.

Just as the boat was about to push off, Duthie, the eldest 'prentice, came scrambling down the side ladder, and jumped for the after thwart. He landed, and sat down, laying the rifle which he had brought, in the stern; and, after that, the boat put off for the barque.

There were now ten in the boat, and all well armed, so that the Mate had a certain feeling of comfort that he would be able to meet any situation that was likely to arise.

After nearly an hour's hard pulling, the heavy boat had been brought within some two hundred yards of the barque, and the Mate sung out to the men to lie on their oars for a minute. Then he stood up and shouted to the people on the barque; but though he repeated his cry of "Ship ahoy!" several times, there came no reply.

He sat down, and motioned to the men to give way again, and so brought the boat nearer the barque by another hundred yards. Here, he hailed again; but still receiving no reply, he stooped for his binoculars, and peered for awhile through them at the two vessels—the ancient derelict, and the modern sailing-vessel.

The latter had driven clean in over the weed, her stern being perhaps some two score yards from the edge of the bank. Her jibboom, as I have already mentioned, had pierced the green-blotched superstructure of the derelict, so that her cutwater had come very close to the grass-grown side of the hulk.

That the derelict was indeed a very ancient vessel, it was now easy to see; for at this distance the Mate could distinguish which was hull, and which superstructure. Her stern rose up to a height considerably above her bows, and possessed galleries, coming round the counter. In the window frames some of the glass still remained; but others were securely shuttered, and some missing, frames and all, leaving dark holes in the stern. And everywhere grew the dank, green growth, giving to the beholder a queer sense of repulsion. Indeed, there was that about the whole of the ancient craft, that repelled in a curious way—something elusive—a remoteness from humanity, that was vaguely abominable.

The Mate put down his binoculars, and drew his revolver, and, at the action, each one in the boat gave an instinctive glance to his own weapon. Then he sung out to them to give-way, and steered straight for the weed. The boat struck it, with something of a sog; and, after that, they advanced slowly, yard by yard, only with considerable labour.

They reached the counter of the barque, and the Mate held out his hand for an oar. This, he leaned up against the side of the vessel, and a moment later was swarming quickly up it. He grasped the rail, and swung himself aboard; then, after a swift glance fore and aft, gripped the blade of the oar, to steady it, and bade the rest follow as quickly as possible, which they did, the last man bringing up the painter with him, and making it fast to a cleat.

Then commenced a rapid search through the ship. In several places about the maindeck they found broken lamps, and aft on the poop, a shot-gun, three revolvers, and several capstan-bars lying about the poop-deck. But though they pried into every possible corner, lifting the hatches, and examining the lazarette, not a human creature was to be found—the barque was absolutely deserted.

After the first rapid search, the Mate called his men together; for there was an uncomfortable sense of danger in the air, and he felt that it would be better not to straggle. Then, he led the way forrard, and went up on to the t'gallant fo'cas'le head. Here, finding the port sidelight still burning, he bent over the screen, as it were mechanically, lifted the lamp, opened it, and blew out the flame; then replaced the affair on its socket.

After that, he climbed into the bows, and out along the jibboom, beckoning to the others to follow, which they did, no man saying a word, and all holding their weapons handily; for each felt the oppressiveness of the Incomprehensible about them.

The Mate reached the hole in the great superstructure, and passed inside, the rest following. Here they found themselves in what looked something like a great, gloomy barracks, the floor of which was the deck of the ancient craft. The superstructure, as seen from the inside, was a very wonderful piece of work, being beautifully shored and fixed; so that at one time it must have possessed immense strength; though now it was all rotted, and showed many a gape and rip. In one place, near the centre, or midships part, was a sort of platform, high up, which the Mate conjectured might have been used as a "look-out"; though the reason for the prodigious superstructure itself, he could not imagine.

Having searched the decks of this craft, he was preparing to go below, when, suddenly, Duthie caught him by the sleeve, and whispered to him, tensely, to listen. He did so, and heard the thing that had attracted the attention of the youth—it was a low, continuous shrill whining that was rising from out of the dark hull beneath their feet, and, abruptly, the Mate was aware that there was an intensely disagreeable animal-like smell in the air. He had noticed it, in a subconscious fashion, when entering through the broken superstructure; but now, suddenly, he was aware of it.

Then, as he stood there hesitating, the whining noise rose all at once into a piping, screaming squeal, that filled all the space in which they were inclosed, with an awful, inhuman and threatening clamour. The Mate turned and shouted at the top of his voice to the rest, to retreat to the barque, and he, himself, after a further quick nervous glance round, hurried towards the place where the end of the barque's jibboom protruded in across the decks.

He waited, with strained impatience, glancing ever behind him, until all were off the derelict, and then sprang swiftly on to the spar that was their bridge to the other vessel. Even as he did so, the squealing died away into a tiny shrilling, twittering sound, that made him glance back; for the suddenness of the quiet was as effective as though it had been a loud noise. What he saw, seemed to him in that first instant so incredible and monstrous, that he was almost too shaken to cry out. Then he raised his voice in a shout of warning to the men, and a frenzy of haste shook him in every fibre, as he scrambled back to the barque, shouting ever to the men to get into the boat. For in that backward glance, he had seen the whole decks of the derelict a-move with living things—giant rats, thousands and tens of thousands of them; and so in a flash had come to an understanding of the disappearance of the crew of the barque.

He had reached the fo'cas'le head now, and was running for the steps, and behind him, making all the long slanting length of the jibboom black, were the rats, racing after him. He made one leap to the maindeck, and ran. Behind, sounded a queer, multitudinous pattering noise, swiftly surging upon him. He reached the poop steps, and as he sprang up them, felt a savage bite in his left calf. He was on the poop deck now, and running with a stagger. A score of great rats leapt around him, and half a dozen hung grimly to his back, whilst the one that had gripped his calf, flogged madly from side to side as he raced on. He reached the rail, gripped it, and vaulted clean over and down into the weed.

The rest were already in the boat, and strong hands and arms hove him aboard, whilst the others of the crew sweated in getting their little craft round from the ship. The rats still clung to the Mate; but a few blows with a cutlass eased him of his murderous burden. Above them, making the rails and half-round of the poop black and alive, raced thousands of rats.

The boat was now about an oar's length from the barque, and, suddenly, Duthie screamed out that they were coming. In the same instant, nearly a hundred of the largest rats launched themselves at the boat. Most fell short, into the weed; but over a score reached the boat, and sprang savagely at the men, and there was a minute's hard slashing and smiting, before the brutes were destroyed.

Once more the men resumed their task of urging their way through the weed, and so in a minute or two, had come to within some fathoms of the edge, working desperately. Then a fresh terror broke upon them. Those rats which had missed their leap, were now all about the boat, and leaping in from the weed, running up the oars, and scrambling in over the sides, and, as each one got inboard, straight for one of the crew it went; so that they were all bitten and be-bled in a score of places.

There ensued a short but desperate fight, and then, when the last of the beasts had been hacked to death, the men lay once more to the task of heaving the boat clear of the weed.

A minute passed, and they had come almost to the edge, when Duthie cried out, to look; and at that, all turned to stare at the barque, and perceived the thing that had caused the 'prentice to cry out; for the rats were leaping down into the weed in black multitudes, making the great weed-fronds quiver, as they hurled themselves in the direction of the boat. In an incredibly short space of time, all the weed between the boat and the barque, was alive with the little monsters, coming at breakneck speed.

The Mate let out a shout, and, snatching an oar from one of the men, leapt into the stern of the boat, and commenced to thrash the weed with it, whilst the rest laboured infernally to pluck the boat forth into the open sea. Yet, despite their mad efforts, and the death-dealing blows of the Mate's great fourteen-foot oar, the black, living mass were all about the boat, and scrambling aboard in scores, before she was free of the weed. As the boat shot into the clear water, the Mate gave out a great curse, and, dropping his oar, began to pluck the brutes from his body with his bare hands, casting them into the sea. Yet, fast almost as he freed himself, others sprang upon him, so that in another minute he was like to have been pulled down, for the boat was alive and swarming with the pests, but that some of the men got to work with their cutlasses, and literally slashed the brutes to pieces, sometimes killing several with a single blow. And thus, in a while, the boat was freed once more; though it was a sorely wounded and frightened lot of men that manned her.

The Mate himself took an oar, as did all those who were able. And so they rowed slowly and painfully away from that hateful derelict, whose crew of monsters even then made the weed all of a-heave with hideous life.

From the Tarawak came urgent signals for them to haste; by which the Mate knew that the storm, which the Captain had feared, must be coming down upon the ship, and so he spurred each one to greater endeavour, until, at last, they were under the shadow of their own vessel, with very thankful hearts, and bodies, bleeding, tired and faint.

Slowly and painfully, the boat's crew scrambled up the side-ladder, and the boat was hoisted aboard; but they had no time then to tell their tale; for the storm was upon them.

It came half an hour later, sweeping down in a cloud of white fury from the Eastward, and blotting out all vestiges of the mysterious derelict and the little barque which had proved her victim. And after that, for a weary day and night, they battled with the storm. When it passed, nothing was to be seen, either of the two vessels or of the weed which had studded the sea before the storm; for they had been blown many a score of leagues to the Westward of the spot, and so had no further chance—nor, I ween, inclination—to investigate further the mystery of that strange old derelict of a past time, and her habitants of rats.

Yet, many a time, and in many fo'cas'les has this story been told; and many a conjecture has been passed as to how came that ancient craft abroad there in the ocean. Some have suggested—as indeed I have made bold to put forth as fact—that she must have drifted out of the lonesome Sargasso Sea. And, in truth, I cannot but think this the most reasonable supposition. Yet, of the rats that evidently dwelt in her, I have no reasonable explanation to offer.

Whether they were true ship's rats, or a species that is to be found in the weed-haunted plains and islets of the Sargasso Sea, I cannot say. It may be that they are the descendants of rats that lived in ships long centuries lost in the Weed Sea, and which have learned to live among the weed, forming new characteristics, and developing fresh powers and instincts. Yet, I cannot say; for I speak entirely without authority, and do but tell this story as it is told in the fo'cas'le of many an old-time sailing ship—that dark, brine-tainted place where the young men learn somewhat of the mysteries of the all mysterious sea.

FANTASTIC TALES

The Derelict

William Hope Hodgson

"It's the material," said the old ship's doctor—"the material plus the conditions—and, maybe," he added slowly, "a third factor—yes, a third factor; but there, there—" He broke off his half-meditative sentence and began to charge his pipe.

"Go on, doctor," we said encouragingly, and with more than a little expectancy. We were in the smoke-room of the Sand-a-lea, running across the North Atlantic; and the doctor was a character. He concluded the charging of his pipe, and lit it; then settled himself, and began to express himself more fully.

"The material," he said with conviction, "is inevitably the medium of expression of the life-force—the fulcrum, as it were; lacking which it is unable to exert itself, or, indeed, to express itself in any form or fashion that would be intelligible or evident to us. So potent is the share of the material in the production of that thing which we name life, and so eager the life-force to express itself, that I am convinced it would, if given the right conditions, make itself manifest even through so hopeless seeming a medium as a simple block of sawn wood; for I tell you, gentlemen, the life-force is both as fiercely urgent and as indiscriminate as fire—the destructor; yet which some are now growing to consider the very essence of life rampant. There is a quaint seeming paradox there," he concluded, nodding his old grey head.

"Yes, doctor," I said. "In brief, your argument is that life is a thing, state, fact, or element, call it what you like, which requires the material through which to manifest itself, and that given the material, plus the conditions, the result is life. In other words, that life is an evolved product, manifested through matter and bred of conditions—eh?"

"As we understand the word," said the old doctor. "Though, mind you, there may be a third factor. But, in my heart, I believe that it is a matter of chemistry—conditions and a suitable medium; but given the conditions, the brute is so almighty that it will seize upon anything through which to manifest itself. It is a force generated by conditions; but, nevertheless, this does not bring us one iota nearer to its explanation, any more than to the explanation of electricity or fire. They are, all three, of the outer forces—monsters of the void. Nothing we can do will create any one of them, our power is merely to be able, by providing the conditions, to make each one of them manifest to our physical senses. Am I clear?"

"Yes, doctor, in a way, you are," I said. "But I don't agree with you, though I think I understand you. Electricity and fire are both what I might call natural things, but life is an abstract something—a kind of all-permeating wakefulness. Oh, I can't explain it! Who could? But it s spiritual, not just a thing bred out of

a condition, like fire, as you say, or electricity. It's a horrible thought of yours.
Life's a kind of spiritual mystery —"

"Easy, my boy!" said the old doctor, laughing gently to himself. "Or else I
may be asking you to demonstrate the spiritual mystery of life of the limpet,
or the crab, shall we say." He grinned at me with ineffable perverseness.
"Anyway," he continued, "as I suppose you've all guessed, I've a yarn to tell
you in support of my impression that life is no more a mystery or a miracle
than fire or electricity. But, please to remember, gentlemen, that because
we've succeeded in naming and making good use of these two forces,
they're just as much mysteries, fundamentally as ever. And, anyway, the
thing I'm going to tell you won't explain the mystery of life, but only give you
one of my pegs on which I hang my feeling that life is as I have said, a force
made manifest through conditions—that is to say, natural chemistry—and
that it can take for its purpose and need, the most incredible and unlikely
matter; for without matter it cannot come into existence—it cannot become
manifest—"

"I don't agree with you, doctor," I interrupted. "Your theory would destroy
all belief in life after death. It would —"

"Hush, sonny," said the old man, with a quiet little smile of comprehension.
"Hark to what I've to say first; and, anyway, what objection have you to material
life after death? And if you object to a material framework, I would still have
you remember that I am speaking of life, as we understand the word in this
our life. Now do be a quiet lad, or I'll never be done:

"It was when I was a young man, and that is a good many years ago,
gentlemen. I had passed my examinations, but was so run down with overwork
that it was decided that I had better take a trip to sea. I was by no means well
off, and very glad in the end to secure a nominal post as doctor in the sailing
passenger clipper running out to China.

"The name of the ship was the Bheospse, and soon after I had got all my
gear aboard she cast off, and we dropped down the Thames, and next day
were well away out in the Channel.

"The captain's name was Gannington, a very decent man, though quite
illiterate. The first mate, Mr. Berlies, was a quiet, sternish, reserved man,
very well-read. The second mate, Mr. Selvern, was, perhaps, by birth and
upbringing, the most socially cultured of the three, but he lacked the stamina
and indomitable pluck of the two others. He was more of a sensitive, and
emotionally and even mentally, the most alert man of the three.

"On our way out, we called at Madagascar, where we landed some of
our passengers; then we ran eastward, meaning to call at North-West

Cape; but about a hundred degrees east we encountered very dreadful weather, which carried away all our sails, and sprung the jibboom and foret'gallantmast.

"The storm carried us northward for several hundred miles, and when it dropped us finally, we found ourselves in a very bad state. The ship had been strained, and had taken some three feet of water through her seams; the maintopmast had been sprung, in addition to the jibboom and foret'gallantmast, two of our boats had gone, as also one of the pigstys, with three fine pigs, these latter having been washed overboard but some half-hour before the wind began to ease, which it did very quickly, though a very ugly sea ran for some hours after.

"The wind left us just before dark, and when morning came it brought splendid weather—a calm, mildly undulating sea, and a brilliant sun, with no wind. It showed us also that we were not alone, for about two miles away to the westward was another vessel, which Mr. Selvern, the second mate, pointed out to me.

"'That's a pretty rum-looking, packet, doctor,' he said, and handed me his glass.

"I looked through it at the other vessel, and saw what he meant; at least, I thought I did.

"'Yes, Mr. Selvern,' I said. 'She's got a pretty old-fashioned look about her.'

"He laughed at me in his pleasant way.

"'It's easy to see you're not a sailor, doctor,' he remarked. 'There's a dozen rum things about her. She's a derelict, and has been floating round, by the look of her, for many a score of years. Look at the shape of her counter, and the bows and cutwater. She's as old as the hills, as you might say, and ought to have gone down to Davy Jones a good while ago. Look at the growths on her, and the thickness of her standing rigging; that's all salt encrustations, I fancy, if you notice the white colour. She's been a small barque; but, don't you see, she's not a yard left aloft. They've all dropped out of the slings; everything rotted away; wonder the standing rigging hasn't gone, too. I wish the old man would let us take the boat and have a look at her. She'd be well worth it.'

"'There seemed little chance, however, of this, for all hands were turned to and kept hard at it all day long repairing the damage to the masts and gear; and this took a long while, as you may think. Part of the time I gave a hand heaving on one of the deck capstans, for the exercise was good for my liver. Old Captain Gannington approved, and I persuaded him to come along and try some of the same medicine, which he did; and we got very chummy over the job.

"We got talking about the derelict, and he remarked how lucky we were not to have run full tilt on to her in the darkness, for she lay right away to leeward of us, according, to the way that we had been drifting in the storm. He also was of the opinion that she had a strange look about her, and that she was pretty old; but on this latter point he plainly had far less knowledge than the second mate, for he was, as I have said, an illiterate man, and knew nothing of seacraft beyond what experience had taught him. He lacked the book knowledge which the second mate had of vessels previous to his day, which it appeared the derelict was.

"'She's an old 'un, doctor,' was the extent of observations in this direction.

"Yet, when I mentioned to him that it would be interesting to go aboard and give her a bit of an overhaul, he nodded his head as if the idea had been already in his mind and accorded with his own inclinations.

"'When the work's over, doctor,' he said. 'Can't spare the men now, ye know. Got to get all shipshape an' ready as smart as we can. But, we'll take my gig, an' go off in the second dog-watch. The glass is steady, an' it'll be a bit of gam for us.'

"That evening, after tea, the captain gave orders to clear the gig and get her overboard. The second mate was to come with us, and the skipper gave him word to see that two or three lamps were put into the boat, as it would soon fall dark. A little later we were pulling across the calmness of the sea with a crew of six at the oars, and making very good speed of it.

"Now, gentlemen, I have detailed to you with great exactness all the facts, both big and little, so that you can follow step by step each incident in this extraordinary affair, and I want you now to pay the closest attention. I was sitting in the stern-sheets with the second mate and the captain, who was steering, and as we drew nearer and nearer to the stranger I studied her with an ever-growing attention, as, indeed, did Captain Gannington and the second mate. She was, as you know, to the west-ward of us, and the sunset was making a great flame of red light to the back of her, so that she showed a little blurred and indistinct by reason of the halation of the light, which almost defeated the eye in any attempt to see her rotting spars and standing rigging, submerged, as they were, in the fiery glory of the sunset.

"It was because of this effect of the sunset that we had come quite close, comparatively, to the derelict before we saw that she was all surrounded by a sort of curious scum, the colour of which was difficult to decide upon by reason of the red light that was in the atmosphere, but which afterwards we discovered to be brown. This scum spread all about the old vessel for many hundreds of yards in a huge, irregular patch, a great stretch of which reached out to the eastward, upon the starboard side of the boat some score or so fathoms away.

"'Queer stuff,' said Captain Gannington, leaning to the side and looking over. 'Something in the cargo as 'as gone rotten, and worked out through 'er seams.'

"'Look at her bows and stern,' said the second mate. 'Just look at the growth on her!'

"There were, as he said, great clumpings of strange-looking sea-fungi under the bows and the short counter astern. From the stump of her jibboom and her cutwater great beards of rime and marine growths hung downward into the scum that held her in. Her blank starboard side was presented to us—all a dead, dirtyish white, streaked and mottled vaguely with dull masses of heavier colour.

"'There's a steam or haze rising off her,' said the second mate, speaking again. 'You can see it against the light. It keeps coming and going. Look!'

"I saw then what he meant—a faint haze or steam, either suspended above the old vessel or rising from her. And Captain Gannington saw it also.

"'Spontaneous combustion!' he exclaimed. 'We'll 'ave to watch when we lift the 'atches, 'nless it's some poor devil that's got aboard of 'er. But that ain't likely.'

"We were now within a couple of hundred yards of the old derelict, and had entered into the brown scum. As it poured off the lifted oars I heard one of the men mutter to himself, 'Dam' treacle!' And, indeed, it was not something unlike it. As the boat continued to forge nearer and nearer to the old ship the scum grew thicker and thicker, so that, at last, it perceptibly slowed us.

"'Give way, lads! Put some beef to it!' sang out Captain Gannington. And thereafter there was no sound except the panting of the men and the faint, reiterated suck, suck of the sullen brown scum upon the oars as the boat was forced ahead. As we went, I was conscious of a peculiar smell in the evening air, and whilst I had no doubt that the puddling of the scum by the oars made it rise, I could give no name to it; yet, in a way, it was vaguely familiar.

"We were now very close to the old vessel, and presently she was high about us against the dying light. The captain called out then to 'in with the bow oars and stand by with the boat-hook,' which was done.

"'Aboard there! Ahoy! Aboard there! Ahoy!' shouted Captain Gannington; but there came no answer, only the dull sound his voice going lost into the open sea, each time he sung out.

"'Ahoy! Aboard there! Ahoy!' he shouted time after time, but there was only the weary silence of the old hulk that answered us; and, somehow as he shouted, the while that I stared up half expectantly at her, a queer little sense of oppression, that amounted almost to nervousness, came upon me. It passed, but I remember how I was suddenly aware that it was growing dark. Darkness comes fairly rapidly in the tropics, though not so quickly as many fiction writers seem to think; but it was not that the coming dusk had perceptibly deepened in that brief time of only a few moments, but rather that my nerves had made me suddenly a little hypersensitive. I mention my state particularly, for I am not a nervy man normally, and my abrupt touch of nerves is significant, in the light of what happened.

"'There's no one on board there!' said Captain Gannington. 'Give way, men!' For the boat's crew had instinctively rested on their oars, as the captain hailed the old craft. The men gave way again; and then the second mate called out excitedly, 'Why, look there, there's our pigsty! See, it's got Bheospse painted on the end. It's drifted down here and the scum's caught it. What a blessed wonder!'

"It was, as he had said, our pigsty that had been washed overboard in the storm; and most extraordinary to come across it there.

"'We'll tow it off with us, when we go,' said the captain, and shouted to the crew to get down to their oars; for they were hardly moving the boat, because the scum was so thick, close in around the old ship, that it literally clogged the boat from moving. I remember that it struck me, in a half-conscious sort of way, as curious that the pigsty, containing our three dead pigs, had managed to drift in so far unaided, whilst we could scarcely manage to force the boat in, now that we had come right into the scum. But the thought passed from my mind, for so many things happened within the next few minutes.

"The men managed to bring the boat in alongside, within a couple of feet of the derelict, and the man with the boat-hook hooked on.

"''Ave ye got 'old there, forrard?' asked Captain Gannington.

"'Yessir!' said the bowman; and as he spoke there came a queer noise of tearing.

"'What's that?' asked the Captain.

"'It's tore, sir. Tore clean away!' said the man, and his tone showed that he had received something of a shock.

"'Get a hold again, then!' said Captain Gannington irritably. 'You don't s'pose this packet was built yesterday! Shove the hook into the main chains' The man did so gingerly, as you might say, for it seemed to me, in the growing dusk, that he put no strain on to the hook, though, of course there was no need—you see the boat could not go very far of herself, in the stuff in which she was imbedded. I remember thinking this, also as I looked up at the bulging side of the old vessel. Then I heard Captain Gannington's voice:

"'Lord, but she s old! An' what a colour, doctor! She don't half want paint, do she? Now then, somebody, one of them oars.' An oar was passed to him, and he leant it up against the ancient, bulging side; then he paused, and called to the second mate to light a couple of the lamps, and stand by to pass them up, for darkness had settled down now upon the sea.

"The second mate lit two of the lamps, and told one of the men to light a third, and keep it handy in the boat; then he stepped across, with a lamp in each hand, to where Captain Gannington stood by the oar against the side of the ship.

"'Now, my lad,' said the captain to the man who had pulled stroke, 'up with you, an' we'll pass ye up the lamps.'

"The man jumped to obey, caught the oar, and put his weight upon it; and as he did so, something seemed to give way a little.

"'Look!' cried out the second mate, and pointed, lamp in hand. 'It's sunk in!'

"This was true. The oar had made quite an indentation into the bulging, somewhat slimy side of the old vessel.

"'Mould, I reckon,' said Captain Gannington, bending towards the derelict to look. Then to the man:

"'Up you go, my lad, and be smart! Don't stand there waitin'!'

"At that the man, who had paused a moment as he felt the oar give beneath his weight began to shin' up, and in a few seconds he was aboard, and leant out over the rail for the lamps. These were passed up to him, and the captain called to him to steady the oar. Then Captain Gannington went, calling to me to follow, and after me the second mate.

"As the captain put his face over the rail, he gave a cry of astonishment.

"'Mould, by gum! Mould—tons of it. Good lord!'

"As I heard him shout that I scrambled the more eagerly after him, and in a moment or two I was able to see what he meant—everywhere that the light from the two lamps struck there was nothing but smooth great masses and surfaces of a dirty white coloured mould. I climbed over the rail, with the second mate close behind, and stood upon the mould covered decks. There might have been no planking beneath the mould, for all that our feet could feel. It gave under our tread with a spongy, puddingy feel. It covered the deck furniture of the old ship, so that the shape of each article and fitment was often no more than suggested through it.

"Captain Gannington snatched a lamp from the man and the second mate reached for the other. They held the lamps high, and we all stared. It was most extraordinary, and somehow most abominable. I can think of no other word, gentlemen, that so much describes the predominant feeling that affected me at the moment.

"'Good lord!' said Captain Gannington several times. 'Good lord!' But neither the second mate nor the man said anything, and, for my part I just stared, and at the same time began to smell a little at the air, for there was a vague odour of something half familiar, that somehow brought to me a sense of half-known fright.

"I turned this way and that, staring, as I have said. Here and there the mould was so heavy as to entirely disguise what lay beneath, converting the deck-fittings into indistinguishable mounds of mould all dirty-white and blotched and veined with irregular, dull, purplish markings.

"There was a strange thing about the mould which Captain Gannington drew attention to—it was that our feet did not crush into it and break the surface, as might have been expected, but merely indented it.

"'Never seen nothin' like it before! Never!' said the captain after having stooped with his lamp to examine the mould under our feet. He stamped with his heel, and the mould gave out a dull, puddingy sound. He stooped again, with a quick movement, and stared, holding the lamp close to the deck. 'Blest if it ain't a reg'lar skin to it!'

"The second mate and the man and I all stooped and looked at it. The second mate progged it with his forefinger, and I remember I rapped it several times with my knuckles, listening to the dead sound it gave out, and noticing the close, firm texture of the mould.

"'Dough!' the second mate. 'It's just like blessed dough! Pouf!' He stood up with a quick movement. 'I could fancy it stinks a bit,' he said.

"As he said this I knew, suddenly, what the familiar thing was in the vague odour that hung about us—it was that the smell had something animal-like in it; something of the same smell, only heavier, that you would smell in any place that is infested with mice. I began to look about with a sudden very real uneasiness. There might be vast numbers of hungry rats aboard. They might prove exceedingly dangerous, if in a starving condition; yet, as you will understand, somehow I hesitated to put forward my idea as a reason for caution, it was too fanciful.

"Captain Gannington had begun to go aft along the mould-covered main-deck with the second mate, each of them holding their lamps high up, so as to cast a good light about the vessel. I turned quickly and followed them, the man with me keeping close to my heels, and plainly uneasy. As we went, I became aware that there was a feeling of moisture in the air, and I remembered the slight mist, or smoke, above the hulk, which had made Captain Gannington suggest spontaneous combustion in explanation.

"And always, as we went, there was that vague, animal smell; suddenly I found myself wishing we were well away from the old vessel.

"Abruptly, after a few paces, the captain stopped and pointed at a row of mould-hidden shapes on each side of the maindeck. 'Guns,' he said. 'Been a privateer in the old days, I guess—maybe worse! We'll 'ave a look below, doctor; there may be something worth touchin'. She's older than I thought. Mr. Selvern thinks she's about two hundred years old; but I scarce think it.'

"We continued our way aft, and I remember that I found myself walking as lightly and gingerly as possible, as if I were subconsciously afraid of treading through the rotten, mould-hid decks. I think the others had a touch of the same feeling, from the way that they walked. Occasionally the soft stuff would grip our heels, releasing them with a little sullen suck.

"The captain forged somewhat ahead of the second mate; and I know that the suggestion he had made himself, that perhaps there might be something below worth carrying away, had stimulated his imagination. The second mate was, however, beginning to feel somewhat the same way that I did; at least I have that impression. I think, if it had not been for what I might truly describe as Captain Gannington's sturdy courage, we should all of us have just gone back over the side very soon, for there was most certainly an unwholesome feeling abroad that made one feel queerly lacking in pluck; and you will soon see that this feeling was justified.

"Just as the captain reached the few mould-covered steps leading up on to the short half-poop, I was suddenly aware that the feeling of moisture in the air had grown very much more definite. It was perceptible now, intermittently, as a sort of thin, moist, fog-like vapour, that came and went oddly, and seemed to make the decks a little indistinct to the view, this time and that. Once an odd puff of it beat up suddenly from somewhere, and caught me in the face, carrying a queer, sickly, heavy odour with it that somehow frightened me strangely with a suggestion of a waiting and half-comprehended danger.

"We had followed Captain Gannington up the three mould covered steps, and now went slowly along the raised after-deck. By the mizzenmast Captain Gannington paused, and held his lantern near to it. 'My word, mister,' he said to the second mate, 'it's fair thickened up with mould! Why, I'll g'antee it's close on four foot thick.' He shone the light down to where it met the deck. 'Good lord!' he said. 'Look at the sea-lice on it!' I stepped up, and it was as he had said; the sea-lice were thick upon it, some of them huge, not less than the size of large beetles, and all a clear, colourless shade, like water, except where there were little spots of grey on them.

"'I've never seen the like of them, 'cept on a live cod,' said Captain Gannington, in an extremely puzzled voice. 'My word! But they're whoppers!' Then he passed on; but a few paces farther aft he stopped again, and held his lamp near to the mould-hidden deck.

"'Lord bless me, doctor,' he called out, in a low voice, 'did ye ever see the like of that? Why, it's a foot long, if it's a hinch!'

"I stooped over his shoulder, and saw what he meant; it was a clear, colourless creature about a foot long, and about eight inches high, with a curved back that was extraordinarily narrow. As we stared, all in a group, it gave a queer little flick, and was gone.

"'Jumped!' said the captain. 'Well, if that ain't a giant of all the sea-lice that ever I've seen. I guess it's jumped twenty foot clear.' He straightened his back, and scratched his head a moment, swinging the lantern this way and that with the other hand, and staring about us. 'Wot are they doin' aboard 'ere?' he said. 'You'll see 'em—little things—on fat cod an' such-like. I'm blowed, doctor, if I understand.'

"He held his lamp towards a big mound of the mould that occupied part of the after portion of the low poop-deck, a little foreside of where there came a two-foot high 'break' to a kind of second and loftier poop, that ran away aft to the taffrail. The mound was pretty big, several feet across, and more than a yard high. Captain Gannington walked up to it.

"'I reck'n this's the scuttle,' he remarked, and gave it a heavy kick. The only result was a deep indentation into the huge, whiteish hump of mould, as if he had driven his foot into a mass of some doughy substance. Yet I am not altogether correct in saying that this was the only result, for a certain other thing happened. From the place made by the captain's foot there came a sudden gush of a purplish fluid, accompanied by a peculiar smell, that was, and was not, half familiar. Some of the mould-like substance had stuck to the toe of the captain's boot, and from this likewise there issued a sweat, as it were, of the same colour.

"'Well?' said Captain Gannington, in surprise, and drew back his foot to make another kick at the hump of mould. But he paused at an exclamation from the second mate:

"'Don't sir,' said the second mate.

"I glanced at him, and the light from Captain Gannington's lamp showed me that his face had a bewildered, half-frightened look, as if he were suddenly and unexpectedly half afraid of something, and as if his tongue had given away his sudden fright, without any intention on his part to speak. The captain also turned and stared at him.

"'Why, mister?' he asked, in a somewhat puzzled voice, through which there sounded just the vaguest hint of annoyance. 'We've got to shift this muck, if we're to get below.'

"I looked at the second mate, and it seemed to me that, curiously enough he was listening less to the captain than to some other sound. Suddenly he said, in a queer voice, 'Listen, everybody!'

"Yet we heard nothing, beyond the faint murmur of the men talking together in the boat alongside.

"'I don't, hear nothing,' said Captain Gannington, after a short pause. 'Do you, doctor?'

"'No,' I said.

"'Wot was it you thought you heard?' the captain, turning again to the second mate. But the second mate shook his head in a curious, almost irritable way, as if the captain's question interrupted his listening. Captain Gannington stared a moment at him, then held his lantern up and glanced about him almost uneasily. I know I felt a queer sense of strain. But the light showed nothing beyond the greyish dirty-white of the mould in all directions.

"'Mister Selvern,' said the captain, at last, looking at him, 'don't get fancying, things. Get hold of your bloomin' self. Ye know ye heard nothin'?'

"'I'm quite sure I heard something, sir,' said the second mate. 'I seemed to hear —' He broke off sharply, and appeared to listen with an almost painful intensity.

"'What did it sound like?' I asked.

"'It's all right, doctor,' said Captain Gannington, laughing gently. 'Ye can give him a tonic when we get back. I'm goin' to shift this stuff.' He drew back, and kicked for the second time at the ugly mass which he took to hide the companionway. The result of his kick was startling, for the whole thing wobbled sloppily, like a mound of unhealthy-looking jelly.

"He drew his foot out of it quickly, and took a step backward, staring, and holding his lamp towards it. 'By gum,' he said, and it was plain that he was generally startled, 'the blessed thing's gone soft!'

"The man had run back several steps from the suddenly flaccid mound, and looking horribly frightened. Though of what, I am sure he had not the least idea. The second mate stood where he was, and stared. For my part, I know I had a most hideous uneasiness upon me. The captain continued to hold his light towards the wobbling mound and stare.

"'It's gone squashy all through,' he said. 'There's no scuttle there. There's no bally woodwork inside that lot! Phoo! What a rum smell!'

"He walked round to the after side of the strange mound, to see whether there might be some signs of an opening, into the hull at the back of the great heap of mould-stuff. And then:

"'Listen!' said the second mate again, in the strangest sort of voice.

"Captain Gannington straightened himself upright, and there succeeded a pause of the most intense quietness, in which there was not even the hum of talk from the men alongside in the boat. We all heard it—a kind of dull, soft thud, thud, thud, thud, somewhere in the hull under us, yet so vague as to make me half doubtful I heard it, only that the others did so, too.

"Captain Gannington turned suddenly to where the man stood.

"'Tell them—' he began. But the fellow cried out something, and pointed. There had come a strange intensity into his somewhat unemotional face, so that the captain's glance followed his action instantly. I stared also as you may think. It was the great mound at which the man was pointing. I saw what he meant. From the two gapes made in the mould-like stuff by Captain Gannington's boot, the purple fluid was jetting out in a queerly regular fashion, almost as if it were being forced out by a pump. My word! But I stared! And even as I stared a larger jet squirted out, and splashed as far as the man, spattering his boots and trouser legs.

"The fellow had been pretty nervous before, in a stolid, ignorant sort of way, and his funk had been growing steadily; but at this he simply let out a yell, and turned about to run. He paused an instant, as if a sudden fear of the darkness that held the decks, between him and the boat, had taken him. He snatched at the second mate's lantern, tore it out of his hand, and plunged heavily away over the vile stretch of mould.

"Mr. Selvern, the second mate, said not a word; he was just staring, staring at the strange-smelling twin-streams of dull purple that were jetting out from the wobbling mound. Captain Gannington, however, roared an order to the man to come back, but the man plunged on and on across the mould, his feet seeming to be clogged by the stuff, as if it had grown suddenly soft. He zigzagged as he ran, the lantern swaying, in wild circles as he wrenched his feet free with a constant plop, plop; and I could hear his frightened gasps even from where I stood.

"'Come back with that lamp!' roared the captain again; but still the man took no notice.

"And Captain Gannington was silent an instant, his lips working in a queer, inarticulate fashion, as if he were stunned momentarily by the very violence of his anger at the man's insubordination. And in the silence I heard the sounds again—thud, thud, thud, thud! Quite distinctly now, beating, it seemed suddenly to me, right down under my feet, but deep.

"I stared down at the mould on which I was standing, with a quick, disgusting sense of the terrible all about me; then I looked at the captain, and tried to say something, without appearing frightened. I saw that he had turned again to the mould, and all the anger had gone out of his face. He had his lamp out towards the mould, and was listening. There was another moment of absolute silence, at least, I knew that I was not conscious of any sound at all in all the world, except that extraordinary thud, thud, thud, thud, down somewhere in the huge bulk under us.

"The captain shifted his feet with a sudden, nervous movement, and as he lifted them the mould went plop, plop! He looked quickly at me, trying to smile, as if he were not thinking anything very much about it.

"'What do you make of it, doctor?' he said.

"'I think—' I began. But the second mate interrupted with a single word, his voice pitched a little high, in a tone that made us both stare instantly at him.

"'Look!' he said, and pointed at the mound. The thing was all of a slow quiver. A strange ripple ran outward from it, along the deck, like you will see a ripple run inshore out of a calm sea. It reached a mound a little foreside of us, which I had supposed to be the cabin skylight, and in a moment the second mound sank nearly level with the surrounding decks, quivering floppily in a most extraordinary fashion. A sudden quick tremor took the mould right under the second mate, and he gave out a hoarse little cry, and held his arms out on each side of him, to keep his balance. The tremor in the mould spread, and Captain Gannington swayed, and spread out his feet with a sudden curse of fright. The second mate jumped across to him, and caught him by the wrist.

"'The boat, sir!' he said, saying the very thing that I had lacked the pluck to say. 'For God's sake —'

"But he never finished, for a tremendous hoarse scream cut off his words. They hove themselves round and looked. I could see without turning. The man who had run from us was standing in the waist of the ship, about a fathom from the starboard bulwarks. He was swaying from side to side, and screaming, in a dreadful fashion. He appeared to be trying to lift his feet, and the light from his swaying lantern showed an almost incredible sight. All about him the mould was in active movement. His feet had sunk out of sight. The stuff appeared to be lapping at his legs and abruptly his bare flesh showed. The hideous stuff had rent his trouser-leg away as if it were paper. He gave out a simply sickening scream, and, with a vast effort, wrenched one leg free. It was partly destroyed. The next instant he pitched face downward, and the stuff heaped itself upon him, as if it were actually alive, with a dreadful, severe life. It was simply infernal. The man had gone from sight. Where he had fallen was now a writhing, elongated mound, in constant and horrible increase, as the mould appeared to move towards it in strange ripples from all sides.

"Captain Gannington and the second mate were stone silent, in amazed and incredulous horror, but I had begun to reach towards a grotesque and terrific conclusion, both helped and hindered by my professional training.

"From the men in the boat alongside there was a loud shouting. and I saw two of their faces appear suddenly above the rail. They showed clearly a moment in the light from the lamp which the man had snatched from Mr. Selvern; for, strangely enough, this lamp was standing upright and unharmed on the deck, a little way foreside of that dreadful, elongated, growing mound, that still swayed and writhed with an incredible horror. The lamp rose and fell on the passing ripples of the mould, just—for all the world—as you will see a boat rise and fall on little swells. It is of some interest to me now, psychologically, to remember how that rising and falling lantern brought home to me more than anything the incomprehensible dreadful strangeness of it all.

"The men's faces disappeared with sudden yells, as if they had slipped, or been suddenly hurt; and there was a fresh uproar of shouting from the boat. The men were calling to us to come away—to come away. In the same instant I felt my left boot drawn suddenly and forcibly downward, with a horrible, painful grip. I wrenched it free, with a yell of angry fear. Forrard of us, I saw that the vile surface was all amove, and abruptly I found myself shouting in a queer, frightened voice, 'The boat, captain! The boat, captain!'

"Captain Gannington stared round at me, over his right shoulder, in a peculiar, dull way, that told me he was utterly dazed with bewilderment and the incomprehensibleness of it all. I took a quick, clogged, nervous step towards him, and gripped his arm, and shook it fiercely. 'The boat!' I shouted at him. 'The boat! For God's sake, tell the men to bring the boat aft!'

"Then the mound must have drawn his feet down, for abruptly he bellowed fiercely with terror, his momentary apathy giving place to furious energy. His thickset, vastly muscular body doubled and writhed with his enormous effort, and he struck out madly dropping the lantern. He tore his feet free, something ripping as he did so. The reality and necessity of the situation had come upon him brutishly real, and he was roaring to the men in the boat, 'Bring the boat aft! Bring 'er aft! Bring 'er aft!' The second mate and I were shouting the same thing madly.

"'For God's sake, be smart, lads!' roared the captain, and stooped quickly for his lamp, which still burned. His feet were gripped again, and he hove them out, blaspheming breathlessly, aud leaping a yard high with his effort. Then he made a run for the side, wrenching his feet free at each step. In the same instant the second mate cried out something, and grabbed at the captain.

"'It's got hold of my feet! It's got hold of my feet!' he screamed. His feet, had disappeared up to his boot-tops, and Captain Gannington caught him round the waist with his powerful left arm, gave a mighty heave, and the next instant had him free; but both his boot-soles had gone. For my part, I jumped madly from foot to foot, to avoid the plucking of the mould; and suddenly I made a run for the ship's side. But before I could get there, a queer gape came in the mould between us and the side, at least a couple of feet wide, and how deep I don't know. It closed up in an instant, and all the mould where the cape had been vent into a sort of flurry of horrible ripplings, so that I ran back from it; for I did not dare to put my foot upon it. Then the captain was shouting to me:

"'Aft, doctor! Aft, doctor! This way, doctor! Run!' I saw then that he had passed me, and was up on the after raised portion of the poop. He had the second mate, thrown like a sack, all loose and quiet, over his left shoulder; for Mr. Selvern had fainted, and his long legs flogged limp and helpless against the captain's massive knees as he ran. I saw, with a queer, unconscious noting of minor details, how the torn soles of the second mate's boots flapped and jigged as the captain staggered aft.

"'Boat ahoy! Boat ahoy! Boat ahoy!' shouted the captain; and then I was beside him, shouting also. The men were answering with loud yells of encouragement, and it was plain they were working desperately to force the boat aft through the thick scum about the ship.

"We reached the ancient, mould-hid taffrail, and slewed about breathlessly in the half-darkness to see what was happening. Captain Gannington had left his lantern by the big mound when he picked up the second mate; and as we stood, gasping we discovered suddenly that all the mould between us and the light was full of movement. Yet, the part on which we stood, for about six or eight feet forrard of us, was still firm.

"Every couple of seconds we shouted to the men to hasten, and they kept on calling to us that they would be with us in an instant. And all the time we watched the deck of that dreadful hulk, feeling, for my part, literally sick with mad suspense, and ready to jump overboard into that filthy scum all about us.

"Down somewhere in the huge bulk of the ship there was all the time that extraordinary dull, ponderous thud, thud, thud, thud growing ever louder. I seemed to feel the whole hull of the derelict, beginning to quiver and thrill with each dull beat. And to me, with the grotesque and hideous suspicion of what made that noise, it was at once the most dreadful and incredible sound I have ever heard.

"As we waited desperately for the boat, I scanned incessantly so much of the grey white bulk as the lamp showed. The whole of the decks seemed to be in strange movement. Forrard of the lamp, I could see indistinctly the moundings of the mould swaying and nodding hideously beyond the circle of the brightest rays. Nearer, and full in the glow of the lamp, the mound which should have indicated the skylight, was swelling steadily. There were ugly, purple veinings on it, and as it swelled, it seemed to me that the veinings and mottlings on it were becoming plainer, rising as though embossed upon it, like you will see the veins stand out on the body of a powerful, full-blooded horse. It was most extraordinary. The mound that we had supposed to cover the companionway had sunk flat with the surrounding mould, and I could not see that it jetted out any more of the purplish fluid.

"A quaking movement of the mound began away forrard of the lamp, and came flurrying away aft towards us, and at the sight of that I climbed up on to the spongy-feeling taffrail, and yelled afresh for the boat. The men answered with a shout, which told me they were nearer, but the beastly scum was so thick that it was evidently a fight to move the boat at all. Beside me, Captain Gannington was shaking the second mate furiously, and the man stirred and began to moan. The captain shook him again, 'Wake up! Wake up, mister!' he shouted.

"The second mate staggered out of the captain's arms, and collapsed suddenly, shrieking: 'My feet! Oh, God! My feet!' The captain and I lugged him off the mound, and got him into a sitting position upon the taffrail, where he kept up a continual moaning.

"'Hold 'im, doctor,' said the captain. And whilst I did so, he ran forrard a few yards, and peered down over the starboard quarter rail. 'For God's sake, be smart, lads! Be smart! Be smart!' he shouted down to the men, and they answered him, breathless, from close at hand, yet still too far away for the boat to be any use to us on the instant.

"I was holding the moaning, half-unconscious officer, and staring forrard along the poop decks. The flurrying of the mould was coming aft, slowly and noiselessly. And then, suddenly, I saw something closer:

"'Look out, captain!' I shouted. And even as I shouted, the mould near to him gave a sudden, peculiar slobber. I had seen a ripple stealing towards him through the mould. He gave an enormous, clumsy leap, and landed near to us on the sound part of the mould, but the movement followed him. He turned and faced it, swearing fiercely. All about his feet there came abruptly little gapings, which made horrid sucking noises. 'Come back, captain!' I yelled. 'Come back, quick!' As I shouted, a ripple came at his feet—lipping at them; and he stamped insanely at it, and leaped back, his boot torn half off his foot. He swore madly with pain and anger, and jumped swiftly for the taffrail.

"'Come on, doctor! Over we go!' he called. Then he remembered the filthy scum, and hesitated, and roared out desperately to the men to hurry. I stared down, also.

"'The second mate?' I said.

"'I'll take charge doctor,' said Captain Gannington, and caught hold of Mr. Selvern. As he spoke, I thought I saw something beneath us, outlined against the scum. I leaned out over the stern, and peered. There was something under the port-quarter.

"'There's something down there, captain!' I called, and pointed in the darkness. He stooped far over, and stared.

"'A boat, by gum! A boat!' he yelled, and began to wriggle swiftly along the taffrail, dragging the second mate after him. I followed. 'A boat it is, sure!' he exclaimed a few moments later, and, picking up the second mate clear of the rail, he hove him down into the boat, where he fell with a crash into the bottom.

"'Over ye go, doctor!' he yelled at me, and pulled me bodily off the rail and dropped me after the officer. As he did so, I felt the whole of the ancient, spongy rail give a peculiar, sickening quiver, and begin to wobble. I fell on to the second mate, and the captain came after, almost in the same instant, but, fortunately, he landed clear of us, on to the fore thwart, which broke under his weight, with a loud crack and splintering of wood.

"'Thank God!' I heard him mutter. 'Thank God! I guess that was a mighty near thing to going to Hades.'

"He struck a match, just as I got to my feet, and between us we got the second mate straightened out on one of the after fore-and-aft thwarts. We shouted to the men in the boat, telling them where we were, and saw the light of their lantern shining round the starboard counter of the derelict. They called back to us to tell us they were doing their best, and then, whilst we waited, Captain Gannington struck another match, and began to overhaul the boat we had dropped into. She was a modern, two-bowed boat, and on the stern there was painted 'Cyclone, Glasgow.' She was in pretty fair condition, and had evidently drifted into the scum and been held by it.

"Captain Gannington struck several matches, and went forrard towards the derelict. Suddenly he called to me, and I jumped over the thwarts to him. 'Look, doctor,' he said, and I saw what he meant—a mass of bones up in the bows of the boat. I stooped over them, and looked; there were the bones of at least three people, all mixed together in an extraordinary fashion, and quite clean and dry. I had a sudden thought concerning the bones, but I said nothing, for my thought was vague in some ways, and concerned the grotesque and incredible suggestion that had come to me as to the cause of that ponderous, dull thud, thud, thud thud, that beat on so infernally within the hull, and was plain to hear even now that we had got off the vessel herself. And all the while, you know, I had a sick, horrible mental picture of that frightful, wriggling mound aboard the hulk.

"As Captain Gannington struck a final match, I saw something that sickened me and the captain saw it in the same instant. The match went out, and he fumbled clumsily for another, and struck it. We saw the thing again. We had not been mistaken. A great lip of grey-white was protruding in over the edge of the boat—a great lappet of the mould was coming stealthily towards us—a live mass of the very hull itself! And suddenly Captain Gannington yelled out in so many words the grotesque and incredible thing I was thinking: 'She's alive!'

"I never heard such a sound of comprehension and terror in a man's voice. The very horrified assurance of it made actual to me the thing that before had only lurked in my subconscious mind. I knew he was right; I knew that the explanation my reason and my training both repelled and reached towards was the true one. Oh, I wonder whether anyone can possibly understand our feelings in that moment? The unmitigated horror of it and the incredibleness!

"As the light of the match burned up fully, I saw that the mass of living matter coming towards us was streaked and veined with purple, the veins standing out, enormously distended. The whole thing quivered continuously to each ponderous thud, thud, thud, thud, of that gargantuan organ that pulsed within the huge grey-white bulk. The flame of the match reached the captain's fingers, and there came to me a little sickly whiff of burned flesh, but he seemed unconscious of any pain. Then the flame went out in a brief sizzle, yet at the last moment I had seen an extraordinary raw look become visible upon the end of that monstrous, protruding lappet. It had become dewed with a hideous, purplish sweat. And with the darkness there came a sudden charnel-like stench.

"I heard the matchbox split in Captain Gannington's hands as he wrenched it open. Then he swore, in a queer frightened voice, for he had come to the end of his matches. He turned clumsily in the darkness, and tumbled over the nearest thwart, in his eagerness to get to the stern of the boat; and I after him. For we knew that thing was coming towards us through the darkness, reaching over that piteous mingled heap of human bones all jumbled together in the bows. We shouted madly to the men, and for answer saw the bows of the boat emerge dimly into view round the starboard counter of the derelict.

"'Thank God!' I gasped out. But Captain Gannington roared to them to show a light. Yet this they could not do, for the lamp had just been stepped on in their desperate efforts to force the boat round to us.

"'Quick! Quick!' I shouted.

"'For God's sake, be smart, men!' roared the captain.

"And both of us faced the darkness under the port-counter, out of which we knew—but could not see—the thing was coming to us.

"'An oar! Smart, now—pass me an oar!' shouted the captain; and reached out his hands through the gloom towards the on-coming boat. I saw a figure stand up in the bows, and hold something out to us across the intervening yards of scum. Captain Gannington swept his hands through the darkness, and encountered it.

"'I've got it! Let go there!' he said, in a quick, tense voice.

"In the same instant the boat we were in was pressed over suddenly to starboard by some tremendous weight. Then I heard the captain shout, 'Duck y'r head, doctor!' And directly afterwards he swung the heavy, fourteen-foot oar round his head, and struck into the darkness. There came a sudden squelch, and he struck again, with a savage grunt of fierce energy. At the second blow the boat righted with a slow movement, and directly afterwards the other boat bumped gently into ours.

"Captain Gannington dropped the oar, and, springing across to the second mate, hove him up off the thwart, and pitched him with knee and arms clear in over the bows among the men; then he shouted to me to follow, which I did, and he came after me, bringing the oar with him. We carried the second mate aft, and the captain shouted to the men to back the boat a little; then they got her bows clear of the boat we had just left, and so headed out through the scum for the open sea.

"'Where's Tom 'Arrison?' gasped one of the men, in the midst of his exertions. He happened to be Tom Harrison's particular chum, and Captain Gannington answered him briefly enough:

"'Dead! Pull! Don't talk!'"

"Now, difficult as it had been to force the boat through the scum to our rescue, the difficulty to get clear seemed tenfold. After some five minutes pulling, the boat seemed hardly to have moved a fathom, if so much, and a quite dreadful fear took me afresh, which one of the panting men put suddenly into words, 'It's got us!' he gasped out. 'Same as poor Tom!' It was the man who had inquired where Harrison was.

"'Shut y'r mouth an' pull!' roared the captain. And so another few minutes passed. Abruptly, it seemed to me that the dull, ponderous thud, thud, thud, thud came more plainly through the dark, and I stared intently over the stern. I sickened a little, for I could almost swear that the dark mass of the monster was actually nearer—that it was coming nearer to us through the darkness. Captain Gannington must have had the same thought, for, after a brief look into the darkness, he jumped forrard, and began to double-bank the stroke-oar.

"'Get forrid under the oars, doctor,' he said to me rather breathlessly. 'Get in the bows, an' see if you can't free the stuff a bit round the bows.'

"I did as he told me, and a minute later I was in the bows of the boat, puddling the scum from side to side, and trying to break up the viscid, clinging muck. A heavy almost animal-like smell rose off it, and all the air seemed full of the deadening, heavy smell. I shall never find words to tell anyone on earth the whole horror of it all—the threat that seemed to hang in the very air around us, and but a little astern that incredible thing, coming, as I firmly believed, nearer, and scum holding us, like half-melted glue.

"The minutes passed in a deadly, eternal fashion, and I kept staring back astern into the darkness but never ceasing to puddle that filthy scum, striking at it and switching it from side to side until I sweated.

"Abruptly Captain Gannington sang out: 'We're gaining, lads. Pull!' And I felt the boat forge ahead perceptibly, as they gave way with renewed hope and energy. There was soon no doubt of it, for presently that hideous thud, thud, thud, thud had grown quite dim and vague somewhere astern and I could no longer see the derelict, for the night had come down tremendously dark and all the sky was thick, overset with heavy clouds. As we drew nearer and nearer to the edge of the scum, the boat moved more and more perceptibly, until suddenly we emerged with a clean, sweet, fresh sound into the open sea.

"'Thank God!' I said aloud, and drew in the boathook, and made my way aft again to where Captain Gannington now sat once more at the tiller. I saw him looking anxiously up at the sky and across to where the lights of our vessel burned, and again he would seem to listen intently, so that I found myself listening also.

"'What's that, Captain?' I said sharply; for it seemed to me that I heard a sound far astern, something, between a queer whine and a low whistling. 'What's that?'

"'It's wind, doctor.' he said in a low voice. 'I wish to God we were aboard.' Then to the men: 'Pull! Put y'r backs into it, or ye'll never put y'r teeth through good bread again!' The men obeyed nobly, and we reached the vessel safely, and had the boat safely stowed before the storm came, which it did in a furious white smother out of the west. I could see it for some minutes beforehand, tearing the sea in the gloom into a wall of phosphorescent foam; and as it came nearer, that peculiar whining, piping sound grew louder and louder, until it was like a vast steam whistle rushing towards us. And when it did come, we got it very heavy indeed, so that the morning showed us nothing but a welter of white seas, with that grim derelict many a score of miles away in the smother, lost as utterly as our hearts could wish to lose her.

"When I came to examine the second mate's feet, I found them in a very extraordinary condition. The soles of them had the appearance of having been partly digested. I know of no other word that so exactly describes their condition, and the agony the man suffered must have been dreadful.

"Now," concluded the doctor, "that is what I call a case in point. If we could know exactly what the old vessel had originally been loaded with, and the juxtaposition of the various articles of her cargo, plus the heat and time she had endured, plus one or two other only guessable quantities, we should have solved the chemistry of the life-force, gentlemen. Not necessarily the origin, mind you; but, at least, we should have taken a big step on the way. I've often regretted that gale, you know—in a way, that is, in a way. It was a most amazing discovery, but at the same time I had nothing but thankfulness to be rid of it. A most amazing chance. I often think of the way the monster woke out of its torpor. And that scum! The dead pigs caught in i! I fancy that was a grim kind of a net, gentlemen. It caught many things. It —"

The old doctor sighed and nodded.

"If I could have had her bill of lading," he said, his eyes full of regret. "If—It might have told me something to help. But, anyway —" He began to fill his pipe again. "I suppose," he ended, looking round at us gravely, "I s'pose we humans are an ungrateful lot of beggars at the best! But—but, what a chance? What a, chance, eh?"

THE
END

A Life & Works

William Hope Hodgson

A phenomenal writer of the earliest weird fiction, Hope Hodgson specialized in heart-stopping moments of terror, built on pages of tense, supernatural menace. The majority of his work focused on the lurking horrors of the ocean but his explorations of dread and panic were much admired by those who built on such themes, and acknowledged by the giants of twentieth century gothic and fantasy fiction, including the influential H.P. Lovecraft, Clark Ashton Smith and August Derleth.

Early Life

Born in 1877 in a less-than-bucolic English village, isolated and vulnerable to the elements, Hodgson was one of twelve children, born to a vicar and his wife. Three of his siblings died in their first few years. The life of a churchman could be peripatetic at best and Samuel Hope Hodgson's family was moved to several new homes during young William's early life. One of these unsettling locations was Ardrahan in County Galway, Ireland where the family was despatched to a bleak rural community of native Gaelic speakers who resented the missionary objective of the English church and their ambassadors. The wind-swept chill of homes, scattered across the landscape close to the sea, inspired what many regard as Hodgson's finest novel, *The House on the Borderland*.

Throughout these early years Hodgson yearned to run away to sea, attempting several times, only to be returned in shame. Eventually he gained a place in the merchant navy, and he trained and set sail for four years. He hated every second of it. Far from being the romantic getaway from his tough and lonely life on land, he spent most of his watch being bullied. This has led to almost every biographer drawing the obvious conclusion that Hodgson's bitter and horrific stories of sea-faring fear can be traced back to his miserable time in the merchant navy.

His return to the mainland in 1902 saw a move to Blackburn in Lancashire where he worked variously as a photographer, fitness instructor (using the skills he had learned in order to survive the abuse endured at sea) and journalist. Increasingly, he turned to fiction in an attempt to support himself and, like other writers of the fantastic and modern gothic, Hodgson's dark themes were driven by the narrow confines of his particular landscape: H.P. Lovecraft lived at home for ten years, enduring the consequences of a nervous breakdown; Robert E. Howard dreamed of ancient Cimmeria from the desolated sweeps of

Texas; Arthur Machen was inspired by the Stygian, supernatural romance of the welsh countryside.

It is interesting to speculate that Hodgson's particular circumstances, the bleak, lonely upbringing, the years at sea, the habitation of an industrial Northern city, kept him away from the dramatic changes in culture, society and politics of the day. With modernism sweeping through high society, challenging the elite and the social order, Hodgson conducted an everyday life of determined survival.

Works & Writing

In common with many of his era and education Hodgson, when he began writing, thought of himself primarily as a poet (as did Lovecraft), but it is hard to find much, if any, distinction. However, it is his prose fiction – four novels and countless short stories – for which he is chiefly remembered. Of the novels, *The House on the Borderland*, published in 1908, is often regarded as the most influential, with its dark terror and hints of the cosmic supernatural. *The Night Land* of 1912 is an early science fiction classic which although invoking Mary Shelley's own novel of slow decline, *The Last Man* (1826), also prefigures the dystopian novels of the 20th century (Aldous Huxley's *Brave New World*, Suzanne Collins' *Hunger Games*), with its future of frightened humanity surrounded by evil in a burnt out world.

Most of Hodgson's work is based on the sea, his two other novels *The Boats of the Glen Carrig* (1907) and *The Ghost Pirates* (1909), and the series of short stories comprising the *Sargasso Sea*. 'The Derelict', 'From The Tideless Sea' and many other dark tales are drenched in the choking depths of the unknown and the nameless monsters that swim within.

Perhaps Hodgson's most well-known creation was Thomas Carnacki, a supernatural detective who delighted in debunking the fake and fraudulent by use of scientific and photographic methods, his tales being recounted by a group of friends at dinner in Cheyne Walk in Chelsea, London. Such stories were popular at the time, with Algernon Blackwood's John Silence and Conan Doyle's masterful detective Sherlock Holmes indulging in similar activity. Carnacki was published in magazines (*The Idler* and *New Magazine*), and as a chapbook and has been much reprinted over the decades since Hodgson's death; the first collected publication was in 1913, as *Carnacki, the Ghost Finder*.

Endings and Beginnings

Hodgson suffered an early death. He volunteered to serve in the First World War and, having survived one attack, he was one of six hundred thousand young men killed in a two-month period, ending in April 1918 at Ypres. Had he survived the war, this industrious and imaginative man would have benefited from the dramatic changes in social order that shifted the economic balance in Europe and saw, amongst many other changes in reading habits, a flowering of the fantastic in pulp magazines of the 1920s and 30s.

Lovecraft's assessment of Hodgson's legacy is generous and accurate. Writing in his 1926 publication, 'Supernatural Horror in Literature' he says:

'Of rather uneven stylistic quality, but vast occasional power in its suggestion of lurking worlds and beings behind the ordinary surface of life, is the work of William Hope Hodgson, known today far less than it deserves to be. Despite a tendency toward conventionally sentimental conceptions of the universe, and of man's relation to it and to his fellows, Mr. Hodgson is perhaps second only to Algernon Blackwood in his serious treatment of unreality. Few can equal him in adumbrating the nearness of nameless forces and monstrous besieging entities through casual hints and insignificant details, or in conveying feelings of the spectral and the abnormal in connexion with regions or buildings.'

Victorian & Gothic Fiction

A Glossary of Terms

A

abacus: wooden device that helped Victorian children to count by sliding colored discs or beads along a column

abbess: nun in charge of a convent; female brothel keeper, a madame

abode: place where people live; period of living somewhere

afford: to provide, allow or supply something

afterlife: existence after death; eternal life

alderman: term for a half-Crown; senior local government official

ale: alcoholic drink made from hops and fermented malt, stronger and heavier than beer

almshouse: privately funded lodgings for the poor (often by the church), as opposed to the workhouse, which was publicly funded

apoplexy: a crippling cerebral stroke, sometimes fatal; a fit of anger

apothecary: pharmacist; one who prepares drugs and medicines and gives medical advice; lowest order of medical man

apprentice: someone who works under a skilled professional for a specific amount of time (usually seven years) in order to learn a trade. When one finished his apprentice, he became a journeyman and would get paid for work himself

area: servant's entrance in the front of many London town-houses, often below-ground

area diving: sneaking down area steps to steal from the lower rooms of houses

automaton: someone who resembles a machine by going through motions repetitively, but without feeling or emotion

B

bank notes: paper currency; promissory notes of a bank to pay upon presentation of the note

banns: announcement or notice of a forthcoming marriage in a parish church, proclaimed on three consecutive Sundays

bathing machine: horse-drawn covered wagon used to haul people into the sea for them to enter the water in bathing clothes without being seen (men and woman swam separately)

beak: magistrate

bearer up: thief with a female accomplice who would distract the victim for the crime to be performed

beating: repeatedly hitting someone; scaring birds from bushes out into the open for shooting parties

Bedlam: nickname for the Hospital of St Mary of Bethlehem, a London psychiatric hospital; place or situation full of noise, frenzy and confusion

beg to: wish to

bird scaring: Victorian children were employed to scare birds away from eating farmer's crops by chasing them off or shouting

boarder: person paying rent for a bed, a room, and usually meals in a private home or boarding house

blackboard: wooden board painted black or a dark color on which the teacher would write on in white chalk

blackleg: someone who works during a strike, often criticised by those who obey the strike (also known as a 'scab')

blag: to steal something, often by smash-and-grab; to trick or con someone

bloodletting: reducing the volume of blood in the body by either opening a vein or by applying leeches as a way of restoring health, used from ancient times up to the nineteenth century

bludger: violent criminal who often uses a bludgeon or heavy, stout weapon

blue bottle: policeman

bob: cockney slang for a shilling or five-pence piece

body-snatching: the act of stealing corpses from graves, tombs or morgues, usually for dissection or scientific study

borough: town that had been given the right to self govern by royal charter; in Victorian London, Southwark was referred to as 'the borough'

Bow Street Runners: detective force in London who pre-dated the police, organized by novelist Henry Fielding and his brother John in 1750 up to 1829, when Robert Peel founded London's first police force

buck cabbie: dishonest cab driver

bug hunting: stealing from or cheating drunks, especially at night in drinking dens

bull: cockney slang for five shillings

C

cant: present, often a free meal; language or vocabulary spoken by thieves or groups of people perceived to be common

caper: criminal act; dangerous activity

cash carrier: pimp or whore's minder, who would literally hold the money earned by soliciting

chavy: child

census: official list of the British population, including address and details of age, gender, occupation, and birthplace, carried out every ten years since 1841

cesspool: hole or pit in the ground for receiving waste matter or sewage from houses

charwoman: cleaning woman

chilblains: red, itchy swelling to parts of face, fingers and toes caused by exposure to cold and damp

chink: money (from the noise coins make when they knock against each other)

chiv/ shiv: knife, razor or sharpened stick used as a weapon

choker: clergyman, referring to the clerical collar worn around the neck

cholera: disease of the small intestine, often fatal, marked by symptoms of thirst, cramps, vomiting and diarrhoea, caused by drinking water tainted with human waste. Victorians were hit with several cholera epidemics before sanitation conditions were improved

choused: to have been cheated

christen: to remove identifying marks from; to use for the first time; to make something like new again

claustrophobia: abnormal dread of being imprisoned or confined in a close or narrow space

cly faking: to pick someone's pocket

coal scuttle: metal pail for carrying and pouring coal

commencement: the beginning or start of something

cop/copper: policeman

costermonger: street peddler, usually selling fruits or vegetables

cracksman: safecracker, someone who cracks or breaks locks

cravat: scarf or band of fabric worn around the neck and tied in a bow

crib: building, house or lodging; location of a gaol

crow: lookout during criminal activities; doctor

crusher: policeman

cudgel: heavy stick used as a weapon

cursory: quick, superficial and not very thorough

D

daffy: small measure, usually spirits; medicine for children, consisting of senna often mixed with gin

daresay: venture to say; think probable

day boarder: someone who spends the day at school but lives at home, as opposed to someone who boards at the school

deadlurk: empty premises

deaner: shilling

despatch: send something; to send someone to carry out a task

device: tuppence; an emblem or motto

deuce hog: two shillings

devil: the Devil, as depicted in Christianity and some other religions, stands as the enemy or opposite to God and tempts people to sin so that they go to Hell; the actual term 'Devil' comes from the Latin diabolus, meaning slanderous. Gothic characters are often tempted by agents of the Devil

dewskitch: giving someone a beating

diligence: public stagecoach; taking care or attention over something

ding: to throw something away; to take something that has been thrown away

diphtheria: infectious disease caused by germs in the throat, causing difficulty in breathing, fever and damage to the heart and nervous system

dispatches: loaded dice; to send someone to carry out a task

dollyshop: unlicensed, often cheap, loan or pawn shop

don: eminent, professional or clever person; leader or head of a group

Doppelgänger: literally translated from German as 'doublegoer'; the ghostly apparition of another, living person; double or alter ego

down: cause suspicion or doubt; to inform on a person, when used in the expression 'to put down on someone'

do down: to beat someone with fists, especially as a punishment

double-knock: applied to the door by a confident visitor, one who was known to the family and comfortable with the purpose of his visit (a single-knock signified a more timid caller, often of an inferior class)

dowager: widow with an inherited title or property from her deceased husband; distinguished, respected older woman

dragsman: someone who steals from carriages or coaches

draught: check or bill of exchange; a small quantity of liquid drunk in one mouthful

dreadnought: warm, thick, tightly woven woollen fabric

dressing: decorating something, such as a Christmas tree

duckett: street dealer or vendor's licence

duffer: someone who sells allegedly stolen or worthless goods, also known as a 'hawker'

E

East India Company: private trading company established by the British government to trade with India, a country it effectively governed until the Indians fought back against the British in 1857

ecod: mild curse, most likely derived from 'My God'

economy: cheapness; giving better value

employ: to hire someone to work for you; if you were in the employ of or employed by someone, you worked for them

entrapment: imprisoning someone; incarcerating or trapping someone, often in dark, strange or claustrophobic surroundings

epidemic: illness that spreads rapidly and extensively, affecting most of people who come in contact with it

E.O.: fairground gambling entertainment

escop/eslop: policeman

establishment: shop, place of business

exorcism: act of forcing the Devil, a demon or evil spirits from the body of someone who is possessed, done through religious prayer or rituals

expectations: chance of coming into an inheritance, property or money

F

fadge: slang term for farthing

fakement: sham or trick, often used when begging

fan: to feel surreptitiously under someone's clothing while they are wearing it, searching for objects to steal

farthing: monetary unit worth quarter of a penny; something almost worthless or of the lowest value

fawney-dropping: trick where a criminal pretends to find a ring (which has no actual value) and sells it as an item of possible worth

fen: marsh or bog

finny: slang term for five pound note

flam: lie or deception

flash: to show off or try to impress; something special or expensive-looking

flash house: public house with criminals as clientele

flimp: snatch stealing or pick pocketing from a crowd

flue faker: chimney sweep, usually young boys

footman: servant in livery, usually in a mansion or palace; a servant who serves at table, tends the door or carriage, runs errands

forfeits: parlour games where each player needs to supply a correct answer and has a forfeit if the answer is not given

furlong: unit of measurement equal to 201 m (660 ft), the length of the traditional furrow or plough trench on a farm

furtherance: helping or advancing the progress of something

gaff: show or exhibition; cheap, smutty theatre; hoax or trick

G

gaiters: cloth or leather covering extending from the waist to the lower leg, usually buttoned up the side

gammon: misleading comment, meant to deceive

gammy: someone false, who is not to be trusted

gaol: jail

garret: fob pocket in a waistcoat; room at the top of the house

gattering: public house

general post: mail that was sent from the London Post office to the rest of England

ghost: phantom or spirit of somebody who has died and who has possibly not gone on to the afterlife, which often inspires fear or terror

gibbet: post with a projecting beam for hanging executed criminals, often done publically as a warning to the public

gig: light, open, two-wheeled carriage drawn by a single horse

gill: unit of liquid equalling a quarter of a pint

glim: light or fire; a source of light; begging by saying you are homeless due to fire; venereal disease

glock: slow, half-witted person

gonoph: petty, small time criminal

gothic: style of architecture, music, art or fiction generally associated with strange, frightening occurrences and mysterious or supernatural plots, characters or locations

gout: disease mainly affecting men, causing inflammation and swelling of the hands and feet, arthritis and deformity; caused by excess uric acid production

governess: woman employed to teach and care for children, in a school or home

greatcoat: long, heavy overcoat worn outdoors, often with a short cape worn over the shoulders

grog: mixture of alcohol, often rum, and water, named after an English admiral who diluted sailors' rum

grotesque: misshapen or mutated character; something or someone unexpected, monstrous or bizarre

gruel: watery, unappetising porridge, popular with the owners of the workhouse or orphanage due to its cheapness

guinea: gold coin, monetary value of twenty-one shillings or one pound and one shilling

gulpy: someone gullible or easy to fool

H

haberdasher: someone who sells personal items, often accessories such as thread or ribbons

hackney coach: carriage for hire

half inch: steal, rhyming slang for pinch

hammered for life: married

hansom cab: two-wheeled, horse-drawn carriage where the driver sat on a high seat at the back, so that the passengers had a clear view of the road

haunted: to be visited by a ghost or supernatural being

haybag: derogatory term for a woman

haymaking: cutting and gathering hay to make haystacks

Haymarket Hector: pimp or whore's escort; especially those working in Haymarket and Leicester Square in London

hob: metal shelf or rack over a fireplace where the pans or kettle could be warmed

hoisting: shoplifting; to lift something up

hopping: picking hops, used for making beer

humbug: something insincere or nonsensical, meant to deceive or cheat people; used to express disbelief or disgust; a hoax or fraud

hykey: pride, arrogance

I

incubus: name for a male demon, thought to be a fallen angel, who forces himself sexually upon sleeping women, which often resulted in the birth of a demon or deformed, half-human child

influenza/flu: viral illness, causing aching joints, fever, headaches, sore throat, cough and sneezing, even followed by death in Victorian times

inkwell: holes or wells in classroom desks that were used to hold the ink for writing

Inquisition: organization founded by the Catholic Church charged with the eradication of heresy or acting against God, by which those found guilty were often put to death

interred: buried

ironmonger: someone who sells metal goods, tools and hardware

irons: guns, usually pistols or revolvers

J

Jack: detective; term sometimes used to address a stranger

jemmy: housebreaker's tool used on locks; someone smart or superior

joey: slang term for fourpence piece

jolly: disturbance or brawl; to be cheerful or happy

journeyman: skilled worker who has finished an apprenticeship and is qualified to hire himself out to work

Judy: term for a woman, usually a prostitute

jump: ground floor window, or a burglary committed by entering through the window

K

kecks: slang term for trousers

ken: house, lodging or public house

kidsman: organizer of child thieves

kith: someone's friends, neighbours or relatives

knapped: pregnant

knaves: jacks in a deck of cards

knee breeches: trousers that reach the knee

knock up: to bang loudly on someone's door to wake them up

know life, to: to be familiar in criminal ways; to be street-wise

L

lackin, lakin: slang term for a wife

ladybird: slang term for a prostitute

lag: convict; someone sentenced to transportation or gaol

larder: cool food storage area

laudanum: solution of opium and alcohol used as pain relief or to aid sleep, highly addictive

lavender, **in**: to hide from the police; to pawn something for money; to be dead

leg: dishonest person, cheat

liberal: generous; tolerant or open-minded

link boy: boy who carries a torch to light a person's way through the dark streets

lodger: person paying rent to stay in a room (or bed) in somebody else's house

logbook: book in which a teacher would comment on pupils' attendance, behaviour, learning progress, etc.

luggers: ear rings

lumber: wood used for building or woodworking, often second-hand furniture; to pawn something; to go to gaol

lurker: criminal; beggar or someone who dresses as a beggar for money

lush: alcoholic drink; someone who drinks too much alcohol; luxurious

M

macer: cheat

mag: slang term for a ha'pence piece

magistrate: judge over trials of misdemeanours; civil officer who upholds the law

maid-of-all-work: usually a young girl, hired as the only servant in the house and required to do any job asked of her

mail coach: carrier of the mail and a limited number of passengers, replaced mid-nineteenth century by the railroad

malt: grain such as barley, that has been allowed to ferment, used for brewing beer and sometimes whiskey

mandrake: homosexual; type of plant

mark: the victim of a crime

market day: the regular day each week when country people would bring their livestock and goods to sell in town

market town: town that regularly held a market, usually the largest town of a farming area

masochism: psychosexual perversion where someone gains erotic pleasure by having pain, abuse or humiliation inflicted on them

materially reduced: having your circumstances and/or finances reduced or lessened

mist: cloud of water particles that condense in the atmosphere, often used in Gothic literature to obscure objects or to prelude something or someone terrifying

mead: fermented alcoholic drink made of water, honey, malt, yeast and sometimes spices

mecks: alcohol, usually wine or spirits

messrs: plural of Mr, used when referring to more than one man

metamorphosis: change or complete transformation in physical form, shape or structure, thought to be caused by supernatural powers

Michaelmas: Christian festival celebrating the archangel Michael, celebrated on 29 September, one of the four quarters of the year

middle class: people who earn enough money to live comfortably, often in a skilled profession such as doctors and lawyers

mizzle: steal or disappear; fine rain

mobsman: conman or pickpocket, usually smartly dressed

mollisher: woman, often associated with a criminal

moniker/ monniker: signature; first name

mortality: death-rate; the number of deaths in a given time or given group

moucher, moocher: rural vagrant or beggar, someone who lives on the road

mourning clothes: black garments worn after a relative dies, the length of which depended on your relationship to the deceased

muffler: scarf

mug-hunter: street thief or pick pocket, from which the modern term 'mugger' comes

mutcher: pickpocket who usually steals from drunks

muck snipe: someone down on their luck

mutton: meat from a sheep, cheaper and less tender than lamb

N

nail: steal; to catch someone who is guilty of a crime

necromancy: black art of conversing with the spirits of the dead, usually done to predict or influence the future, also for making the dead perform tasks for you; witchcraft or sorcery

nethers: charges or rent for lodgings

netherskens: cheap, unsavoury lodging houses, flophouses

nib: point of a pen, often a fountain pen

nibbed: arrested

nickey: slow or simple-minded

nightmares: frightening or unsettling dream, often used in Gothic literature to heighten drama or fear; a malign spirit thought to haunt or suffocate people during sleep

nobble: to inflict severe pain or bodily harm

nose: informant or spy; to try to find something out

nosegay: small bunch of flowers

notions : small personal items, such as a handkerchief or snuffbox

numerous: many in number; frequent

O

occult: relating to the supernatural, witchcraft or magic; something not capable of being understood by ordinary people, but known only by the initiated

occupation: job, means of earning a living

odour: smell

omnibus: single or double-decker bus which was pulled by horses, capable of carrying lots of people

opium: drug extracted from the dried juice and seeds of the opium poppy, which is highly addictive

outdoor relief: charity for the poor which did not require them to enter the workhouse, eliminated in 1834 by the New Poor Law to stop people playing the system

on the fly: while in motion, moving quickly; something done quickly or spontaneously

orthodox: following established rules of religion or society; proper way of behaving

out of twig: unrecognizable, in disguise

outsider: instrument used for opening a lock from the wrong side; stranger or interloper

P

paddingken: tramp's lodgings

page: boy or young man working as a servant or running errands

palsy: medical condition producing uncontrollable shaking of the muscles

pall: detect; become dull or fade; gloomy atmosphere or mood

palmer: shoplifter; someone who 'palms' items to steal them

parlour: living room, usually for guests

patterer: someone who earns a living by recitation or hawker's sales talk, convincing people to buy goods

peach: inform against someone or give information against someone, often leading to imprisonment

pea-coat: short, heavy double-breasted overcoat worn by seamen, usually dark blue or black

peelers: nickname for the new London police force, organized by Sir Robert Peel in 1829

penny-farthing bicycle: bicycle with a large front wheel, to which the pedals were attached, and a much smaller back wheel

phenomenon: fact or occurrence that is out of the ordinary or hard to believe, even though it can be seen

pertaining to: concerning or to do with

picnic: any informal social gathering for which each guest provided a share of the food; informal meal eaten outside

pidgeon: victim; also known as a plant

pig: policeman, usually a detective

pleurisy: inflammation of the lungs producing a fever, hacking cough, sharp chest pain and difficulty in breathing

poorhouse: place where poor, old or sick people lived, where anyone able was put to work, also known as the workhouse

portrait: likeness of an individual or group created through photography or in paintings

possession: being controlled by an evil, demonic or supernatural force

postboy: someone working at a post house or inn, who helps to change the horses on coaches on long journeys

post chaise: enclosed, four-wheeled, horse-drawn carriage, used to transport mail and passengers

postern: small back entrance or gate

posting: travelling in a coach or carriage, stopping along the way in post houses or inns to change horses

prater: idle, foolish talk; bogus preacher

proctor: court officer who manages the affairs of others, answering to an attorney or solicitor

prodigious: great in amount or size; a lot

proprietor: owner of a commercial or business enterprise

puckering: jabbering; speaking in an incomprehensible manner

punishers: men hired to give beatings or 'nobblings'

pursuit: the act of chasing after someone, usually to attack or catch them, often inspiring fear

push: slang term for money

Q

quadrille: card game for four players using forty cards; dance

quarter days: four days of the year when quarterly payments were made; Lady Day (25 March), Midsummer (24 June), Michaelmas (29 September), and Christmas (25 December)

quay: wharf or platform in a port or harbour where ships are loaded or unloaded

quick-lime: white, corrosive alkaline substance consisting of calcium oxide, acquired by heating limestone

quid: slang term for pound

R

racket: illicit or dishonest occupation or activity

reader: pocketbook or wallet

ream: someone superior, real or genuine

rag and bone shop: shop that bought and sold rags that were made into paper, and bones used for manure

repeater: pocket watch that chimed on the hour or quarter past the hour, making it easier to tell the time in the dark

resurrectionist: body snatcher; someone who steals corpses from graves, usually to sell to medical students. Legally, only the bodies of criminals could be used, but demand for corpses was so high that resurrectionists dug up graves the of recently dead

revenant: dead person who has returned to terrorize or to avenge a score with someone living

revenge: act of avenging or repaying someone for a harm that the person has caused; to punish someone in retaliation for something done to them or to a loved one, carried out by humans or by spirits; a popular theme in Gothic literature

ribald: vulgar, lewd humour, often involving jokes about sex

roller: thief who robs drunks; prostitute who steals from her (usually drunk) customers

Romanticism: arts and literature of the Romantic movement, characterized by the passion, emotion and often danger of love and associated feelings

rookery: urban slum or ghetto; nesting place for rooks

Rothschild, to come to the: to brag that you are rich

rozzers: policemen

ruin: to go out of business; lose all your money or possessions

ruffles: slang term for handcuffs

S

saddle: loaf; cut of meat

sadism: perversion where one person gains sexual gratification by causing physical or mental pain on others, first coined to describe the writings of the Marquis de Sade; delight in torment or excessive cruelty

salubrity: health or well-being

Salvation Army: worldwide religious organization founded by William Booth in 1865; it provided aid to the poor, helped those in need and sought to bring people back to God

saveloy: highly seasoned, spicy, smoked pork sausage, sold as a snack ready to eat

scaldrum dodge: gaining sympathy, begging by means of fake or self-inflicted wounds

scarlet fever: infection usually suffered by children, causing a red rash and high fever; also called Scarlatina

scran: slang term for food

screever: forger; writer of fake documents

scullery: area for dish washing, preparing food and storing dishes

sealing wax: wax that is soft when heated, used to seal letters – red for business letters, black for mourning and other colours for general correspondence

sedan chair: covered chair to which two long poles were attached and on which a person was carried around by chairmen

servant's lurk: public house used primarily by crooked or dismissed servants

shake lurk: begging under false pretences, usually those of being a shipwrecked, out of work seaman

sharp: conman, card swindler

shilling: unit of money equal to five pence in today's money

shirkster: layabout, work-shy

shofulman: someone who makes or passes bad money

slap-bang job: public house frequented by thieves, where no credit is given

slate: used to teach children to write; they would write on black slates with white chalk, instead of the paper used today

slum: ghetto; false or faked document; to cheat someone or pass money you know to be bad or false

smasher: someone who passes bad or false money

smoking bishop: drink made at Christmas from heated red wine or port flavoured with oranges, sugar and spices, named because of its deep purple colour and traditionally heated with a red-hot poker

snakesman: small boy used for housebreaking, as they could enter a house through a small gap

snoozer: someone who steals from sleeping guests in hotels

snowing: stealing clothes that have been hung out on a washing line to dry

somnambulism: sleepwalking, a dissociated mental state that occurs during deep sleep, where, in Gothic literature, people would do things they would not normally do

spike: slang term for the workhouse

sponging-house: temporary prison for those who cannot pay their debts, prior to someone being sent to a prison such as Marshalsea in London

srew: skeleton key, for use in burglaries

stricken: affected by; suffering or struck by

sublime: to be awed, moved or transported by something, such as religion, beauty or emotions; used in Gothic literature as the thrill of being terrified, because fear inspires such strong emotions

subscription: collection of money paid over a period of time; fee to be paid; donation given to a charitable cause

succubus: female demon, counterpart of the incubus (*q.v.*)

supernatural: phenomena or events that seem unbelievable or cannot be explained by natural laws; occurences relating to magic or the occult

superstition: deep-seated but often irrational belief in something, such as an action or ritual, thought to bring good or bad luck

sweep: chimney sweep, often small boys who could easily fit in chimneys; it became a crime in 1842 for an apprentice under the age of 16 or anyone else under the age of 21 to be forced up a chimney

sweetmeat: sweet treat, such as candy or candied fruit, often served at the end of a meal

swell: elegantly or stylishly dressed gentleman; expensive dress

T

tallow: hard, fatty substance from sheep or oxen, used to make candles or soap

taper: small, slim wax candle, narrower at the top than the bottom

taproom: bar room in a public house where working class people ate and drank, as opposed to the parlour, used by the middle classes

teetotaller: someone who completely abstains from alcohol, an activity which gained in popularity in the middle classes during Victorian times

tea leaf: rhyming slang for thief

thicker: slang for sovereign or pound

thick 'un: slang term for sovereign

thriving: to be profitable or successful; flourishing

toff: elegantly or stylish gentleman; someone rich or upper class

toffken: house in which well-to-do, upper-class people lived

toke: slang term for bread

tooling: experienced pickpocket

topped: to be hung

tradesman: man in a skilled trade, such as a carpenter or plumber; shopkeeper; someone who buys and sells goods

transportation: when exiled British criminals were sent to the colonies, usually Australia, as punishment

turnkey: jailor; keeper of keys

turnpike: toll road that people paid to travel on; the money from which was used to keep the road in good condition

twirls: keys, usually skeleton keys

typhoid: serious, often fatal, illness caused by drinking polluted water (contaminated by sewage)

U

uncanny: something or someone too strange, weird or eerie to be natural or human; supernatural under and over: fairground game, often used to swindle people

union workhouse: workhouse for the poor, which parishes were obligated to provide after the 1834 New Poor Law

unprovided for: left with no money or security

upper class: people from rich, moneyed families, such as landowners or aristocracy

V

vamp: to steal; pawn something; to seduce or manipulate someone

vampire: supernatural being of a malignant nature, believed to suck the blood of the living for sustenance, from European folklore

vapour: steam

vespers: evening church service, prayers

viands: tasty articles of foods

vie with: compete with someone; strive for superiority

vintner: wine maker or merchant

W

ward: child or youth under the care and control of a guardian

washhouse: building where clothes were washed, often shared

wassail: spiced ale or wine served at Christmas or other festive occasions

watch: men chosen to guard the streets at night, periodically calling out the time and ensuring that no crimes were being committed

weeping willow: rhyming slang for pillow

werewolf: someone who is human by day and turns into a wolf at night, living off humans, animals, or even corpses, from European folklore

whistle and flute: rhyming slang for suit

wholesome: healthy, clean-living; decent

whooping cough: infectious disease, often affecting children, that causes heavy coughing and makes it hard to breath

witchcraft: spells and magic performed by a witch; in Gothic fiction the witch is usually depicted as an old, hag-like crone or a beautiful, seductive young woman

without: outside, usually referring to outside the house in which someone is

work capitol: to commit a crime punishable by death

working class: those in heavy manual labor, usually for low, hourly wages, such as farm laborers, factory workers and builders

workhouses: place where the sick, poor, old and those in debt went or were sent for food and shelter. The New Poor Law (1834) made the workhouse almost a prison for the poor, who had to work hard in miserable conditions, often fed on gruel only and separated from their families

whist: popular card game, know known as bridge

worrit: worry; worry-wort

Y

yack: slang term for a watch

yennap: slang term for a penny

yeoman: independent farmer who cultivated, and often owned, his own small area of land

Other Titles and Recommended Reads

A range of Gothic novels, horror fiction, crime,
mystery, fantasy and science fiction: available
and forthcoming from Flame Tree 451

1936	*The Shadow Out of Time*	H.P. Lovecraft	Science Fiction
1936	*At The Mountains of Madness*	H.P. Lovecraft	Science Fiction
1818	*Frankenstein*	Mary Shelley	Horror, Gothic
1826	*The Last Man*	Mary Shelley	Science Fiction
1868	*The Moonstone*	Wilkie Collins	Crime, Mystery
1878	*The Haunted Hotel*	Wilkie Collins	Crime, Mystery
1911	*The Lair of the White Worm*	Bram Stoker	Horror
1897	*Dracula*	Bram Stoker	Horror
1886	*Jekyll & Hyde*	R.L. Stevenson	Science Fiction
1912	*The Lost World*	Arthur Conan Doyle	Science Fiction
1929	*The Metal Monster*	Abraham Merritt	Science Fiction
1930	*Belshazzar*	H. Rider Haggard	Fantasy
1908	*The Ghost Kings*	H. Rider Haggard	Fantasy
1887	*She*	H. Rider Haggard	Fantasy
1895	*The Time Machine*	H. G. Wells	Science Fiction
1898	*War of the Worlds*	H. G. Wells	Science Fiction
1897	*The Invisible Man*	H. G. Wells	Science Fiction
1900s	*Short Story Collection: Ghosts*	Various	Horror, Mystery
1900s	*Short Story Collection: Mystery*	Various	Crime, Mystery
1900s	*Short Story Collection: Gothic*	Various	Gothic
1900s	*Short Story Collection: SF*	Various	Science Fiction
1900s	*Short Story Collection: Crime*	Various	Crime, Mystery
1900s	*Short Story Collection: Horror*	Various	Horror
1911	*The Centaur*	Algernon Blackwood	Gothic
1909	*Jimbo*	Algernon Blackwood	Gothic
1874	*The Expressman and the Detective*	Allan Pinkerton	Crime, Mystery
1794	*The Mysteries of Udolpho*	Ann Radcliffe	Gothic
1878	*The Leavenworth Case*	Anna Katharine Green	Crime, Mystery
1895	*The Three Imposters*	Arthur Machen	Horror, Mystery
1906	*The House of Souls*	Arthur Machen	Horror, Mystery
1917	*The Terror*	Arthur Machen	Horror, Mystery
1894	*Martin Hewitt, Investigator*	Arthur Morrison	Crime, Mystery
1909	*Black Magic*	Marjorie Bowen	Horror, Mystery
1903	*The Jewel of Seven Stars*	Bram Stoker	Horror, Mystery
1934	*Murder Monster*	Brant House	Horror
1938	*Power (G-Men)*	C.K.M. Scanlon	Crime, Mystery
1798	*Wieland*	Charles Brockden Brown	Gothic
1799	*Ormond, or The Secret Witness*	Charles Brockden Brown	Horror, Mystery
1852	*Bleak House*	Charles Dickens	Crime, Mystery

1820	*Melmoth the Wanderer*	Charles Maturin	Gothic
1794	*The Banished Man*	Charlotte Smith	Gothic
1913	*The Poison Belt*	Arthur Conan Doyle	Fantasy
1928	*When the World Screamed*	Arthur Conan Doyle	Fantasy
1902	*Hound of the Baskervilles*	Arthur Conan Doyle	Crime, Mystery
1890	*The Sign of Four*	Arthur Conan Doyle	Crime, Mystery
1915	*The Valley of Fear*	Arthur Conan Doyle	Crime, Mystery
1887	*Study in Scarlet*	Arthur Conan Doyle	Crime, Mystery
1959	*The Galaxy Primes*	E. E. Smith	Science Fiction
1928	*Skylark of Space*	E. E. Smith	Science Fiction
1926	*The Moon Maid*	E. R. Burroughs	Science Fiction
1918	*Red Hawk*	E. R. Burroughs	Science Fiction
1918	*The Land That Time Forgot*	E. R. Burroughs	Fantasy
1912	*Tarzan of the Apes*	E. R. Burroughs	Fantasy
1913	*Return of Tarzan*	E. R. Burroughs	Fantasy
1917	*John Carter, A Princess of Mars*	E. R. Burroughs	Fantasy
1919	*John Carter, A Warlord of Mars*	E. R. Burroughs	Fantasy
1913	*Trent's Last Case*	E. C. Bentley	Crime, Mystery
1908	*Lord of the World*	R. H. Benson	Science Fiction
1909	*Necromancers*	R. H. Benson	Science Fiction
1831-49	*Short Stories 1*	Edgar Allan Poe	Crime, Mystery
1831-49	*Short Stories 2*	Edgar Allan Poe	Crime, Mystery
1831-49	*Short Stories 3*	Edgar Allan Poe	Crime, Mystery
1831-49	*Short Stories 4*	Edgar Allan Poe	Crime, Mystery
1831-49	*Short Stories 5*	Edgar Allan Poe	Crime, Mystery
1831-49	*Short Stories 6*	Edgar Allan Poe	Crime, Mystery
1936	*Red Nails*	Robert E. Howard	Fantasy
1934	*The People of the Black Circle*	Robert E. Howard	Fantasy
1935	*The Hour of the Dragon*	Robert E. Howard	Fantasy
1935	*Short Stories Selection 1*	Robert E. Howard	Fantasy
1935	*Short Stories Selection 2*	Robert E. Howard	Fantasy
2011	*Greek Myths*	J. Jackson (ed.)	Myths & Fables
2011	*Celtic Myths*	J. Jackson (ed.)	Myths & Fables
2011	*Native American Myths*	J. Jackson (ed.)	Myths & Fables
2011	*Indian Myths*	J. Jackson (ed.)	Myths & Fables
2011	*Chinese Myths*	J. Jackson (ed.)	Myths & Fables
2011	*African Myths*	J. Jackson (ed.)	Myths & Fables
2011	*Viking Myths*	J. Jackson (ed.)	Myths & Fables
2011	*Scottish Myths*	J. Jackson (ed.)	Myths & Fables

1828	*Pelham*	Edward Bulwer-Lytton	Crime, Mystery
1842	*Zanoni*	Edward Bulwer-Lytton	Horror, Mystery
1862	*A Strange Story*	Edward Bulwer-Lytton	Horror, Mystery
1807	*The Demon of Sicily*	Edward Montague	Gothic
1868	*The Huge Hunter*	Edward Sylvester Ellis	Science Fiction
1861	*East Lynne*	Ellen Wood	Crime, Mystery
1847	*Wuthering Heights*	Emily Brontë	Gothic
1876	*The Man-Wolf*	Erckmann-Chatrian	Horror, Mystery
1886	*The Mystery of a Hansom Cab*	Fergus Hume	Crime, Mystery
1874	*Temptation of St. Anthony*	Gustav Flaubert	Horror, Mystery
1811	*Undine*	Friedrich Heinrich Karl	Gothic
1811	*Sintram*	Friedrich Heinrich Karl	Gothic
1911	*The Innocence of Father Brown*	G. K. Chesterton	Crime, Mystery
1907	*The Mystery of the Yellow Room*	Gaston Leroux	Crime, Mystery
1940	*The Ghost Strikes Back*	George Chance	Science Fiction
1846	*Wagner-The Wehr-wolf*	George W. M. Reynolds	Horror, Mystery
1919	*Door of the Unreal*	Gerald Biss	Horror
1927	*Color out of Space*	H. P. Lovecraft	Science Fiction
1898	*The Turn of the Screw*	Henry James	Horror, Mystery
1764	*The Castle of Otranto*	Horace Walpole	Gothic
1905	*A Thief in the Night*	E. W. Hornung	Crime, Mystery
1892	*The Big Bow Mystery*	Israel Zangwill	Crime, Mystery
1818	*Northanger Abbey*	Jane Austen	Gothic
1927	*Witch Wood*	John Buchan	Horror, Mystery
1953	*The Black Star Passes*	John W. Campbell	Science Fiction
1791	*Tancred: A Tale of Ancient Time*	Joseph Fox	Gothic
1864	*Journey to the Centre of the Earth*	Jules Verne	Science Fiction
1904	*Master of the World*	Jules Verne	Science Fiction
1886	*Robur the Conqueror*	Jules Verne	Science Fiction
1936	*The Undying Monster*	Jessie Douglas Kerruish	Horror
1927	*The Dark Chamber*	Leonard Lanson Cline	Horror, Mystery
1920	*Voyage to Arcturus*	David Lindsay	Science Fiction
1862	*Lady Audley's Secret*	Mary Elizabeth Braddon	Crime, Mystery
1795	*The Abbey of Clugny*	Mary Meeke	Gothic
1908	*The Circular Staircase*	Mary Roberts Rinehart	Crime, Mystery
1796	*The Monk*	Matthew Lewis	Gothic
1907	*The Exploits of Arsene Lupin*	Maurice Leblanc	Crime, Mystery
1919	*The Three Eyes*	Maurice Leblanc	Science Fiction
1851	*The House of the Seven Gables*	Nathaniel Hawthorne	Horror, Mystery

1850	*The Scarlet Letter*	Nathaniel Hawthorne	Horror, Mystery
1860	*The Marble Faun*	Nathaniel Hawthorne	Horror, Mystery
1936	*The War-Makers*	Nick Carter	Crime, Mystery
1935	*Odd John*	Olaf Stapledon	Science Fiction
1930	*Last and First Men*	Olaf Stapledon	Science Fiction
1937	*Star-Maker*	Olaf Stapledon	Science Fiction
1859	*Elsie Venner*	Oliver Wendell Holmes	Horror, Mystery
1890	*The Picture of Dorian Gray*	Oscar Wilde	Gothic
1907	*The Red Thumb Mark*	R. Austin Freeman	Crime, Mystery
1897	*The Beetle*	Richard Marsh	Gothic
1939	*Almuric*	Robert E. Howard	Science Fiction
1872	*Erewhon*	Samuel Butler	Science Fiction
1918	*Brood of the Witch-Queen*	Sax Rohmer	Horror, Mystery
1872	*In a Glass Darkly*	Sheridan Le Fanu	Crime, Mystery
1783	*The Recess: A Tale of Other Times*	Sophia Lee	Gothic
1768	*Bradford Abbey*	Susan Minifie Gunning	Gothic
1919	*The Moon Pool*	Abraham Merritt	Science Fiction
1845	*Varney, the Vampyre*	Thomas Preskett Prest	Horror, Mystery
1910	*The Return*	Walter de la Mare	Horror, Mystery
1908	*Mystery of the Four Fingers*	Fred M. White	Science Fiction
1839	*Amber Witch*	Wilhelm Meinhold	Horror, Mystery
1859	*The Woman in White*	Wilkie Collins	Crime, Mystery
1786	*History of the Caliph Vathek*	William Beckford	Gothic
1799	*St. Leon*	William Godwin	Horror, Mystery
1794	*Caleb Williams*	William Godwin	Crime, Mystery
1908	*The House on the Borderland*	William Hope Hodgson	Horror, Mystery
1907	*The Boats of the "Glen Carrig"*	William Hope Hodgson	Horror, Mystery
1909	*The Ghost Pirates*	William Hope Hodgson	Horror, Mystery
1801	*The Magus*	Francis Barrett	Horror, Mystery

A TASTE FOR THE FANTASTIC

The Return by **Walter de la Mare**

Arthur Lawford falls asleep against the tomb of suicide victim Nicholas Sabathier. Feeling invigorated upon waking, Lawford hurries home only to be dealt a chilling shock. It is a stranger's face that peers back at him from the mirror! Discovering that his new face is that of the dead Sabathier, Lawford skulks in the shadows, questioning who he is and who he might become. A psychologically thrilling tale of the occult from Walter de la Mare's masterful imagination.

Wieland by **Charles Brockden Brown**

Penned by the skilful hand of Charles Brockden Brown, *Wieland* was one of the first American Gothic novels and is a fantastic piece of horror fiction. The terror begins when Clara Wieland's family starts being plagued by mysterious voices and a stranger named Carwin appears in their lives. From a zealously religious father who one day spontaneously combusts in a temple, to entrancing voices encouraging madness and murder, Clara's fear intensifies as she tries to escape the atmosphere of doom that surrounds her family.

The Monk by **Jessie Matthew Lewis**

An original gothic masterpiece of madness, lust and terror. Matthew Lewis introduces us to the sinful world of Ambrosio, a monk in an ominous Madrid monastery. The seemingly pious Ambrosio reveals himself to have a less than admirable character as he lusts after one of his students. As the horror escalates, it seems the devil himself has had a hand at every turn. Ambrosio's hopes of redemption diminish with every breath and every repulsive act…until he is forced to face the very evil he commands.

For information on these as paperbacks and ebooks please visit
www.flametree451.com or www.flametreepublishing.com